THE SURVIVALIST
THE LEGEND

"Hold me!" Rourke shouted below, feeling Natalia's hands grab him as he wedged himself into the corner of the moon roof. He swung the energy weapon to his shoulder like a shotgun, settled the front sight on the center of the lead chopper and fired, then fired again in the same breath.

The helicopter, close now, was suddenly aflame, the fireball rushing toward the staff car. Rourke twisted and threw himself downward, his arms going around Natalia to protect her lest the fireball be sucked in through the open driver's side door.

The car rocked, Rourke's skin hot, then cold. He was up, Natalia shouting "Be careful!" He lifted the energy weapon again, feeling her hands on him, swung the weapon to his shoulder and fired on the next helicopter.

He missed.

The chopper was pounding the air overhead, hovering as it fixed the staff car in its gunsights.

There was time for only one more shot.

And no time to aim . . .

The Survivalist series by Jerry Ahern published by New English Library:

The Survivalist
The Legend

Jerry Ahern

NEW ENGLISH LIBRARY
Hodder and Stoughton

A CIP catalogue record for this title is
available from the British Library

ISBN 0-450-57101-7

Printed and bound in Great Britain for
Hodder and Stoughton Paperbacks, a
division of Hodder and Stoughton
Ltd., Mill Road, Dunton Green,
Sevenoaks, Kent TN13 2YA (Editorial
Office: 47 Bedford Square, London
WC1B 3DP) by Clays Ltd., St Ives plc.

Author's Note

At the ten year mark for THE SURVIVALIST, a few words seem in order. As a boy, like most kids of my generation, I had a lot of heroes, both in reality and in fiction, from 'rough riding' President Teddy Roosevelt to the Lone Ranger and Tonto to Mike Hammer. An odd group, admittedly, but I saw and still see one common thread which unites them all, unites them with the Wyatt Earps, the Madame Curies, the Louis Pasteurs, the Jesse Owenses, the Audie Murphys, the Winston Churchills and all the great heroes of fact and fiction: fair was fair, right was right, good was good and evil was evil and, while life and breath remained, giving up was out of the question, no matter what the odds.

When I was ten years old (No! This isn't the story of my life), I taught myself how to type (and I still type that way!) and decided I wanted to be a writer. Every time a teacher assigned a short story in class, mine was never short. I took creative writing classes in high school under a teacher named Jim Norris. Mr. Norris, a Faulkner fan, was never exactly fond of my penchant for good guys versus bad guys, heroes versus villains, with a few beautiful babes tossed in for good measure, but he taught me a lot about perspective for which I'll always be grateful. And, he said something which was probably intended as a cut but I took as a compliment; it turned out to be prophetic. It was something like, "Ahern's got it down, and he'll probably be able to sell this stuff someday."

I took that as a compliment because I took my heroes seriously and still do. Perhaps I'm naive, but I sincerely believe to this day that good will always triumph in the end, no matter how long it takes, no matter what the odds, and that evil, no matter how strong it seems, will eventually succumb to courage, determination and right. Couple this conviction with an equally strong belief in individual freedom and initiative based on a personal sense of right and wrong and John Rourke's character begins to emerge.

As associate editor of *Guns* Magazine for a couple of years, I had the opportunity to write for a living rather than a hobby, and learned how to deal with deadlines (meet them if you can, ignore them if you can't, but use the pressure to do the job better). I also became acutely aware of two very important sociological phenomena: People saw themselves, in the event of catastrophic disaster, rising to the occasion rather than lying down, dying and becoming a statistic; to facilitate this vision, people were spending time, money and energy on all aspects of survivalism, from cannisters in which to bury supplies to firearms with which to defend one's family and nation, to property to be turned into survival retreats to something as basic as growing one's own vegetables in a truck garden as a source of chemical free food.

Sharon and I were Cold War kids. Like other people of our generation, we grew up with sirens sounding air raid drills and were taught how to stand in the school corridors, well away from windows, with our coats covering our faces to protect us from flash burns when the BOMB was dropped, something kids these days rarely if ever think about, and hopefully the kids of the next century will look back on as some sort of kinky version of recess. As a teacher in the late sixties and early seventies, I managed my own share of school evacuations because of bomb threats, saw more than my own share of what were euphemistically called 'mass civil disturbances' or just plain 'dislocations.' I realized that if the unthinkable ever became reality, those who survived would not be able to rely on others, but would have to rely on themselves.

I did a lot of things for a living: teaching, writing magazine articles on everything from firearms to vampire researchers; wholesaling for two of the nations then-largest firearms jobbers, etc. And, I met lots of interesting people with very colorful backgrounds and picked up a considerable amount of knowledge in some rather odd disciplines.

Sharon and I began kicking around the idea of what the world might really be like if something came about to cause the total collapse of society. And what would a man with the perfect combination of the skills necessary for survival do?

Getting THE SURVIVALIST published was a task fitting for John Rourke himself. We were told emphatically and often that a series of books taking place after World War III would be too depressing, that no one would want to read it. Yet, Sharon and I were convinced that out of darkest adversity comes humanity's finest moments, most truly shining hours, and that people would want to read about such times and such deeds.

Zebra Books, to whom we are eternally grateful, decided to gamble. THE SURVIVALIST #1, TOTAL WAR, debuted in 1981.

Since that time, in multiple printings, THE SURVIVALIST has been translated into French and Japanese, turned up in bookstores outside Oxford University and base exchanges in places like Greece and Korea, developed a loyal following of men and women of all ages from all walks of life, quite literally all over the world.

As this is written, thank God, the possibility for World War III seems to grow progressively more remote. Yet, injustice and tyranny still run rampant in the world at large, the potential for environmental catastrophe of epic proportions increases by the hour, and terrorists, drug dealers and street criminals still initiate deadly violence for everything from psychotic whim to just turning a fast buck.

The likelihood of a man such as John Rourke, or men and women such as ourselves, having to fight the good fight against impossible odds has not diminished, whatever the immediate cause might be. As long as there is good and there is evil there will be conflict, whether it is met with fists, guns or votes on election day.

A story is as strong as its characters, no more, no less. It is gratifying to us through reader letters, when we attend science fiction conventions, when we do book store signings, visit gun or knife shows, etc., that people talk to us about the Rourke family as real people, care what happens to them, count them as friends.

We've always felt that way, too.

In THE LEGEND, a major new saga begins for THE SURVIVALIST. Thanks for staying with us all these years, from the Ahern Family and the Rourke Family.

JERRY AHERN
Commerce, Georgia

Prologue:
Warfare

The matte black German gunships closed up tightly around his own craft. John Rourke wheeled the captured Soviet machine 180 degrees on its main rotor axis and fell into the center of their formation. Flak fired from mobile anti-aircraft, batteries exploded around them and shoulder-fired surface to air missile launches, were increasing by the second. Several of the German gunships were already damaged, one of them aflame, but, as yet, none brought crashing down to the icefield which stretched in all directions below them as far as Rourke could see.

German J-7V vertical take-off and landing fighter bombers with fresh coatings of arctic camouflage screamed out of the snow-heavy clouds from the north and across the airfield in high speed, low altitude strafing runs. The Allied goal was to keep as much as possible of the massive Elite Corps installation at Gur'Yev (where the Ural River met the Caspian Sea) intact so that, once taken, the field and its extensive synth-fuel dumps could be utilized as a staging area for the impending Allied assault on the Soviet Underground City in the Ural Mountains. This thrust, in conjunction with a simultaneous attack on the Soviet underwater facility in the Pacific, if successful, would be the last battle of the war which had raged across the planet now for more than five centuries..

From the main portion of the fuselage behind him, albeit well back from the cockpit, Rourke heard the sounds of his son Michael and his friend Paul Rubenstein reloading their weapons, their justifiably anxious talk concerning the the demolitions work all four of them—Michael, Paul, John Rourke himself and Natalia—had accomplished in preparation for the attack. Below Rourke, visible

9

through the Soviet gunship's chin bubble, the main helicopter hangar, the smaller hangar which had accommodated Soviet fighter bombers and the field's main control tower all lay in still fiery ruins.

In the co-pilot seat beside John Rourke, Natalia Tiemerovna removed the short blonde wig she'd worn when they'd infiltrated the base disguised as Soviet Elite Corps personnel. Her real hair beneath the wig—so dark a brown it was almost a true black and very beautiful—cascaded to her shoulders. She shook her hair free, then put the headset back to her ear and resumed tuning the frequency scanner on the radio. Their eyes met, her eyes' almost surreal blueness holding him. But, making a conscious effort, Rourke looked away from Natalia and back to what he should be looking at, the controls of the helicopter he piloted.

"John!" Natalia was normally an alto, but the excitement in her voice edged the pitch higher. "Listen. It's Sam! I'll put this on speaker." She had been working the radio, hunting for transmissions from the commando teams which went after Gur'Yev's primary anti-aircraft batteries, the teams led, respectively, by Major Otto Hammerschmidt of New Germany and U.S. Marine Corps Captain, Sam Aldridge of Mid-Wake.

Aldridge's voice came up on the speaker. "I say again. Knockout One to Snowbird Leader. We have total control of Objective Alpha. I repeat, total control of Objective Alpha. Over."

There was a burst of static, then Colonel Wolfgang Mann's voice. "Knockout One, this is Snowbird Leader. Knockout Two reports similar results. Can you hold your position? Over."

"Snowbird Leader, this is Knockout One. Resistance minimal. We can hold but would appreciate air support against platoon strength enemy unit approaching rapidly from map co-ordinates G-15. Need that ASAP. Enemy unit is armed with at least one energy weapon and we are currently receiving moderately heavy incoming mortar fire. Please advise. Knockout One, Over."

John Rourke took up Natalia's headset. "Snowbird Leader, this is Rourke in Soviet Helicopter KH R 333 658. We can interdict enemy force at co-ordinates G-15 if Knockout One can talk us in. Over."

"Yes, Herr Doctor. But—" Mann's voice seemed to hesitate, then, "Do you copy this, Knockout One? Over."

"Affirmative, Snowbird Leader. We can talk the doctor in. Over."

"Very well, Doctor. Snowbird Leader, Out."

"Sam, ETA's about two minutes. Over."

"I copy that, Doctor. Knockout One, Out."

"Rourke, Out." John Rourke handed back the headset.

"Can I change frequencies for a minute?" Natalia asked.

"Sure," Rourke nodded to her.

She flicked back to the main German frequency. There was chatter between the air strike units and the heavier aircraft coming in at considerably higher altitude, co-ordinating the pull-back of the J-7Vs to allow for the landing of German paratroopers on the field itself.

Michael leaned over between their seats. "Going to try the energy weapon, Dad?"

"That's what I'm thinking, Mike." He'd called his son by his nickname perhaps three times in his life. Michael clapped him on the shoulder.

From the rear of the fuselage, Paul called out, "John. After that energy pulse we took a couple of minutes ago, you think the wiring'll stand using the energy weapon we have aboard?"

Natalia shouted back to him, "As best I can tell, the rotation of the main rotor is constantly recharging the power supply, Paul. We should be all right, even on emergency power as we are, because the systems shouldn't interconnect."

"All I wanted to know!"

Rourke had been climbing the machine since Mann gave the go-ahead and he was well enough above the German gunships now that he could bank to starboard and clear the other helicopters. The J-7Vs were moving out to the south, the lead elements of the attack formation already manuevering into position for a second strafing run, but selective this time, in support of the paratroopers once the men touched down. Already, through the overhead bubble, Rourke could see the first of the chutes starting to open in the sky well above their machine.

Many of these "parachutists" weren't parachutists at all, only drones, similar in concept and purpose to those used by the Allies during pre-dawn portions of the D-Day invasion in June of 1944, near the close of World War Two. Articulated dummies, miniaturized to perfect scale with their smaller parachutes, they were air dropped in conjunction with actual paratroopers, providing a greater number of targets to draw fire from enemy personnel on the

11

ground, thereby minimizing the potential for real casualties while at the same time deceiving the enemy into believing that he had to deal with an even larger force.

More chutes were opening now, and Rourke heightened the Soviet machine's speed so he could clear the area before any of the chutes neared his operational deck.

"I'm switching back to Sam's frequency, John," Natalia announced.

"Paul and I can set up doorguns," Michael offered.

"Go for it," Rourke nodded, checking his compass coordinates Rourke rasped to Natalia, "Get Sam to talk us in on that enemy platoon."

Natalia started calling for Sam Aldridge now, and Rourke, the machine he piloted well out of range of the fray at the airfield, began descending, following terrain to minimize the enemy's chances for establishing visual contact.

At last, Sam Aldridge's voice came over the speaker, reciting coordinates, the sound of detonating mortars in the background at times deafeningly loud. John Rourke activated the gunship's headsup display, searching for the correct map grid, finding it, then making a mental fix on the relative position of the advancing enemy platoon. He locked the auto-navigator system on the co-ordinates, for the first time since leaving the immediate vicinity of the airfield looking fully behind him along the interior of the fuselage.

Soviet heavy machine guns, mounted on rotating tripods, were going up on either side of the aircraft just inside the open doors. Paul and Michael wrapped seatbelt webbing around the mounts to secure the guns once the relatively steady flight pattern changed to the erratic pattern of battle. The floors of the Soviet machines were fitted with cleats to accommodate bipods, but no bipods were apparently present in the machine, these machine guns just being hauled rather than intended for combat use.

Rourke's eyes flashed to the headsup display. Auto navigation was bringing the gunship in along a broad arc from the west to the south that would intersect the enemy unit's assumed line of movement, but he suddenly had a better idea. John Rourke adjusted the unit's controls, no need for his full attention to navigation just yet. The helicopter banked slowly, evenly to port now Rourke's goal in modifying the flight plan was to come upon the attacking Soviet platoon from the rear. He had no desire to test the capacity of the enemy energy weapons against his own machine, the potential for a duel serving no purpose.

"I see them, John," Natalia said after a minute or so passed. Rourke only nodded, seeing them, too. He switched off auto-navigation and went to manual. "We have a full charge on the energy weapon," Natalia added.

From aft by the open fuselage doors, Paul shouted out over the slipstream's roar, "We're ready, John!"

John Thomas Rourke had never liked war, felt that no rational man did. Violence was the last resort when reason failed, and reason had failed dismally in the days immediately prior to The Night of The War.

And reason had done nothing but fail ever since.

And now, in seconds, he would bring the liberated Soviet gunship screaming in over the heads of men who were, to him, total strangers, then attempt with all his abilities and the technology of the aircraft he flew to cut them down.

He hated war.

Soon this war would end.

"We're going in," John Rourke almost whispered, banking the Soviet gunship to port, then levelling off as he took control of the energy weapon fire mechanism. "Power full?"

"Power full," Natalia said from beside him.

There were three dozen men below him, men in enemy uniforms.

John Rourke pushed the fire control. The machine guns on both sides of the gunship opened up.

The earth below him seemed to incinerate, bodies vaporizing as the blue wave of energy passed across the ground, machinegun bullets rippling across the bodies as yet untouched.

And John Rourke pulled up, satisfied that the energy weapon in possession of the enemy ground force was no longer functional.

He didn't look at anyone as he levelled off, letting the machine rotate 180 degrees on its axis, his eyes narrowed and focused on the fleeing enemy forces beneath him.

Two thirds of the platoon strength enemy unit was dead, what remained of their bodies smoldering on the snowy ground beneath him.

Sam Aldridge's voice came over the speaker. "You got 'em, Doctor Rourke! The rest of them are withdrawing! Can you intercept—"

John Rourke cut off the radio speaker and when he said the word "Enough" he almost whispered it . . .

This was the stuff that legend would be made of in the Earth's future, if indeed the Earth had a future.

An army like no other one ever assembled was forming now near the entrance to the Soviet Underground City in the Urals, much of the force on a high snow-covered plain swept by icy winds which never ceased to blow. Perhaps, at some point in human history, there had been larger armies preparing for an ultimate battle, but not even in World War Two had an alliance been formed which was so unique, Paul Rubenstein thought.

Tanks were being flown in swinging on cables beneath large, powerful cargo helicopters, trucks and armored personnel carriers were moving everywhere, men and equipment in such great abundance that he did not attempt a tally of any sort.

The alliance here was of men, really, not of nations. A unit of Icelandic police, battalions of Germans born and raised under Nazi dictatorship who, with a taste of freedom, now committed their all to its cause, a few Americans, the Chinese who had remained faithful to the sweep of change and democratization which started, then stalled, then split the very fabric of China, even—although precious few of them—men from the Wild Tribes of Europe, not trained in fighting, nor skilled in technology, most of them unable to communicate verbally in any real sense, but doing their part by moving crates of ammunition and disposable rocket launchers, aiding in whatever manner they could.

Paul Rubenstein would have liked to just sit in the prefabricated tower which controlled air traffic for the field and use that time jotting down notes for his journal; but, instead, he too was busily working. As time went on in this war which, he prayed, would now end, he had become something of the 'expert' concerning Soviet computers, on several occasions jury-rigging Russian-made instruments because the job needed doing and no one else was available. Now, he worked with Natalia, what he witnessed over the landing field only possible for him to watch because he had needed to rest his eyes from the green of the screens he had been staring at for more hours than he wanted to consider.

"I think I have it, Paul!" Natalia called up to him. Paul Rubenstein sighed heavily, rubbed at his aching back, dropped to his knees on the tower floor beside her and rubbed his balled fists over his eyes. Indeed, it appeared she had at last made the critical connection linking the auto-navigation broadcast system aboard the captured Soviet gunships into the German navigational computer used by the tower controllers. If the system worked, it would be possible—in theory, at least—to track every single Soviet helicopter gunship that would be sent against them on computer, then link that system into missile targeting.

The result would be obvious. A computer operator could locate, track and destroy each of the Soviet gunships at whim merely by locking a missile onto each individual gunship's auto-navigation evasion program. By the time the Soviet pilots caught on that their own evasive action was homing a missile on to them, it would be too late. Eventually, the better pilots would realize what was happening, but by that time, it would be too late to save the majority of the Soviet gunships.

"You've got it," Paul agreed, checking the screen "So, let's try it out." He crossed to the other side of their private corner of the tower and took up the radio microphone, beginning to signal to Michael Rourke who was airborne over the ice more than five miles downrange . . .

"This is Sitting Duck, reading you loud and clear. I will commence evasive pattern starting now. Sitting Duck Out." Michael Rourke punched in the standard Soviet evasion program and watched as his instruments, on auto-navigation, suddenly seemed to have a mind and will of their own, moving the Soviet helicopter he flew to a higher altitude and commencing a zig-zag pattern.

On his incoming radar, in what seemed like seconds but was at least a minute, he saw the predicted missile, the blip very small at first, but growing larger and larger by the micro-second. And the Soviet machine which he no longer piloted saw it, too.

He thought of his talk with his father before taking off. "You've gotten pretty good with one of these things, Michael, but never think you're too good. Once the missile is on target and the machine is responding with evasive action and the missile seems locked on regardless, cut out of the auto-nav mode, dive the machine and call in to Natalia and Paul to give the destruct code for the missile. You don't need that thing crawling down your neck to prove the system works."

"I can handle it, Dad."

His father smiled. "I know you can handle it. Otherwise, you wouldn't be doing it."

Michael Rourke hadn't quite understood his father's meaning with that remark, realizing full well that John Rourke could have meant it several ways.

He checked his instruments again. The Soviet gunship was playing out its heart, really, and Michael Rourke could feel that in his stomach, the climbing, the diving, the rapid direction changes. But the growing blip of missile still moved inexorably nearer to the center of the green screen with the yellow grid. And the radar screen itself was that center.

He decided to hang on a while longer, really giving the new system the test it deserved. If the system worked, countless allied lives could be saved, because the Soviet gunships would, themselves, call on target the missiles sent to destroy them.

Michael Rourke watched the blip, the blip growing larger because it was coming closer.

In his peripheral vision, he saw the snow, the sky—the sky was just a darker white—and, at last, he saw a contrail.

"Sitting Duck to Guardian Angel, Sitting Duck to Guardian Angel. Come in, Guardian Angel. Over." Michael Rourke switched off auto navigation and cancelled auto pilot interlock, starting the gunship into a high speed dive. "Sitting Duck to Guardian Angel. Come in, Guardian Angel. Over."

"This is Guardian Angel, reading you loud and clear, Sitting Duck. Over."

"Execute destruct sequence now. I say again, execute destruct sequence now. Over!"

Michael Rourke had let the missile get too close, he realized. And he banked the Soviet gunship hard to starboard, starting a maximum acceleration climb to avoid the consequences of his error in judgment. The missile itself was visible as a blurred streak of darker gray against the sky, a snow white contrail snaking after it, zig-zagging maddeningly but ever nearer.

At the high point of his acceleration, Michael Rourke dove, the missile visibly streaking past him just over his main rotor. He glanced right, the missile making a near right angle turn, still homing in.

Michael Rourke grabbed for the knife given him in Lydveldid Island by old Jon, the Swordmaker. It was an identical duplicate, copied faithfully over five centuries, of the Crain Life Support System I, smaller than his father's original Life Support System X in both blade and handle. And now, it was his only hope. There was something wrong with his auto navigation system, had to be, and in another second or two the missile, still homing in on him, would be remotely exploded. The concussion, at this range would be great enough to damage the Soviet chopper Michael Rourke flew and bring the machine down.

Michael Rourke took the knife in his right fist and, awkwardly working the machine's controls with his left, hammered the butt of the Crain knife against the auto navigation console, smashing into it. Michael Rourke wheeled the nine-inch blade knife in his fingers and stabbed into the wiring, the knife flying from his grip, the helicopter's control consoles starting to smoke.

The missile shot past him as he wrenched the helicopter out of the dive and slipped to port.

The missile exploded now, the machine rocking, trembling around him.

But the controls still worked, although all electronics were dead. The important thing Michael Rourke thought, smiling was that he was not . . .

The temperature inside the hermetically sealed tent was, he knew on a rational level, comfortable; yet, in contrast to the outside temperature, it seemed stiflingly warm. He clamped his cigar between his teeth, just keeping it there rather than lighting it.

He was entering a moment, as it were, for which he had been waiting five hundred years. The Night of The War had come, despite the fact that those persons who considered themselves wise and informed had proclaimed that peace was at hand and that World War Three would never occur. And, after The Night of The War, there had been no time to do anything but react. First, the search for his wife and children, with his unexpected but welcome ally, Paul Rubenstein, who was now not only his best friend but his son-in-law. Shortly after beginning his search for his family, he had met Natalia, and his world changed again. He remembered her from the espionage game they had both played out in Latin America, but on opposite sides. And, Natalia too had become his friend and ally and something more. He was in love with her, and she with him. But that fact had no bearing on his search for his family.

He found them, barely made it into the Retreat with them alive before the ionization of the atmosphere took full effect and the sky literally caught fire. Deliberately while his wife, Sarah, his friend Paul and Natalia too, rested through the centuries in cryogenic sleep, John Rourke awakened, awakened his children, taught them, then returned to the Sleep. He at once performed a disservice to his wife, for which he could never make amends, and do the right thing. She lost her childhood, but now Michael, their son, and Annie, their daughter who was now Paul's wife, were adults, fully capable of shouldering their share of the burden of survival and of helping to propagate the species.

But, the Eden Project, mankind's supposed last hope, returned, and over the course of the days and weeks and months following the Awakening from cryogenic sleep in the safety of The Retreat, John Rourke's 'family' was no longer alone on the earth, the Eden returnees, others as well who had, by various means, survived the holocaust. Including two colonies of the enemy, survival communities of KGB-led hardline Soviet Communists still intent on world domination, even at the risk of global destruction.

John Thomas Rourke looked around the table as his son, Michael, approached the table, then sat down. Although everyone told John Rourke that he and his son looked sufficiently alike to be twins, Rourke only considered that well-meant flattery. Yet, because of the tricks with human aging he had played through use of the cryogenic chambers, although their birthdays were decades apart, there was now less than a decade's gap between their actual ages. He looked directly at Michael Rourke. "How's your knife?"

"Didn't get hurt, Dad."

Wolfgang Mann, already seated, said, "Doctor, the meeting is yours."

John Rourke nodded to his son, exhaled, then sat down, saying, "Gentlemen, this will be our last briefing before those few of us who are going inside move out. I don't know the overall attack plan of Colonel Mann, nor do I desire to know it. Should any of us who will be entering the Underground City be taken alive, such knowledge could endanger too many others. So, this will be a little one-sided.

"Timed to coincide with the Mid-Wake attack on the Soviet Underwater Complex," John Rourke went on, "it has been the intent since events began shaping up for what is about to occur that, in order to minimize casualties, commando raids would be launched simultaneously on the Underground City and the Soviet Underwater Complex just before the main attacks take place. My team and I will be leaving—" John Rourke rolled back the cuff of the black knit shirt that he wore to read the face of the Rolex on his left wrist—"in approximately fifteen minutes. It is our intention to penetrate the Underground City, utilizing the energy weapons created especially for that purpose as based on the Soviet technology. Once inside, we will fight our way toward the central control complex, where, according to our most recent intelligence data, we should be able to locate and neutralize both the main entrance controls and the primary radar system which co-ordinates surface to air missile responses."

He hoped . . .

Jason Darkwood broke surface under the dome of the lagoon, cocooning his wings around him. High clouds hung beneath the dome, clouds of water vapor and God only knew what else, clouds that were always there, giving the air above the appearance of being a sky. But on the other side of the dome was the sea, the entire Soviet Complex on a ridge beside an undersea volcanic vent providing its geothermal power source.

Far away beneath the sea, sharing the same volcanic vent for the same purpose, lay Mid-Wake, the American undersea colony established five centuries before, only a moment in history before The Night of The War.

Jason Darkwood, Captain, United States Navy, Commanding United States Attack Submarine *Ronald Reagan*, had gambled, and with the twenty-three U.S. Marines of his commando team, he'd won. The computer banks of the most recently captured Soviet Island Class submarines contained the latest safe route into the lagoon which was the harbor and central docking area for the Soviet Underwater Complex. The gamble was that the Soviets who controlled the complex would not have had the time to change the route beneath the dome and into the lagoon in time.

There was always the possibility that the Soviets had, of course, left the route unchanged as part of a trap, but the purpose such a trap might achieve was unfathomable to him, and the risks were great. He could have brought two hundred men in with him, or more than that.

A slip up had been on the part of the Soviet Marine Spetznas who co-ordinated security for the Complex. That he'd made it into the lagoon and stuck his helmet up above the surface without getting his head inside of that helmet blown off was concrete evidence of that.

Now, Darkwood was tired of holding his breath—the hemosponge through which he breathed under the water was useless in atmosphere—and he was as certain as circumstances allowed that he and his men were undetected. So, he ducked under again, allowing his wings to unfold, then twisting his body into a downward roll, toward the shoaled area just beneath the main dock.

His twenty-three commandoes waited for him, in a classic wedge-shaped defensive posture, their liberated Soviet shark guns poised and ready.

With hand and arm signals, Darkwood communicated that all above seemed well and his intention, as planned, to assault the dock—now.

The Marine lieutenant—Stanhope from the *Reagan*—and two Marine sergeants broke off toward the other dock ladders, taking five men apiece, five men falling in behind Darkwood himself.

The old, rusty AKM-96 that had been there the one previous time he had entered the Soviet Underwater Complex was still there, if anything rustier. Darkwood wondered if the Marine Spetznas trooper who had lost it had finished paying for it yet. And, he smiled. With the wages the Marine Spetznas were paid in the lower enlisted ranks, he seriously doubted it.

One way or the other, today, he hoped to bring that man debt relief . . .

Soviet uniforms would have availed them no element of surprise, and certainly no entry to the Soviet Underground City in the Ural Mountains, because the Soviets would be using daily issue passes and regularly changed code phrases. Of that, John Thomas Rourke was sure. With the Allied Army camped virtually on their doorstep, they would have been fools to do otherwise.

But, on the plus side, Soviet uniforms would get them to the main entrance unmolested.

The system they used was exactly the same which had worked successfully for them at Gur'Yev. Paul drove the ATV staff car, Michael sat beside him, Natalia sat on the driver's side in the rear passenger seat, John Rourke beside her, all of them in appropriate Soviet uniform attire. The exception this time was they were more heavily armed, and secreted under the rear seat and behind it were explosives and the four German-made energy weapons.

Paul turned the staff car onto the icy road heading toward the outer boundary gate for the Underground City, Soviet vehicles all around them, Soviet air power—fighters and gunships—in the sky above them.

As they settled onto the road, the outer boundary gates just barely in sight and several minutes away on the ice-slicked roadway, Paul held up a tape recorder, the small, hand held kind businessmen five centuries ago had sometimes used for dictation.

As he pushed the play button, then looked back at John Rourke and smiled, the music started. The sound quality left much to be desired, but the message the music made was clear.

They were driving through the New Mexico desert five centuries ago in a red '57 Chevy, unwittingly on their way to their first real fight side-by-side at a wrecked jetliner against Brigand bikers. It was the same music playing now through the little tape machine as had played through the Chevy's tape deck then.

The Beach Boys.

John Rourke smiled at his best friend. "Trigger control." It was the only thing John Rourke could tell this man who was more a brother to him than if they had come from the same womb.

And Paul Rubenstein just nodded that he understood . . .

Jason Darkwood dropped to his knees behind crates of explosives stacked there on the dock. By now, he was nearly gasping for breath, his helmet still on. As he freed himself of the helmet, he sank forward on the palms of his gloved hands.

There was a sentry on the dock who hadn't been there when he'd broken surface for a quick look only moments before, and it was imperative now to remove that sentry before the rest of his team could break surface. If anyone from the other three teams broke surface and were spotted—Darkwood remembered the old expression from archival videotapes of pre-War movies: "There goes the ballgame."

He shrugged out of his wings as quickly as he could, out of his flippers as well, no time to shed the rest of his swimming gear.

He reached to his side for the Randall Smithsonian Bowie. It wasn't really that, of course, but an identical duplicate of the Randall which his ancestor had brought to Mid-Wake five centuries before. But something existed now which had not existed then. It was a type of field blue that was also an anti-corrosive sealant. It coated the high carbon steel blade of his knife, killing the shine and protecting it against seawater.

Darkwood fisted the knife as he peered around the corner of the little fort of packing crates within which he hid.

The sentry would not be coming back toward his position for at least two minutes, and in those two minutes the teams would already have begun coming onto the dock and the ballgame would be gone.

Darkwood looked quickly up and down the dock, seeing no other signs of guard personnel except those on the Island Classers themselves which were at dockside. But their decks were so high above the docks that, if luck were with him, he might not be seen at all.

Darkwood gambled again, moving out from the walled structure of ammo crates and along the dockside itself, moving as quickly and as silently as he could, the Randall tight in his right fist in a rapier hold, ready to chop or thrust. He gambled for the same reason he usually gambled—there was no choice.

Steel and flesh. The first time he was taught the techniques, the idea of using a knife on a man was an abstraction. Unlike most of his fellow Mid-Wake submarine commanders, however, he had never been able to sit idly and relatively safely by, aboard his vessel, while the Marines assigned to him went into man-to-man battle. Therefore, the abstraction had become reality for him quite some time ago. And the reality revolted him, more so because he was good at it.

Darkwood kept moving, the reality approaching again as he approached the man he was about to kill. His eyes shifted from the imaginary spot he had picked just beyond his target (one never, he was taught, watched the intended victim), to the knife.

If they succeeded here today and in the hours to come, and if similar success were in the cards for Doctor Rourke and the land forces, then the war would be over. If they failed, he would almost certainly die.

There would be much killing. But, why this killing . . .

Jason Darkwood rolled the handle of the Randall in his fist, bringing the knife edge upward, just as effective for a thrust into the kidney or a cut to the spine. But even more effective for something else.

He remembered watching some of the old mysteries, where the heroes—men like Bogart or Cagney—would get struck on the head and awaken experiencing no ill effects. That was absurd, at least usually. So, what he planned for the Soviet sentry was not all that humane—days or weeks in a hospital, perhaps side effects, perhaps not—but it would cheat death.

Jason Darkwood was about three yards from the man when he quickened his pace. The man turned around.

Jason Darkwood struck with the heavy spine of the Randall's blade, going for the base of the neck behind the right ear, missing because the man turned, striking the right shoulder instead, a curse from the Marine Spetznas sentry's lips then . . .

No choice, no cheating of death.

Jason Darkwood's left hand grabbed the man's face as his right hand raked the knife's primary edge across the throat of the Spetznas just as the man was about to cry out.

There was no cry.

Death got what it wanted.

"Shit."

Jason Darkwood rolled the dead man over to the dock's edge, jerking his body over and into the water, controlling the fall as best he could to minimize the noise. Gloved hands reached up out of the water, taking the body, to weight it down, weight it down with junk from beneath the dock.

And Jason Darkwood had the strangest thought as he clung there just below the dock level, in the shadow of one of the Soviet Island Class submarines—perhaps this was the Marine Spetznas who had lost the rusting away AKM-96 in the water just below.

Perhaps the man and his weapon, both of them spent, would be united again . . .

Paul Rubenstein cut off the tape player, hit the eject button, pushing the player under the skirt of his open greatcoat, dropping the tape into an interior breast pocket of his Soviet Elite Corps uniform jacket as he began to slow the ATV staff car.

For another day, if there was one, perhaps another adventure.

Here he was, Paul Rubenstein thought, the junior editor from a New York magazine turned freedom fighter all because he got on one airplane instead of another and survived the Night of The War while everyone else in New York City, including the girl he'd been dating, thinking seriously about, just died in one blinding microsecond.

He was married, to the daughter of his best friend who, chronologically, was just his junior, despite the fact they'd been born a quarter century apart.

And she was magnificent, his wife, John's daughter, Annie.

And now he might lose all that he had in her, all his future, their future together.

He had never considered turning away from his course when once he'd started it.

That would have been cowardly and stupid. He'd never considered himself that terribly brave at all, but he'd never considered himself stupid, either.

As he braked and the ATV skidded just slightly near the guard post on the Underground City's outer gate, his right hand moved under the skirt of his greatcoat again, but not for the tape recorder. He was more heavily armed than he had ever been since he first took up a gun to fight beside John Rourke that day five centuries ago, when they'd returned to the crashed jetliner, only to find that some segments of humanity were not sufficiently glutted on death, wanted more.

The German MP-40 sub-machine gun, which he still called a Schmiesser just because it had become a running joke between John and himself, was slung under the coat. The battered old Browning High Power he'd taken from a pile of Brigand weapons after the battle at the jetliner was still with him, as was its newer, less blue worn twin, which he'd acquired later.

Aside from the Gerber MkII fighting knife which he habitually carried, now inside a slit of his greatcoat, he carried two other handguns, these courtesy of John's stockpile at The Retreat, where he and the rest of the family had weathered five centuries in cryogenic sleep together.

What would become of the 'family' now, should this war end today?

Natalia?

Natalia loved John, but she would never intentionally come between John and his wife, Sarah.

Paul Rubenstein closed his fist over one of the two handguns from the Retreat. One was a Beretta 92F, originally from the Eden stores, the cache of weapons, material and survival necessities located with strategic reserves in various locations throughout what was once the United States. That was stuffed in his belt beneath his uniform beside the newer of his two Brownings, just a spare for the job at hand. But the other gun, the one he held in his right fist now, was one that he had decided he would keep, use.

Even if the war ended today, Paul Rubenstein realized he'd become too much of the veteran campaigner to expect that weapons could be melted down into plowshares.

The gun was a Smith & Wesson Model 681, the short-lived fixed sight production version of the four-inch stainless steel L-Frame .357 Magnum. It was another of the seeming myriad guns which John's old pal, Ron Mahovsky had made up before The Night of The War.

Metalifed—an electrostatic chrome binding process—over the stainless steel, round butted to accept Goncalo Alves combat stocks, action tuned to buttery smoothness, it was perfect for the job at hand.

The Elite Corps guards approached the staff ATV. There were two of them.

Paul Rubenstein rolled down the staff ATV's passenger window and pointed the gun at them, firing point blank into the head of the nearest man, then two shots to the chest of the one farthest away.

He threw the revolver down onto the seat beside him and stomped the gas pedal, heading off road to punch through the electrified fence and evade the deflection barriers. "Here we go! Don't touch anything metal!"

The ATV seemed to hesitate for a split second, then was through.

Jason Darkwood was stripped of his environment suit, making a last equipment check on the black penetration suit he wore beneath it. Around him, Marine Raiders were in various stages of shedding their Sea Wings and environment suits, two of Stanhope's men detailed to Darkwood keeping watch, PV-26 shark guns and 2418 A2 pistols with thirty-round magazines at the ready.

Darkwood swapped magazines for his pistol, pouching the fifteen-shot stick and putting a thirty up the well, the chamber already loaded, of course. His knife was already sheathed to his right leg.

Darkwood approached the two Marines on guard, nodded for them to get out of their gear while he took the watch. Another Marine, Lance Corporal Mondragon, joined Darkwood there at the edge of the packing crate fort.

Darkwood rolled back the left cuff of his penetration suit and studied the dual analog/digital display of his Steinmetz. They would commence their attack in just under two minutes. If all went well, in under seven minutes, the first U.S. submarine ever to move into the lagoon would start through the entry tunnel, clear it in under a minute more and surface in the Soviet Underwater Complex.

If all went well . . .

Paul wheeled the staff car along the the slope into the hairpin. Natalia could feel the ATV's rearend skidding, slipping, clutched at John's arm as she started skidding herself, along the rear seat.

"Hang on," John whispered quietly beside her.

They were into the curve now, and as she clutched more tightly to John Rourke, she could see out the car's rear window. Two trucks, a half track and another staff car pursued them. Soon, there would be a helicopter, then another and another.

"Is it time?"

They were out of the hairpin. John Rourke nodded.

Then, there was only one thing to do.

Natalia Anastasia Tiemerovna, Major, Committee for State Security of The Soviet, Retired, pulled the pin.

Then, with both hands, she took the ridiculous Soviet uniform hat from her head, throwing it down to the floor. Next came the short blonde wig. But, already, she was dropping to her knees beside John as he began pulling the seat out. She pushed the poorly fitting skirt up along her thighs for more freedom of movement, her hands moving to the seat cushion, helping John to pull it outward and up.

The first thing she saw was one of the energy weapons. With these, they stood a chance, even against helicopters. And, as she looked up and through the rear window, she saw the first of the Soviet gunships on its way, coming after them . . .

As they crossed along the rear of the dock, Jason Darkwood could see a crane in operation over the missile deck of one of the Soviet Island Class submarines, the one at the farthest end of the dock. A warhead was being lowered into one of the Island Classer's missile tubes. The shape and size of the warhead was considerably different from any Darkwood had ever seen before on captured Soviet vessels.

And he realized, a chill running up his spine, that it had to be nuclear.

The damned fools were ready to start it all again, and this time destroy the entire planet in the process.

Darkwood and his team of Marine Raiders reached the end of the dock. Each sabotage team had its own mission, and the mission of Darkwood's own team was arguably the most difficult and at once the most vital.

The central control complex for the lagoon itself. Once neutralized, the defense systems prohibiting unauthorized entry by submarines into the lagoon itself would be down.

Jason Darkwood longed to see the *Reagan*'s sail rising out of the lagoon, see her reinforced full complement of United States Marines and German Long Range Mountain Patrol and Commando personnel swarming across her decks, each man with his motorized scooter unit which would get him to the docks, to the decks of the Island Classers.

And the invasion of the Soviet Underwater Complex would have begun.

Darkwood huddled against a wall of crates, these larger than the ammunition crates he'd seen before. And, as if he'd needed the reminder, stenciled on the crates in black and yellow paint was the universal symbol for radioactivity.

Nuclear warheads.

"Captain, you see—

"I see it, Mondragon," Darkwood nodded, trying to control the mixture of fear and loathing so his voice would not betray his emotions. "They won't get the chance to use them. Trust me on that, son. Move it, now!" And Darkwood hustled his five Marines along toward the gates which guarded the dock area of the lagoon, and the high rise structure just inside the fence.

It was the control center . . .

Michael Rourke reached up to the roof panel, unlocking it on the passenger side, Natalia doing the same on the driver's side. "Ready, Michael?"

"Let her go!"

Natalia almost broke a nail letting loose of the panel, the staff car's slipstream sucking it away from them, the panel bouncing over the trunk lid and into the ice-slicked road surface behind them. The 'moon roof' was a custom modification to the staff car, not a standard feature. But, under the circumstances, it would be very useful.

John was nearly into the pack for the energy weapon, movement of any kind in the rear seat cramped because of the modest leg room to begin with and the added problem of the removed seat.

She helped him fasten the last buckle for the pack around his chest, then squeezed back against the door so she could give John more room. He rose to his full height, threading his tall, muscular frame through the opening in the roof, dragging the energy weapon itself with him.

Natalia twisted herself around and wrestled open the door, the slipstream catching her hair, suddenly chilling her legs, her skirt up to her thighs. She clawed at the seat, pushing it outward, through the open doorway and out, the ATV bumping as it rolled over it. From under her greatcoat, she pulled the German sub-machine gun, pushing it forward, the sling still wrapped over her body beneath her coat. And she stabbed the sub-machine gun through the open door, wedging it open with her right knee, opening fire now on the nearest of the enemy vehicles, the half track.

Men clung to its superstructure, returning fire, Natalia drawing back.

"Look out! Grenade outgoing!" She glanced behind her for a split second, catching a quick glimpse of Michael hanging out the passenger side door, pitching the grenade. The only time she ever wished to be a man was when she needed to throw a grenade. She could never get the distance Michael got, the grenade hitting the roadbed and rolling under the front of the APC she'd swapped shots with, then detonating. The APC lost a tread as it careened toward the shoulder, men falling from it into the roadbed.

The vehicles behind the lead APC did not swerve to avoid casualties, but ran over the hapless trooper's bodies instead.

"Let's see if this works," John called out.

There was a hum, a crackle and, as she watched a tongue of bluish white energy like a lightning bolt move toward the staff car that was right behind them. And the staff car exploded, a fireball, black and orange and yellow, belching skyward, then engulfing the APC that drove through it . . .

All of the security was on the gates themselves, but Jason Darkwood and his five commandoes were already inside the fence. They started for the stairs leading up to the harbormaster's tower. From there, as best intelligence estimates indicated, the sonar net and the sharks which guarded the entire area except the new sonar free tunnel were controlled.

The sharks were controlled electronically by the Soviets and used like the sentry dogs. Darkwood had seen them in video movies from before the Night of The War. But the sharks were, literally, controlled; there not just to alert their masters of an incoming diver, but to attack and devour that diver. Darkwood and the twenty-three Marines had entered through the new sonar tunnel, a necessity for the Soviets so the sharks could enter and leave without putting the entire sonar net on alert. But no ship could pass through such a small tunnel.

If control for the movement of the sharks and the sonar net itself was based in the tower above, and that tower could be taken over, then American vessels could enter beneath the Soviet domes, surface in the lagoon and do so in total surprise. To destroy the tower would have been easy enough, but the element of surprise, critical to any hope for success against the superior numbers beneath the Soviet domes, was crucial.

Admiral Rahn's plan was brilliant—seize the submarine bays, blocking access to the docks from within the domes and set up a perimeter defense to block any Island Classers on patrol from getting back inside. Then, form a *cordone sanitaire* through which Mid-Wake vessels could travel, bringing in more and more troops, most of these German, eventually taking the city, block by block if need be.

There was always the chance the masters here would detonate explosives which would collapse the domes, thus destroying not only the enemy but themselves as well. If that happened, at least Mid-Wake would survive.

Jason Darkwood neared the steps leading up into the tower. There were two guards stationed at the base, with AKM-96 rifles at port arms.

It was serious business even to consider firing a conventional projectile type weapon beneath the Soviet domes because of the possible catastrophic damage which might result. Mid-Wake engineers had perfected an effective anti-personnel round which would not penetrate the dome material itself, but there was nothing to suggest the Russians had a similar round.

For one of these sentries to open fire, only the most dire circumstances could be the justification.

9mm Lancer Caseless rounds, however, would not penetrate the dome material; or, at least, that was what the engineers said. Indeed, no handgun round could, not even the .44 Magnum (which was still in use by some firearms hobbyists at Mid-Wake). Yet, by way of example, Darkwood and the commando unit had been told that even the relatively anemic 5.56mm round in use by the United States Military during the Viet Nam and post-Viet Nam era could penetrate.

A single penetration in the domes might not bring catastrophe, but if the penetration hit at an architectural stress point, or there were several such penetrations, one of the domes might fracture. Then they would all go, and the sea would rush in, the air suddenly compressed and domes rupturing outward.

Disaster.

The only solution to the problem of the two guards, since there were no suppressed pistols available, was the PV-26 shark guns or knives.

The shark guns were relatively silent, but not silent enough, with more Marine Spetznas personnel dangerously close by. Darkwood handed off his pistol to a young Marine near him. Holstering the Lancer would have been grossly impractical because of the thirty-round extension magazine. Swapping magazines to the shorter one would have been too noisy, the clicking of the magazine's being re-seated possibly loud enough to betray them to the guards they would have to kill. He drew the Randall from his leg sheath instead, (the closure was an advanced hook and pile fastener system which was essentially noiseless), gestured with his knife toward the two guards, then looked from man to man. All five Marines drew their issue blades by way of volunteering.

Despite the circumstances, Jason Darkwood smiled. But, he wasn't surprised. After all, the men with him were United States Marines . . .

The wind, unremittingly, bitingly cold, numbed the back of his neck and tore at his hair as he stood in the ATV's roof opening, the energy weapon locked in both fists. John Rourke fired the energy weapon. There was the hum, the crackle, but there was no recoil felt, no pushing back against him nor was there any muzzle rise. Accuracy from the hip was outstanding.

The APC was there one instant and gone in a ball of flames the next.

He twisted the weapon upward as the Soviet gunships—the second one had joined the first only a moment ago—started trying to outflank them. It was a classic Soviet maneuver, and an effective one. Once both machines were in position—a matter of seconds only now—they would most likely fire their inboard missiles, the objective to literally shatter the object they wished to destroy between the tandem explosions. He doubted they'd perfected tactical use of the energy weapons with which they were doubtlessly armed, doubted they would try the same tactic.

But John Rourke had no intention of waiting to find out.

He swung the energy weapon to his shoulder. The stock's length was too short and the comb was too low for a proper spotweld, but he did the best he could, steadying himself as he squeezed the trigger, only a crude switch.

A bolt of the plasma energy lightning lashed outward and upward, toward the Soviet gunship on his left, missing. But the gunship drew back. Submachinegun fire from within the car, Natalia firing at the choppers as well, either that or Michael using Paul's MP-40.

The second chopper fired a missile and John Rourke threw the upper half of his body flat over the staff car's roof, protecting his face and chest as best he could and, at the same time, covering the energy weapon.

The explosion of the missile so close to him was ear-shattering, and a shower of dirt and debris crashed over him, the car swerving maddeningly.

Rourke raised himself upward, shouting to Natalia below, "Steady me! Steady me!"

He felt her hands on his thighs and hips now as he wedged himself into a corner of the roof opening, bracing himself for maximum steadiness.

Rourke fired, missing. It wasn't just the bumpiness, but the sights were off, Rourke realized it as he turned the weapon in his hands, shouting to Natalia, "Let go of me and duck!" He threw himself forward again, protecting the weapon and protecting his face as another missile fired, this time impacting still closer, the entire fabric of the staff car pulsing with it.

Rourke's squinted eyes flashed to the energy weapon's rear sight. A screw had worked out, the sight blade slid all the way left. "Damnit!" There was no time to secure another of the energy weapons from inside the car. The next missile strike would have them, and the first chopper was coming back.

"Hold me again!" Rourke shouted below, feeling Natalia's hands on him once more as he wedged himself into the corner of the roof opening. The rear sight be damned, he told himself, almost verbalizing it as he swung the weapon to his shoulder like a shotgun, settling the front sight on the center of the chopper and firing, then firing again on the same breath.

The helicopter, close now, was suddenly aflame, the fireball rushing toward the roof of the staff car. Rourke twisted and threw himself downward, his arms going around Natalia to protect her lest the fireball be sucked in through the open driver's side rear door.

The car rocked, Rourke's skin hot, then cold. He was up, Natalia shouting to him, "Be careful!" He grabbed up the energy weapon again, feeling her hands on him, swung the weapon to his shoulder and fired on the first helicopter.

He missed.

He fired again, then again, catching the machine at the tail rotor, the tail rotor seeming to melt, then a line of flame running back from the tail rotor engine toward the fuel tanks, the fireball belching outward. Rourke threw himself down again, the staff car almost upending with the concussion.

John Rourke, holding Natalia Tiemerovna against him, looked up.

No more choppers.

"We're almost at the main gate, John!" Paul Rubenstein shouted.

John Rourke twisted around, still holding Natalia, his eyes focusing on the entrance to the Underground City.

This was the moment . . .

Jason Darkwood moved along beneath the open steps, no kick panels fitted to them. He could see the the feet of the two guards. If all he wanted was to kill, it would have been ridiculously simple. A slash across an artery and the man would be done for, but not so quickly that he couldn't raise an alarm with a scream of pain or a wild shot—and with a stray rifle bullet, there was always the possibility of doing considerably worse damage.

The young Marine beside him—Lance Corporal Mondragon—looked at him.

Darkwood's raised the palm of his free hand toward Mondragon, gesturing for patience.

And Darkwood's eyes tracked along the steps themselves. When he and Mondragon had left the other three Marines, the guards had been standing by the base of the steps, easier prey. But while Darkwood and the Marine circled around the tower's legs to get at the guards, they moved, one on the lowest step, leaning against the handrail, the other on a step about midway along the length of the upward run.

Darkwood exhaled, nodded to himself.

He signalled to Mondragon, to wait until he—Darkwood—made his play. And Darkwood sheathed the Randall, flexed his shoulders and jumped. He jumped only a few inches, resisting the impulse to go for the next higher step, knowing that the vibration might alert the men he stalked. He swung there, waiting for something to happen, which never did—he was unheard. And he started climbing, hand over hand, from step to step, upward.

His old injuries from New Germany plagued him as he moved, not all his muscles back in tone and some of his wounds not fully healed.

But, Darkwood kept climbing, slowly, his hands on the same tread as the farther away of the two guards now. The man moved, started to turn around. Darkwood held his breath, that the guard would not look down and back and see gloved hands on the same step on which he stood and that Lance Corporal Mondragon would not overreact, opening fire or in some other way trying to take out the guard.

Darkwood hung there, his fingers stiffening, his shoulders and the horseshoe muscles of his upper arms screaming at him. The guard's feet shifted, and there was no more movement.

Jason Darkwood waited for another few seconds, then began again to climb, running out of strength, moving as quickly as he could. He judged himself to be just below the landing, looked up and confirmed that. He shifted his left hand to the landing surface, then his right, chinning himself with considerable difficulty, glancing upward along the second set of steps, seeing no movement from the door leading into the harbormaster's tower, but realizing full well that someone could be inside, just beyond one of the many windows, watching the loading of the Island Classers, perhaps grabbing a cigarette. If such a person looked down, he—Darkwood—would be seen instantly.

It was a chance he had to take.

34

Darkwood swung there, then pushed upward, changing his hand positioning, getting his right knee over onto the landing, then clambering up, sliding beneath the hand rail.

Darkwood rose into a crouch.

He drew the Randall Smithsonian Bowie.

On the balls of his feet now, keeping to the side of the steps along the near handrail to minimize any possible creak from the steps themselves, Jason Darkwood started down, the Bowie in a rapier hold, his left hand outstretched.

He was counting on Mondragon's training coming to the fore. If it were Sam Aldridge waiting down there, Sam would know what to do. But Sam was in Europe, fighting with the Mid-Wake contingent of the Allied force attacking the Soviet stronghold in the Ural Mountains.

Would Mondragon have the presence of mind to wait for the precise instant that Darkwood attacked the guard at the middle of the steps, then attack the guard at the steps' base?

Darkwood focused his concentration on the point of his knife, admiring its symmetry, the blade geometry which gave strength and beauty to it.

The trick was to focus the mind on anything besides the man you approached. Somehow—it almost made one a believer in extra-sensory perception—it seemed that by concentrating on the target, the target was alerted.

He was two steps up behind the man he was about to kill.

There was no choice but to look at him now, the exact position of the sentry's rifle, how to counter the gun's being dropped or fired, all the nuances of the thing.

Darkwood mentally shrugged, then jumped, grabbing for the sentry's right ear with his left hand as he crossed the man's body, Darkwood's forearm going over the man's mouth and jerking the head back as Darkwood's right arm pistoned forward, driving the blade in his hand into the spine to kill as quickly as he could. Darkwood's wrist moved with the vibration as steel met bone, pain moving up Darkwood's right forearm.

There wasn't a sound.

As Darkwood, leaving the knife where it was, grabbed for the body, the guard just below was turning around and Darkwood started to grab for the dead Marine Spetznas' Sty-20 dart gun. But

Mondragon had the second sentry, hand over the mouth, blade into the chest, drawing it out again, slitting the throat.

As Mondragon dragged the sentry down, Darkwood eased his man onto the steps.

Darkwood licked his dry lips, braced his left knee against the dead man's back, then wrenched the Bowie knife from the man's spinal column.

And Darkwood looked toward the landing and up along the length of steps toward the door to the harbormaster's tower.

So far, he thought, so good . . .

The main gates were reinforced and there were deflection barriers before them and there was no way to drive around either.

John Rourke twisted round, getting as low as possible to the staff car's roof line as he aimed the rear-sightless energy rifle toward the gate, Natalia below him calling out, "On three! One . . ."

There was a specially built platform that folded out of the passenger side front door, forming a step. Michael was on that step now behind the armor plated door, armed identically to John Rourke, but hopefully his weapon still possessed of an operational rear sight.

"Two . . ."

The idea was a simple one, like the entire plan. Blast down the deflection barrier and the gate behind it, then get inside.

"Three!"

John Rourke fired for the center of the deflection barrier, Michael for the center as well, streams of blue light moving as bolts from their weapons, blindingly bright if looked at the right way, this another detriment to good marksmanship. John Rourke fired again as Natalia counted to three again, both of them aiming for the same spot in the deflection barrier, the center of the synth-concrete barricade already smoldering. The idea was to excite the atoms sufficiently. John Rourke smiled at the thought, that if the atoms in the deflection barrier were male, all that would have been necessary to excite them would have been for Natalia to smile.

On three, Rourke fired still again, the deflection barrier shimmering where the beams impacted it. "Keep firing continuously until it goes!" John Rourke shouted, firing at will, realizing Michael was doing the same. Their wonder weapons weren't destroying the synth-concrete of the deflection barrier and Paul wouldn't be able to turn the staff car to avoid it.

John Rourke kept firing, feeling the power pack that was strapped to his back starting to warm. He kept firing. The barrier glowed now, vehicles behind it exploding, metal fence struts just beyond it melting. John Rourke kept firing, Michael firing too.

If he ever built another Retreat and natural granite was unavailable or impractical, this synth-concrete would be ideal. It was the material's density, Rourke realized, that made the synth-concrete disintegrate. His thoughts were cut off as he fired, a group of Soviet Elite Corps personnel almost literally throwing themselves across the barricade, firing automatic weapons.

Paul swerved the staff car as Rourke fired toward the Elite Corps personnel, missing. But Rourke swung the muzzle of the energy weapon left, firing again, Michael firing too, now, and the rattle of Natalia's sub-machine gun from below. Bullets whined off the deflection barricade, two of the Elite Corpsmen going down, the beam from Rourke's energy weapon striking two of the men, their bodies torching for an instant, then vaporized.

Michael's energy weapon was aimed again at the barricade, and firing. Rourke fired too, the staff car mere meters from it.

The deflection barrier seemed to glow brighter than it had, and there was a crack louder than the heaviest caliber rifle shot John Rourke had ever heard, and the glow turned into an arc, the synth-concrete barrier exploding.

Rourke's ears rang from the cracking sound, but he could faintly hear Paul's voice as Paul shouted, "We're going through!"

Bullets zinged and whined off the staff car's coach work, what was left of the glass in the vehicle shattering. John Rourke swung the muzzle of the energy weapon in his hands toward the greatest concentration of Elite Corps personnel and fired . . .

The remaining four Marine Raiders mounted the steps, their Soviet AKM-96s, ready. Once inside the harbormaster's tower, guns could be fired with relative impunity as concerned the integrity of the dome above, on the other side of which was the sea. But the noise would alert Marine Spetznas personnel nearby of an attack, and that was to be avoided if at all possible, lest the important element of surprise be lost. Jason Darkwood was on the right side of the door at the height of the steps, Lance Corporal Mondragon on the left.

The lead man of the four Marines returned Darkwood's 2418 A2, Darkwood press checking the slide, confirming the still-chamber were in loaded condition.

And Darkwood gave the nod, the last of the Marine Raiders in place.

Mondragon and one of the other men readied their rifles, three of the Marines with specially prepared gas grenades. Mondragon was already lacing a strip of black adhesive against the doorlock, connecting power leads to the battery pack brought up by one of the other four Marines. It was an offshoot of the technology used by the terrestrial Soviets in the construction of their energy rifles. The same plasma energy could be used to melt the lockplate on the doorway.

Darkwood stepped over the railing, down two steps along the outside. He watched as Mondragon powered up, hissing under his breath to the three grenadiers, "Be ready. Masks up!" Darkwood pulled his gas mask from the the bag at his side, snapped it over his face, popping the cheeks and making a seal.

There was a crackle, then a muted pop and a clang as the door's lockplate fell away.

"Grenades!"

Each of the three Marines with the gas grenades hurtled a pair of the grenades each, the instant the word left Darkwood's mouth. Rifles ready now from the three grenadiers, Darkwood and Mondragon and the sixth man broke through the doorway, STY-20 pistols in hand. Darkwood fired one of the Soviet dart pistols point blank into the chest of a burly figure coming at him through the cloud of gas, then fired a second and third dart, putting the figure down.

Marine Spetznas personnel were rising from their consoles, staggering blindly, eyes streaming tears, coughing, starting to collapse, grasping for belted weapons as they fell.

Darkwood crashed the butt of his pistol down across the neck of a man, wrestled a woman down, snatching her gun from her holster.

The harbormaster's tower, with no bloodshed inside, was taken, but it had to be secured.

As Darkwood moved toward the control panels, he ordered, "Administer the injections and make certain they're disarmed and cuffed."

"Yes, sir!"

Special sedation kits had been prepared for the tower personnel, and plastic disposable cuffs were brought along to bind the tower personnel, hand and foot.

"Secure the tower, Mondragon! On the double!"

"Yes, sir!" And Mondragon began shouting orders to the remaining four Marines from the raiding party.

The door leading to the steps was closed. Already, two of the Marines were stripping off their penetration suits, beneath them Marine Spetznas uniforms already worn so the guards on the steps could be replaced.

No gunfire, no alarms, nothing to indicate that the other raiding parties were faring poorly in their work seizing controls of other parts of the port facility. The gates to the mini-sub pens might already be closed.

Now the hard part, Jason Darkwood thought, as he sat at the sonar net controls and tried to determine which dials and switches to work to shut down just half of the sonar net. If he killed the entire net, alarms would automatically sound. If he killed the wrong side, the *Reagan* and the other vessels coming in after her would activate the sonar system and the entire Underwater Complex would be on alert in a matter of moments.

Darkwood rubbed his thumbs against the tips of his fingers, then started working the controls . . .

The control center for the Underground City's anti-aircraft defenses, according to intelligence data that was as impeccable as could be, was located just beyond the main personnel access tunnel which fed directly into the city itself.

Paul Rubenstein wheeled the shot-up staff car to a halt just inside the gates, the tires smoking, smoke streaming from the seam where the hood met the fenders on all sides of the engine.

As he stepped out of the car, he shrugged the German MP-40 submachine gun forward on its sling, racking the bolt and opening fire as Elite Corps personnel from just inside the gates, streamed toward them.

John was still atop the car, firing the energy weapon again, a beam of the bluish white light, like a bolt of lightning, flickering from the weapon's muzzle and outward, like the hand of death, vaporizing a half dozen of the Elite Corps troopers as they closed toward the staff car.

Natalia rolled out of the passenger seat, another of the energy weapons with her, but the backpack not yet on. With the backpack beside her, she opened fire toward a knot of Elite Corps electric cars, power arcing off their batteries as the beam would strike, the cars exploding in the next instant.

Paul scrambled into the back seat, getting the last of the four energy weapons, pulling on the backpack harness, powering up.

John was off the car now and, shoulder to shoulder with Michael, advancing on the Elite Corps guards. It was only a matter of time — minutes at best — before Soviet energy weapons would be brought to bear against them.

But Paul Rubenstein was already moving, Natalia on her knees near the rear of the car, getting her arms into the pack straps, Paul helping her to at stand and get the pack into position. She buckled up, Paul doing the same as he checked the energy weapon's power level.

Full.

"Let's go, Paul," Natalia urged.

Natalia at his left, Paul Rubenstein started forward, widening the arc of fire John and Michael had begun, the access tunnel into the city less than a half of a city block from them now . . .

The moment Nicolai Antonovitch had waited for had arrived.

And he was still uncertain what to do.

Centuries before, he had sworn allegiance to a madman who had wrested from what could have been an era of peace and global cooperation, a holocaust unlike any in human history.

The office was soundproofed, but there had been three calls, and the red light on his desk was flashing, indicating that an incursion against the city was underway.

He typed a last few words into the computer on the disk that he had begun when the light first started flashing several moments ago.

To prevent the immediate recognition of his words by Soviet personnel, yet attract the attention of any Allied personnel who might subsequently locate the disk, he wrote in English. It was more difficult for him, but that could not be helped. "I discovered that then Colonel Vladmir Karamatsov, in conspiracy with higher ranking officers among the Soviet General Staff who were in sympathy with the policy of war against the West, personally ordered the airborne firing of a stolen nuclear missile from an unmarked Soviet aircraft at the Tallinn radar installation on the Gulf of Finland. As the missile struck, a pre-fabricated tape was broadcast, as though coming from the Tallinn installation, that an American B-52 had penetrated Soviet air space and had launched what appeared to be a Cruise-type missile.

"Because of this missile firing and the taped message, presumably a last message from the crew of the facility before it was obliterated with a direct nuclear strike, Moscow was alerted to American nuclear attack and responded with a retaliatory launch.

"That night, Vladmir Karamatsov precipitated what was nearly the total destruction of humankind. I have borne this knowledge for some time now, and it eats away at my soul. Now, the masters of this city plan a pre-emptive nuclear strike against our allied enemies from the missile tubes of the nuclear submarines based in the Pacific.

"If this should occur, all of humanity will most assuredly be destroyed. The atmospheric envelope is too fragile to sustain even one high megatonnage range nuclear detonation according to the computer models of our best scientists. Yet, the leadership of the Underground City ignores the danger. I cannot. For this reason, I shall now betray Communism in order that I do not betray my country."

He filed the data, then extracted the small hard disc and pocketed it in his uniform tunic.

He stood up, belting on his pistol.

Presumably, when he'd sent plans out for the energy weapons, he had been successful, because, clearly, this type of weapon was being utilized now by the attack force. A small group, although there was no information concerning identities, he wagered with himself that Doctor John Rourke, and perhaps Major Tiemerovna as well, were among them.

Antonovitch walked to his door, unlocked it, opened it.

41

Two junior officers stood open-mouthed in the outer office. "Comrade Marshal—the city—"

"I am aware of such matters, Captain."

"But orders—"

"You will both accompany me."

He walked past them, trying to ignore the questions they shouted after him, into the corridor beyond the outer office. He hoped the two were following him, simply to keep them from other duties. Men and women ran along the corridor, many of them armed, others carrying computer discs, still others seeming just confused.

Antonovitch turned off the main corridor and toward the office of the Premier.

Only the Premier himself could give the order that must be given now . . .

Natalia Tiemerovna paused just inside the tunnel entrance, John and Paul and Michael exchanging fire with an Elite Corps Unit which had pursued them from beyond the main gates. She kicked out of the low heeled shoes that went with her uniform, throwing down first one then the second of the two shoes that had been stuffed into the interior pockets of her greatcoat. They were the modern-day German equivalent of high fashion track shoes, closed quickly enough with the hook and pile fasteners. And, she could run in them.

She kicked the uniform shoes away and picked up her weapon, starting down the tunnel ahead of the three men, toward the control center at its opposite end. As soon as the radar system was down, the Underground City's air defense system would be neutralized and the Allies would be able to attack.

It was poor tactics to run on ahead, but it was also a compulsion, a need within her to which she had no choice, other than to respond.

Ever since she had started thinking for herself, started fighting on the side that was right in this war which had lasted now for five centuries, something had nagged at her soul. And perhaps it had nagged at her soul even before then.

If the Soviet cause had been wrong, if Communism was a lie, a terrible deceit perpetrated on the impoverished masses, could there be any other immediate cause for the nuclear terror which had all

42

but obliterated humanity?

And she had been a part of it, a small part, but an important part. She had worked to subvert the western democracies, had worked to further Communist revolutionary aims throughout the world, had done her part and more. She had the decorations—she still possessed them—to prove it.

She was one of the precious few women to achieve field grade rank. No doubt, part of that was because of her uncle, Ishmael Varakov, who subsequently became Commander of the North American Army of Occupation. Part of that, too, was her then-husband's influence.

But she'd been good, very good, and distinguished herself in what then she had thought was service to the Soviet people and the downtrodden of the world.

It was her fight more than it was anyone's fight.

If she helped to start it, she should help to finish it. And, if she died doing this, then another problem was solved.

She had no death wish, but death was preferable to being alone, and once this war ended, John and Sarah could enjoy the blessings of peace, raise the child that was even now in Sarah's womb.

And, if she lived, she would go her own way. She had already considered that. The Wild Tribes of Europe, children's children of a French survival colony that could not stay out of the atmosphere long enough and had been forced prematurely back to the deadly surface, desperately needed help. Education of even the most basic sort was unknown to those few who survived, the infant mortality rate over seventy percent because of lack of medical care and poor sanitation. She had considered this as her alternative, and realized that perhaps somehow she might at last have found the impoverished masses that the philosophy of Marx and Engels had taught her to serve.

Natalia Anastasia Tiemerovna reached the end of the tunnel.

There were KGB Elite Corps troops stationed there and they opened fire on her with energy weapons . . .

John Rourke ran, the energy rifle at high port in his hands, Michael and Paul holding the near end of the tunnel which accessed into the city. In the distance, toward the end of the tunnel, he could just make out Natalia, flat on the tunnel floor, energy pulses impacting the tunnels walls around her, the pops of small explosions as tunnel wall material exploded, the bolts of bluish white lightning crackling everywhere.

But John Rourke had planned ahead. Technology was fine, but some things were never out of date. From the belt beneath his tunic, John Rourke pulled a grenade. It wasn't gas, it wasn't sound and light. It was a copy of the American M-67 fragmentation grenade with a four to five second delay fuse. The classic baseball grenade, a good man with a good arm could throw it forty yards and the casualty radius when the body of the grenade itself fragmatized on impact was at least fifteen yards was ready. John Rourke could see Natalia now, lying there in the tunnel mouth, unmoving. And fear like he had never known suddenly gripped his stomach, nearly loosening his bowels.

Hugging along the wall now moving steadily forward, he pulled the wire clip which was the second safety for the grenade, all that remained, to pull the split ring at the end of the cotter pin and lob the grenade. If Natalia were dead, he asked himself, what had any of this profited him? What would he do? Her death would solve his greatest dilemma by the simplest means, but John Rourke had never sought the easy way and simple solutions carried with them terrible peril.

There was still no movement from Natalia as he neared the tunnel mouth. When he first learned about grenades, concurrently he had also learned that sometimes bowling a grenade toward its target was the most effective means of getting a grenade where you wanted it when shorter distances were concerned, rather like the underhand throwing of a knife at close range. The energy weapon hanging from its sling by his right side, John Rourke pulled the pin and lobbed the grenade underhand, past Natalia, out of the tunnel mouth and toward the knot of energy weaponed armed Elite personnel. Rather than throwing himself to the tunnel floor to protect himself he stabbed the energy weapon toward the Elite corpsmen and fired, pumping the trigger as fast as he could, dashing toward Natalia. Inside his head, he counted the seconds. The maximum delay would be five. It was at three seconds that he let the energy weapon fall to his side and threw his body on Natalia's, covering Natalia's head and his own with his hands and arms. The roar of the M-67 so close to the tunnel mouth caused an echo effect, his ears ringing with it.

But beneath him, he heard a sound sweeter than anything he had ever imagined. "What—"

Natalia's voice.

She lived.

"Can you move?" He didn't wait for an answer, looking toward the end of the tunnel. The KGB defenders were dead or dying, their energy weapons no longer a threat. But that situation would change in seconds as more of their number reached the site. And, beyond the tunnel, he could see the Air Defense Command Center.

All he had to do was reach it. If he could plant the charges that he wore beneath his coat, he could neutralize it. If he could not plant those charges, he could neutralize the facility at any event, detonating it on his body.

Paul wore a similar set of charges, as did Michael.

John Rourke had refused Natalia's request for the same.

But she could not be left on her own now, barely able to stand, weaving as she sagged against him, a darkening bruise marring the perfect alabaster of her left temple. He dragged her onward, looking back only once. Paul and Michael were pinned down by the entrance to the tunnel, energy weapons impacting the tunnel walls.

And, maybe, this time would be the end.

Since The Night of The War, he had cheated death more times than he could remember. As he half-carried Natalia beside him, he wondered if this time death might finally win the game . . .

So far, so good, Darkwood said under his breath. The phrase was becoming his watchword for this operation. Not a shot had been fired to alert the Marine Spetznas guarding the lagoon, which would, in turn, sound a general alert throughout the complex.

The sonar net had not registered entry of a submarine, yet; yet, the time was long since past for the *Ronald Wilson Reagan*, Sebastian at the con, to have penetrated the entry tunnel to the lagoon beneath the domes.

"Sir!"

"What is it, Mondragon?" Darkwood responded, his eyes never leaving the control panels he monitored.

"Three Marine Spetznas bigshots on the way up, Sir!"

"Mondragon, we don't refer to officers of opposing forces as 'big shots.' They are officers and should be accorded all due respect for rank; unless, of course, circumstances indicate we should kill them. But, we kill them respectfully."

"Yes, sir. Sorry, sir." And there was a slight hint of a laugh.

"Get out of sight and let them in," Darkwood ordered. "Don't react until I give the word or they try to shoot me. Clear?"

"Yes, sir."

Darkwood glanced over his shoulder, then over to the console nearest him, to the Lancer 2418 A2 within reach of his right hand.

He exhaled, listened for the door to open behind him, heard the voice in Russian snapping, "What is this?"

In English, Darkwood responded, "What's it look like, Comrade?" And Darkwood looked over his shoulder. Three Marine Spetznas officers, the highest ranking among them only a captain. But a naval captain, Darkwood's rank, was field grade, the equivalent of a full colonel, so he had the senior-most one of them considerably outranked. "You should be saluting a senior officer, gentlemen; but, I won't tell if you won't tell."

"Take your hands from that equipment!"

Darkwood glanced at the console, then into the lagoon. Nothing yet. "Gentlemen, has it crossed your collective minds—and I use the term 'collective' intentionally—that if I'm in here, and I'm not bothering to try to run or fight, you are outnumbered? I suggest relaxing. Consider the smoking lamp as lit. You might care to surrender your weapons, too. You've just been outflanked."

He heard the scratchy sound of a plastic Sty-20 scraping against a plastic Soviet issue holster. Since captured Sty-20s were so often utilized by American forces, there was inventoried a fabric holster for use with the pistols, vastly better designed and considerably less noisy.

Darkwood said to the three Marine Spetznas officers behind him, "If you shoot me with one of those, the Marines that are in here with me will shoot you, then slit your throats for good measure. And, the two men on the steps aren't yours; they're mine."

Before there was a response, Darkwood saw the black monolith that was the sail of the *Reagan* break surface in the lagoon. A smile crossed his lips as he turned in his seat and looked at the three men.

Their Sty-20s were aimed at his chest. "I suggest setting down your weapons; you have that choice or death. I won't bring it up again."

The two junior officers looked at the captain, who stood between them.

The captain lowered his weapon, then lowered his body into a crouch and set the Sty-20 on the floor by his feet. As he rose back to his full height, the other two officers set down their weapons and Mondragon and the two Marines inside the harbormaster's tower came from hiding behind two of the equipment racks, their AKM-96s at high port.

Jason Darkwood turned back toward the lagoon. The deck of the *Reagan* was just surfaced and her hatches were opening, men and equipment pouring from them.

So far, so good . . .

Nicolai Antonovitch walked past the wall-to-wall staff officers in the Premier's outer office, reached over just under the lip of the secretary's desk and pushed the button which provided access through the double doors into the Premier's office.

The secretary, a pretty, if somewhat severe looking girl in her mid-twenties, looked up at him, brown eyes wide.

"Everything will be better from now on," Antonovitch told her, smiling at her.

The door lock buzzed and Antonovitch entered.

The Premier stood before an illuminated map table which showed the interior and immediate exterior of the Underground City. He looked up from the table, saying, "You should have been announced. Why are you late?"

"I was considering several strategic and tactical options."

"And?"

Nicolai Antonovitch drew the pistol at his belt—it was a Tokarev he'd carried and used for years—and pointed it at the Premier, then began pulling the trigger . . .

Heavy conventional gunfire—automatic weapons and some pistols—along with the bluish white lightning bolts from Soviet energy weapons poured toward them, craters in the ground around their position and the walls near them blackened from energy weapons strikes, pockmarked from bullets.

John Rourke held Natalia, still slightly ill-looking, but able to hold a gun, held her close beside him.

Time was running out.

But he would never choose death while an alternative remained.

"Help me," Rourke told her. "Keep up steady answering fire, but don't work for accuracy. Just keep them busy, like they used to say in the old western movies."

"We're not going to make it," Natalia whispered.

"Yes we are," Rourke smiled, the words holding more conviction than he genuinely felt. As soon as the radar controls for the anti-aircraft batteries were knocked out, there would be an attack against the Underground City of unprecedented magnitude. Then there would be a chance.

The structure at the base of which they huddled for protection from fire was the command center for the Underground City's air defenses. If he could neutralize the structure—John Rourke's mind raced. Already, he was pulling hand grenades from his gear, but the hard way, by twisting open the plastic hangers rather than pulling pins.

The command center was a concrete block building some thirty feet high with no access at all at ground level except via a driveway with a heavy looking metal door at the far end where trucks could enter and leave. There was access above, but that meant traversing an open staircase leading to a main door, and there was already gunfire from above.

John Rourke had anticipated being able to enter the building via conventional means with the help of the energy weapons, then destroy the radar guidance equipment which controlled the air defense response. He had not anticipated the rapidity of the resistance response.

But, he had planned ahead for emergencies.

The explosives he wore, powerful new German plastique, could destroy much of the building, probably do the required amount of damage if detonated from the outside. But, to do that, it would almost certainly be necessary to die in the process.

He'd spent his life telling himself that there had to be a better way, and he was trying to convince himself now that he'd just thought of it. The plastique, unaffected by a bullet strike, unaffected by flame, etc., was only capable of being detonated electrically. Its intended purpose, after reaching the air defense control center and hitting the equipment with the energy weapons, was to blow the entire complex from within, so nothing could be hastily repaired that would allow the system to become operational again.

He eyed the door at the end of the downward leading driveway.

If the idea he had worked, the mission would be accomplished and they just might live through it. His hands had been busy, pulling the second safety from each of the grenades he wore. Natalia, trading occasional shots from her energy weapon with the enemy personnel, seemed to be reviving somewhat.

A bolt from one of the enemy weapons hit the wall near them, a rain of synth-concrete dust falling on them. Rourke, grateful now for the synth-concrete's resistance to the energy weapons, leaned back against the wall, telling Natalia, "Here's what we're going to do. The explosives I'm carrying can be detonated only electrically. I'm betting that a steady stream of shots from one of these," and he patted what corresponded to the receiver area of the energy weapon, "can detonate the plastique and heighten its effect. I'm running down, while you cover me."

"Where? The driveway! You could be—"

"It's not all that healthy waiting here, is it?" Michael and Paul, as best he could tell just through hearing, were still pinned down by the other end of the tunnel. As long as he—Rourke—and Natalia held out here, no one could get into the tunnel from this end to catch Paul and Michael in a crossfire. "But the company's marvelous," and he touched his lips to Natalia's forehead. "I can't detonate even half the stuff from up close without getting killed, so I'm leaving my energy weapon with you. Keep the Elite Corps concentrated on this position as best you can, but don't take any needless chances. Try to pin them down. Make certain you don't deplete the batteries on both guns, though. We'll need one to activate the explosives.

"Once I've got the charges dumped—there wouldn't be time to set detonators or precise charge placement—I'll start running back. Once I'm a safe distance away, start shooting at the plastique. If it goes up, the door will come down. We use the energy weapons and conventional weapons to shoot our way inside, and we use these." And Rourke nodded to the grenades beside him. "The remainder of the plastique should do the trick inside to destroy enough of the building's electrical systems that we can temporarily cripple the equipment. Using it in conjunction with the energy weapons against a synth-concrete load bearing wall, we might be able to collapse the building. Not as good as the original plan, but it should get the job done."

"How do we avoid getting blown up with it?"

"We use the energy weapons to detonate the plastique, then the energy weapons, more grenades and conventional weapons to get a far enough distance away that we'll have a chance of staying alive." The alternative was certain death and failure in their mission if they waited it out here. There was no need telling Natalia that, however, because she knew as much about this sort of thing as he did.

"It could work. I'm moving better. I'll make it." And Natalia leaned across to him, rose up on her knees and held his face in her hands, then kissed him hard on the mouth. "I will love you forever, John."

"I love you. You know that." And he smiled. "Keep a good eye on our grenades, huh?"

He gave a squeeze to her hand, then started shifting out of the backpack for his energy weapon . . .

Nicolai Antonovitch stood over the Premier's body. With the double doors closed, the shots would not have been heard outside in the secretarial suite. The Premier's office, conveniently enough, was soundproofed.

From a spare magazine pouch on the holster itself, he took a fresh load for the pistol, pocketing the empty magazine.

Several options presented themselves now, but the most likely one to succeed in bringing this thing to a close with minimal loss of life was to cut all power for the City. It seemed obvious that the small team, which even now was presumably still fighting, wished to reach the controls for air defense radar. Killing the power would kill the air defense radar. That could only be done at the main power station or at Commissariat for Special Contingencies, at the headquarters for the civil police, about a quarter mile from the Premier's office along a series of tunnels through which he should, he presumed, still be able to travel easily enough because of his position.

50

The Commissariat for Special Contingencies was a crack team of anti-riot police on constant alert for quelling civil disturbances, which there rarely were. Recently, however, there had been small groups of dissenters within the City, protesting the continuation of the war. On the wall inside the inner sanctum of the commissariat there was an illuminated map which showed all power grid sectors, and a series of switches which could shut them off one at a time as necessary, or all of them at once.

Antonovitch walked to the double doors, the trick now was to get out of the office without anyone seeing the dead body lying inside . . .

John Rourke, three of the now precious grenades in his pockets, the plastique parcel cut in half, the strips—the material smelled faintly like bleach—wound around his shoulders in long ropes, drew both Scoremasters from beneath his belt.

Natalia could see him, he knew, just as he could see her. He gave her a nod. She blew him a kiss.

John Rourke broke into a dead run toward the driveway leading down to the massive garage door. The color of the door stuck in his mind for some reason; the color was green, a very deep, yet bright green.

Behind him and to his right, he could hear the sounds of energy weapons being fired, the hum, the buzz, then sometimes what sounded like an explosion.

There was some conventional weapons fire, but none of it so far aimed toward him, because where he ran now he was beyond sight level for the enemy personnel swapping shots with Natalia and, so far at least, none of the personnel from the air defense center had apparently noticed him.

But that changed in the next instant, automatic weapons fire pouring down into the synth-concrete roadbed over which he ran. Rourke punched both .45s upward, toward the source of the gunfire, firing the ScoreMasters simultaneously. Accurate return fire was impossible for him now, but if he could get close enough he could drive them back and keep them from firing at him anymore.

That was working, both ScoreMasters empty in his hands, their slides locked back. Leaving them that way, he thrust both pistols into his belt, grabbing for one of the three grenades he'd taken from the pile. He pulled the pin, broke stride and hurtled the grenade toward the small balcony from which the personnel of the air defense command were firing at him.

It was a lucky throw and Rourke knew it, the grenade going over the balcony rail, the explosion coming in the next instant, bits of people and equipment and the balcony itself raining down around him. He raised his left forearm over his head to protect his eyes. With his right hand, he drew one of the little Detonics CombatMasters from the double Alessi shoulder rig beneath his uniform tunic.

As the shower of debris abated, he drew the second of the twin stainless Detonics .45s.

He was into the driveway now, the downward pitch of the driveway itself drawing him downward at an even faster rate than his normal running speed. He kept going, eyes back on the green garage door.

The nearer he came to it, the more massive it appeared.

But he could not afford to use all the new German plastique to get inside the building, because then there would be no point to the exercise, no way to destroy the equipment which controlled the Soviet anti-aircraft defenses.

Energy weapons were being fired at him now, the synth-concrete near him taking the hits, blackening as the blue-white flashes of plasma energy passed, the surface beneath Rourke's feet vibrating with the concussion.

He kept running, eyes on the green door, pistols in his hands.

Conventional small arms fire came at him again from above. But Rourke kept running this time. To have slowed at all might give the Elite corpsmen who were firing the energy weapons at him just enough time to make an accurate hit.

Machinegun fire rippled across the synth-concrete near his feet, Rourke squinting his eyes, averting them as the dust rose around him. He kept running for the door. A bullet struck his left thigh and he stumbled, but didn't fall, pressing his hand and the butt of the pistol in it against the wound to staunch the blood.

He heard the sound of a grenade exploding, realizing it must be Natalia, trying to cover for him.

And, at last, Rourke was at the green door . . .

Antonovitch entered the Commissariat offices, the first time he had ever done so. He was struck by their austerity. There was the customary photograph of the Premier (now late Premier) and the photo of Lenin painted in an heroic pose, chin whiskers pointing defiantly forward.

"Comrade Marshal!" The receptionist was on her feet at attention, her flat chest under her loose fitting uniform singularly unappealing. And Antonovitch still resented this artificial rank which had been bestowed upon him, which he did not feel he had earned, but this was not the time to ignore her, appear odd in any way.

"Comrade. To combat the emergency precipitated by the emergency near the main gate section, I require access immediately to the power grid controls."

"I shall—"

"You shall summon no one because there is no time. Were there time to waste do you think, girl, that I would have come here myself?"

"No, comrade Marshal, but I have—"

"And now you have new orders. Be quick. Lives are at stake here!"

She fetched a small book from within the center drawer of her desk, leafing through it quickly enough as she said, "Follow me, please, Comrade Marshal." And she started down a narrow corridor with its origins to the right of her desk.

Antonovitch followed her, watching her rather skinny legs for a moment; her stockings—heavy, disgusting looking, very typically Russian—were actually loose on those spindly legs.

And, for some reason, he thought of Major Tiemerovna.

Now, there was a woman, well-practised in a woman's art, beautiful, perfectly dressed, yet it all seemed so natural for her.

And Antonovitch felt a flash of remorse for the time when he had abetted Major Tiemerovna's maniacal late husband in entrapping her for torture and death.

He had respected her then, respected her more now.

The receptionist stopped before a vault-like door, with a standard touchtone security lock in place beside it.

She looked at him, imploring, "But Comrade Marshal—"

Nicolai Antonovitch cut her off mercilessly. "Open the door now, girl."

She turned on her heel, the movement almost provocative, a body gesture which would have been provocative in any other woman under any circumstances other than these, but not with her, not under any circumstances.

And he realized suddenly, as she tapped out the door entry code, that he was transferring to this girl with the faded blond hair and pale pimply skin, all of the disgust he harbored for the system which had built this girl, made her what she was, made him what he was, too.

She opened the door. Lights came on with an audible click and buzz.

He started to walk past her, but turned and looked into her faded brown eyes. "I am sorry if I spoke rudely to you, but there is something I must do that cannot wait."

She seemed shocked, and there was the hint of a smile in her eyes that might almost have made her barely pretty if she had allowed it to fully happen.

She did not. She was not.

Antonovitch walked into the room, the lights on the map just as he had been told they looked, just as he had pictured them.

And, encased under a plexiglas cover, there was a set of switches.

He crossed the room and walked toward these.

The cover was merely set in place over the switches.

He started to lift it.

"Comrade Marshal!"

He didn't look at the bland girl, merely told her, "Go away."

He never bothered to look if she did.

He tripped the switch and the entire room was in darkness, just as he knew the entire city would be.

He drew his gun, stood there in the total darkness and waited for the girl to stop screaming at him long enough to grope her way back down the corridor and summon help. By the time all that was done and they came and he shot it out with them, the Allies would have done their work, if they were clever.

If they were not clever, nothing would help them. He tried to think of something happy, knowing these would be the last thoughts of his life.

And he started to cry, because he could think of nothing happy at

John Thomas Rourke froze.

No lights, total darkness except for the flash of the energy weapons, and those were few and far between in these last few seconds.

He was beside the door, and he bent awkwardly, setting out the plastique, wondering why there were no lights, and was the power failure general.

Rourke heard Natalia's voice from the darkness, shouting to him, "It could be a trick!"

He knew she would not expect an answer.

Although he always carried at least one flashlight, he moved in darkness now, his only light the occasional futile flash of the hoped for lucky shot with one of the energy weapons the Elite Corps still fired sporadically.

Rourke's left thigh pained him badly, but the flow of blood, as best he could tell in the darkness, had eased; and, since he was not dead yet, he theorized that the bleeding was not arterial.

He kept moving, dragging his left leg slightly, focusing his attention on the job at hand instead of the pain. If all the power in the city were out, either the Hand of Providence had hit the switch or something unfathomable had occurred.

It was possible, just possible, that the power inside the air defense center was down, too . . .

Natalia moved quickly along the edge of the barricade behind which she had hidden. The jacket of her uniform was off, the grenades inside, the sleeves of the jacket tied together forming a bundle with which to carry them. Already, the air inside the mountain was stuffy, smelled badly, and made her feel slightly nauseated.

She was confident that she could find her way back to their original position where she had left the energy weapons, despite the surrounding darkness which was almost total. She carried a small flashlight in her purse, the purse slung cross body like a musette bag now. And, if she could not find her way back, or time did not allow that, if what she planned succeeded, she would have access to all the energy weapons she needed.

In the darkness, with no sounds of electrical equipment and no flow of fresh air, she could hear tiny noises, and thus moved more carefully. The Soviet uniform skirt was poorly designed and even more poorly executed and impeded her movement as she crept forward. So, the Bali-Song knife already out and silently opened in her hand, she found the side seam by her left thigh and eased the knife's primary edge against it, splitting the skirt to her hip. The slip beneath it was already bunched up and out of the way, and it was her own so she had no desire to cut it.

She kept moving, her objective a simple one: To reach the enemy position which had been the source of the energy weapon fire and neutralize the men there . . .

A good three dozen men of the raiding parties—U.S. Marines, German Long Range Mountain Patrol and Commando personnel, Chinese from the Second City, all fighting side-by-side against the common enemy—rallied around Jason Darkwood. Darkwood raised his right arm, sweeping hand and arm forward in a broad arc as he shouted, "Follow me!"

Darkwood started toward the fence gates which separated the lagoon docks from the domes of the Soviet city itself, his Lancer pistol in his left hand, his Randall knife in his right.

Gunfire from the men around him was deafening, and the thought crossed his mind that he hoped the newly-developed low penetration round these men were firing was as safe to fire under the domes as testing indicated. Otherwise, a stray shot and they could all die.

Black uniformed Marine Spetznas personnel held the gates, returning fire with Sty-20s, PV-26 shark guns and AKM-96 assault rifles. Men fell on either side of Jason Darkwood.

A young black Marine near to Darkwood, left arm limp at his side and streaming blood from a shoulder wound, did something then that took Jason Darkwood totally by surprise.

He started to sing.

The Marine hymnn.

Under normal circumstances, Jason Darkwood would have started looking for people to join him in "Anchors Aweigh," but instead he joined the young man, and others did, too. Some of the Germans and Chinese mumbling were words that didn't fit, but keeping to the tune.

They were at the gates now, the electric gullwing car that was their battering ram, punching through the fence, its windows riddled with bullets, the man driving it probably dead.

The Soviet forces fell back from the fence, but held their ground near a knot of gullwing cars parked near to the gates.

Darkwood didn't know the second verse to the song, just started singing the first verse again.

Everyone was singing, now, and the words no longer were even distinguishable and, as they ran, weapons firing, they fell into step, charging toward the Soviet Marine Spetznas position.

They closed with the enemy.

At point blank range, Jason Darkwood fired the Lancer 9mm pistol into the chest and neck of a Marine Spetznas officer coming at him with an AKM-96. Two enlisted men charged toward him and Darkwood backstepped, firing the Lancer again, putting down one of the men, sidestepping and using the knife in his hand like a club, crashing the blade flat down across the skull of the second man.

Two Marine Spetznas officers were inside an already moving gullwing car, the doors open.

Darkwood thrust his pistol into his belt and picked up an AKM-96, fisting the weapon in his right hand, bracing the stock between his right elbow and hip. He fired, spraying out the magazine in three-round full-auto bursts, killing the man behind the wheel of the gullwing, the car crashing into the tunnel wall just beyond.

From the corner of his eye, Darkwood spotted the senior among all the Marine Spetznas officers he had seen so far, and Darkwood summoned two of the Marines near him, racing toward the man. A Soviet enlisted man lunged with his bayonet, just missing Darkwood's right rib cage. Darkwood fired out the last half-dozen rounds in the AKM-96's magazine, putting the man down.

The Marine Spetznas officer, back to a gullwing car, raised his hands and shouted in Russian, "Do not shoot!"

Jason Darkwood threw down the emptied Soviet assault rifle and pointed the muzzle of his pistol toward the Soviet officer. "Sir, in the name of the United States Government of Mid-Wake and Allied Expeditionary Force command, I order you to instruct your men to lay down their arms and cease hostilities at once or suffer the consequences."

Darkwood cocked the hammer on the pistol and smiled.

With a tremulous voice, the Marine Spetznas officer began to shout to his men.

And Jason Darkwood decided it was safe to lower the hammer on his pistol . . .

She was already through the knees of her stockings, and her bare knees were cold against the street surface as she crept toward the very faint outline of a man. Although every light was out, some very diffused illumination came through the tunnel from the gray outside, and when she was very careful, she could make out some shapes.

This shape was clearly human.

She went after it with her knife . . .

His light sensitivity had always been a problem for him during daylight hours, requiring him to use sunglasses ever since his early teens whenever he was in strong sunshine. But, on the plus side, his night vision had always been superb.

He could see now, just barely enough to know that he had his plastique reasonably evenly spaced along the massive green door.

And he stood beside the door, with much difficulty because of his wounded left thigh.

The quickest way to one of the energy weapons was to walk straight up the middle of the driveway. Of course, if the lights came back on, he would be a sitting duck.

He decided to risk it, while his leg still held out. With the added time the darkness had given him, he'd been able to utilize all the plastique in a manner which would obviate ever having to go inside the building.

The pattern and density with which he had been able to plant the charges would do the job he'd intended to do with the other half of his plastique and the grenades, destroying the very bowels of the building and possibly bringing down a wall.

He was walking right up the middle, the twin Detonics mini-guns in his hands, the reloaded Scoremasters in his belt beneath the uniform tunic, elsewhere on his body the suppressor-fitted Smith &

Wesson 6906 and the A.G. Russell Sting IA Black Chrome knife, the S&W Centennial revolver in his hip pocket.

Rourke did not run because he could not run with any degree of comfort, limping badly on his stiffening left leg. The thigh wound had all but stopped pumping and he suspected that the bullet was out, that the wound was just a very deep graze.

He kept moving.

If the anti-aircraft defenses were out, Colonel Mann and his forces would know and German air power would be starting its attack at any moment — ground forces from New Germany, Mid-Wake, the Second Chinese City and the Icelandics (a small contingent of Icelandic police) storming toward the city. Nearly as small a force as the men of Lydveldid Island were, the few persons from the Wild Tribes of Europe, these not fighters at all, but cargo handlers and the like, doing what they could to further the cause of freedom.

John Rourke kept walking.

At last, he neared the position where he had left Natalia, slowing his pace, knowing her night vision was good but not as good as his, not wanting to surprise her.

But when he reached the spot, Natalia was no longer there.

The grenades were gone, but both energy weapons and their power source backpacks were there.

"Shit," John Rourke observed.

He picked up one of the energy weapons, slipping into the straps for the backpack. He powered up the rifle, brought it to his shoulder, squinted his eyes against the flash from the first of two shots he intended to make, the first to light the target for the second.

He shouted in Spanish to Natalia through the darkness, reasoning that there were probably twenty people alive on Earth who spoke that rich and musical tongue now and none of them were here. "Be careful! I am firing now! Keep down!"

And he touched the trigger of the energy weapon . . .

Natalia's left hand was over the man's mouth, her right knee crashed against his spine, the knife in her right hand gouging into the side of his neck as she heard John Rourke's voice.

She gave the knife a twist and dove toward the nearest wall, drawing the suppressor-fitted Walther PPK as she did so, covering her face and eyes as the hum and buzz of the energy weapon came and went, the faint sound of synth-concrete taking the hit.

There was no explosion, and she realized there should not have been. John would be firing his first shot to illuminate the target area.

The second shot came, and a roar followed it, her eardrums pulsing with it.

"He used it all," she verbalized to her unhearing ears . . .

John Rourke raised up from the prone position he'd dropped to, but with considerable difficulty.

Fire burned within the base of the air defense control center now, the fire burning so brightly because there were trucks parked within the below ground area, and the synth-fuel tanks they carried, had caught. The fires licked upward around the exterior of the structure, but synth-concrete did not burn.

While the fires spread—they would be short-lived, he knew—John Rourke hauled himself to his knees behind cover, firing the energy weapon he'd used to detonate the plastique on the green door while he still had sufficient light. This time, his targets were the windows of the structure. Any damage he could do to the equipment inside was a plus, now.

And, from far to his right, there was more energy weapon fire, but not directed toward him.

"John!"

It was Natalia.

Rourke shouted back to her as he fired, "I'm working the windows. Help Michael and Paul, then get out of here! I'll be right behind you!"

There was no answer, but after a flurry of quick shots from Natalia's direction, her firing ceased.

The flames from the fire in the substructure of the air defense center were already dying, but Rourke kept shooting, smaller fires started by the energy weapon hits already visible through several of the shot through windows.

Behind him, toward the tunnel where Michael and Paul were pinned down, he heard the muted roar of a grenade, then another.

The energy weapon in Rourke's hands died, the last burst missing its target completely and impacting the synth-concrete driveway.

John Rourke shrugged out of the packstraps, putting his arms into the straps for the second weapon, shouldering the pack, then hauling himself to his feet. A spasm of pain shot through him from his leg, settling in his stomach for an instant. He shook his head to clear it, then started away from the synth-concrete wall where he'd taken cover. There was not enough light to check the energy level on his new weapon, but there should be a dozen or more full-charge shots left in it he guessed, he hoped.

Rourke started toward the tunnel.

The first impact came, a conventional explosive missile or bomb, he realized, striking near the main gates. The floor beneath him vibrated with it and the tunnel wall near him cracked, the tunnel ceiling above cracking as well, and synth-concrete dust showering down on him.

Rourke ordered himself to ignore the pain, breaking into a run.

Another impact, the sound of this explosion rattling through the tunnel itself, but from behind him. German missiles, hitting the side of the mountain itself, knocking out the air defense batteries that now, apparently, were without radar guidance.

There was another explosion, the tunnel shaking violently, Rourke nearly stumbling, his left leg nearly buckling with pain.

"Bleeding again. Damn," Rourke almost whispered, still running.

Ahead of him, he saw Michael firing a conventional Soviet assault rifle, but no sign of Natalia and Paul. Michael's right arm was limp at his side, the assault rifle at his hip.

Rourke quickened his pace as much as he dared, nearing the tunnel entrance now. Another explosion came, the tunnel starting to break up, massive chunks of synth-concrete falling from the tunnel ceiling.

Rourke grabbed at his thigh, pressing his hand and the pistol in it against the wound to staunch the flow of blood.

He was almost to the tunnel entrance now, Michael firing again. In the distance, well out from the tunnel, Rourke caught a glimpse of Natalia and Paul, running out ropes of German plastique.

There was another missile strike, the floor of the tunnel splitting. Michael turning around and looking back down the tunnel, then shouting to him—not loudly enough to be heard—and gesturing to him to hurry.

John Rourke threw himself into the run, lightheadedness and nausea sweeping over him from blood loss.

As the roar of the explosion died, he could hear Michael shouting, ". . . waiting for you! Gonna blow!"

Rourke wasn't thinking straight, he realized.

He lurched along the last portion of the tunnel, sagging against the tunnel wall and his son calling. "Dad—"

"I'll be all right, Michael. They're mining the area between here and the entrance—right?"

"Come on!" And Michael Rourke drew his father's left arm across his shoulder with his own left hand.

"Your arm."

"Bullet broke the radius, I think. Hurts like hell. Come on, Dad. You shoot, I'll carry. "

John Rourke looked at his son, his friend, and smiled. "Got a deal, Michael."

John Rourke leaned his weight on Michael, the two of them starting through the tunnel entrance now, gunfire from Paul and Natalia providing covering fire.

Two Elite corpsmen started from behind an overturned truck and Rourke stabbed one of the twin stainless Detonics .45s toward them, firing a double tap into one of the men, dropping him; the second man going down with a burst of 9mm from Paul's sub-machine gun.

The gates at the main entrance were partially destroyed, partially pristine, a portion of the synth-concrete entrance collapsed over them. But there was still a clear path in and out.

Another missile strike, incredibly louder here, and as it died, the sound of J7-Vs roaring past, strafing the ground outside.

Natalia's voice. "I'm detonating Michael's and Paul's plastique on five! Get out!"

There was enough of the German plastique to bring the entire entrance area down, Rourke realized. He looked back, Natalia looking toward him.

"Don't die," John Rourke whispered.

He limped on, the weight that would have been on his left leg across his son's shoulders.

Outside, in the numbing cold and wind, the sky rained death, missiles and bombs pulverizing everything on the ground.

And, from behind him, John Rourke heard the roar of the explosion starting, plastique enough to—He shivered, telling himself it was blood loss, cold and shock.

German helicopter gunships were closing toward the city, the J7-V's backing off now. German paratroopers bailed out overhead, the canopies of their chutes opening white against the blue gray of the sky. Vehicles all around them were aflame. From the south, the west and the east, Allied ground forces—armor and infantry—closed on the Underground City. J7-V's engaged the comparatively few Soviet aircraft which had launched in aerial dogfights, missiles exploding everywhere in the clouds.

As blackness swept over him, John Rourke said to his son, "So, this is Armageddon."

Part One

Separate Ways

One

He placed the diaphragm of his stethoscope against her abdomen, then helped her to position the ear tips of the binaurals. "Can you hear now?"

"Ohh, my God!"

The hesitant look that had been in her eyes a few seconds earlier was gone, replaced by a smile which radiated from her eyes, lighting her entire face.

He helped her to remove the stethoscope, telling her as he gestured with his right first finger toward her hugely swollen abdomen, "That, my dear woman, is the healthy heartbeat of a healthy baby. And I should know! Not only am I a doctor, but I have two grown children of my own and my wife and I have our third child on the way. Now, will you get some rest?"

She licked her pale lips, her eyes casting down, her skin slightly clammy looking under the glare of the light over her bed. He took a damp cloth and gently rubbed it over her forehead, over her cheeks. "I'm acting like the baby, aren't I?"

John Rourke shrugged his shoulders. "When it comes to pregnant women of my experience, you're no more concerned than average. And since no man has ever had a baby, I can't comment further. The baby is healthy. You're healthy, too. If you rest and do what you're supposed to, you'll be walking out of here with your baby in your arms in a few more days."

"You wife is lucky, Doctor."

John Rourke found that last remark amusing. "Why is she lucky?"

"Well, I mean, you—" Color was coming back into her cheeks so rapidly it seemed like a blush. "I mean—"

He dried her face with a small towel, then said, "You get some sleep so I can get some sleep, okay?"

"Okay. You're a nice man. Thank you. I—"

It was horribly unprofessional, of course, but he'd never really worried much over having an image. As he stood up, John Rourke leaned over the bed and kissed the girl lightly on the forehead. "Now, don't open your eyes."

And he walked away from her bed, down the corridor formed at the center of the long, wide room by the beds on both sides and toward the double swinging doors at the far end. He needed his rest tonight, but Lieutenant Martha Larrimore was so nervous, so pathologically terrified that her baby would be stillborn, he had camped out in his office just to be near her.

A nurse could have done the stethoscope routine, of course, could have held her hand for a while, could have reassured her, but inside himself he'd known it wouldn't be the same for Martha Larrimore or for him. Her baby would be over two months premature when it came. He could have C-sectioned her and been done with it, but this was a harsh new world and she would have more babies because she was healthy and wanted children and a C-section now would mitigate strongly against normal deliveries in the future. And, the longer the baby could remain within her, the stronger the child would be when it was born.

He hadn't told her, but tomorrow morning he would begin to induce her with pitosin and, if he guessed correctly, she'd be a mother by noon.

He hoped.

He did not want to miss the wedding, or the party afterward.

John Rourke let himself into his small office, took the stethoscope from his neck and sat down in the chair behind his desk, then poured a cup of the fresh coffee which Doctor Munchen had brought with him from New Germany that afternoon. The coffee, from a Mid-Wake microwave coffemaker, was hot and good.

He took a cigarette from the package he kept in his desk for the occasional time when he really wanted a smoke but was too busy or too tired to go outside and light a cigar.

The clinic was built like the spokes of a wheel, four spokes to be exact, his office and the other offices and labs at the center or hub, patient accommodations, ward and private for those few difficult cases, filling the spokes.

New Germany had built the clinic for him, and he would be eternally grateful to Colonel Mann, Deiter Bern (President of New Germany) and the German engineers who had built it. As he lit the non-carcinogenic cigarette in the blue-yellow flame of his Zippo, he considered the fact that he should be grateful to Commander Dodd, as well. Dodd, asshole that he was, could have said no to the clinic, but didn't.

In a way, that had bothered Rourke since the beginning. There was all but concrete proof that Dodd conspired with the neo-Nazis for the overthrow of both the Government of New Germany and Eden Base. So, why had he allowed the clinic to be built?

When the war came to its end, the politics began and John Rourke opted out.

Throughout his life prior to the Night of the War, he had been perpetually amazed and bemused that anyone would enter politics of his own accord, because the seeking of public office in America had long ago ceased to be a duty, reluctantly entered into by those whom honor and responsibility called to serve. There were, then, some few who still viewed their quest for public office as a means of performing public service, but they were a fast-fading breed.

Instead, politics had become the means by which the small-minded sought to gain power over their fellow man.

All but gone was the concept of representing the voters; replacing it was the tantalizing prospect of ruling prince-like, the lives of others.

Tantalizing to some, disgusting always to him.

He rubbed at his left thigh, remembering how a shot had brought him around from unconsciousness and, despite the fact he couldn't walk too well, with Michael's and Paul's help he'd gotten himself aboard one of the German mini-tanks and re-entered the battle for the Underground City.

The explosives he and Natalia had used against the air defense center had done more of a job than he knew then. Nicolai Antonovitch, the commander of Soviet forces, had been the one who cut the power. After holding out for what seemed, as best evidence indicated, several hours, Antonovitch was overcome and killed, but only after neutralizing the city's electrical supply, during a critical period and assassinating the Underground City's leader.

When the electrical power was restored, had the explosives Rourke and Natalia used not done their work, air defense radar would have come back on line. It never came back, however.

The explosives Natalia and Paul planted near the main entrance and which Natalia subsequently detonated, served to trap the majority of Soviet ground forces, not already in the field, inside the Underground City egress, through various smaller points limited.

All tolled, discounting the considerable loss of life, the commando raid the four of them—Paul and Michael and Natalia and himself—had conducted, was more successful than could have been imagined.

John Rourke stubbed out the cigarette, turning his lighter over in his hands as he looked toward the cot along the far wall of his office.

He set down his lighter, reached under his white lab jacket and pulled out the little Hip-Gripped Smith & Wesson Centennial and put the revolver on the floor beside the cot. Old habits died hard, and he'd rather carry a gun and never need it, than need a gun and realize it was some critical distance away, in a drawer someplace.

He sat on the end of the cot and leaned over to untie his boots. The Mid-Wake issue boots were comfortable and he had a sufficient number of pairs—they were black, similar in appearance to G.I combat boots—that he could wear a fresh pair every day for a week without repeating.

He lay back on the cot and reached up with his right hand to turn down the light switch, then reached down for a last touch at the little gun.

He closed his eyes, opened them, and stared at the grayness of the ceiling.

The battle for the Underground City endured for nine days.

That was three months ago, now, and still there was no accurate casualty figure.

On the ninth day, Rourke's leg so well restored that he had just returned from a commando raid against a Soviet artillery battery, and the decision had just been made to bring up captured Soviet Island Class submarines as close in as possible along the Med, the Arabian or the Berents Sea with conventional warheads targeted against the City.

But the announcement came from the Soviet high command that the city would surrender.

John Rourke, in his reluctant capacity of Brigadier General as appointed by the President of Mid-Wake (and also the United States, technically), was asked to receive the surrender documents.

With Wolfgang Mann, field commander for the Allied Forces and commander of the Army of New Germany, John Rourke and a party of fifteen officers, met with twelve Soviet officials, both KGB Elite Corps, Army and civilian, a mile out from the main entrance of the Underground City.

And he would always remember the words of the ranking Elite Corps officer. "Your people did not win, Doctor. Nor did your ideology. You won. Will you call yourself king or president or premier? But, as the Englishman, Shakespeare said, I believe, . . . a rose by any other name."

John Rourke had wanted very much to hit the man, a major, one of the survivors from before The Night of The War, one of the original men from Vladmir Karamatsov's KGB Elite Corps.

But he did not.

Instead, following the ceremony he left, returning at first to New Germany, to his wife, Sarah, and his daughter, Annie, Paul's wife.

Doctor Deiter Bern conferred upon him the Knight's Cross of New Germany, the country's highest order.

And Doctor Munchen, over a drink following this second accursed ceremony, asked him, "Herr Doctor, I have been asked by Deiter Bern—but I would myself have asked it—to offer you a professorship at the University. You can teach whatever you like, work with our finest doctors, live the life you deserve after all you have endured on mankind's behalf."

"I didn't do anything on mankind's behalf, Doctor. I did it for me. The United States needs rebuilding. There's work there I want to do. If I can get the materials and supplies—"

"A hospital?"

"Yes," Rourke told him.

"And what of Commander Dodd, the fellow who wants to be a god or a king?"

"He's technically the leader of a nation, Eden. He's subject to that nation's laws, and Eden doesn't have any. I intend to correct that."

"You? I would have thought—"

"That law isn't something I'm fond of?"

"Well," Munchen smiled, taking a cigarette from his case, apparently remembering to offer one—Rourke refused it—then lighting. "I mean that—"

"I know what you mean. I mean the Constitution of the United States. We don't need any other laws beyond that, Doctor. There's bound to be an election, because Dodd won't have any choice. And Akiro Kurinami will stand against him—"

"But you—may I call you John?"

"Yes; me, what?"

"You could—"

John Rourke smiled, lit one of the thin, dark tobacco cigars he preferred, telling the German military physician, "No one would ever vote for me, and if anyone would, I wouldn't want it. I'm no politician. Anyone who supposes he's capable of running somebody else's life is a fool or a would-be despot. I'll live my life the way I can and tell no man how to live his; I don't expect the same treatment, but I'll damned well get it."

"Then why not stay here, John?"

"I have to do what I feel is the right thing; you wouldn't do any less, would you? You were never a Nazi, always on the side of the people who supported Deiter Bern and freedom, weren't you?"

Munchen looked down at the tip of his cigarette, molded it free of ashes, the tip glowing as he raised it to his lips and inhaled. "Dodd, if he is working with the neo-Nazis, as you call them, will kill you. You know?"

"I suspect he'll try," John Rourke smiled, inhaling on his cigar, holding the smoke in his lungs, then exhaling it through his nostrils.

"And what will you do after you have Kurinami elected and your hospital is running perfectly well and Michael is married and Annie and Paul have a child—and the baby your wife carries is born? Then what will John Rourke do? Grow old and fat?"

"Hardly fat, hopefully old," Rourke laughed.

"After five centuries of one life, how—"

"I've never been a violent man, but violence has so often been required of me." And he smiled again. "Imagine what's out there," John Rourke said, gesturing toward the world beyond the cocktail lounge in which they shared a ridiculously small round table. "The pyramids are still standing, in Egypt, and I bet in Mexico. Mysteries that your science could solve, that mine could never solve. Great underground repositories of books and records and sound re-

72

cordings that would have survived in the capitals of the world. Time capsules. Maybe other people, people who somehow managed to survive."

And Rourke laughed at himself.

"Why are you laughing, John?"

He shook his head, saying, "I guess I've always craved adventure. Silly of me, I know, but I suppose there's a little boy inside every man who wants to find what's lost and explore things undreamed of."

John Rourke closed his eyes, and sleep finally came.

Two

Annie Rourke Rubenstein sat with her hands bunched tight in her lap, staring out the window of Wolfgang Mann's private J7-V. It had been flown all the way from New Germany (Argentina, Before The Night of the War) to Lydveldid Island, where she and Paul worked to help restore the Hekla community, picked them up and now was flying them all the way back, to what was once the United States.

She felt like she was coming home.

Sunshine washed over across the landscape, low with the dawn, reflections rising from rivers and streams and lakes, dancing like the sparkle of the diamonds in the little earrings Natalia had sometimes worn.

The Retreat was here, in Georgia, somewhere in the snow-capped mountains below them now. She could have found it from an aerial photograph, but the J7-V's altitude was too great and its speed too fast for recognition by casual observation. And the home she'd been born in—well, she'd actually been born in a hospital—had been near here, too, but down in the piedmont, not up in the mountains.

The house had been burned the morning after The Night of The War, but even its skeletal remains were certainly turned to ashes when the ionization effect within the atmosphere rose to such a level that, one morning at dawn, fire swept the skies just behind the sunrise and almost everything on the surface was destroyed.

But this was home, in the physical sense, only partly now in the emotional sense. She was no longer a little girl, but a married woman, and far closer to thirty than twenty. Talk about a baby was frequent with Paul, and they were planning to try to have one soon.

Yet, her father and her mother lived here, near Eden Base, although not in Eden Base proper.

And then there was her brother, Michael. Michael had been in New Germany since the war ended, there with Maria Leuden.

Maria was a nice girl, but not like a sister to her, as Michael's late wife, Madison, had been.

"Whatchya thinking about?"

She looked at Paul and, as she did, his hand moved off the armrest between them, closed over both of hers in her lap.

"Everything," she smiled.

Paul laughed. "If I know you, you just realized that all the stuff you packed wasn't enough and you left the one dress that you really needed at home."

There it was again, that word, "home," she thought.

She smiled, leaning her head against his shoulder "No. I brought enough."

She was becoming a clothes horse, she realized. After all the years of living just with a brother, before The Awakening, then being in the field so much with the Family; she had never had the chance to just be a woman. Now she did and she enjoyed it, and she loved clothes.

"What were you thinking about?"

"Ohh, I really was thinking about everything, sort of. It's only been weeks, really, but it seems like an eternity since we left here."

"Well," Paul told her, holding her hands still, "Akiro and Elaine's wedding makes a good excuse, doesn't it?" She laughed a little. "And," he went on, "you get to be a bridesmaid."

"I hope I don't screw it up, being a bridesmaid, I mean."

"All you have to do is just look pretty, right? You do that all the time, so no big deal."

She punched his arm and looked out the window again, smoothing her skirt across her thighs, trying to see if she could just maybe locate The Retreat anyway . . .

The really special thing about any marriage was the fact that two people were pledging their lives and futures to one another, but she supposed there was something historic to the proceedings as well.

Akiro Kurinami and Elaine Halverson were the first two people from the Eden Project to return to the surface of the planet, after five centuries.

And now Akiro and Elaine were being married.

Sarah Rourke looked at herself in the mirror.

Her hair, longer than she had ever worn it before The Night of the War, was down, and she felt so fat that she couldn't comfortably do anything else with it. And she tried telling herself she didn't look like a blimp, that she was just pregnant, but that didn't work.

The mirror didn't accept excuses.

She couldn't get into any of the clothes she'd worn while the war was still going on. Her feet were a little swollen and even her shoes felt tight. She couldn't have bent over far enough to lace up combat boots if her life depended on it.

She'd felt like an idiot, but her toenails had needed cutting so badly she was putting holes in her socks. In the end, she'd asked John to cut them for her.

"Baby," she said, not certain if she were talking about the child in her womb or herself . . .

John Rourke had started the pitosin I.V. at seven a.m.

It was ten and he was just through with his morning rounds when he heard his beeper kick in.

Martha Larrimore's face was bathed in sweat, despite what appeared to be valiant efforts on the part of the German nurse. "Doctor Rourke! Thank God."

"Relax. You'll be fine," John Rourke told her, looking at the continuous echo sound digital display on the monitor at the head of her bed, positioned just properly so she couldn't see it.

The baby, perfectly formed, moved almost violently within her body. John Rourke placed his hand on her abdomen, feeling the baby with his fingertips as he watched it—clearly a boy—moving in the birth canal.

"How many centimeters?" Rourke asked the nurse, a blond haired woman somewhere in her fifties, her face perennially stern, her eyes equally warm.

"Nine and one-half, Herr Doctor. And she is better than ninety-five percent effaced."

John Rourke nodded, telling Martha, "You hear that? You'll be delivering in a very little while now. How's your breathing?"

"I'm trying. I'm—" She screamed and grasped John Rourke's hand. The American nurse, from Mid-Wake, who was acting as her labor coach, was panting in unison with her.

"I'm going to wash up—it won't take long at all—and then I'll be back and we'll help you to deliver your baby, okay?"

"Ohh—Hurry!"

John Rourke nodded, checked the echo sound digital display again. Despite being premature, the baby was well formed, large. And she was small. This would not be the easiest birth, and as he looked at the German nurse, he wrote on the pad at the top of Lt. Larrimore's chart that she should be given a very mild sedative, nothing that would put her to sleep, but just enough to relax her so that she could aid in the delivery process, something to take the edge off her near-hysteria . . .

Jason Darkwood brushed an imaginary speck from the spit-shined brim of his hat, then looked below them at the ground. Here, there was nothing but radioactive desert, he knew, and should the German J7-V in which he, Maggie Barrow, Sam Aldridge and Sebastian now flew crashed, even if they survived the impact, they would never survive the exposure.

Parts of the earth, the scientists said, would be uninhabitable for generations.

That thought chilled him and he reached out and took Maggie's hand.

"What's the matter, Jase?"

"Just thinking about something."

"What?"

Darkwood shrugged his shoulders and smiled. "Well, with what's happened, there's already talk about our people returning to the land, at least in part; but, in a way, haven't we been lucky living under the sea?"

Her pretty eyes looked back at him strangely. He felt the pressure of the engagement ring he'd placed on her finger weeks before beneath his hand. "I mean," he told her, "the sea is clean and fresh and we could go anywhere except for worrying about the Russians, and now we don't have to worry about them anymore. Every Island Classer and every missile in their inventory is under our control now. They couldn't hurt us if they tried. But here, I don't know, too many memories of what happened, what went before."

"Not looking forward to Hawaii?"

He laughed. "You've never had to deal with snow, Maggie. It looks great in old videos and at first it's a novelty. But when you have to work in it day after day, it loses its charm. The Oceanographic and Atmospheric specialists are saying that it snows at least once a day in the islands."

"Maybe we can learn how to ski?"

Darkwood just shook his head, then held her hand more tightly. When he looked around the J-7V's cockpit, he could still see Sebastian, sitting in the co-pilot's seat, learning how to fly the aircraft.

Clearly, some of Mid-Wake's citizens would adjust better to the new world than would others . . .

The head crowned, Rourke astonished really at just how well formed the child was.

The edge he'd had taken off Martha Larrimore with the mild sedative did the trick. She was holding her own with the breathing, controlling her pain so well that, if he hadn't known better, he would have thought she were having a second or third child rather than a first.

"How—how—"

"He's healthy looking, Martha," Rourke answered her, easing the first shoulder out, then telling her, "I need another good push and we'll have him. Talk about shoulders! You'll have to send this boy down to Mid-Wake so he can play football!"

She pushed, and suddenly the child filled John Rourke's hands.

He raised the baby by its heels and it wasn't even necessary to slap it on the behind to start it crying. The German nurse helped and John Rourke placed the little boy in his mother's arms as he set about to cut the umbilical cord.

And the symbolism of what he did was not lost to him.

A cord had been cut for all the world, five centuries of war, suddenly ended in the total defeat of the enemy.

And now the task of rebuilding, the hardship of reclaiming the land, the challenge of day-to-day life, lay before everyone who had survived.

When he cut the infant boy's cord, the child cried.

Three

The headpieces—silly little round things like small crowns—worn by the bridesmaids incorporated a short veil which fell just below eye level. Gazing through the netting, all the world looked to have a pink cast to it.

Except the flowers.

And there were flowers by the score, flown in from Lydveldid Island, beautiful flowers, unlike anything Natalia had seen since before The Night of The War.

There was a wooden platform erected, with timbers from New Germany, labored over by the small contingent of Mid-Wake Marines that she understood were now permanently stationed on the New Germany base beyond the confines of Eden. It looked very much like the deck that had overlooked the yard of the small American suburban house she had occupied very briefly five centuries ago as part of the cover for a mission with Vladmir inside the United States.

The Mid-Wake equivalent of a boom box played the works of Chopin, a special recording made by German audio engineers to function in the American system, the pianist from Lydveldid Island, the speakers adapted to the unit with some minor difficulty, she understood, because they came from the Chinese Second City.

Chopin was a favorite of both Elaine and Akiro.

She watched Commander Dodd's expression as the Revolutionary Etude began to play, wondering if his knowledge of Chopin were good enough to know the Etude in C minor, Op. 10, No. 12's, more common title. That he had come at all was an anomaly in itself, because the election that would name the first President of Eden was in progress, Dodd pitted against Akiro Kurinami and Dodd's chances for electoral success dwindling by the moment.

She fluffed the skirt of the floor length pastel pink dress she wore. There were enough yards of chiffon in the skirt to make one of the hermetically sealed German field tents, she thought, smiling, picturing a group of German soldiers taking shelter inside a see-through tent that was colored pink. Annie never did things by half measure, of course, and Annie had made all three bridesmaid's dresses, Annie's yellow, Sarah's blue.

The Presbyterian minister from Mid-Wake who would read the marriage vows that, in turn, Akiro Kurinami and Elaine Halversen would repeat after him, stood ready.

Elaine wore a classically flowing white wedding dress, puff sleeved and high necked with tiers of lace in its skirt; the dress made for her in New Germany. The tiara which supported her veil was the same one worn by the mother of Mid-Wake's Marine Captain, Sam Aldridge, for her wedding to Sam's father, the veil itself of lace, crafted in Lydveldid Island. The silk shoes she wore originated in the Chinese Second City.

Natalia Anastasia Tiemerovna, Annie Rourke Rubenstein beside her, stepped up behind Sarah Rourke as Sarah, Elaine's matron of honor, started down the aisle, a pretty little child from New Germany with ringlets of strawberry blond hair carrying Elaine's train as carefully as if it were made of crystal.

Natalia's mind was on everything but doing a good job as a bridesmaid, and there wasn't really that much to do anyway, just stand there and look pretty and decorative. She had left behind seven classes of eager, scruffy, wonderful children from the Wild Tribes of Europe, children to whom she taught everything from basic hygiene to basic math, children who had taught her that her natural woman's instinct toward motherhood was alive and well and yearning. But the women from New Germany who aided her at the school would see to the welfare of her precious charges for a while, she told herself.

There was the permanent school which was being built, Soviet prisoners of war doing the labor, problems with design changes and the like. She would be happy when the school was finished, but even happier when the last prisoner was repatriated. That would be several months yet.

And she was very tired, putting in eighteen hard hours before boarding the aircraft to Eden, sleeping only fitfully on the aircraft. But the time spent was necessary, so much to do to make certain that everything ran fluidly in her absence.

It was the thought of seeing John again which drove her, both as an added inducement for traveling here, back to Georgia, and immersing herself in her work even more so than usual.

Because he was never out of her mind.

And, as she looked up, John stepped forward, taking Elaine's arm; and John looked toward her and their eyes met and she looked down at her dress just to control her breathing.

In a moment, John would give the bride away, then sit down again.

Natalia would be standing less than six feet from him.

As Natalia looked at the little bouquet clutched in her hands, the petals of the flowers there trembled . . .

John looked—Natalia had no words to form the thought.

There was a little weariness in his eyes, but he looked happy, and the uniform of a brigadier general of Mid-Wake's Marines (all the men of the wedding party wore military dress uniforms) became him, although she knew he was uncomfortable wearing it.

Sam Aldridge, a very good looking man, wore the same uniform, more ribbons, less rank, but somehow it didn't look the same on Sam.

Dress blue.

He looked—She smiled, looking away.

"Natalia."

She turned, faced him.

John's hands touched gently at her upper arms and his face bent over hers and she raised her chin, his mouth touching at her lips, then gone. He held her close for the briefest instant. "You look exquisite," he told her.

"So do you," she laughed, looking down at her hands. They trembled, and her breathing was short, shallow, and her face felt warm and flushed.

"Would you walk with me?"

82

"Yes."

He placed her right hand into the crook of his left elbow and they started across the floor, toward the doorway which would lead into the nearly completed corridor. The room—the wedding and now the reception filled it—would someday be the seat of Eden's new government, the only portion of the structure fully completed, the complex begun by Dodd but never finished.

They passed Jason Darkwood, Jason coming to attention, bowing slightly to her. Paul and Annie were huddled in a corner with Elaine and Akiro and Colonel Mann and Sarah (thank God John had told her about it and through John she had come to believe in, that Sarah didn't look).

At the doorway, John leaned forward, opening a door for her which she passed through, gathering her dress around her, John behind her. The door closed, and she felt his hands on her arms, turning her around. She was powerless to say or do anything.

"You look well, Natalia."

His brown eyes were so deep, so clear.

"You look just tired and happy enough to be enjoying your new hospital."

He smiled. "I am." She shivered, half from the feelings just having him look at her gave her, half from the colder air here.

Almost instantly, John began unbuttoning his uniform jacket, slipped out of it, folded it around her shoulders, enormous on her, the warmth of his body still in the fabric. She saw the butt of the little Smith & Wesson revolver on its Barami Hip-Grip just to the left of the center of his body. Some things never changed. She drew the coat tightly around her. She wanted him to say that he missed her, that he loved her, knew that perhaps he had said it when he told her she looked well. And she cursed herself for loving him, but wouldn't have wanted not to love him, because loving him, was that around which, her entire existence pivoted, had ever since she had opened her eyes in the desert after he and Paul found her; perhaps ever since she had seen him that very first time in Latin America when they were agents on opposing sides for countries locked in conflict.

Natalia could not look at him anymore without dying inside, but if she turned around he might touch her and she would fall apart and cry. "I will be leaving sometime tomorrow. They tell me, Colonel Mann's personal plane is dropping off Paul and Annie and then flying on to Europe with me."

"If you want to teach, soon there'll be children enough here. I just delivered one this morning, a boy."

"The first of the Eden children? Premature?"

"Yes, but healthy, both mother and son. I avoided a C-Section, for the obvious reasons. She was a little afraid, but that's perfectly natural."

Sometimes, when she thought about children, her breasts ached. But the only man whom she had ever met, whose children she wanted to bear, was married to one of the two finest women she had ever met, that woman's daughter, Natalia's best friend. "I am happy it worked out, John. You would like the doctor the Germans have sent us to help with the Wild Tribe children, a very fine and patient man."

"That's marvelous. May I come and see your school sometime?"

"Ohh, I would love that, and the children would love to meet the hero of the War. They talk about you—they like to practice talking every chance they get—and the boys, especially, sometimes they play at war and I don't like it, but all the boys want to be you. You are their hero, but then you are my hero as well."

John looked embarrassed.

She started to laugh.

He asked, "What's so funny?"

"You and I are very funny, aren't we?"

And John reached out and held her hands and if she used all her concentration maybe she could keep them from trembling, keep herself from swooning like some silly girl in a romantic novel. "I wish I had something fresh to say, something new that would resolve—"

"We don't have a problem, John. You live here and I live there. Sarah looks radiant. And very pregnant. You are the most fortunate of men."

"I know that, at least sometimes I think I do."

She bit her lower lip, leaned her head against his chest and he took her into his arms and she felt his breath on her skin and wanted to drown in it . . .

He could not count on support from the Neo-Nazis as long as there was the significant likelihood that Akiro Kurinami would be elected President of Eden. The election could be done away with easily enough, of course, but there was the matter of the damnable, Doctor John Thomas Rourke, his insistent interference in support of outmoded values, the critical factor that could not be dismissed.

The idea of people being sufficiently mentally fit to govern themselves had ended in disaster the last time, nearly wiping out all of humanity and could not be allowed to take control again under any circumstances now.

Commander Christopher Ignatius Dodd sat at the command console of Eden One, hands on the armrests of his command chair, his eyes peering at his own image reflected there in the windshield against the stormy darkness, the command compartment surrounding him. The effect was like that of a beacon in the night. He would be that beacon to the true people.

Five centuries ago, he had learned the truth, that the incipient weakness in the United States was the result of racial inferiors inbreeding with the Aryan people. And then, without knowing it, he became taxi driver supreme to the racial inferiors, helping the mongrels to return to Earth to destroy it again.

And John Rourke disgusted him.

That Rourke, as Aryan certainly as any man could be, despite his Irish surname, had allowed his only daughter, a beautiful white woman, to marry the Jew Rubenstein was nauseatingly indicative of the degeneracy which had caused the United States to be driven to destruction. And Rourke, all but singlehandedly, toppled the government of New Germany, giving the weakling, short-sighted fringe members of that once-glorious society, their disgusting democracy, deposing a man whose very essence so perfectly defined Aryan superiority as to make him godlike.

As long as John Rourke survived, to support the Japanese who had just married the black, the mongrelization of the new Earth would progress unabated. That a yellow man fucked a black woman by sanction of a pseudo-religion that had no resemblance to the true Christianity was of little concern, but that they should live to threaten the order which mankind so desperately required was an abomination against nature.

And the power which he, Dodd, so justly deserved, based on ability and service and, perhaps, Divine Providence, would be unjustly denied.

Without his—Dodd's—leadership and courage, not a single one of the shuttle fleet which had been launched on The Night of The War and travelled an eliptical course to the edge of the solar system and back while computers maintained life support and the crew of 120 slept, not a single vessel of the fleet would have returned, no one would have have survived. Not even John Rourke or Akiro Kurinami would have disputed that.

But how quickly that was forgotten.

Because of Rourke.

It could rightfully be said he—Dodd—had given life to the planet. Mid-Wake, with its blacks and Jews and orientals and mongrelized so-called whites was not a fit starting place for life, nor were either of the Soviet enclaves, on land or beneath the sea. Only New Germany had been a chance for humanity, but thanks to Rourke—

With Rourke out of the way, Kurinami could be liquidated in a convincing manner and no one would be the wiser, he—Dodd—could step in, lead, eventually weeding out the racial inferiors, and bring about a new order on this reborn earth.

The Russians were powerless now, their land forces demobilized and disarmed, their undersea forces so pacified that no submarine warships remained to them and their mini-subs were strictly monitored.

Eventually, the Russians—Slavs and, as such, racial inferiors—could be dealt with.

The new power would grow, Eden its center of energy, and New Germany, its first logical convert.

But it all hinged on Doctor John Rourke, strutting about in his Mid-Wake brigadier general's uniform, courting the Communist Bitch, Tiemerovna, before the very eyes of Rourke's pregnant wife.

Sarah Rourke was strong, so if he could liquidate her as well, all the better.

The Jew, Rubenstein, would protest, would accuse, but could be dealt with like any Jew.

The key was John Rourke, and tonight that key would be turned.

Forever . . .

She felt like a giant blue Easter egg, and standing still, hurt her back more than walking.

So, with her lined German field jacket over the bridesmaid's dress she wore, she walked, alone along the single street which had formed between the shelters erected by the Eden Project Crew. She had slipped out of the reception, then slipped out of her Chinese shoes, into her combat boots.

She looked down at herself and laughed, thinking perhaps that although she felt like a giant blue Easter egg, she looked more like a fat man in drag.

It was cold, the street, the literal embodiment of the term "windswept."

Sarah Rourke understood the symbolic meaning of Akiro's and Elaine's wedding being held in Eden, but it would have been a vastly more comfortable affair had it been held at the recently restored and expanded German base just outside Eden. The heat was better, the washrooms (pregnant women became connoisseurs of toilet facilities) better, too.

She considered the name, "Eden."

Perhaps history did repeat itself, and perhaps the snake in the Garden had been less literal than figurative.

There was a logical candidate for snake here, the same man who was the candidate for President running opposite Akiro Kurinami.

Yet, if this cold, dreary place with its political uncertainty and petty jealousies were "Eden," it would be hard to imagine why Adam and Eve would have be discouraged to be tossed out on their ear.

A hell in the making, perhaps, but not an Eden.

Of course, neither she nor John could vote, because neither of them was an Eden Project survivor. Up until 1920, of course, as a woman, she could not have voted anywhere in the United States, except the state of Wyoming.

About one hundred people, all the survivors remaining from

87

the Eden Project and only they, would determine what would certainly be the future of the United States, someday perhaps the destiny of this new world.

She had actually heard one of the Eden survivors, whom logic and common sense would have dictated to be too intelligent to harbor such thoughts, murmuring under his breath, "Think of the children" as Akiro, a Japanese, had married Elaine, an Afro-American.

Think of the children indeed, with brilliant and courageous parents who would love and nurture them, teach them, respect them, prepare them to make this new world a better place than the old one had been.

Think of the children of the man who had made that remark, growing up to inherit a father's mindless bigotry.

Sarah Rourke dug her hands into the jacket's muff pockets, walking toward her husband's hospital where, in a short while, she would deliver the baby she carried within her . . .

John Rourke smoked one of Natalia's cigarettes, sitting beside her just inside the entrance to what would someday be the seat of Eden government. He was a little cold, but Natalia required his jacket, so he dismissed the cold, smoked the cigarette.

There were so many things he wanted to tell Natalia.

Yet there were so many reasons why he could tell her nothing.

He loved Natalia Tiemerovna and he loved Sarah Rourke, loved them equally. And Sarah was his wife.

Natalia leaned her pretty head against his shoulder. "Do you think there is anything to what the Hindus believed?"

He just looked at her, not quite taking her meaning because he had been into his own thoughts.

Natalia whispered, "That perhaps in another life we—"

"Transmigration of souls?" Rourke smiled. "I don't know. I long ago taught myself to discount no theory until it had been thoroughly disproven, so I won't discount the possibility. Why?"

Natalia laughed. "Men are amazing."

"I don't think that was a compliment."

"It wasn't, John. Why would I be thinking about another life instead of this one?"

He thought that he might suspect an answer, but it would be such a terribly conceited sounding thing to say.

Natalia said, "Men can be so emotionally obtuse, at times, it is hard to comprehend. I meant that if there is another life in store for us, I hope that then, maybe, we will be able to be together. This life is no longer a viable proposition."

"I really messed you up, and I'm sorry."

"No, John, there's nothing you should be sorry for. And the only person whose fault any of this is, is mine."

" 'The fault, dear Brutus, lies not in our stars, but in ourselves,' " Rourke whispered, exhaling smoke, but unable to see any stars through the doors at the end of this cold and dark corridor.

"Julius Caesar?"

"Yes," Rourke nodded.

"You used to watch the stars a lot, John, on those nights out in the desert. What were you thinking?"

John Rourke extinguished his cigarette beneath his heel, held Natalia's right hand in both of his, exhaled. "I was trying to convince myself that there was something better out there. I didn't know about the Eden Project then, and I wouldn't exactly say we've been touched by the finger of God in their return."

"Are you that much of a cynic, or only on certain subjects?"

"Only on certain subjects," he laughed. "For example, I think the New York Stock Exchange will never rebound."

Natalia started to giggle like a little girl, saying through it to him, "Be serious, John."

"Well, as an ex-Communist you should be familiar with the cyclical view of history."

"And?"

"Well, I sometimes wonder if we came in at the end of one cycle and lived through into the next."

"Do you think that years from now two people like us will sit here having this same conversation, John?"

"Maybe, or maybe two people already did," Rourke told her.

Natalia hugged his left arm very tightly. "Would you tell me that you love me just one more time?"

He looked at her, touched his fingertips to her chin, raised her face, said, "I love you now and will always love you. But stop loving me—"

"If I love you? That's a logical absurdity, just like it would be to stop loving you."

John Rourke kissed Natalia Tiemerovna, telling himself that he would never kiss her like this again, inside himself hoping that what he was thinking would be a lie.

Four

Natalia Tiemerovna pressed her palm against it and pushed open one of the two exterior doors, passed through the foyer, then the inside doorway. "Heat," she whispered to herself. But there wasn't enough warmth that she was tempted to remove her coat, just let it fall open.

The coat was a relic of her past, and in that respect she detested it. But it was both very warm and very beautiful, and for that reason she kept it. Russian sable, the very best, ankle length, full enough that she could almost wrap it round her body twice, could have been wearing her double holster rig with the stainless L-Frame .357 Magnum revolvers beneath it and no one looking at her would have been the wiser.

The shawl she'd thrown over her head against the biting wind she now tugged down to her shoulders.

And her hands had been warm enough in her gloves.

But her toes were stiff with the cold, the Chinese silk shoes terribly ill-suited for the near arctic conditions here in American Georgia.

She had never been inside this hospital of John's and she stood now just inside the inner doorway, looking around.

"May I assist you, Fraulein?"

Natalia looked toward the desk at the far side of the hallway. Beneath a desk lamp's light, she could see a woman's face, plain but with a pleasant smile. "You must be Magda."

"Yes, Fraulein—but—"

"John—Doctor Rourke, I mean. He said you might know where his wife was."

91

"She's in her husband's office. I can show you—"

"It's Fraulein Tiemerovna—Natalia. And if you'll just point the way for me, I'm certain I'll be all right."

The nurse directed her down a corridor and Natalia told her how John had spoken so highly of her, then started toward John's office.

There were lights burning inside and she knocked, hearing Sarah say, "Come in."

Natalia entered and saw Sarah behind John's desk, sitting there with a .45 in her right hand. "Hi."

Sarah smiled, lowered the pistol. "Sorry."

"You're like John, still carrying a gun," Natalia noted.

Sarah shrugged her shoulders, a German arctic parka draped across them. "Aren't you?"

Natalia moved her left leg forward, then lifted her dress, revealing the Walther PPK/S, sans its usual suppressor, in the black fabric Galco thigh holster. As she let her clothes fall back in place, she gestured to the small beaded bag she carried "My Bali-Song. I guess old habits—"

"Not just old habits," Sarah told her. "John hasn't been elaborating on what's going on here, has he?"

Natalia didn't wait to be asked to sit down, merely did, opposite Sarah. "What do you mean? I know that the election between Dodd and Akiro is—"

"Bitter? Maybe that's too mild a word. John refuses to take it seriously, but I think Dodd sees John as a threat and wouldn't stop at trying to kill him."

"That is the reason for the gun, then," Natalia nodded. "No. John said nothing about things being that bad."

Sarah turned the gun around on the desk blotter. "He thinks I'm being a worrier. Maybe I am funny," Sarah smiled, still looking at the gun. "before The Night of The War, I wouldn't touch a gun except to move it so I could dust. God, how things change us."

"Maybe events merely awaken us to necessity," Natalia suggested. "Will it bother you if I smoke?"

"So long as it's not one of John's cigars," Sarah laughed.

Natalia took cigarettes and lighter from her purse, fired the lighter, looked at Sarah as she exhaled smoke. "How are you feeling?"

"Fat." Natalia was momentarily taken aback. But then Sarah laughed. "You remember Michael and Annie when they were little." There was a slight catch in Sarah's voice, but then she went on. "You should have seen me when I was carrying Michael. He weighed nine and a quarter pounds at birth. I looked like the Goodyear Blimp. I don't think this little guy's gonna be as big."

"Then it will—"

"Amniocentesis? Me? A needle in my navel?"

Natalia laughed, remembering the reason she had come here. "Akiro and Elaine will be getting picked up in a little while. John wanted to know if you'd like to come and see them off."

"My back was killing me, just standing. Not used to even a little heel like these things anymore," Sarah said, gesturing toward her shoes as she stood up . . .

They moved along the street now, walking side by side, Natalia walking more slowly than she would have liked, but terrified that Sarah would slip on the icy road surface and fall and hurt herself or the baby.

"Ever hear the acronym D.R.E.A.D.?"

Natalia had heard it. "I assumed it was just disinformation."

"John said he assumed the same. By the way, thanks for being a friend, especially now."

"What do you mean?" The wind was blowing stronger, colder, Natalia huddling her shoulders deeper into her coat, her feet starting to go on her again. But it wasn't that far a walk to the Eden headquarters, so she told herself her toes would be fine. "What do you mean?"

"About which?"

"Being your friend. I mean, I think we are, friends."

"I mean with John, now, then. He's a strong man, but he could have been pushed." And Sarah laughed "Did you see a lot of American movies?"

"Every one I could. I had to pretend to be American often enough and they helped a lot."

"Ever notice, with rare exceptions of course, women were never shown to be buddies?"

And then Natalia laughed. "You and I should have been fighting over him?"

"Yes, scratching each other's eyes out and that sort of dumb stuff."

"I couldn't see either of us doing that."

"But if we were really buddies, just like guys," Sarah smiled, laughing again, "we would have flipped a coin over him, letting the best 'man' win."

"I suppose. I don't know. You are the best 'man', and you have him already. I am happy for you both." She wanted to change the subject. "What did you hear about D.R.E.A.D.?"

"I can't see how you ever passed the spy school course in lying, Natalia, because you're terrible at it. But you're nice to try," and Sarah reached out and took Natalia's hands in hers. "You are a good friend."

Natalia leaned forward and kissed Sarah's cheek, very cold from the wind, but that didn't matter. They held each other for a moment, neither of them saying anything . . .

The helicopter was arriving, one of the German machines from the base just outside Eden. The wind was rising, too, and she stabbed her already gloved hands into the pockets of her coat, drawing the garment more tightly around her, pushing her knees together more tightly as the helicopter's downdraft ricocheted off the landing pad and the icy cold blew up under her dress.

But Natalia smiled, thinking how interesting it would have been if someone had thought to invoke the old American custom of tying tin cans (had there been any) to the wedding car (the helicopter). But, of course, the honeymoon was to be a little out of the ordinary, too. No Niagara Falls, instead a quick flight to the German base, then by J7-V to the floating landing field the Germans had just erected over Mid-Wake.

John had offered them the Retreat, she understood, but advised them against its use. The only peace they would have would be at Mid-Wake, because it was the only place on Earth with totally controlled access.

It was no way to start a life together, in fear.

Sarah had only said that John believed there really had been a project with the code name D.R.E.A.D., and that Akiro would search the duplicate Eden computer files while he and Elaine were at Mid-Wake (they were stored there now) in order to know for certain.

She recalled D.R.E.A.D. well, the acronym somehow more chilling than the cold which surrounded her: Defense Recovery Emergency Armed Deterrent. It was an arsenal of nuclear weapons put away for the proverbial rainy day.

And John, according to Sarah, felt that Commander Dodd wanted it under his control.

The man would have to have been insane.

Suddenly, she felt movement beside her. It was John, one arm around Sarah, the other going around her.

She huddled close against him, and when she saw Sarah's face, Sarah smiled.

Akiro and Elaine, Elaine with an arctic parka over her wedding dress, emerged from the complex, waving at their friends. Elaine throwing her bouquet, Natalia didn't even try.

Five

Young Martha Larrimore was having trouble—tension, John Rourke surmised as the problem's root cause, no more than that—getting her child to take her breast.

Sarah and Natalia flanking him, he walked along the street toward the hospital, considering the old aphorism about 'a rose between two thorns.' In reality, it never seemed to work that way, and tonight he was indeed the thorn between two roses.

"You, Natalia, are not getting off without being around here after the baby comes. You're just going to have to make time," Sarah was saying. "And John and I have already decided, if you don't mind, that if we have a girl, well, we want to name her after you."

Natalia said, "Ohh, Sarah, you don't have to—"

"We want to," Sarah responded. "And you'd better get used to the idea that, boy or girl, you'll be 'Aunt Natalia', if—"

"I've never been an aunt before."

John Rourke revised his estimate of the situation. Rather than a thorn between two roses, he felt more like the net at the center of one of the ping pong tables in the recreation hall at the German base.

He stopped trying to look from one woman to the other, to follow the conversation, merely looked straight ahead, toward the hospital.

Somehow, and he wasn't quite certain why (which annoyed

him, of course), he felt happier than he had been in longer than he could remember. At least he would still have Natalia as his friend, and Sarah and Natalia seemed better friends than ever.

That was good.

Soon, Akiro would know if the D.R.E.A.D. weapons system was a reality, and something which Dodd might realistically hope to obtain. And the election would come and Akiro, respected by almost everyone, would surely win the Presidency.

The only potential for war, now, was minor, the still surviving Neo-Nazi group that was headquartered somewhere in the remote regions of what had been Paraguay. German Long Range Mountain Patrol units searched for them even now, and it was only a matter of time until they were captured or killed.

Annie and Paul had found a true home in helping Madame Jokli to rebuild the Hekla Community in Lydveldid Island.

"God's in his Heaven and all's right with the world," John Rourke said aloud, both of the women he loved just looking at him . . .

There was a knock at the hatchway of the Shuttle. Commander Christopher Dodd took the Beretta pistol from the console near his hand and stood up, walking toward the hatchway lock, twisting it open with one hand and stepping back as the hatch moved.

There was a cyclone of swirling snow and wind.

In the doorway stood a solitary man, face obscured by snow goggles and a toque, the hood of his parka snorkled close.

He was a big man, powerfully built, that apparent despite the arctic gear.

In his lightly gloved right hand was a semi-automatic pistol.

"Herr Commander Dodd, I am Deitrich." The man's voice was a rich baritone, the German accent more of a lilt. And he gave the code phrase then, a Latin phrase Dodd had never heard in the original, until the Nazi hierarchy had decided upon it. *"Alea jacta est."*

But he knew its English translation well, the words that Julius Caesar supposedly uttered when, against orders, he prepared to cross the Rubicon river with his army: The die is cast.

Dodd lowered his weapon . . .

"Your baby is lovely. And he's so well developed."

Martha smiled, touching the child's face with her fingertips. "He is beautiful."

"Now it's your turn to keep your fingers crossed for me," Sarah said.

Natalia looked at Martha Larrimore and then at Sarah.

Lieutenant Larrimore was putting her baby to her breast again. The advice John had given her had helped, and the baby seemed to be feeding well now. Natalia thought of her own breasts, useless throughout her life for their intended function and destined to remain so.

The more she thought of it, the more she wanted a baby; but, it would have to be John's baby, and that could never be. She had sometimes pictured herself holding such a child, nursing it, loving it, watching it grow to adulthood in his image.

Such thoughts, although she tried to keep them from her heart, were always there . . .

Michael Rourke began to undress. "Wasn't she a beautiful bride, Michael?" Maria Leuden asked him.

"Yes, Elaine was very beautiful." And he turned around to face Maria, already in her nightgown, sitting on the edge of the bed in the guest officer's quarters. "Would you like to get married?"

"Michael?" Her green eyes—she still wore her glasses—went

wide, her shoulders raising, arms at her sides, tiny fists pressing down against the bed.

"Will you marry me?"

She licked her lips, then ran from the bed and into his arms and he held her against his bare body. He didn't love her, but she loved him, and he liked her so very much.

He knew the difference.

He had loved Madison, always would. And Michael Rourke was convinced that true love came only once in a lifetime, at least for him . . .

John Rourke inspected the medical imaging results from the examination of Sergeant Reimensschnieder once again. Rourke could try the therapy here, of course, but the cancer was too far along to take any risks. At Mid-Wake, to accomplish the therapy, would be the proverbial piece of cake.

He began the memo to the German base commander, recommending that the sergeant, a likeable old guy if ever there was one and very close to his retirement, be flown at once to Mid-Wake for treatment.

Many types of cancer, especially in the early stages, could be instantly and permanently eradicated with drugs developed in Mid-Wake, now available to all the Allies and their former enemies. But some—like pancreatic cancer, always a tricky type to deal with—required specialized implant techniques. To accomplish these in a normally equipped hospital meant major surgery, but the time release drugs could be inserted through special appliances at Mid-Wake, where the medical imaging equipment was vastly advanced over anything possessed even by the Germans in their most advanced facilities.

After a few days in the hospital at Mid-Wake, the sergeant's condition would be vastly improved. In a few weeks, he would be in total remission, the damage already done by the disease undone through the miracle of Mid-Wake's gene splicing technology.

Finished with the memo, John Rourke looked at the Rolex on his left wrist and realized it was nearly one a.m. And he also realized that he was very tired . . .

Annie sat bolt upright beside him, awakening Paul Rubenstein instantly.

Annie's nightgown was wet with perspiration, and she was breathing very rapidly.

He didn't turn on a light, but could see her well enough in the faint light which came through the windows of the officer's quarter billet.

His right hand went to her thigh, his left hand to the battered Browning High Power on the floor beside their bed. "What is it? What's wrong, baby?"

"It's momma and daddy. They're in terrible trouble."

He sat there in the darkness beside her, collecting his thoughts for an instant longer. In a television sitcom from five centuries ago, the exhausted husband would have rolled over and gone back to sleep, dismissing his wife's fears as groundless nervousness.

But Annie Rourke Rubenstein, ever since the Awakening, possessed what some would call a gift and others would call a curse. At a library in Germany on a videofiche of an English language book, he had discovered the proper term for it: Remote Viewing, as distinguished from Clairvoyance.

She could not see the future, but she could see the present, wherever she was, if it somehow affected someone she loved.

He swung his feet over the edge of the bed, grabbed his pants from the chair nearby and started into them, telling his wife, "Get some clothes on." Maybe things had been quiet too long for the Family.

And then a thought came to him which chilled him.

For the first time since the War against the Russians had ended, the entire Family—John and Sarah, Natalia, Michael, Annie and himself—were together.

Ever since childhood, when he had heard the stories of how Hitler had guided his armies by astrological projections, he had rejected the idea that there was any such thing as Fate.

But if there was, it was at work here tonight.

Fate . . .

Michael Rourke's lips touched at Maria Leuden's nipples and he sagged against her, his body still pulsing from the moment passed, her breathing hard. "I love you," Maria whispered.

The telephone rang.

Michael Rourke stared at it, then picked up the receiver, reaching across Maria as he did so, her lips caressing his chest, his shoulder. "This is Michael Rourke."

"Me, Annie. Momma and daddy are in trouble. We're going to the hospital. They aren't at their quarters and Paul tried calling the hospital. Either they're talking to somebody or the terminal has been disconnected or something."

"They set it up so it thinks it's talking to itself, and nothing gets through but it gives the caller a busy signal. I'm on my way. You guys be careful."

He pushed the off button to sever the connection and pushed up from between Maria's legs. "What is it, Michael?"

"There might be a problem with mom and dad. You stay put and lock the door after me." He knew better than to ask if Paul or Annie had called the authorities, because the hospital was under the jurisdiction of Eden and, if there was a problem, the current leader of Eden would be behind it. And he knew better than to ask Maria to accompany him. She would have, as the expression went, followed him into hell, but when they got there she wouldn't have been much help, despite loyalty, sincerity, and desire to try. She was a wonderful, intelligent and talented girl, but in the ways of violence no amount of desire could compensate for her lack of abilities.

But there was something she could do. "Call Colonel Mann. Give me about five minutes, then tell him to think up some pretext for entering Eden."

His sister's psychic flashes had the annoying proclivity for accuracy.

Six

Natalia heard something.

Her left hand swept over the pink chiffon and silk that was the skirt of her bridesmaid's dress, her right hand moving toward the Walther PPK/S, in the black fabric Galco, thigh holster.

The little stainless .380 pistol was in her hand in the same instant, her right thumb working the slide mounted thumb safety up and off.

And then she stood stock still, waiting.

Her little gun was loaded with German fabricated duplicates of the Federal 90-grain jacketed hollow point load she had used in the gun ever since the first day she had taken it out of its black plastic box. Not long after that, the barrel was threaded (losing about a quarter inch of rifling at the muzzle) to accept a suppressor. The suppressor, along with the shoulder holster in which she so frequently carried the Walther, was in her suitcase, back at the bachelor officers quarters at the German base outside Eden.

If she needed to use the gun, waking up some of John's patients would be unavoidable.

She still listened for the sound to come again.

And it came again, like something scratching at the synthglass windows.

The medium heel shoes she wore had hard heels and would click as she walked.

She stepped out of them, the hem of her dress tumbling over her toes. The gun in her right hand, her dress pinched between the thumb and first finger of her left hand, Natalia started toward the windows, her stockinged-feet-cold against the corridor floor.

Young Lieutenant Larrimore's baby had started spitting up, and although John had not thought anything was wrong, to humor an anxious first time mother he had agreed to examine the baby in greater detail and observe the child until it was asleep.

John's trouble as a physician was exactly the same as his trouble during the War: John Rourke could not remain uninvolved or uncaring. And his trouble was also his greatest virtue.

She peered through the windows into the swirling snow of the night, seeing nothing but her own reflection because of the work light over the reception desk, well down the corridor.

The trouble with a hospital or a hotel or motel or anything like that was the multiplicity of doors behind which someone could hide. She started along the corridor. A door opened to her right and she wheeled toward it, realizing instantly that she had made a fatal error when she heard the sound of another door opening behind her.

Natalia recognized the smell immediately, the classic scent of bitter almonds. Cynanide.

Automatically, Natalia turned her face away from the cloud of gas that billowed toward her from the doorway and pulled the trigger of her pistol as she collapsed to the floor, having used a cyanide gas pistol enough herself in the days prior to The Night of The War, to realize that she was a dead woman . . .

Munchen lifted the receiver of his telephone, automatically opening his case and extracting one of the custom blend non-carcinogenic cigarettes. "This is Munchen."

"This is Colonel Mann, Herr Doctor. I may need you. Bring your bag and your pistol. A corporal will be in to collect you in a moment."

The line clicked dead, and in the same breath as Munchen exhaled smoke, there was a knock at his door.

John Rourke looked away from the baby as he wheeled toward the doorway, the Centennial coming into his hand from the waistband of his uniform trousers in the same motion . . .

It was clearly the sound of a pistol shot, nothing else.

And her husband's little office was suddenly a very vulnerable place, with too many windows, no secure door, very little potential for covered positions from which to return fire.

Sarah Rourke's right hand groped for the Trapper Scorpion 45 in the pocket of her German arctic parka, the garment draped over the back of her husband's chair.

The pistol's chamber was already loaded and she thumbed back the hammer as she stood.

Pain shot through her, from groin to chest.

She was cold and hot at once.

Fluid burst from her, spraying downward between her legs and onto the floor, her water bag broken.

Her knees went weak.

As she upped the safety on the .45 and doubled forward over the desk, choking back a scream, she realized the baby was coming early . . .

It sounded like a shot. Annie fell into a run at the same moment her husband did, with her left hand catching up the skirts of the nightgown and robe she wore beneath her parka, drawing the Scoremaster from the holster cinched about her waist with her right hand and cocking back the hammer . . .

Michael Rourke's hands moved under his open parka, tearing first from the leather, the Beretta 92F beneath his left armpit, then the one from beneath his right, flicking off both safeties as he broke into a dead run for the hospital . . .

A burst of automatic weapons fire, the sound of synth-glass shattering.

There was a dull thudding sound at the far end of the corridor, metal or ceramic bouncing over a hard surface, John Rourke halfway along the corridor's length when he heard it. He felt a cold draft of wind, a synth-glass window punched through. An explosion, and a fireball filled the corridor there, the fireball blown along its length, rolling toward him on the air current from the destroyed window.

Rourke threw his body weight against a patient door, hitting the floor in a roll, coming down hard on his left shoulder, the flames gusting past him.

And he was up, framing himself just inside the doorway, the Smith & Wesson revolver in his right hand, his left hand moving to his trouser band where the A G Russell Sting IA Black Chrome was sheathed, snapping it free. The sprinkler system switched on, Rourke instantly soaked in icy cold water, the spray like a very heavy rain.

The fireball was gone, but flames licked everywhere along the corridor, hissing as the water from the sprinklers contacted them, but the fire was still spreading.

The building's fire alarms were sounding.

John Rourke tentatively stepped into the corridor, the little .38 Special revolver tight at his right hip, the knife in a rapier hold along the outside of his left thigh. Gunfire tore along the wall near him, a sub-machine gun from the sound of it, and he ducked back.

Who had fired that first shot?

But the more important concerns now were his wife, their unborn child, Natalia, Lieutenant Larrimore and her baby and the other patients.

To deal with those concerns effectively, he had to get out of the room, capture a more effective weapon if possible, and at least neutralize the attackers sufficiently, that he could act.

There was a bedpan, stainless steels wrapped in its sanitization seal, on the sliding table near the foot of the hospital bed. John Rourke turned toward the patient room's window and fired the Smith & Wesson, twice, the synth-glass taking the bullet holes but not shattering, merely spiderwebbing around them.

But the webs of fractured synth-glass interwove and Rourke seized up the bedpan, the Sting IA clamped between his clenched teeth; his left fist, the bedpan armoring it against the glass, punching through the window between the two bullet holes, making a hole roughly circular and about eighteen inches in diameter. Rourke let the bedpan fall through the opening, drew his hand back inside, shoved the Hip-Gripped revolver into his waistband and tore the pillow off the bed.

Icy wind licked through the opening, chilling Rourke instantly, but his mind was elsewhere. Using the pillow like a giant padded mitten, he reached into the hole, closing his eyes and averting his face as he pried back, a´ huge chunk of the synth-glass snapping inward. He threw it to the floor, grabbing the next piece, prying again, the razor sharp wedge splitting free.

Rourke threw it down and the pillow as well, grabbed the visitor chair from the foot of the bed, put it beside the window, stepped up and clambered through the opening, jumping down into the drifted snow beside the wall.

The cold thoroughly numbed him now, but Rourke started moving nonetheless, opening the cylinder of the little five shot .38 Special, dumping its contents into his hand, discarding the two spent cases, pocketing the three live rounds, in the same movement recovering the Safariland speedloader. He rammed the five 158-grain lead hollow points into the charging holes, the speedloader releasing as its center piece, contacted the ejector star. He dropped the empty loader into his pocket, moving along the side of the building wall, the fully loaded revolver tight in his right fist.

More gunfire, but no sounds of fire or emergency equipment (German origin) from Eden Base.

"Dodd," Rourke rasped through his teeth, the knife still clamped there, ready for use and helping to keep his teeth from chattering together.

Beside the corner where the outer walls met, Rourke stopped, belting his revolver again, taking the three left-over rounds, inserting them casehead first into the speedloader, then pressing the bullets against the wall while he turned the locking knob to secure the rounds in the loader.

At least now he could reload quickly, but with only three rounds.

The revolver still in his belt, the knife back in his left hand, Rourke peered around the corner.

Four men with sub-machine guns, German issue, all four swathed in arctic gear. The men stood near the flames licking from the doorway. They were taking grenades from their web gear.

There was a fifth man, apparently standing watch, some distance back toward Eden's single street.

Rourke dropped to his knees and elbows, taking advantage of the high drifts of snow as concealment, crawling away from the corner and along the driveway toward the fifth man.

This was his logical target, the fifth man carrying an M-16.

Instinct told him that this gun's serial number would match up with the list of those M-16s missing from the Eden Project stores.

Dodd, again.

Rourke moved as quickly as he could, fingers stiffening, his ears numbing; a scream from inside the hospital making him quicken his pace beyond what he'd thought was possible.

He was at the end of the driveway now, roughly parallel to the man with the M-16, still about ten yards from him.

It would have been an easy shot, even with his hands trembling slightly from the cold. But the shot would be heard despite the crackle of the orange flames which now licked across the hospital roofline.

Instead, Rourke raised up from his knees into a crouch, rolled over and moved partially through the snowdrift, coming up to his full height.

There was no time for finesse or some exercise in technique.

He threw himself into a dead run, the knife in his right hand now, his quarry starting to turn around. Rourke jumped toward him, his left hand grabbing the man over his ski-toqued mouth, his right ramming the knife into the man's carotid artery.

As they fell to the frozen ground that formed the driveway surface, Rourke moved his left hand, grabbed a handful of the parka hood, snapped the man's head back and slammed his face into the ground.

Tearing the knife from the dead man's neck, Rourke raked it across the M-16's sling, tearing the Colt assault rifle free of the body, wheeling the muzzle around as his thumb found the selector, moving it to full auto.

Rourke fired, cutting down the first of the four men near the hospital's main entrance just as the man lobbed a grenade through the flames, two of the others doing the same. He fired as the men started to turn toward him to return fire, but too late.

He caught the second man along the spine and in the left kidney, swinging the muzzle left, catching the third man in the neck, fighting the M-16's muzzle down, another short burst into the man's groin.

Explosions rocked the hospital, a portion of the north wing's roof collapsing.

Rourke fell left as assault rifle fire tore into the snowbank beside him, rippling across the driveway surface toward him.

The M-16 stitched a pattern from abdomen to face on the

fourth man, the fourth man's gun firing out full auto into the snowy darkness above.

The rifle was empty.

Rourke threw it down, already to his feet and running for the flaming entrance to the hospital . . .

More explosions were coming from the hospital, earlier sounds like grenades or small bombs, these were somehow different, perhaps the flames reaching combustible liquids.

Annie fell to her knees, Paul wheeling toward her "No! It's momma—she's having the baby. I can feel it. And she's in pain! Hurry! I'm coming."

Paul was already running on.

Annie knelt in the snow, her hands clasped to her abdomen and her groin, the empathic pain she experienced as real and devastating as if it were her own.

Flames rose from the hospital roof, licking hungrily skyward.

Sarah Rourke, her pistol clutched in her right hand, fought against the cramping which seized her, consumed her, dragging herself along the floor now, into the corridor, dragging herself because she could not walk. The first of the explosions had knocked her to the floor.

On her knees beside the corridor wall, she sagged, felt the movement of the baby.

It had to be a boy, racing to the sound of battle just like his father had always done, but not now!

She tried to get to her feet but could not rise.

Smoke filled the corridor, acrid smelling, filling her lungs and the baby's blood stream, too, she knew.

But the back door to the hospital, the emergency entrance, was only a few yards away, she told herself, only a few yards.

Where was John? Natalia? Where was Natalia?

And Sarah Rourke shivered, because if neither John nor Natalia had come for her, that meant they were perhaps in greater danger than she . . .

Michael Rourke started to slow down as he neared his sister, shouting to her, "Annie?"

"I'm all right. Mom's having the baby. Help Paul! Go on!"

Michael Rourke, hands clutching his pistols, arms out at his sides, chest thrown forward, ran full out toward the flames . . .

"John! Don't! Don't go in—" But it was too late. John Rourke ran into the flames, into the burning hospital.

And Paul Rubenstein, his eyes flooding with tears knew why and kept running toward the building, to do the same . . .

Deitrich Zimmer went from right to left through the doorway, his two lieutenants already through ahead of him. The fire was spreading more rapidly than he had supposed it would.

But his mission was clear and could not be sacrificed for concerns of personal safety.

Seventeen patients had escaped through the emergency entrance, but escaped only to death. They were all followers of Deiter Bern and, as such, unworthy of life.

The woman, Sarah Rourke was not among them.

It was for her now that he searched . . .

Smoke so thick he could barely breathe or see, John Rourke stumbled over a body in the corridor just inside the doorway. A woman's body.

He felt for a pulse.

There was none, not even a weak one that he could detect. And, as his hand drifted along the wrist, he felt the face of a watch, the shape of which was quite familiar.

"Natalia!"

She was dead.

His eyes already streamed tears from the smoke, but as he swept her up into his arms, more tears came. There was a gun locked in her hand. He already had it free, the hammer dropped. Pulling her coat up over her as much as possible to protect exposed skin, he started back through the fiery doorway, just in case there was a chance she still lived.

Near the doorway, he could see Paul, starting through.

Rourke shouted to his best friend, "Stay back!" And Rourke was through, dropping to his knees with Natalia, Paul kneeling beside him. "I think she's dead, but don't give up on her. Try CPR. Don't give up."

And John Rourke started to his feet, doubling over and gagging.

Paul Rubenstein grabbed at him. "You can't go in there, John! You can't!"

John Rourke shoved Paul's hands away.

Paul grabbed at him again, trying to turn him around. John Rourke straight-armed Paul in the chest, sending him sprawling, then vaulted through the doorway again, into the inferno . . .

Deitrich Zimmer followed the sounds of the screams. For a moment, as he stepped through the doorway, he thought he had found Sarah Rourke.

A woman with a hospital gown up past her hips huddled in the far corner, clutching an infant to her breast.

But the woman was not Sarah Rourke.

She appealed to him in English, "Please help us!"

Something moved Deitrich Zimmer. Not compassion, but inspiration . . .

112

John Rourke was nearer to the room occupied by Lieutenant Larrimore and her infant son than he was to his office, and Sarah was mobile, had probably escaped already.

He started toward Lieutenant Larrimore's room.

There was a terrible scream and the sound of a shot.

John Rourke, staggering from the effect of the smoke, ran toward the sounds.

As he neared Lieutenant Larrimore's doorway, three men wearing gas masks and oxygen breathing apparatus emerged, the third stepping back inside quickly as the other two turned toward Rourke. Rourke already had his revolver in hand, firing, then firing again, putting down one of the men with a double tap into the throat and head.

As Rourke wheeled on the second man and fired, the second man lobbed something toward John Rourke.

Rourke's shot struck and the man went down, Rourke throwing himself forward to escape the grenade, but the explosion starting, the walls around John Rourke, already smoldering, crashed down around him in flames as he fell into darkness . . .

There was an explosion and the forward central section of the hospital caved in on itself from both walls, then the ceiling collapsing.

Michael Rourke stripped away his parka, throwing it into the snow, shrugging out of his shoulder holster as well, Paul already packing snow over his own parka.

Annie knelt beside Natalia. Natalia dead.

"Daddy is dying! He's—"

"We're going in. Keep up the CPR until help comes. Maybe we can save her," Paul shouted, throwing his coat over his head and neck and shoulders.

Michael Rourke did the same, both Berettas in his waistband

now.

Paul Rubenstein beside him, they dashed through the scant break in the wall of flames . . .

Wolfgang Mann stomped the accelerator of his staff car, cutting the wheel into the turn, easing the gas as he downshifted, upshifting and accelerating as he turned out of the curve.

Beside him, Munchen gasped, "Look at the flames, Wolf!"

The night sky was orange, where the hospital walls had been, only sheets of flames were now.

Mann's hands clenched the wheel more tightly. The only emergency sirens which could be heard over the crackling of the flames were those of the vehicles following him.

Nothing was coming from Eden Base . . .

Sarah Rourke leaned with her back against the wall, her legs squatted beneath her.

On one level of consciousness, she told herself that American Indian women—African women, women for centuries had delivered their own children this way.

But that level was very small and very far away.

Her fingernails gouged into the wall and she shrieked her pain to the flames around her, the smoke making her cough and gag, but the baby's head crowned, blood oozing along her thighs, her flesh ripping.

"John!"

The baby.

Something enormous was pushing through her, tearing at her, sending waves of pain through her body no matter how she tried to regulate her breathing.

"John!"

More pain than she had ever known, and then it was gone, and blood and fluid dripped from her, but her baby's head was out. She bore down with her shoulders, her rib cage, her pel-

114

vis, pushing as hard as she could, unable to move her hands to help herself lest she fall.

She drew herself in and pushed down.

Movement.

A shoulder. It had to be. She pushed. And she could feel her child alive and moving and she let herself slide down along the length of the wall as her hands grasped for the baby, drawing the child—her child, John's child—the rest of the way from her body.

As she raised the new life toward her—a boy—he simultaneously screamed and urinated.

"Very impressive, Frau Rourke."

Tears filling her eyes, she looked up toward the mechanical sounding voice.

It had come to her through some sort of mask.

Her baby's body was slick and at the same time sticky, the umbilical cord still attached, blue and pulsing.

The man who had spoken to her had a gun in his hand. "This is for your crimes against National Socialism, Frau Rourke."

She screamed, "John!"

She saw a flash from the muzzle of the gun . . .

Michael Rourke beside him, Paul Rubenstein fell back from the flames, collapsing to his knees in the snow. Michael slumped in the snow as well. "We have to get in there!" Paul coughed.

"Around to the back."

Annie was screaming incoherently, her face buried in her hands, body doubled over, head nearly in her lap; Natalia's body in the snow beside her.

Paul Rubenstein wanted to take his wife into his arms, but instead pushed himself to his feet, starting to run along what remained of the burning north wall of the building, to reach the rear entrance, realizing every second lost could mean death . . .

The Rourke child wrapped in the dead woman's coat and carried under his left arm, screaming into the night, its umbilical chord still attached, Deitrich Zimmer ran through the snow. A helicopter would be waiting over the rise.

Inspiration was what differentiated some few men from their inferiors.

And this child, taking this child of Fate, was inspiration on the grandest scale . . .

There were dead strewn everywhere near the entrance, patients in hospital gowns and robes, bodies stitched with bullet holes, slaughtered.

The rear entrance was clear. Both Berettas in his hands, Michael Rourke ran toward it, Paul ahead of him.

Through the doorway, the air inside unbreathable, but going on, anyway.

A body.

The smoke swirled in a vagrant current of fresh air from the open doorway.

Michael saw her.

His mother lay in a pool of blood, blood between her legs, blood covering her face, a bullet wound by her left temple.

Michael Rourke fell to his knees beside her.

She had had the baby.

The baby was gone.

Paul shouted, "God damn them! I'll look for your father!"

Michael thrust his pistols into his waistband, then lifted his mother into his arms and wept as he carried her from the burning building . . .

Paul Rubenstein, despite the saturated parka to filter the air he breathed, coughed, his eyes streaming tears, but not all the tears because of the smoke.

Sarah.

She was dead.

After all of this, Sarah and Natalia in one night.

And his hands shook, with rage, because if John had not prevented what happened to Sarah, that meant that John was—

Paul Rubenstein kicked away a burning sheet of plaster board, his trouser leg catching fire. He tore the coat from his head, holding his breath against the heat and smoke, beating out the flames, then running on, dragging the coat over him again.

The corridor took a bend and he was at John's office.

The door was open.

There was no one inside.

"The woman and her—" Paul leaned against the office wall, trying to get a breath.

John would have gone to find Lieutenant Larrimore, whose baby he had just delivered this very morning, thinking that Sarah could make it out herself, perhaps.

Paul moved along the corridor, trying to orient himself, turning to his left.

The corridor walls and ceiling were collapsed and there was a wall of flame between him and the debris.

"John! John! Where are you? John!"

The walls and ceiling creaked. In seconds, Paul Rubenstein knew, the bulding would be entirely collapsed.

All hope would be dashed.

The Germans and the Americans at Mid-Wake did wonders with skin grafts these days, he knew.

Inhaling as deeply as he could, pulling the coat tight around his head, Paul Rubenstein ran toward the flames and jumped, his trousers on fire, his left arm aflame. And he was through. He threw himself against the wall, rolling against it to extinguish the fire, beating at his legs with his coat, his left arm cold with pain.

He could hardly see, but there was a pile of rubble just ahead of him.

He staggered toward it.

"John?"

It was John, beneath pieces of the walls and ceiling, some of these aflame.

"John!"

Paul Rubenstein, on his knees beside his friend, threw his weight against the rubble, sending chunks of it skidding away, his hands grabbing at the still hot pieces of steel, blistering as he touched them.

"John!?"

John's upper body was free, a huge fragment of steel protruding from John's back.

Paul Rubenstein leaned over his friend, protecting John Rourke's body with his own, kicking at the rubble which pinned John's legs, kicking at it, pulling at John's upper body, praying he was doing the right thing, not killing his friend by moving him.

Paul Rubenstein fell back, John pressed against him.

"God, save him!"

Paul dragged himself to his knees, pulling at John, pulling him up. Paul bent forward as low as he could, getting his right shoulder beneath John, then trying to kneel, Paul's burned and blistered hands grasping at the wall, at anything for support.

He stood, swaying.

Flames were on his right.

There was an open doorway along the corridor.

Paul held John close, sagging under his friend's weight, moving along the wall, toward the doorway, not knowing if safety might lie beyond it.

To the doorway.

Flames almost danced along the floor, up the wall. The window was smashed.

Cold air.

118

He moved toward it.

The air made him light-headed, faint.

He staggered, but did not fall.

To the window.

He pushed John's body up, off his shoulder, over the sill, through and into the snow, the creaking of the walls, of the entire structure, louder now; fire covering the ceiling of the room, rolling toward him.

Paul Rubenstein stepped up onto a chair, threw himself through the opening and into the snow . . .

Annie Rourke Rubenstein cried, her eyes aching with the tears, her fingers knotting into her hair as she wept and screamed and shouted damnation to the men who had done this, shrieked this to the vaults of Heaven.

Part Two
The Child of Fate

One

Paul had been sedated, his hands so badly burned that, in conjunction with the burns on his legs and left arm, he would require surgery and the only relief from his pain would be in sleep.

Annie, arms hugged close against her, sat on the edge of a straight back chair, her smoke smudged nightgown all but in tatters, a blanket wrapped round her hunched-forward shoulders, a blank look in her eyes, her mouth downturned.

The door opened.

Hair pulled straight back, face as pale as death, eyes filled with hate, Natalia entered the room. She wore German fatigue pants, surgical scuffs and a khaki T-shirt.

"You shouldn't be up."

"Don't tell me what to do; you're not your father."

"Sit down before you fall down," Michael countered. She glared at him, but sat on the remaining vacant chair. Michael Rourke watched her. "Are you all right?"

"My lungs were flushed, my stomach was pumped and they stimulated my heartbeat with high voltage. I have bruises all over my chest and my left breast. I am just fine. And I want to throw up but there isn't anything in my stomach." She looked away, started to light a cigarette, broke it in half and threw it into the ashtray on the desk near her. "How are you?"

Michael Rourke wished he smoked.

And he didn't want to answer her.

When the medical team which accompanied Colonel Mann arrived, Doctor Munchen was already injecting Natalia with drugs designed to regulate her heartbeat, Michael Rourke had been told. Her heartbeat had been so low, so erratic, that she had been mistaken for dead.

And the medical team had had so much to do, had they done anything else right, Michael wondered? But, he told himself, they had done everything right, done everything that was possible to save the lives of his father and mother.

Natalia was by the front entrance—what had been the front entrance. Hence, she was the first of the casualties to be attended to.

He closed his eyes, sat on the edge of Doctor Munchen's desk and waited.

But his mind could not rest.

What happened to his father was less deliberate than the fate which had befallen his mother, a deliberate assassination.

And, where was the child?

Doctor Munchen entered the office and stood in the doorway.

Michael stared at him.

Annie did not move.

Natalia said, "Well?"

"The child was a boy. We were able to tell from amniotic fluid residue scrapings taken from Sarah's thighs. There is no reason to suppose that anything was wrong with the child. That is the good news."

There was an old joke his father had told him years ago, something his father had heard on television or in a movie or something like that, and Michael Rourke remembered it now: A doctor entered his patient's room, the patient recovering from surgery. "I have good news and bad news. The good news is that the man in the next room would like to buy your slippers. The bad news is that we amputated the wrong leg."

Annie didn't look up when she spoke. "Tell them."

Michael stared at her, wondering if she already knew.

Munchen cleared his throat. "The bullet which penetrated Sarah Rourke's skull essentially killed her."

124

Michael Rourke stood up, his hands trembling. "What the fuck does essentially mean, damnit!"

Munchen lit a cigarette from his case. His eyes were very tired. "There is nothing in our power now that can alter the state of your mother's condition for any positive result, but she is still perfectly alive in the physical sense."

"Jesus," and Michael as he made the sign of the cross.

"The bullet entered the brain in such a manner that its path evidently did little damage, and there is a remarkable tendency for the brain to heal itself, for one portion of the brain to take over the function of a portion which has been damaged. But the bullet is buried within an area of the brain which is inaccessible in a living patient by any means at our disposal. To remove the bullet, without going into medical explanations none of you—and I mean no offense by this, of course—but that none of you would understand, would precipitate her physical death instantly. Researchers in both New Germany and Mid-Wake have been studying the brain in great detail for the past five centuries; as, of course, have Soviet researchers. This is nothing new, certainly. The brain, as the seat of personality, of being who we are, is the ultimate quest in medicine.

"We have known," Munchen said through a cloud of exhaled smoke, "for centuries that the brain feels no pain, yet makes its own pain killers to assist those portions of the body which do feel pain. Brain surgery was not even undertaken in modern medicine until the early 1900s, although primitive societies undertook brain surgery of a sort in ancient times by various means, often just drilling into the skull. Enkaphalins, endorphins and other natural drugs are just a part of the chemical defenses the brain can muster to support the host body during times of stress. Because Sarah had just given birth, her body was pumped with natural chemicals, things to give her greater endurance, things to give her greater strength, things to help her control the pain and discomfort of her sudden childbirth.

125

"Add to this," Munchen said, "that she was already in another crisis situation, namely the burning hospital, the fact that she had to be uncertain about John, Natalia as well. Then, as all these chemicals are beginning to rebalance in her body and her brain, along comes whoever the assassin was and there is an instantaneous surge of various of these chemicals as the brain and the body try to prepare for an anticipated, known trauma."

"But Momma isn't dead," Annie almost whispered.

"No, she is not," Doctor Munchen responded almost immediately. "But she is comatose and, in light of current technology, there is no way to remove the bullet which has precipitated this condition. 'Dead' and 'alive' cease to have meaning in such a situation as this. With X-ray tomography, we have located the bullet, but seeing it and getting at it are two different things.

"The bullet is lodged in almost the very center of the epencephalon, near the post-nodular fissure on the under surface of the cerebellum. No tool can reach it, let alone extract it, without killing Sarah. No technique of micro-surgery currently known, nor laser surgery, nor any method currently under development can effectively assist Sarah Rourke."

"What about Dad?" Michael asked, watching Munchen's face.

"Your father suffered burns, none of them serious; he suffered various traumatic bruises, which will heal. Unlike your mother, he suffered no penetration of the brain or the body, yet very like your mother, he is comatose. Evidently, the roof materials which crashed down on him caused several incidents of trauma to the brain, concussion. But all of these will eventually heal.

"John Rourke's problem," Munchen said, lighting another cigarette, "is more complex. To have a chance of saving Sarah Rourke, we need the right tools and procedures. These do not exist. But for John, I do not know. He could awaken in ten seconds, or he might never awaken. I am not a specialist in these matters, but I know the literature. Like your mother, he may have assumed at the instant that the explosion or structural collapse caught him, that this was, in fact, the end, that he was dead. Add to that, the peculiar nature of John Rourke's personality and the problem we may face begins to take shape.

"John Rourke, like any man, would reject death. But, unlike most men, he has an almost pathological sense of duty. It is likely he suspected that Sarah might still be in the building. From where he was found, he was evidently en route to locate Lieutenant Larrimore and her baby in order to effect a rescue. Death meant more to him than the loss of his life, something he had risked on occasions too numerous to count; it meant the inability to do what he must do. It meant failure. I may be very wrong, and I certainly hope that I am. Yet, I suspect that what makes John Rourke comatose is his inability to accept the fact that just this once he did not succeed. In effect, his brain is rejecting contact with reality, almost angry with his body for failing to shrug off the building materials which collapsed upon him and drove him into unconsciousness, so angry with the body that it may well have disassociated itself from the body."

"What are you talking about?" Natalia asked him, coughing, staring down at her hands; they were shaking.

"For a human being to function, brain and body must work together. The brain controls the body, but the body affects the brain, because the brain is physical, is an organ like any other in that respect. The brain has defenses, for the body and for itself. One ultimate defense is the total rejection of what surrounds it. This only occurs in cases of severe trauma coupled with great stress. John Rourke had a mission. He was unable to fulfill this mission. Somewhere, deep inside his psyche, his brain is rejecting awakening because of this perceived failure. His brain is giving all the appearances of shutting down the biological system which supports it. John Rourke's blood pressure, heart rate, everything is declining, as if death were imminent. Brain activity, measured electrically, is subsiding

127

rapidly to death. We can keep him alive on machines, as we do now, but that is not the answer, nor is it even an effective temporary solution. He can only decline so far before this lack of co-operation between his inner self and his physical being will begin to take its toll on the brain as an organ, in a way that is very physical.

"He would still be alive," Munchen added, "but he would be nothing more than a shell, never to awaken again, merely living on, solely because of the machines which support him even as we speak."

Annie said very quietly, "I'm getting nothing from Mom. It's like she's dead. But Daddy, there's something there, but I keep losing him and then he comes back. And each time, it's worse, what I feel is weaker, harder to reach."

"What about what John did when I was ill?" Natalia asked, looking at Munchen.

"That was most ingenious and daring and inventive, and thankfully quite effective. However, Fraulein Major, the situations are totally dissimilar."

"He's right," Annie murmured. "I couldn't reach into Daddy's mind, and neither could you."

"The concept of 'mind' is the key to understanding, here. There is a tendency to look at the brain as some mystical thing. It is a physical organ, and what occurs occurs because of physical processes, some from within the brain itself and some from without, internal and external stimuli, if you will."

"So. What are we supposed to do? Let mom be brain dead and dad just die?" Michael said slowly.

But before Doctor Munchen could answer, Wolfgang Mann and Commander Dodd, an odd pairing to be sure, Michael thought, appeared in the outer office. Munchen turned toward them.

"Colonel?"

"Commander Dodd wishes to speak with all of you; I thought it best to accompany him, under the circumstances."

Dodd entered the inner office, stood just inside the doorway,

Colonel Mann, worn looking, sad-eyed, stood in the doorway just behind him.

Dodd put his hands on his hips.

"What is it that you want?" Natalia asked.

"I came to express my condolences on your bereavement. What a fine and brave family to endure such terrible emotional hardships. Doctor Rourke and his wife will be sorely missed."

Michael cleared his throat. Otherwise, the room was as silent as the grave.

Dodd went on. "I have a responsibility to the citizens of Eden which, however onerous, must be carried out."

"What?" Annie asked him, the hatred for him ill-disguised in her voice.

"There has been a crime. The person or persons responsible must be apprehended if society is to continue, if there is to be civilization here rather than chaos."

"I agree. We need to take the killer and kill him, hard," Michael said, standing, looking at Dodd, taking a step toward him.

Dodd stood his ground. "I'd never thought a Rourke would feel differently. That's why I must do what I must do."

"And what the hell is that?" Michael Rourke snapped.

"To thoroughly investigate this crime, we need evidence. And, as far as I am able to ascertain, Doctor and Mrs. Rourke died intestate."

"They are not dead," Natalia hissed, standing, throwing her shoulders back.

"Their deaths are a matter of time, if I properly understand their conditions. Therefore, I am officially requesting Colonel Mann that their bodies be released to me so that at the instant of death, Eden's resident physician can conduct a proper autopsy on each of them to assist in accumulating evidence."

"Against whom?" Annie asked him.

"That is another reason I have come."

Wolfgang Mann spoke. "He has six armed men of Eden

with him. He intends to arrest the Fraulein Major on suspicion of murder."

Michael Rourke jumped toward Dodd, hands going for Dodd's throat, Michael's right knee smashing upward into Dodd's groin, hammering the man to the floor, Michael was atop him now, fingers closing more tightly around Dodd's neck.

Dodd's pudgy face was starting to discolor.

Michael felt hands on his arms and shoulders, his eyes so tightly focused on Dodd, willing the man to die, that he saw noone else.

"Mike!"

He looked up.

Into Natalia's eyes.

She knelt beside him, her hands on his arm. "Not now."

The only person who had ever called him 'Mike' was his father, and only a few times, in their too short lives together.

Michael looked to his left. Annie and Doctor Munchen held his other arm.

Michael looked back at Natalia.

For once in his life, his father had misdiagnosed, thought she was dead, but had 'planned ahead' as he always did, in the event that he was wrong—getting her from the fire, protecting her from additional smoke inhalation in the process. If she had not gotten instant care, the cyanide gas would surely have claimed her. She had saved herself, and had to have turned away the instant death that came for her, or otherwise the amount of the gas would have been such, she would have died on the spot, in that very instant.

And he realized something else.

Whether his parents lived or died, he had the mantle of his father's responsibility now.

Lieutenant Larrimore and her baby were burned to ashes, a few of Lieutenant Martha Larrimore's bones likely all that would be found. The other patients, all of them German, were dead.

But the child to whom his mother gave birth only seconds before she was shot in the head, might still live.

He had to find that child, and find the killers who assaulted the hospital.

If he murdered Dodd now, who could not possibly have been physically responsible for what occurred (although doubtlessly was in whole or in part behind it), he might sever the last possible link to the actual culprits, to his just born brother.

He released Dodd's throat and stood up from the floor.

Dodd lay there, Munchen examining Dodd's throat briefly, taking Dodd's pulse, then rising, saying, "You appear well, Herr Commander."

Dodd looked up from the floor, into Michael's eyes, but never quite holding Michael's gaze. "I wasn't going to bring this up now, but I will. With your father and mother near death, and no clear will—"

"Will?" Annie repeated.

"It is my duty as leader of Eden to impound the Retreat and its contents until such time as proper legal proceedings can be established to dispose of the estate."

"You can fuck off and die before you get my father and mother into your hands to kill them," Michael Rourke told him. "And the Retreat doesn't belong to you. And you don't know the way inside, you schmuck." It was Yiddish for prick, that word, something he had picked up from Annie, whom Michael assumed had, in turn, learned it from her husband.

Colonel Mann cleared his throat, then said, "Commander, you may or may not have the right to seize the possessions and property of the Herr Doctor and Frau Rourke, but this base constitutes the embassy of The Republic of New Germany in Eden, and as such cannot be subject to your civil authority. You cannot remove the Rourkes, nor can you arrest Fraulein Major Tiemerovna. John and Sarah Rourke will be flown away from here as soon as Doctor Munchen considers it medically advisable, then to New Germany or Mid-Wake

131

where they will be given the finest care to be had in the hopes of their full and complete recoveries. And, although it is not my place to comment, once Akiro Kurinami bets you in a free election, were I you, I might think of where on this small Earth of ours to hide from the wrath of God and man.

"It is you, Herr Commander, and Nazi conspirators whom I think must be responsible for what has happened here this night. Once that is proven, you will be the sworn enemy of every free man and woman. Enjoy your moment, for it will be your last."

Dodd was on his feet now, starting for the door. And Wolfgang Mann interposed himself within the doorway between Dodd and the outer office. "I personally, Herr Commander, count Frau Rourke as one of the finest persons I have ever known. That you authorized or ordered or even condoned what was done to her is beyond despicable. Were I a private citizen, I would kill you now, you disgust me so."

"Where's our brother, Dodd?" Michael Rourke's hands trembled with rage, his fists balling closed, opening, balling closed again.

"I am not responsible to you."

Wolfgang Mann said, "Once you leave this facility, Herr Commander, I would walk quickly, and I would never keep myself alone, nor be without a weapon in instant reach, and avoid dark places."

Dodd looked at Natalia. "Will you chose to surrender yourself to me for trial?"

Natalia lit a cigarette, blew the smoke in his face. "I am not religious, but I am struck by the Biblical story of Eden, Commander Dodd. There was a temptor. There were the tempted. But you have simultaneously offered the apple and eaten it yourself. Perhaps, if I were to cut off your arms and legs, you could then crawl on your belly as you should."

Wolfgang Mann stepped aside.

Dodd walked out.

Michael Rourke looked out the office window. Perhaps there

was symbolic meaning behind it, although he doubted that. But, the sun definitely rose.

"Paul should be well enough to travel in a few days," Annie said emotionlessly from behind him.

Natalia asked, "Doctor Munchen, what is their fate?"

Michael Rourke closed his eyes, no longer wishing to see the sunrise.

Munchen's voice came to him through the darkness.

"To prevent John's condition from further deteriorating, and to keep Sarah alive until, someday, there may be a procedure by which she can be saved, there is only one choice, a gamble at best.

"But they are man and wife, and at least they will sleep together."

"The Sleep," Michael Rourke said, not opening his eyes.

Two

Wind swept over the field, light snow falling, driving hard against them.

The J7-V which would transport them was waiting at the center of the field. Three more of the craft circled overhead, waiting as escort for the flight and now as sentries against the unexpected.

Jason Darkwood and Margaret Barrow would accompany John and Sarah Rourke to Mid-Wake, where German doctors were already waiting to consult with their American colleagues. A Russian specialist from the Underground City had volunteered his services as well.

Paul and Annie, Paul's hands swathed in bandages and a large patch bandage on his left cheek, stood at the edge of the pad; Annie's long skirts blowing in the wind.

And Natalia looked suddenly at Michael Rourke who stood beside her when he reached out and took her hand. She let him hold her hand, not knowing why she let him do so nor why he wanted to.

Beneath hermetically sealed half-cylinders, John and Sarah were brought out onto the field. Doctor Munchen walked beside them.

Natalia could see their faces clearly, despite the fact that the left side of Sarah's face was heavily bandaged.

She looked asleep, and so did John.

Colonel Mann—had he secretly fallen in love with Sarah? Natalia wondered, saddened at the thought as the honor guard was called to attention.

A tape was begun, the Star Spangled Banner.

As the United States national anthem played, John and Sarah were wheeled across the field. Colonel Mann ordered present arms.

Rifle salutes from the men and women ranked on three sides of the field.

Colonel Mann rendered a hand salute.

Tears flooded Natalia's eyes and she cursed her sex for the emotions being so close to the surface, sometimes so hard to control. She needed to be hard, more than ever before, to avenge the terrible act which wrought this, to find John and Sarah's missing child.

But her heart was ripped from her, and she could barely stand.

Michael's arm went around her and she leaned her face against his chest and wept.

Michael whispered to her, "Let it go. Let it go."

Her tears flowed more freely now than she could ever remember having cried before, even as a little girl. And she felt more alone than she had ever felt in her life.

But Michael held her.

Twenty-one persons, men and women of Mid-Wake and of New Germany, ranked behind the flags of the United States (and Mid-Wake) and of New Germany, fired their assault rifles skyward as Natalia looked.

"I swear to your God, John and Sarah, I will never rest until we find the child and kill the men who did this."

Beside her, Michael, his voice hoarse, tight, tears running down his cheeks, his body shaking, whispered, "Amen."

135

Three

The election would be in a matter of days, the election for leadership of Eden, a mere handful of persons deciding the future of what was once the United States, to follow Akiro Kurinami, who stood for honor and courage, or Dodd, who was vile and despicable.

Annie Rourke Rubenstein, her eyes burning with exhaustion and tears, dressed herself for the ordeal now facing them, where climate, as much as anything else would be the adversary. Chinese silk tights, heavy and black, like her spirit. A cream colored silk teddy, of the kind Natalia always wore, also Chinese. Then, over the tights, heavy stockings, of coarse black wool, elasticized at the thighs to stay up. She stepped into a heavy silk slip, elasticized at the waist, the garment coming to mid-thigh level.

If—when—they found—What exactly were these people? Killers? Certainly, but not of her parents, not yet, because her parents both lived in a strange, horrible way. Was life like that better than death?

It would be a matter of a few days only before the decision would have to be made to put her mother and father into cryogenic sleep, the same procedure which had saved all their lives, allowing them to sleep for five centuries while the Earth became at least slightly habitable again, while they waited for the return of the Eden Project.

What irony, she thought, that the humans for whom she and her brother—especially her brother—had watched in the night sky each and every night, well over a decade, should return to bring them this horror.

She buttoned her blouse, white, long sleeved, heavy cotton, buttoning it fully to the neck.

Annie stepped into her skirt, nearly ankle length, moderately full, charcoal gray-lined wool. Smoothing the tails of her blouse beneath the waistband, she zipped and buttoned it at her side. She pulled on her sweater, long-sleeved, crew-necked, charcoal gray like her skirt. She pulled the little round collar of her blouse from beneath the neck of her sweater.

The logical starting place was Dodd, of course.

It had to be Dodd.

Akiro had volunteered to return, as had Elaine, but Michael and Paul had insisted that they should not, not until the eve of the election, and only then if he kept as close as possible under German security.

She stepped into her boots, began completing the lacing.

The first step would be Commander Dodd, learning from him who had her unnamed brother, where they hid him.

Between them—herself, her husband, her brother, Natalia—they had not yet decided what to do about Dodd. Kill him?

Or let the election throw him out, ruin him, reveal him. Let the new laws which would be made, bring him to book.

Her boots tied, she began to don her weapons.

The little cold steel Mini-Tanto. Sheathed in the special rig made for her in Lydveldid Island, she secured it to the inside of her left calf. She buckled on her gunbelt, the Detonics Scoremaster .45 in one holster, the Beretta 92F she'd taken from a man who had kidnapped her and tried to rape her, in the other. Spare magazines for both pistols—two for each—were arrayed in pouches on the belt, the rest of the magazines for her handguns, along with other miscellaneous gear, in a leather musette bag she carried, which doubled as a purse, with her hairbrush and other necessities.

Annie Rourke Rubenstein looked at herself in the mirror.

She always felt slightly ridiculous suited up for the wilderness or for battle, and usually both.

Since her girlhood, when their father had awakened them early from the cryogenics chambers, to which both her father and mother might soon return, perhaps forever, she had felt compelled to express herself as female in a world where, then, the only two other humans were male, father and brother.

Desire had become habit and on those few occasions, when the extremes of climate demanded, she had to wear trousers, she felt terribly uncomfortable, unnatural almost.

For the first time since the attack on her parents, she almost laughed, seeing herself in the mirror, skirt and combat boots, peter pan collar and gunbelt.

She sat down in front of the mirror and put on her earrings . . .

"You will be killed."

"So?"

"So?"

"So."

"Colonel Mann can organize—"

"Colonel Mann can't do what needs to be done. He knows it and so do I."

"But, Michael, the war is over."

"Only a major engagement, Maria; that's all that's over. The wars never end. There's an occasional truce, a lull in the fighting, and sometimes a shifting of alliances. But the war goes on forever, if you think about it."

"What are you telling me, Michael?"

"That you love me and I care a great deal for you, but I don't know when I'll be back, or even if. And I think you'd be better off without me."

"Michael!"

"I'm sorry, but not for what I am."

Michael Rourke did not kiss Maria Leuden, simply looked

138

at her one more time and left the room, walked along the corridor, taking his gunbelt from his shoulder and cinching it at his waist.

He could hear his father's voice inside his head: "You behaved like an asshole toward her, Michael; she loves you."

He didn't love her.

And that was a fact he could not escape.

And Michael Rourke wondered what his father would say if he could see just what was in his son's mind and heart right now, at this very instant.

He doubted very much that John Rourke would like what he saw very much at all.

Four

Natalia Anastasia Tiemerovna set down the receiver of the radio telephone.

Frau Bruner had put Jea on the line. "Natalia?"

"Yes. Did they tell you?"

"No like."

"You help Frau Bruner, okay?"

"Yes, no like."

"Are we friends, you and I?"

"Yes."

"Would you help me?"

"Yes.

"Then, help me now. And understand why I help my other friends, okay?"

"Yes. Love much."

And he had handed the receiver back to Frau Bruner.

They spoke for several minutes about the school, about Jea, about when Natalia might be back.

"I do not know, Frau Bruner. I may never be back."

"But, Fraulein Major!"

"I have asked you to call me just Natalia, or Fraulein Tiemerovna, or whatever you like but that." But, why argue that now? "Anyway, Frau Bruner. You can run the school not just as well as I, but better. And we both know that, don't we?"

Frau Bruner was silent for a moment, and Natalia almost began to think the transmission was broken. But then her voice came back. "I will miss you, Natalia."

Frau Bruner said Natalia's name with great deliberance, great care.

"I will miss you, Clara. You are my good friend. Bless you." And Natalia hung up.

She stood now in front of the mirror, just looking at herself.

Natalia Anastasia Tiemerovna was back in the world where she belonged, doing what presumably she was born to do, if one believed in Fate.

She took the gunbelt John had searched so hard to find for her, securing it around her waist just over the hips. She picked up the twin stainless steel Smith & Wesson L-Frame .357 Magnum revolvers with their American Eagles engraved on the right barrel flats, holstering them both, the loads already checked after she had completed cleaning them. Then washed her hands several times to rid herself of the odor of the lubricant/cleaner that accumulated beneath her nails.

She took the Null shoulder holster from the back of the vanity chair, slung it on, securing the crossover strap to her gunbelt (more comfortable than attaching it to the loop sewn into the waist of the black jumpsuit she wore). The PPK/S, which John had rescued along with her from the fire, was already holstered, its suppressor in place. Finally, she picked up the Bali-Song from the small table the Germans had provided her.

Her right thumb flipped up the lock, and she wheeled the knife in her hand, steel moving like something alive. She desperately wanted to use the knife, to kill Commander Dodd.

She closed the Bali-Song, securing it inside the sewn-in pouch, along the jumpsuit's right leg.

Natalia caught up her black purse which converted to a day pack, and her parka, too. Black fabric—the lining of the jacket and the hood—synthetic fur as warm and soft and real feeling as the sable of the once glorious coat which was now stained with and smelled of smoke from the fire.

She looked at herself one more time in the mirror.

Had she not averted her face and held her breath, she would have inhaled enough of the cyanide gas that she would be dead now. Five centuries ago, she would never have survived in any event.

She wondered if she was better off now or would have been better off then . . .

Michael Rourke, his pack set on the synth-concrete beside him, stomped his booted feet against the cold.

The night was nothing but stars, no cloud cover, no precipitation, no moon amounting to anything more than an obscure sliver, the blackness like velvet. He remembered the nights before the Awakening, watching the stars with his father and his sister. Then Annie would go to bed.

That was his time, to sit with John Rourke, the hero, the legend, the demi-god, his father.

It was precious time, because in a short while his father would return to the Sleep, to rejoin them once again in what was then a distant future time.

And the future never was nor would it be something one could count on.

"Why do you watch the stars, Dad?"

"Well, beats looking at you, right?" And then his father would laugh, hit him on the the arm or hug him to him and sometimes kiss his forehead. That gesture was embarrassing then, because they were both guys.

Michael Rourke longed for it again, now.

"I like to try to guess what's up there, Michael."

"You mean like the Eden Project?"

"No. They're just men, like ourselves." That sounded pretty good at the time. "I just kind of wonder, that's all."

"So do I."

"What do you wonder about, Michael?"

"What's gonna happen in the future."

His father laughed, puffed on his cigar. "Nobody can tell that. And that's probably a good thing. If we knew all the happy moments and all the sad ones, we'd be so busy trying to rearrange everything, we'd never get anything done and before you knew it all the happy times would be gone."

"What will the happy times be like, Dad?"

"You'll know them, Mike, and the sad times, too."

Michael Rourke took his father's battered old Zippo lighter from his pocket, pulled off his outer glove and the liner. In the light from the airfield, he could just make out the steam rising from the palm of his hand as he shone the lighter on them.

The lighter was the one thing of his father's that he had.

But, that was a lie.

The lighter was only a tangible possession.

He had many things of his father, he told himself, intangible things that were more important than anything physical.

Memories, love, learning.

No Commander Dodd, no assassins, no living death in cryogenic sleep could ever deprive him of such things as these.

He held the lighter very tightly in his fist.

He heard footsteps and looked around, but slowly.

It was Annie, looking for all the world like someone off for a walk in the countryside, yet somehow dressed for battle, too.

Paul, his hands still bandaged under his gloves, Michael knew.

Natalia, beautiful Natalia.

And the last two members of their group, Bjorn Rolvaag, the Icelandic policemen, and his wolf-like dog, Hrothgar.

Natalia said something to him and he nodded, smiled.

Annie gave him a big hug.

Paul made a gesture that was something like a salute.

And everyone looked at him. His eyes met Natalia's eyes, and they held each other's eyes for an instant, and then she cast her eyes down.

And, in that moment, Michael Rourke realized that, for better or worse, he was the leader because he was John Rourke's son and John Rourke could not lead them now.

143

His rifle held easily in his left hand, in his right hand that was inside his pocket he held his father's lighter as he said, "Once we step off the base we're no longer under the protection of New Germany. According to that asshole Dodd, Natalia's wanted. That means we're her accomplices, if I understand that sort of thing correctly. So, it's likely anyone who's in league with Dodd will have orders to shoot us on sight, as criminals.

"Once the election takes place and Akiro is installed in office," Michael Rourke went on, "we'll have the Eden government on our side. But, until that time, we'll technically be criminals. Assuming those were some of his neo-Nazi pals who did the actual dirty work, we'll have them to contend with them, too. Dodd will know that the first place we'll come is after him.

"So, let's not disappoint him." Michael concluded.

"Will we need anything from the Retreat, Michael? I mean, eventually they'll just blow the doors off if they have to, won't they?"

"Annie's right, Michael," Paul nodded. "Now or never for the Retreat."

Michael looked at Natalia again and smiled. "They'll have to work at getting inside, but I agree that they will penetrate the main entrance. We can use one of the escape tunnels to get in or out until they do. If there were the time, yeah, I'd say go in, take what we need, then destroy the rest so Dodd can't get his hands on anything, but there isn't the time to do that and find the baby.

"Priorities," Michael added.

"Agreed," Natalia said. "Anything we might need, the Germans can make for us."

Michael Rourke looked toward the fence. They were going to cut it (with the full knowledge and permission of Colonel Mann) in order to exit the facility, knowing that Dodd would have the entrances to the base watched for their exit.

There were irreplacable family photos at the Retreat, but

memories were more than physical objects could ever be, and this was what his father and mother would want them to do, find the baby.

And that was what they would do, or die in the attempt . . .

Natalia slipped out of her backpack, drew the Bali-Song from the pocket of her jumpsuit, then looked at Michael Rourke. How much like his father he was, she thought.

He was already out of his pack, a Gregory, like his father wore at times.

And he nodded toward her.

Together, they started along the edge of Eden Base, leaving Annie and Paul and Bjorn and his dog, ready to cover their exit if it came to that.

She reminded herself that most of the citizens of Eden would not know what to think. They had been told Dodd's lies, that somehow she was responsible for the fire at the hospital, the deaths of seventeen patients outside the building, the death of Lieutenant Larrimore and her newborn baby and two night duty nurses inside, and the near deaths of John and Sarah.

And, she knew the story Dodd would tell, that finally she couldn't take it any longer, her jealousy so intense that she lost her mind (after all, she had recently had a nervous breakdown, hadn't she?) and she did all of this in order to get John for herself and Sarah out of the way, unaware that John was nearby and would himself be perhaps fatally injured.

The bullet that was buried in Sarah's brain would doubtlessly be a 9mm Browning Short, otherwise known as .380 ACP. It would not have been difficult to find a Walther PP series pistol at New Germany, so many of the people who lived there, possessing firearms from the World War Two period, which had been carried by their ancestors, and the museum at New Germany featured an extensive arms collection, from both prior World Wars and the post-War period.

145

It was good to have friends, who trusted and could be trusted.

As she and Michael dropped into concealment beside a massive piece of earthmoving equipment, she whispered to Michael, "Thank you."

"For what, Natalia?"

"Believing in me. It never crossed your mind once that I might be lying, that Dodd might be right, did it?"

"No. It never did." And his bare right hand closed over her gloved right hand. "Let's go."

They were up and moving again, Michael in the lead. And that seemed very natural.

After navigating a deep, partially dug out ditch where sewer piping was to be placed, they paused behind several sections of the pipe, Natalia looking to right and left, searching for some sign that they had been observed.

There was no such sign.

She carried the Bali-Song locked closed, intending to use it only as a striking instrument unless circumstances were forced otherwise. These people of Eden might believe Dodd, but stupidity was not an adequate reason for killing.

And she suddenly wondered. What if Dodd were able to somehow turn this situation so to his advantage that he defeated Akiro Kurinami for President of Eden?

People could not be that stupid.

To vote in a free election and determine the fate of a nation was a responsibility and a privilege, and she could not fathom people misusing this wonderful gift, this freedom.

They were moving again, Michael's four-inch barreled Model 629 .44 Magnum in his right hand, ready for use as a bludgeon if need be.

They reached the far edge of the solitary street which traversed Eden end to end. To her right, the still smoldering ruins of the hospital, and the sight sickened her.

Inside those ruins were human remains, of people who were not victims of war or anything so involved as that, simply murdered because a man lusted for power.

To the left stretched the street, some considerable distance away a few lights from some of the tents, the shell for the permanent structures well beyond still, not visible from here.

Michael started moving again, and Natalia Timerovna ran beside him.

Five

Her knees were tucked nearly to her chin, and she sat stock still, her skirt pulled down as far as she could get it, against the bone chilling cold of the night.

Annie Rourke Rubenstein felt her father's mind.

She sensed horror, outrage, anguish, despair.

And she felt this, too.

Paul had been talking a lot lately about a baby, and she wanted Paul's baby very badly. But now—She exhaled, steam rising from her breath despite the scarf tied loosely over her mouth against the chill.

Despair, despair over a bright future dashed to darkness and ashes.

She wanted to ask God why it was that after all her mother and father had endured, the Night of the War, the wandering in search of each other, the dangers, why couldn't they now have some little time of happiness?

Instead of something that was worse than death.

The chances were very poor, Doctor Munchen had said, that anything would be able to be done for either of them. They would be placed in cryogenic sleep (risky in itself under the circumstances) and kept on the edge of life until, in some future time, something might possibly be done for her mother and (even more doubtful) for her father if he showed signs of emerging from the coma.

There was a limit beyond which people could endure. Natalia reached that limit and snapped, only because of her inner strength being able to survive it at all and return even stronger.

Someday, that limit would be reached for Michael, for Paul and for herself.

It was her father having reached that limit and not ever knowing it which had brought this about, thrown him so deeply into himself that he could not be revived.

Maybe the German and Mid-Wake doctors and the Russian specialist would be able to do something, find some miracle.

But miracles were not the province of men.

And what of the baby? Her brother? Assuming they found the child alive, she and Paul would raise him, of course, one day tell him about his real parents, teach him—Tears began to flow from her eyes and her nose began to run and she pulled away the scarf, searched for a handkerchief.

But Paul knelt beside her, handed her his handkerchief, and folded her into his arms very tightly . . .

Dodd was not in his tent. That was clear without even entering it, because there were no guards.

"Where could he be?" Natalia whispered.

Michael Rourke looked along the street, past the new construction, toward the soft white shapes in the far distance. "There."

The Eden Project Shuttle Fleet.

"Akiro said Dodd's taken over one of the shuttles as his administrative headquarters, closed the cargo bays, had the interior changed around. He's there. Waiting for us."

Natalia, her face visible in the starlight, a sparkle in her very pretty eyes, said, "Then at least we do not have to worry about who we have to kill, do we?"

Michael Rourke didn't disagree . . .

It was as if they'd been gone forever, but on the other hand it seemed as though they hadn't been gone at all. Annie Rubenstein welcomed the distraction from her thoughts, from her involvement with her father's mind. Reaching him was impossible, but she could still 'read' his feelings. Confusion, anger, a sense of being lost.

Quickly, Michael and Natalia briefed them concerning where Dodd was not and logically had to be.

Then, as quickly as they could, they moved out, Bjorn and his dog moving just ahead of them because Hrothgar might sense a trap, humans would not.

After more than twenty minutes of trudging through the snow drifts, they rested, Annie sinking down beside her husband in a cluster of low rocks, keeping her head down. She took the opportunity to re-tie the scarf that was over her head against the cold, then made a last minute check of her weapons.

Anyone inside the shuttle with Commander Dodd would be fair game, except Dodd himself. He had to be taken alive.

And, although no one had said anything, there was the very real possibility that the baby would be there.

Both the necessity of keeping Dodd alive and the possibility that the baby might be there precluded going in shooting. She had worked over the computers aboard the shuttle fleet, knew the typical shuttle layout very well, as did her husband, her brother and Natalia.

Bjorn did not, but Bjorn and his dog would remain outside, to cover them, alert them to more of a trap than they already expected. Attacking the craft would be a tactical nightmare.

Annie was getting tired of nightmares . . .

Deitrich Zimmer looked down at the baby.

It was asleep in a packing crate cradle.

There were ample supplies of baby formula among the Eden stores and, basic creatures that they are, the baby was easily enough calmed.

With this baby, he could rule the world.

150

Zimmer's academic background lay in genetic surgery.

However important environment was, the genetic stamp was the key. Environment could not mold what was not there. Yet, with the proper environment, and judicious tampering with certain genes, the base material, the raw clay, could become something extraordinary—beneath the hands of the proper sculptor.

And he was such a man.

This child, so physically perfect, the offspring of a man he had never seen except in a moment of violence, of a woman he had shot in the head, this child had locked within it, a potential that was extraordinary.

The tendencies toward such things as academic brilliance, athletic superiority, creativity, inventiveness, all these were inherited, to be capitalized upon or suppressed within a given environment.

His attempts to improve upon nature were what drew him into the Leader inner circle, what made him realize that there truly was such a thing as racial superiority.

But even that could be improved upon, and a race of true supermen created, not men who merely professed to be so. With this child, that race would be born, would spread its seed over the planet, would bring about an age like none in history, would someday spread its seed among the stars and eclipse the glory of this mystical force, the weak called their God . . .

He pushed back the hood of his parka, despite the ski-toque he wore, his head cold in the night air.

During the brief period of peace while he had tried to determine what he would do with his life, Michael Rourke spent much of the time in New Germany, trying to convince himself that Maria should be his wife.

At last he asked her, then in nearly the same breath he walked away from her.

It was being a cad, to use an old word he'd heard first in one of the videotapes at the Retreat, had to look up in one of the dictionaries in order to ascertain its meaning, at that age been shocked at the implication.

He was certain Maria was not pregnant (her menstrual cycle had just begun), so he wasn't being as rotten as that. Had she been pregnant with his child, he would certainly have kept his peace, said nothing, taken her as his wife.

But he had known real love, and although for a time, when there had been an absence of violence, he had convinced himself that he could settle for less.

Here, on the edge of life or death again, he realized it was better to have the real thing or nothing at all.

He looked down at the M-16 in his gloved hands. The caliber—5.56mm—was vastly less than ideal, but he had settled for the rifle out of convenience; he would have preferred something better.

There was no comparison, really between an inanimate object and a human being, but the principle was the same. Maria was as fine a woman as a man could hope to meet, loving and, sometimes it seemed, devoted beyond credulity. To have stayed with her would have been cheating her even more than cheating himself, because she desired the same fervor in return.

Beside him, Natalia asked, "What are you thinking about, Michael?"

He looked at her. "My rifle."

She nodded approval at that.

And, he wondered, wondered if something that had touched at his consciousness fleetingly before, something he had shoved from his thoughts, was partially at work within him. "My favorite rifle, before the Night of The War was the Heckler & Koch, the G-3 or the 91, the semi-, it didn't really matter which. One rarely uses a rifle in the full-auto mode if one's a decent marksman."

"Yes."

"So, the battle rifle or the sporting rifle, to me it was much the same. A solid cartridge in a solid action. I had a G-3 with a scope on it, once, and it was the most accurate rifle I'd ever used. John likes his bolt action, which is fine—" And her voice caught.

Michael looked at her, told her, "My father will survive this. He's that way. Sometimes I think he's immortal."

Natalia laughed softly. "No. He's very mortal. For a time, I thought he was not, and then I realized he had to be, or I could not have loved him in the way that I did."

"What are you going to do, now, I mean?"

"Live for the moment, Michael."

"How do you see me?"

"What do you mean?"

"I mean, do you still see me as a kid? Like I was when we first met? You know, chronologically, I'm a year older than you are, even though I was born almost two decades later."

"Try explaining that to someone," and she laughed softly again. "I don't see you as a little boy. I don't think I did even then, although you were one. When I learned what you did the morning after the Night of the War, to save Sarah from those people who attacked your farm, I realized this was a man inside a boy's body and the body merely had to catch up. But you are not your father."

"What do you mean?"

"Have you read much tragedy, Michael?"

"Shakespeare, the Greeks, yes."

They waited, just the two of them, because they had split into two units for better fire and maneuver function, and waited about two hundred yards from the shuttle, its lights yellow glowing against the palpable icy blackness, there beneath the stars. The shuttle, white, was matte-finished against the shimmering whiteness of the snow.

"The principal character in a tragedy always has a fatal flaw, like MacBeth's ambition. Your father's flaw is his perfection. He is beyond human. Or is it just that after all this time I never understood him."

He was grateful she used 'is' rather than 'was' in reference to his father. "Dad's human," Michael laughed, shaking his head, the smile staying after the laugh went. "He's as uncertain as anybody, but he never shows it. I know I'm not my father. I'm part of each of them, mom and dad, and I'm both and neither of them. Annie's that way, too. She's mom and she's dad and she's both of them at once and neither one of them at all because she's herself." And then he said something he had not planned to say at all. "Until my father's back, you remember something, Natalia; you remember that you are not alone. I'm not my father, but I'll protect you just as he would have done."

And she looked hard at him. It was odd watching her eyes. He could not see their surreal blueness, but only a piercing darkness against the white of her flesh, precious little of that visible beneath the black silk scarf which swathed her lower face, an identical scarf bound over her head and hair, leaving only a wedge of her face visible where one scarf stopped and the other began.

"I don't think of you as a little boy," she told him, pushing back her hood now.

Michael said nothing.

He shifted his gaze toward the approximate position where Annie and Paul should be. After a moment, he saw a flash of red light, no more than a pencil thin pinpoint. It was Annie's Taurus Pt-92 with the laser sight. She carried the gun as a special purpose weapon, and had used it when she and Natalia had defended the Retreat against another group of neo-Nazis.

Michael made his own signal, using the mini-Mag-Lite from his jacket pocket. There was an answering flash of red.

He looked at Natalia now. "It's up to us."

"I'm with you."

Michael nodded, partially unzipping his German arctic parka, drawing out the Beretta 92F pistols from the double shoulder holster he wore beneath it, removing the fifteen-round magazines from first one then the other pistol, inserting twenty-round 93R magazines in their stead after first striking the spine of each magazine against the palm of his hand to make certain the 115-grain 9mm jacketed hollow points were seated as they should be.

He pocketed the fifteen-round magazines, stuffed the two handguns between his gunbelt and his abdomen. The four-inch .44 Magnum Smith & Wesson was in the crossdraw holster between his navel and his left hip. He regloved, but only with the thinner liners, thumbing the M-16's selector to auto.

Natalia was right that a battle rifle should be rarely used on auto, but he would be using his rifle like a sub-machine gun, for sweeping.

"Let's go."

Snow crunched beneath his boots as he started from their place of concealment behind a low ridge. Over their parkas, each of them wore a white snowsmock, but further precautions would have been useless.

The enemy knew they were coming, just not precisely when . . .

Paul Rubenstein edged along the dunes of drifted snow, the Schmiesser in his left hand, the M-16 in his right, his wife in his footsteps, a yard behind him when he looked back.

John was almost dead, and might remain that way, if he lived at all, for days or months or years or decades—perhaps centuries.

He would miss his friend more in those times to come than he did now, he knew, and to gauge a loss more acute than that, which he already felt, was incalculable.

John was friend and brother and mentor.

And Sarah, the deliberateness of what had been done to her, sickened his spirit.

This night, he wanted the enemy to be there, well-armed and ready, and he wanted to kill as many of them as he could.

That would not undo what had been done, and his motives

in wanting the confrontation were purely selfish, he knew, but it would feel good to kill these people, take some measure of revenge, however minuscule. How many of their lives lost forever would compensate for the loss of John Rourke or Sarah Rourke for even a second in infinity?

His wife, John and Sarah's daughter, was consumed with these feelings as well, he realized, and he was happy for that. Because, once these feelings passed, she would feel the loss even more greatly.

If they found the child, would they raise him as their own? Would Annie's brother grow up to think of his sister as a mother, his brother-in-law as a father?

What would they tell the boy. "Your real mom and dad aren't really dead, they're just—" What?

Paul Rubenstein shivered at such thoughts, of death without death, of life without life, going on forever until time stopped, perhaps . . .

Christopher Dodd looked out across the chamber's vastness.

The floor surface of Eden One's cargo bay was nine hundred square feet, and made a fine office to serve his needs of the moment. Among the Eden Project stores were a considerable number of highly sophisticated personal computer terminals, and these could be linked in series to increase their capabilities. It was an arrangement such as this which Dodd now faced, the master terminal linked by cable to the vastly more powerful onboard computer.

With the right software, he could manage a nation, perhaps a world from here, and he could have designed a computer to manage this.

The information on D.R.E.A.D. was now his, as well as other secret information concerning how to access certain underground vault areas, located around the continental United States, in which were hidden even greater supply caches, information repositories, ultra sophisticated computers, weapons—everything from water to smallpox vaccines.

And there was bio warfare material listed there, too.

It was to be hoped that the people of the world would come to accept the natural leadership he offered, but if they failed to do so, utilizing the manpower reserves of the Nazis along with the sophisticated hardware left for his use, he could wrest control, if need be.

The government of New Germany had the beginnings of nuclear weapons technology. It was possible that, someday, the Chinese of the Second City might locate the remainder of the pre-War Peoples Republic nuclear arsenal. But, in either case, there was no workable delivery system.

The Icelandics he totally dismissed, as he did the Wild Tribes of Europe, but for vastly different reasons. The Icelandics would never dream of building or acquiring such weapons, and the Wild Tribes were too intellectually inferior to even consider them as a threat.

The Russians were now disarmed of nuclear weapons.

These were possessed by Mid-Wake.

Talks were underway between the Allies—Mid-Wake, New Germany, Lydveldid Island, The Chinese Second City and Eden—concerning how best to dispose of these weapons so they would never again be a threat to human survival.

Once the Soviet weapons were eliminated, Dodd would quietly prepare his own. The codes for use, as well as such things as location, megatonnage, etc., were all locked within the D.R.E.A.D. program.

He had, so far, been unable to fully access D.R.E.A.D., in order to allow use.

But that would come.

Already, doubt was building among the citizens of Eden, that perhaps Natalia Tiemerovna, out of jealousy, had engineered the destruction at the hospital, and was responsible for the deaths there. And even if John and Sarah Rourke were not fully dead, they were out of the picture, and would pose no threat.

The one obstacle was Kurinami, and as long as Natalia Tiemerovna and the Rourkes could be conveniently blamed for things, it might even be possible to stick them with culpability if Kurinami and his new wife needed to be liquidated.

The Rourke family—what remained of it—would be coming here, tonight or tomorrow night, here to his killing ground in search of information on the baby, and perhaps to seek revenge as well.

Dodd's palms sweated slightly. On the desk in front of him was an M-16, fully loaded and ready for use, and holstered at his side was an M-9 Beretta, chamber loaded.

Hidden within the bowels of Eden One and in the snow drifts outside were enough of Deitrich Zimmer's new SS men to handle the situation.

With John Rourke out of the picture, any Rourke family action was a lost cause . . .

She was taking a gamble, that Michael's being a Rourke, his father's son, would somehow be enough. But if she exercised a leadership function now, he never would; so, she did not.

And, so far, Michael Rourke was, indeed, his father's son in the truest sense.

They were divided into two teams, good basic tactics. Michael had acquired a number of useful items from Colonel Mann to help compensate for the odds that more than likely would be mounted against them.

They waited at the edge of a long, drifted over ridge of dirt, just beside one of the pieces of earth moving equipment.

"Masks," Michael said quietly.

Natalia reached to the bag slung beside her left breast, removing the M-17 gas mask (taken from the supplies at the Retreat) and pulling it on over her scarfed head, pulling down in the same motion, the scarf which covered the lower portion of her face.

She popped the seals at the cheeks, the mask at least serving to warm the air before she inhaled it, oddly comfortable (not usually the case with a gas mask).

Michael pulled his mask over the thin toque which he wore, looking for all the world like an SAS man, attired just as the British Special Air Service sometimes were, all in black; but no SAS man would ever have been caught with an American assault rifle.

He signalled her ahead, and they ran from their position of cover and concealment toward the remains of the bridge that had to be blown before the Eden Project Shuttles had been able to land, so long ago it seemed.

The concrete, jagged shapes, jutting almost angrily toward the stars, was snow packed. They hid behind it.

Strapped to Michael's back beside his pack was a German grenade launcher, not too dissimilar to the old 40mm grenade launchers of five centuries ago, rather shotgun-like in appearance, but firing a vastly wider array of rounds. Natalia observed as Michael broke the launcher's action, then selected a round from the small pack slung from his right side.

There were teargas, sound and light, high explosive and barricade penetration rounds, one of the latter was what he now chambered in the launcher.

He closed the launcher, brought it to his shoulder. The launcher was laser sight fitted, accurate to three hundred meters. She did not ask, but assumed he had set the sight for the barricade penetration round. Since each round had a slightly different weight, trajectory had to be adjusted accordingly.

"Be ready," Michael told her.

She grunted that she was, the remote for the simulators already in her left hand.

Michael fired the launcher.

There was a whoosh, a blur along the same path as the pale red beam of the laser.

The starboard side of the shuttle's cargo bay took the hit, a short, light sounding explosion, and there was a hole in the fuselage large enough for a man to walk through without

159

bending over.

Natalia touched the controls on the remote, the simulators activating immediately from all sides of the shuttle, primer detonations as facsimiles of gunfire, small explosions, mini-mortars whose projectiles exploded on time delay fuses while still airborne, high wattage mini-speakers broadcasting laser audio disc recordings of incoming aircraft, fixed wing and helicopter.

It was like some American movie from before The Night of the War, special effects to such a degree that she almost believed they were real, almost thought that the armies of New Germany and the Marine Corps of Mid-Wake were closing on the position.

Michael just ahead of her, she ran with him toward the hole they had blown in the side of Eden One.

Michael stopped for an instant, closing the action of the grenade launcher he'd been reloading on the run, put the weapon to his shoulder and fired.

No expert marksmanship was required, the hole in the fuselage so large.

As the round struck, gas billowed back from inside the shuttle cargo bay.

By that time, Michael was already loading another round. She knew that this one would be sound and light.

Six

Annie gave a tug at her gas mask, then broke into a dead run, beside Paul as he started toward the shuttle's main access, the explosion from the far side of the shuttle followed up by several more now, all the while the simulators making the night sound suddenly as though rival armies were competing with one another for the loudest possible noise of destruction.

Paul dropped to one knee, firing the grenade launcher the instant it came to his shoulder, a hole opening in the next instant along the portside fuselage. Paul broke the action, loaded, then fired again, Annie averting her eyes slightly because of the coming flash, too far from the explosion to have to hold her ears against the whistling howl of the sound and light grenade.

She ran to her right, her M-16 almost to her shoulder, Paul running left . . .

Paul Rubenstein was on line with the 'entrance' he had shot into the shuttle's fuselage, and he started toward it, zig-zagging a little as he ran.

There were two schools of thought on an evasive running pattern when one was under fire, as John had once explained to him. One held that the fastest trip between point A and point B offered the least chance for incoming fire to strike, while the second method opted for an erratic course between point A and point B lest an enemy shooter should try to lead his target.

Paul, after more experience than he really wanted to remember, had struck on what he always hoped was the happy medium; if it was not, he would be dead and he wouldn't have to worry about it anyway; he ran as rapidly as possible between points of cover, but always varied his course just enough that he couldn't be led.

He hoped.

He was beside the fuselage now, ducking low near the vast craft's underbelly for the added protection of the re-entry tiles lest someone start shooting through the fuselage.

If the baby were inside, the child was a risk, but as much so as other options available to them for entry, less than most.

Annie was in position by Eden One's cockpit, bowling sound and light grenades through the open doorway . . .

Michael Rourke crossed left to right, Natalia right to left, through the hole in the portside fuselage, three sound and light grenades and a gas grenade going in ahead of them. There was the possibility that if his newborn brother were inside, the child might suffer permanent nerve damage and be hearing impaired for life, but even that was a better prospect than death at the hands of Dodd and the Nazis.

Inside the opening, Michael dropped to cover behind the near end of a bank of cable-linked PCUs, the computers sputtering and spitting high voltage sparks. Gunfire tore into the console nearest him, the old-style monitor's vacuum tube exploding with a loud pop and glass flying everywhere as Michael fired a burst from his M-16 across the ceiling formed by the closed shuttle bay doors.

He rolled a teargas grenade along the shuttle bay floor, toward the center of the enclosure, both Berettas coming into his hands as he let the safed M-16 fall to his side on its sling.

Natalia was moving from cover to cover—packing crates—along the aft section of the shuttle bay, both .357 Magnum Smith & Wesson revolvers blazing in her hands.

Michael Rourke started forward, a man rising up from behind the PCUs, to start firing a German assault rifle. Michael fired first, a double tap from each pistol cutting into the man's chest, bowling him back.

Assault rifle fire cut into the decking near his feet and Michael dodged left, firing both pistols from shoulder level, shattering another of the PCU monitors. A man with an M-16, the rifle still firing, but into the decking, tumbled from behind the computers . . .

Paul Rubenstein hurled his last gas grenade and drew the pistol with the grappling hook attachment from the holster-like case beside his empty gas mask bag, taking three steps back, but staying well clear of the opening.

Paul Rubenstein took a last look toward his wife. Annie was still beside the cockpit hatchway, lobbing in more gas grenades.

Paul fired the pistol, the grappling hook spreading open as it punched upward, the thin synthetic rope behind it snaking out, uncoiling.

Paul tugged at the gun, grabbing a hank of rope in his left fist.

The grappling hook had caught.

He hoped permanently.

He ran toward the shuttle fuselage, both the Schmiesser and the M-16 hanging from their slings at his sides. He jumped, reaching for more rope, feet against the fuselage. If anyone fired a sufficiently heavy caliber rifle through the fuselage, he was dead . . .

"Natalia! Look out behind you!"

Natalia Tiemerovna wheeled around, dodging right as she did, her revolvers emptied and in her belt, her M-16 in her right fist.

163

She punched the assault rifle toward the fuselage opening, three men with M-16s firing on full auto, entering there. She fired her own rifle, just locking back the trigger, edging back toward cover.

Michael.

She heard the boom of his .44 Magnum revolver.

She dropped to her knees behind a packing crate, the fiberboard of the crate splintering away. She edged back still farther. As she emptied the M-16, she cut down one of the three, another of them already down thanks to Michael. But gunfire tore into the fuselage bulkhead near her and she dropped flat, letting the M-16 fall away, snapping the PPK/S from the shoulder holster beneath her open coat and stabbing it toward a man with an M-16 who was shooting at her.

She fired the .380 twice, shattering his left cheekbone and blowing out his left eye.

Michael shouted to her, "Catch it!"

She looked up, one of Michael's Berettas arcing toward her.

Under normal circumstances, she would have eschewed anyone throwing a gun, loaded or not, but now she was grateful for it, shifting the PPK/S to her left hand, catching the Beretta with her right.

The gun was safed, had a fifteen round magazine loaded and she assumed that was full as she thumbed off the safety and fired toward the third man in the fuselage opening, a double tap, then another and another, the man's body almost pirouetting as it started to fall.

As she snapped her head left, she caught a glimpse of Michael Rourke, his M-16 in his right hand, the .44 Magnum revolver in his left.

Two men emerged from the far end of the rank of personal computer units in the forward section of the cargo bay, stolen M-16s chattering.

Michael was already firing.

Natalia punched the Beretta toward the men, holding it at shoulder level, firing . . .

164

Paul Rubenstein attained the height of the cargo bay, kneeling there, taking the small charge of German plastique from his gear, slapping it down—it was magnetic—and hitting the arming switch, then the time delay switch. Fifteen seconds.

Paul edged back, almost curling himself into a ball along the tail section, counting down the seconds until detonation of the charge.

The blast came, very small, but he hoped just right for the task. When they had agreed on going after Dodd, they had realized full well that if Dodd were not in his tent, he would be here, and assuming this the more likely spot, planned accordingly.

He ran forward, an opening the size of the manhole covers one had seen in streets everywhere before the Night of The War, blasted into the joint where the cargo bay doors separated. He reached to his belt, hurtling down the rope with his right hand, a gas grenade with his left, shouting through his mask, "Grenade!" in the event that Michael or Natalia might be near enough that its concussion could injure them.

He thought about the baby for a split second.

There was no time to think about the child any more.

Paul Rubenstein threw himself down, the rope going taut, pulsing under his weight as he descended. From the start, trying to rescue the child was putting the child at risk. And there was nothing to do but pray for its safety . . .

Michael Rourke stabbed the .44 Magnum toward the head of a man and fired, the head exploding outward and blood and brains flowing backward from the exit wound in a pinkish gray cloud that was almost enough to make him throw up inside his gas mask—almost, but not quite.

The 629 empty, Michael advanced, one half-loaded Beretta 92F in his left fist.

As Paul descended, three of the enemy defenders opened fire from cover.

Michael snatched a gas grenade from his web gear, popping the pin as he freed the grenade, lobbing the grenade toward a stack of packing crates near the far port side of Eden One's converted cargo bay.

Paul swung from the rope, the Schmiesser in his left hand, the sub-machine gun chattering toward the same target.

Natalia shrieked, "Watch out for me!" and streaked past Michael, her knife in her right hand, a pistol in her left. She dove over the packing crates and was gone from sight.

There was a hideous scream. But it was a man's scream . . .

Paul Rubenstein swung forward on the rope, his feet touching a desk top.

A figure moved behind the desk and Paul, still holding the rope in his right hand, took a half step forward, his right foot snapping out, contacting something hard, like bone.

And then he looked, listened.

Face bloodied, eyes streaming tears, hands over his ears from the stun of the grenades, Christopher Dodd begged, "Please don't kill me!"

Paul Rubenstein's left hand squeezed more tightly on the sub-machine gun's pistol grip, his left index finger against the trigger.

It would have been so easy to kill Commander Dodd.

But then, he would have become like him.

Seven

There was no law to which he could be surrendered except his own, which would not prosecute him. And they were not murderers, which Dodd already knew. Commander Christopher Dodd would live if he talked, and Dodd was not courageous enough to do otherwise.

Paul's eyes met his, and Michael shrugged his shoulders, feeling somehow inadequate because he was chained to a moral code that Dodd was not.

Paul Rubenstein said, "The good die young that they may not be corrupted; the wicked live on that they may have the chance to repent."

"Shakespeare?" Natalia asked.

"The Torah," Paul said quietly, his eyes shifting to settle on Commander Dodd.

Bjorn Rolvaag waited guard outside, Hrothgar at his side, lest more of Dodd's Nazi confederates were in the vicinity, although that seemed unlikely, and to alert them—Natalia, Paul and Annie, and Michael Rourke—should the crowd outside attempt to storm Eden One. So far, they milled around, waiting. People had come from Eden, armed and ready (for what, Michael was uncertain). He addressed them when they were assembled outside. "Commander Dodd and his neo-Nazi sympathizers are responsible for the burning of my father's hospital, the killing of the patients and on-duty staff, the assassination attempts on the lives of my parents and the kidnapping of a newborn infant my mother had just delivered of herself. Don't interfere."

There had been grumbles from some of the persons outside, Dodd sympathizers, but no overt moves of hostility. One voice from the crowd shouted, "Maybe this is just an attempt to discredit the commander so the Jap can win the election."

There were more grunts, no more intelligible words.

Michael retired to the cargo bay then, where he stood now, staring at Dodd.

Annie stood behind Dodd.

Michael said to Dodd, "You have us at no disadvantage, because a single radio message will bring in a German helicopter to pick us up. Your people outside won't be able to whip up a mob and 'arrest' us, or kill us, either. The longer you let this go, the more what's happened here is going to start to smell badly to all those potential voters outside. If you get out there quickly enough, maybe you can lie to them while there's still time."

Dodd's eyes took on a hint of arrogance. "You never voted, did you? You were a little kid when everything happened, too young. You don't know the power of rhetoric. How you can turn things around and people will be saps enough to believe you, vote for you?"

"I can imagine," Michael almost whispered. "Where's mom and dad's baby?"

Dodd sneered.

Natalia's right hand moved in a flash, the Bali-Song making the click-click-click sound, the point of the knife hooking into Dodd's left nostril. "I was trained by the KGB, remember? We actually had courses in making people talk. I always had high marks. First it will be the left nostril, then the right. Then the left side of your mouth, then the right. Then the left outer ear, then the right. By the time I am through with you, the only way you will win votes is out of pity. And, if you do not tell us right now, and the truth, it will not matter to me if you speak after one nostril is gone, or if I am still at work on one side of your mouth. I will do all that I have said, regardless. And, if you refuse to tell us how to find John and Sarah's child after all of that, then I will flail the skin from your testicles and make you eat it."

There was a sound almost too soft to notice.

Michael looked down, then looked away to conceal his amusement. Natalia would never have done such things—at least he assumed she would not.

Commander Dodd's coveralls were dark near the crotch and there was a small puddle on the floor between his legs.

Dodd's voice shook as he said, "Deitrich Zimmer. It was all, all his idea. They reformed the new SS, along the lines of the old one from World War Two. The party has a new leader. The man claims descent from Adolf Hitler, direct lineage. I don't know who he is. Zimmer knows."

"How many are there, in this new SS?"

"Zimmer told me a couple of thousand. A lot of them escaped right after Doctor Rourke overthrew The Leader's regime, more of them drifted out during the weeks afterward. Some of them still live in New Germany, but not revealing their politics."

"Some of the ones who tried to kill Sarah, and then Annie and me, that time," Natalia whispered.

"What's their goal?" Paul asked, breathing hard as he spoke.

Dodd evidently had some of his courage back, because he snapped, "To rid the world of scum like you, Jew, and anyone who isn't white."

Paul smiled, turned away, punched his right fist into his left palm. Without looking at Dodd, he said, "We're the scum? Why don't you look in a mirror, *ubermench.*"

Annie went to Paul, put her arms around him.

Natalia's voice sounded hard. "Where have they taken the baby, and why?"

"I don't know why, and—"

Natalia moved the knife back into his nostril and jerked it slightly, Dodd screaming, blood trickling down over his mouth.

"Where and why were the questions," Michael reiterated.

"I swear to God, I don't know why!" Natalia started to move the knife again. Tears fell from Dodd's eyes and there was the unmistakable sound of the commander's bowels loosening, followed by a fecal smell that was sickening. "I know where!"

"Where?" Natalia hissed.

"They moved their headquarters, Zimmer told me. It's in the high peaks of the Andes Mountains in Peru. But you can only get in there by helicopter and they have anti-aircraft weapons. You don't have a chance. The Leader had the place built in the event of a revolution forcing him out of power. A bunker, that's what it is. You'll never get in there, and if you do, you'll never get out alive. It won't do you any good."

"Are you finished with him?" Natalia asked.

"Let's see if he can pinpoint it on a map," Michael said.

"And then you tell us everything else you can think of about Zimmer, about this secret place, all of it. And maybe I won't turn you into a grotesque."

Dodd looked at Natalia and started to cry even harder.

Eight

Wolfgang Mann's fingers knitted into the shape of a tent.

He looked across those fingers, saying, "The Leader could very well have diverted men and materiel within the structure of the old SS to construct such a thing. It would be highly secure. Dodd may have been right, that you cannot get in or get out. But we will die in the attempt, if necessary. The four of you with Rolvaag helping cannot hope to penetrate such a place."

Natalia lit a cigarette.

Paul paced, Annie perched on the edge of a chair watching him.

Michael Rourke exhaled as he said, "Dodd seemed to be telling the truth. He gave us that set of map co-ordinates just before we called in the chopper to get us out."

"Cartography and Electronic Intelligence is working on the co-ordinates even as we speak, and I have contacted New Germany to begin an exhaustive records search in the hopes of verifying the site, then ascertaining just what has gone on there, what we will be facing."

Michael fingered his father's lighter in his pocket. "Is there anything you can think of, Colonel, that might indicate why Zimmer would want the baby, give us some sort of clue as to what he's planning?"

Colonel Mann swiveled his desk chair to better view the screen of his computer terminal. "Zimmer is a physician and surgeon, a very good one. He specialized, according to this, in genetic micro-surgery, pioneered a variety of techniques I

171

do not understand, but evidently important ones."

"That scares me," Paul volunteered, ceasing to pace for a moment. "The genetic surgery bit."

"And what about this man that Dodd says Zimmer told him claimed descendency from Hitler?" Natalia asked.

Wolfgang Mann laughed, but it was in irony, Michael Rourke surmised. "During World War Two," Mann began, stubbing out his cigarette then quickly lighting another, "there was a program in which the most presumably genetically perfect from among the ranks of the SS were selected to breed with the most genetically perfect German girls that could be found. The children of these unions were known as Reichskinder. The man to whom Commander Dodd referred is named Albert Heimaccher.

"Heimaccher claimed," Mann went on, "that his ancestor, was the illegitimate son of the Fuhrer, and was a part of this program. There may be truth to the claim. Hitler was outwardly quite the moral man, oddly enough, according to the consensus of history, marrying Eva Braun in those last days in the Bunker in Berlin. But there were always those who claimed that Hitler never died there."

Michael volunteered, "I've read quite a bit about that period. I don't claim any expertise, but I was always mildly amazed that Hitler chose to stay in Berlin with the end coming, that he was quite that insane."

Mann shrugged his shoulders. "Insane he most assuredly was, but I agree that remaining in Berlin was tantamount to suicide, which is, of course, what he is credited as having eventually performed."

"He was more afraid of our troops than those of the rest of the Allies," Natalia said. "Because our troops had the memory of Stalingrad."

Colonel Mann said, "This Albert Heimaccher was on the fringe of the Leader's inner circle, part of it but never fully trusted, I think. Heimaccher is an engineer, very talented as an architect as well."

"Does he do water colors?" Paul asked bitterly.

Mann answered, "I know what you are thinking, Herr Rubenstein, that perhaps Heimaccher is some true descendant of the Fuhrer and that he will be able to somehow duplicate the terror of his antecedent. This is a different age."

"Is it?" Michael asked. "But, regardless of any of this, we have to penetrate this redoubt in the Andes and find the child before it is too late. Why they took him is something I still cannot fathom, but conjecture is immaterial at the moment."

Colonel Mann, his face drawn down into a frown, only nodded . . .

Deitrich Zimmer sat at the console of his computer, the program converting videotape of the child's face and body into a digital format.

He punched in that he desired split screen.

On the right hand side of the screen he summoned up the countenance and vital statistics of Albert Heimaccher, the self-proclaimed descendant of Adolph Hitler.

Over Heimaccher's countenance he super-imposed the face, five centuries old which had nearly dominated the entire world, the Fuhrer's face.

There was some superficial resemblance, indeed.

The video of the Rourke baby was fully digitized.

He studied both sides of the screen, simultaneously now.

There was, of course, no Adolph Hitler to study, not even some bit of genetic material.

But, if Heimaccher were a true descendant, as some physical characteristics and talents seemed to suggest, some of that raw material was present, waiting to be discovered and used in a better man.

Deitrich Zimmer lit a cigarette as he stood up, turning away from the computer console, leaving his desk and crossing the room toward the window. The window could be shuttered in the event of attack, the shutters bombproof steel alloy molded and colored to resembled the surface of the mountain itself, in which the Redoubt was set.

173

But now, the shutters back, the view was breathtaking, peaks ranked one after the other toward the north and the south, the very spinal cord of the continent. A glint of early morning sunshine could be seen in the crystalline snows, making what was white, gold against the gray of granite.

He inhaled on his cigarette.

The only problem was to get Heimaccher to agree, of course, because one could not perform such testing without the knowledge of the subject. But for all his shortcomings—he could never lead them, now or ever—Heimaccher did have a sense of history and the very idea of the exercise might just appeal to that sense. The baby had been examined by the very best doctors, was sound, perfect, as fine an example of humanity as one could wish to find.

Zimmer recalled the data concerning the Rourkes.

John Rourke's I.Q. was nearly off the scale, his physical prowess, stamina, dexterity and agility all better than the best of athletes. A physician, a true Socratic man—what a fine party member, what a magnificent commander in the SS, he would have made, embodying all that was perfection.

Sarah Rourke was more 'normal,' of course, but in her way equally as perfect. The baby was the living proof of that.

The child had her eye color, rather than that of the father, but facially the resemblance between the child and the father was otherwise hauntingly close.

If the child had his father's genes, his father's intelligence, his father's athletic abilities, then the child could be molded, to attain still greater heights, to lead . . .

Jason Darkwood shut off the pocket viewer. The news video fiche clicked out and he withdrew it from the viewer, crumpling it in his hand, then looked about for a place to discard it. There was a trash neutralizer on the far wall and he stood up, pocketing the viewer in his uniform and leaving his hat on the sofa.

Mid-Wake Today's banner headlines carried news that medi-

174

cal specialists from Mid-Wake, New Germany, Lydveldid Island and even the Soviet Underground City were working round the clock in an effort to save the lives of John and Sarah Rourke.

Jason Darkwood already knew that, and all the other facts the paper had not gotten to print.

Sarah Rourke's condition, although near death, was stabilized. John Rourke's condition was worsening by the hour. He was slipping away and, at least to the degree that Darkwood could understand the information Maggie Barrow passed on to him, there was virtually no hope.

Admiral Rahn had relieved him—Darkwood—of regular duties until there was a change, for better or worse, placing him in charge of security, but Tom Stanhope was actually handling the details with his Marine guards.

The flags of Mid-Wake flew at full mast, but details stood by to lower them to half-staff at a moment's notice. A friend who worked for one of Mid-Wake's television stations had told him that video obituaries were already fully assembled, merely awaiting update when the time came. There would be security camera footage seized from the Soviet Underwater Complex, footage contributed by the Soviet Underground City that actually showed some scenes from The Night of The War.

The President was already planning to ask Congress—a mere formality—for a national day of mourning to be declared, a statue to be built, all the customary things that were done when a figure or figures of heroic stature, died.

Darkwood pushed the video fiche into the neutralizer, then walked toward the windows.

He could look down from here over much of this sector.

Women in dresses pushed baby strollers.

Flowers grew.

Life went on.

Without John Rourke, there would have be none of that ever again.

Nine

Michael Rourke set down the radio telephone receiver.

"Well?" Annie insisted.

He looked at his sister, then at his brother-in-law, then at Natalia. "Mom's stabilized. Dad is slipping away. The doctors are still trying, but nothing seems to work. Whatever damage was done to his brain when all that rubble fell on him is the cause, but nobody seems to know what to do about it."

Annie just looked away, apparently no tears left.

Natalia closed her eyes, leaned her head back, the pulse in her long, graceful neck visibly moving.

Paul, leaning on Colonel Mann's desk, held to the desk top so tightly his knuckles were white with it.

Annie, without looking at them, asked, "So. Are we going after our brother, or going to Mid-Wake to be with them when he—uhh—when—when." She looked at Michael now, and Michael knew he had been wrong. There were still tears.

Annie had ceased sensing anything from their father, hours before, as if his mind were simply turned off.

Natalia said, "It is your decision, now, Michael."

"She's right," Paul nodded, his voice hoarse, strained sounding. "What do we do?"

Michael Rourke had tried his father's cigars once or twice over the years while his parents and Paul and Natalia had slept. He went to Natalia, reached to the desk top where her cigarettes were, took one, and lit it with his father's battered old Zippo. He inhaled the smoke, remembering why people

176

did such a stupid thing as to take smoke into their lungs intentionally.

It was a diversion.

From reality, for even just a microsecond.

"Mom and Dad, given the options we have, would tell us to go after the baby. Our being at Mid-Wake—" and he forced himself to say it, his throat so tight he thought he would choke. It wasn't from the cigarette. "Our being there when he dies won't make any difference to him or to mom, but if there's an afterlife and somehow he can know, well—" The tears came and he couldn't speak, his chest tight, his body shaking.

Natalia stood up, put her arms around him and let him hold her . . .

"The Rourkes are vicious animals. I'm not talking about John Rourke, God bless that valiant man. Nor Sarah Rourke, the heroic wife and mother. No! I'm talking about Michael Rourke and Annie, his sister, and Paul Rubenstein and the Communist woman, Major Natalia Tiemerovna of the KGB."

The people of Eden sat in the hall where only a short while ago, the yellow man had married the black woman. The thought of this made Dodd's skin crawl. But a substantial portion of the people of Eden were of 'other' races, so he said nothing, would say nothing, concerning his truest thoughts.

"All of you have seen me, seen the way the Russian woman tried to mutilate me the other night with that terrible knife of hers. And why? I'll tell you why. They beat me, killed heroic German nationals who were aiding me in combatting Wolfgang Mann's Nazi plots. They threatened my life—all of that so I would not stand here before you today, to tell you the truth.

"Wolfgang Mann is a Nazi. John Rourke and Sarah Rourke were taken in as his dupes, thinking they were deposing a Nazi regime in New Germany when, in reality, they were only aiding Wolfgang Mann in his power struggle to control the Nazi Party of New Germany. Paul Rubenstein, as a Jew, someone who should have been loyal to the United States because of the United States' unflinching loyalty to the state of Israel in Palestine, is no more a loyal American, than I am a man from Mars. Before the Night of The War, he was a member of the American Communist Party, cleverly assuming the identity of an Anti-Communist in order to better infiltrate American intelligence to bring about the destruction of the United States, by means of a surprise, sneak attack against the United States from the Soviet Union.

"Rubenstein—his real name may never be known—played his role very, very well, feeding information on America's defense secrets to the Soviet KGB through Major Tiemerovna. When Doctor John Rourke and Paul Rubenstein met on that airplane—we've all heard the story—Rubenstein was really on his way to Atlanta for one purpose only: Rubenstein intended to board a waiting private aircraft which would have flown him to safety in Communist Cuba where he could have sat out the misery and death in comfort, eventually returning the the the United States after its conquest as head of the North American Division of the KGB."

There were sounds from the audience, gasps, whispers, even some persons laughing.

Dodd continued, hands gripping the podium. "Both the so-called Rubenstein and Communist KGB Major Tiemerovna realized that they must maintain their charade, only hoping for the day their own ideology would be victorious. Major Tiemerovna and Paul Rubenstein at last realized that Communism had lost. The Communist Rubenstein had and still has some strange hold on the daughter of John and Sarah Rourke. Whatever that is, he swayed her into believing that fighting against the constituted authority of Mid-Wake was the right thing. Somehow, between them, Rubenstein and Tiemerovna hoodwinked Michael Rourke as well.

"How callous could they be?" Dodd asked rhetorically. "Major Tiemerovna was personally responsible for what amounts to the murder of Sarah Rourke, because Major Tiemerovna could no longer control her lust for John Rourke. To cover this horrible act, with Rubenstein's help, she set fire to the hospital and killed all the patients and staff, among the dead our own Lieutenant Martha Larrimore and her newborn baby. What kind of heart must a woman have to murder an infant that is less than a day old?"

There were more whispers from the audience, some heads nodding, others shaking in obvious incredulity.

"I have the cartridge case recovered from Major Natalia Tiemerovna's gun, the gun she struts about the camp wearing, the gun she used to shoot Sarah Rourke after Sarah Rourke had just given birth to John Rourke's child, a child she wanted to bear."

Commander Dodd held up a small plastic bag, a piece of .380 brass inside it (he had gotten it from Zimmer who carried a gun similar to Tiemerovna's to use for the assault on the hospital). "Here is the proof! Anyone can examine it!" Still holding the bag with the brass case inside, he shouted, "But the Communist KGB Major's plans to kill Sarah Rourke and seduce John Rourke failed when one of her own explosive devices claimed John Rourke!"

More murmurs from the audience, heads shaken in disbelief.

Dodd played his ace. "I realize this is hard for you to believe. I could not believe it. But, in order prove this to you, in order to do my duty as a citizen of Eden, I hereby resign the race for the Presidency of Eden and throw my support to the heroic pilot and war veteran, Akiro Kurinami!"

Dead silence, then cheers.

Dodd raised his hands above his head and everyone in the room stood up and applauded—for him.

Ten

Maggie Barrow looked very tired, but as always very pretty. She wore civies, and as she sank down beside Jason Darkwood, on the couch in the waiting room, her pink print sundress rustled and she shrugged out of the white sweater that had been across her shoulders, just leaning her head on his shoulder. "It's going to have to be the cryogenics, Jase. But the medical team is agreed that they doubt Doctor Rourke will survive the process of going under. I think they're doing it just to do something, so they can tell themselves they just didn't stand there and let him die."

Jason Darkwood didn't say anything, just put his arm around her. As medical officer of Darkwood's ship, the *Reagan*, Maggie was unmatched, her skills ideal. But as a ship's doctor only, she was hopelessly out of her league here. She'd told him that from the first. Just as he had been assigned to security, she had been assigned as liaison between the international medical team and the government of Mid-Wake, both jobs only for the sake of keeping the two of them nearby to people who had, over what was really a very brief time, become friends forever.

Maggie kicked out of her shoes and put her feet up on the corner of the coffee table, ankles crossed. "This is just—"

"What?"

"All they went through, and the first chance they would have had to be together, to be happy, just to live a normal life, this shit happens. I mean, I mean—"

"Shh," Darkwood whispered, touching his lips to her hair.

He knew exactly what she meant. Where was the sense of any of it? To go through all that they had gone through, then to die after the war ended because a group of terrorists fire-bombed a hospital, just so a tin-plated martinet could become the leader of a hundred or so people?

And perhaps control a nuclear arsenal, D.R.E.A.D?

"Why do I have the uncomfortable feeling that peace isn't really at hand, Maggie?"

"I don't think there can ever be peace," she answered, shaking her head. "Not ever. Not ever, ever, ever."

"When? The freeze, I mean?"

"Tonight. And then—Hell, I don't know."

"Marry me?" Darkwood asked.

And she looked up at him. "What?"

"You heard me. Marry me."

"You, uhh—you—"

"Yeah, I mean it."

"You mean it," she repeated.

"Damn right. I love you and I don't want to waste any more time," Jason Darkwood told her.

"All right, because I love you, too," she said, "and that's the only reason. You realize I gotta resign my active duty commission?"

"Yeah. But you can stay in the reserves."

"When?"

"Maybe we can do it tonight, or—"

"Look, if I'm marrying you," she told him, looking up at him unwaveringly, "then we're doing it right. Long white dress, the whole shot."

"I don't have a long white dress," he laughed.

"Ohh, shut up. Whatchya got going on Saturday?"

"I'm getting married," Darkwood told her, turning her around, drawing her chin up, kissing her hard on the lips. It would be forever, he realized, and he was happy about that, the forever part.

Eleven

Michael Rourke wondered if his father could somehow have foreseen such a crisis, or if it was merely another case of his father's planning ahead?

Extensive notes, well organized, almost book length, existed regarding use of the existing cryogenic chambers and so did extensive chemical analysis of the serum, without which the cryogenic chambers were merely eternal tombs for the living, living who could never be awakened.

The notes, on both the cryogenic chambers and the serum, existed in original form at the Retreat. But duplicates had been given to both New Germany and Mid-Wake officials.

One cryogenic chamber each had been carefully transhipped to Mid-Wake and to New Germany for a period of thirty days, then returned to the Retreat and put back in storage. During those thirty days, with his father's notes to guide them, scientists and engineers of both countries labored to duplicate the technology.

Michael Rourke, alone, sat in the office used by Colonel Mann, waiting.

At last, the telephone on the desk buzzed and Michael picked it up. Colonel Mann's secretary, a pretty enough young woman named Irene, came on the line. "Herr Rourke, the call from Doctor Munchen has come through. One moment please."

"Yes."

Then he heard Munchen's voice, the transmission clear, despite the fact that it originated half a world away beneath the sea at Mid-Wake. "Michael?"

"Yes, Doctor."

"It has to be the cryogenic chambers. There is no other choice, for either of them."

"I understand. Are you certain that the chambers and the serum are adequate for the task, Doctor?"

"As certain as we can be. The serum is the identical duplicate of that used five centuries ago. Logic dictates that had the serum broken down, your father would not have been able to utilize it again after he awakened to spend those years with you and your sister. So, we are as certain as can be under the circumstances of the formula's integrity. As to the chambers, they are identical to the originals, except they are made of better materials and would endure longer than the originals. And, lastly, the American Marine, Captain Aldridge requested that he be allowed to volunteer to test the chambers and the serum—"

"You shouldn't have—"

"He thinks as highly of your parents as do the rest of us, Michael. As of five minutes ago, all vital signs, all readouts, everything was perfect. We will awaken Captain Aldridge shortly before we inject your parents. That will be—" There was a pause, Munchen presumably looking at his wristwatch. "—in precisely three hours and twelve minutes."

Michael Rourke licked his lips, looked at his own watch, a Rolex like his father's, but the Sea-Dweller, not the Submariner model. "We will be en route at that time, Doctor. Once we are on the ground—"

"I will of course stand ready for your call as soon as it is safe for you to make it."

"What are their chances? Honestly."

There was another pause, then Munchen's voice came back again. "I will not lie to you and your family, Michael. I respect all of you too much for that. The chances are slim at the very best. We are relying on the body's natural recuperative powers to revive your father from the coma into which he slips more deeply by the minute. There is precedent for this

183

hope.

"Paul Rubenstein's eyes are the best example," Munchen went on. "I have seen the glasses he had to wear before The Sleep, as you call it. He was near sighted to a considerable degree. Yet, since The Sleep, his vision is perfect. Your father carried numerous scars on his body from violent encounters, he once told me, yet John Rourke bore none of those scars after The Sleep.

"That is the chance," Munchen concluded.

"And my mother?"

"We put her into The Sleep—well—I have heard your family speak of God, a concept we at New Germany had all but dismissed. If there is a God, then placing your mother in The Sleep is something that we do with a prayer on our lips and in our hearts. I will try it as well, prayer. Her only hope of survival is that someday in the future, micro-surgery will be so advanced that the bullet can be removed from her brain and that somehow, with medical skill and patience, she can be restored. Such processes may never be discovered, most certainly will not be discovered within our lifetimes, Michael.

"Perhaps, in the future, your mother and your father will be able to share the life which they have been denied in this time," Munchen said, a catch in his voice.

"You, uhh, mentioned—mentioned God. Well, God bless you for—" Michael's voice broke, the tears starting, his throat too tight for him to speak.

"I know, Michael. Believe this: All of us, even the Russians, have done all that is in our power. Their lives will soon be out of our hands. And I hope you are right, that there is a God. Goodbye."

The line went dead.

Michael Rourke still held the receiver, his head bent over Mann's desk. His face and his eyes, felt as if they were about to explode.

He leaned his head back, closed his eyes, re-opened them, the tears too strong to keep them closed. He would never see his mother and father again.

And a cold feeling, starting as a hollowness deep in his guts, swept over him.

He was orphaned. What went right went right because of him, and what went wrong was his responsibility, too. And he faced what might be the most difficult task of his life, the attempted rescue of his newborn brother.

If he failed at this, he was not his father's son, not his mother's son.

Michael Rourke stood up, setting down the telephone receiver, his shoulders shaking, his hands shaking. He balled his fists, standing there at the desk, his body racked with sobs. His father and mother would not want him wasting another precious second weeping for them.

Michael hammered his fists against the desk and shouted to God, "All right!"

If men had a Fate, he marched toward his . . .

Paul Rubenstein sat in a chair in the corner of the rooms he shared with his wife. And he wrote in his journal. "My father-in-law, who was my best friend before I married his daughter, and has been my best friend, and will always be, may soon die, if death hasn't claimed him already. I think back a lot these days, because Annie and I are thinking about having children of our own. And what will I tell them about their grandparents?

"My father was an Air Force officer, a man finer and more honorable than I ever suspected while he lived, my mother, a wife and mother and friend, to him, to me. Annie's parents, John and Sarah, were the two most remarkable persons I could ever imagine. How do I tell the children, Annie and I will some day have, about these people? It would be empty and meaningless to merely recount their accomplishments, but just as hollow to say that had my parents and Annie's parents lived, they would have loved these children.

"Of course they would have loved them, taught them, listened to them, cared for them.

185

"Does my wife have the same feelings now inside her as I felt when I realized my parents died along with millions and millions of other people that morning the sky caught fire and scoured the earth of life?

"Annie was closer to her parents, spent her entire life with them until these last weeks, since the War finally ended.

"I have never understood why Annie chose me. She is so beautiful, so intelligent, so brave. I'm just me, and that's what I have always been. Yet she is a Rourke, and she loves me.

"It will be up to us, to Annie and me, to teach our children that being both a Rourke and a Rubenstein means something, that there was something very special about their grandparents, that each of them, in their own ways, was a hero. We will have to teach them what heroes are, and that there are many types of heroes and that any man or woman can be a hero just by trying.

"A few centuries from now, perhaps sooner, the earth will be rebuilt, repopulated. But we must make certain that our children know the stories of these times just past, and of the times before, and never forget either, so they can tell their children, and in turn their children can tell theirs.

"Otherwise, if what has happened is forgotten, it may happen again.

"As I write these lines, we are prepared to fly to what was once Peru, there to meet with a large force from our allies and friends in New Germany, then to launch an assault against a mountain redoubt where we believe the newborn son of John and Sarah is being held. If our enterprise succeeds, it has been agreed that Annie and I will raise this baby as our own child until the day he is old enough to know his heritage.

"May God watch over us all."

Paul Rubenstein laid down his journal and closed his eyes.

Twelve

Himself.

It was up to him.

Michael Rourke dressed, in the black battle dress utilities of Mid-Wake, as his father had in recent times. He stepped into the pants.

To find his brother. That was the issue at hand and all other considerations had to be set aside. They would have to give the boy a name, and he had one in mind—John Thomas Rourke, the second. There could be no finer name, albeit a challenge to live up to.

He pulled on the long sleeved, black knit, placket front, shirt, pushing the sleeves up along his forearms. Maria, whom he had so cruelly treated, had come to see him before returning to New Germany, telling him, "I realize now that you were right, Michael. I will always love you, but I do not think that being married, living together forever, was ever our fate." And she kissed his cheek, then left.

Michael Rourke pulled on his combat boots.

His father's boot size and his own were the same, but not for a moment did he think he would be able to fill his father's shoes in the classic figurative sense. All he could do was make the attempt, however vain or successful such effort might prove to be.

Michael Rourke made a last minute check of his personal weapons, the two Beretta 92F military pistols, the four-inch barreled Model 629, the knife made for him by old Jon, the Swordmaker. The knife's edge was sharp. He holstered each handgun in its turn, dropping the double rig made for him at Lydveldid Island across his shoulders. He secured his gunbelt at his waist, the .44 Magnum Smith & Wesson carried crossdraw, the knife old Jon, the Swordmaker had crafted for him at his right side, the spare magazine pouches for the Berettas and the ammo carriers for the .44 filled on the belt.

He caught up his rifle, checked that the chamber was empty, ran the action several times, finally snapping it off, then placed a loaded magazine up the well.

His father had told him on several occasions that the measure of a man was his desire to do what was right and good, and the sacrifice he would endure in order to fulfill such a desire.

Michael Rourke took his wallet from his trousers, opened it and looked at the small photo of his father and mother that he carried there. He wondered what their thoughts were when the photo was taken five centuries ago, a few months before The Night of The War.

He'd seen happier smiles on his mother's face, and his father's face too.

But there was happiness there, and love, despite complications. As a child, he'd known his mother and father did not quite get along, but he'd never doubted then nor had he since, that they loved each other and loved his sister and him.

It was that image—of love—that Michael Rourke tried to keep in his mind's eye as he left his quarters, not the image of two people who were nearly dead going into cryogenic freeze in a city, thousands of miles away and far beneath the sea . . .

Natalia Tiemerovna packed as she always did for something like this, with a modest amount of everything she might require, all of it fitting into her backpack/shoulder bag.

Clothing could be just as important to a female agent as a gun or knife might be to her male counterpart. For that reason, there was a slip, a skirt, a blouse, a pair of casual shoes.

And a spare black jumpsuit, identical to the one she wore

now.

She buckled on her gunbelt, the belt something John had
looked long and hard to find for her, the holsters, along with
the two stainless steel Smith & Wesson L-Frame .357 Mag-
nums they carried, the gift of the last President of the United
States, Sam Chambers.

Mid-Wake had a President, and he was President of The
United States, but it was a different United States over which
he presided, a different world.

Each of the revolvers carried engraved on the right barrel
flat, an American Eagle.

Natalia had often looked at these images. The American
philosopher and inventor, Benjamin Franklin had wished that
his young country's national symbol would be something besides an heroic appearing vulture. But the American Eagle had
come to mean more symbolity than in reality, the essence of a
proud if sometimes hard to fathom nation of people, who
could be described in exactly the same way, as proud always
and hard to fathom often.

Peace.

What an odd concept.

She should never have given it any credence as long as humanity infested this place called Earth.

She caught up her coat and bag and rifle and the long, thin
black fabric case and started from her quarters, forcing herself
not to consider the fact that thousands of miles away, the only
meaning which had ever been in her life was dead or dying
and would be lost to her forever . . .

Wolfgang Mann stood by his aircraft, smoking a cigarette,
the wind cold but stirring to the blood. Soon, they would be
boarding the aircraft, and with others like it, flying toward a
rendezvous in what had been Chile. The rendezvous was a
staging area, and from the staging area, an assault would be
launched against the mountain redoubt where Albert Heimaccher and Deitrich Zimmer could be found. With them, as best

189

they could guess, would be the Rourke child.

What remained for him then, for Wolfgang Mann?

Duty?

He had done his duty, was prepared to do his duty again.

But, then, after his duty was done?

His wife had been murdered, assassinated by the vile Nazis whom even now he was on his way to fight against again. He had no living children, something which saddened him and always had.

Mann exhaled, smoke and breath mixing in a gray cloud on the frigid air . . .

The cursor on his terminal's screen blinked.

Deitrich Zimmer watched it. His thoughts were not on the printout, nor were they on the data on his screen.

Rather, he was concerned with implications.

Albert Heimaccher's genealogical background checked. Albert Heimaccher was, indeed, the descendant of a Reichskinder whose biological father was Adolph Hitler.

Hitler had not directly fertilized the woman, of course. But data in the official files compiled over centuries of historical research at New Germany confirmed that der Fuhrer, in a moment of great generosity, allowed his sperm sample to be taken. The sperm sample was used, in fact, to fertilize several women. Albert Heimaccher was descended from one of the 'unions' which resulted.

The woman who mothered the child from whom Albert Heimaccher was descended bore the name Maria Clarisse Volkman of Stuttgart. In files of the Reichskinder project, there was a Maria Clarisse Volkman of Stuttgart, named as one of six women impregnated with Adolph Hitler's sperm.

If the essence of Adolph Hitler could somehow be distilled from Heimaccher, all other characteristics excluded, then the extraordinary thing could be done and der Fuhrer could be, essentially, duplicated. Certainly, noone could capture all those subtle nuances of greatness, but the essential elements of the man would be there.

That was what was important.

With the right heredity and the proper environment, history could be re-made.

Zimmer made his decision.

He would do it, and the world would be forever changed, because he did.

Thirteen

He felt stupid in the sterile surgical garb, but he had to be here.

He wore no rubber gloves because he did not have to touch anything, nor did Maggie, who had said she would be his wife.

Jason Darkwood held her hand.

The head of the medical team administered the injections, first to Sarah Rourke, then to John Rourke.

Doctor Munchen, a good-hearted man, stood between the two coffin-like chambers.

Sarah Rourke's face looked incredibly peaceful.

John Rourke's face look disturbed, almost angry.

Lights flickered on within the chambers and in the consoles surrounding them as the lids were brought downward.

In the instant that they closed, clouds of gas, light blue in color, began to fill the chambers' interiors.

Jason Darkwood held Maggie Barrow's hand tighter.

The light within each chamber shone through the gas, making the interior of the chamber seem to glow.

Living people who might never live again were inside, and watching the clouds of gas Darkwood thought, for just an instant, that perhaps the brightness was their souls. But were they freed or imprisoned by what the Rourke Family called 'The Sleep'?

The question was for a philosopher or a priest and Jason Darkwood was neither, nothing but a man. Knowing Doctor John Thomas Rourke had made him appreciate all that being a man implied, more than he had ever understood it before.

The chambers were fully closed, the gas all but totally obscuring the faces of John and Sarah Rourke.

Maggie's hand trembled in his. He looked at her and her eyes were filled with tears. Through her surgical mask, she said, "The first time I saw him, he was like this, more dead than alive."

Darkwood held her hand more tightly, saying, "John Rourke survived then. Maybe they'll both survive this, too. At least we can pray."

And Maggie leaned her head against his shoulder and Captain Jason Darkwood was glad he would make her his wife.

Fourteen

More than fifty German helicopter gunships, black painted, main rotor blades moving gently in the wind from the sea, were ranked along the beach of white sand and snow. Froth-edged breakers crashed against the land, rolling over the black rocks farther out, the wind rising, urging them to greater heights.

Men moved along the beach, German Commandoes and Long Range Mountain Patrol cadre, most of them with conventional weapons, some armed with the newest generation plasma energy rifles, the backpacks which were the power source more streamlined now, like scuba tanks.

Natalia Tiemerovna, hands dug into the pockets of her open black coat, stood just inches from the water, letting the wind tear at her face and her hair, breathing in the life. Michael had just spoken with Doctor Munchen.

John and Sarah were in The Sleep, perhaps forever.

The wind also dried her tears almost as soon as they came. Although she no longer believed as Vladmir had always taught her that any sign of weakness was unforgivable, it was not good to advertise her tears. With Annie, she would be the only other woman on this mission.

She sniffed, blinked, stared. Vladmir and John. From the arms of a devil to the arms of an angel. Why was it, she almost laughed, that her affair with the devil was consummated, while her affair with the angel never was?

She would willingly have accepted death if only John would once had made love to her, penetrated her body with his.

If this was it forever and he never awakened, he should not lie preserved in cryogenic sleep. His body, with all his weapons adorning it, should be placed on a pyre of wood, and a fire set someplace high above the rest of the world, where its glow would be seen by men everywhere, to be remembered, burning into their eyes and hearts, as an image of what was attainable by man.

She had no doubt that if, indeed, although clinically alive he were really dead, that if there were a God and He had a Heaven, John Rourke would be there now, Sarah beside him.

When she thought of Sarah, Natalia felt a cheapness inside her. If John had been willing, no matter that she respected Sarah, loved Sarah as a friend; she would have lain beneath John's body as long and as often as he desired, cheating Sarah.

She was not her own woman while John Rourke walked the earth. But could she now, did she even want to live?

The idea of suicide crossed her mind more than once in the brief time since everything had happened.

Obviously, John would have rejected the very concept. Life was too precious to discard; but, she had no life. She had convinced herself that filling her days—the children of the Wild Tribes, the school, all of that—was filling her life. But she knew better then, knew better now. Living a lie while she could lie to herself that some day, some miracle might happen, was one thing, this another.

John Rourke was out of her life forever.

If she wanted to continue with life, it would be her own doing and noone else's.

As she watched, the sail of an Island Class Submarine broke the surface of the water well out from shore. It would be the *Rogers*, the vessel commanded by Jason Darkwood's second in command, the black man named Sebastian. Two smaller sails broke the surface on either side of the first. These would be the *Reagan* and the *Wayne*, she knew.

The Rogers was equipped with Soviet missiles converted to conventional warheads and, when the Nazi mountain redoubt was penetrated and the results of the raid were known, good or bad, the *Rogers* would fire its missiles until the redoubt was obliterated from the face of the earth, German helicopters confirming that.

If someone were watching the shore from the sail of any of the three submarines, with powerful enough digital imaging computer assist binoculars, her face would be clearly visible. If that person knew her, like Sebastian, or perhaps one of the Marines she'd fought beside, whoever watched her would know why should he or she saw a tear.

But a stranger would wonder, of course, and might, at some later time, ask her, "Why were you crying?"

She would say simply, "Sometimes, when a life ends, one cries; sometimes, too, one cries when a life begins. I think I was crying for both at once, but I am not certain yet. Can I let you know when I know myself how things work out?"

That was the way, of course, to take it an instant at a time and see, see if anything was worth the trouble, the pain. Right now, she was not optimistic. But, the thought of ending her own life was temporarily removed from her list of options. John and Sarah's son was in danger, in enemy hands.

That much and so much more, she owed them both.

Fifteen

Starting from the north, the German helicopter gunships began rising from the sand and snow that was now the coastline of Peru, arcing westward and seaward, passing over the sails of the three submarines, men on the decks waving up at them, gesturing with clenched fists and thumbs up.

American flags flew from each vessel.

The sun was high, but not near to noon.

With the fuselage doors open, the interior of the gunship was frigid.

Paul Rubenstein watched his companions, his family.

His wife, his friend (also his brother-in-law), his other friend.

He wondered about John's plan.

Had events finally forced its existence, its reality?

It had been obvious that John planned to re-populate the earth, if need be, with the life contained within The Retreat. That, more than the other genuine reasons, that adults could better cope with a survival situation than children, that the children (one of them was now his wife) needed an uninterrupted time to acquire an education, than anything else was the reason John Rourke awakened, awakened Annie and Michael, then allowed them to age to adulthood.

John had wanted, all along, to provide for the future of the human race. Three mating pairs rather than one, a husband for his daughter, a wife for his son.

Paul Rubenstein held his wife's hand; her head rested on his shoulder and she seemed to be asleep.

Michael and Natalia sat opposite him.

A German crewman closed the fuselage doors.

Overhead lights came on automatically. Natalia opened her black bag, extracting a smaller bag from inside it. Paul Rubenstein almost laughed when he recognized its contents. The two-gun, knife-wielding, martial arts expert was doing some type of sewing. Embroidery, he thought, assuming that because it resembled the same sort of thing Annie sometimes did to while away the time.

Had Annie taught her?

It certainly wasn't a course in 'spy school' as Natalia sometimes called it. Or, had it been? "Now, Comrades, you shall learn the things that American housewives and mothers do in the event that, someday, while fighting the forces of Imperialism, you must pass yourself off as one of the wives of the Capitalist Exploiters. You must strive to excel, but not to enjoy!" No, he doubted that. Most certainly, it was his wife who had taught her.

He looked at Michael.

To the casual observer, Michael might appear to be the world's slowest reader, because whenever Paul observed Michael Rourke, he was always reading Ayn Rand's, *Atlas Shrugged*. It was John's favorite book, and evidently also his son's favorite. Paul had read it, then read it again several years later, enjoying it even more.

Michael seemed always to be reading it.

There was wisdom in its pages, and Michael loved the pursuit of wisdom with a passion rarely seen.

Paul Rubenstein considered them both.

A man. A woman. So much in common, yet so totally different.

And he wondered, did Natalia see Michael Rourke as John Rourke's flesh and blood ghost?

Paul Rubenstein returned to his journal . . .

Wolfgang Mann surrendered the controls of the gunship, letting the machine's pilot take charge for a time while he studied the maps on his laptop computer.

The Nazi redoubt was atop and partially within a peak designated only as K-17, not the highest in the subrange of which it was a part, but neither was it the lowest. Its elevation at the highest point was nineteen thousand feet above sea level. But, of course, with the glaciation of so much of the northern hemisphere, sea level figures were invariably incorrect.

The structural data was most interesting. Synth-concrete molded into the shape of the mountain rocks, the effective result camouflaging its presence from ordinary aerial observation. The framework was a peculiar form of polymer reinforced spun titanium, the most advanced structural material known to the science of New Germany. As strong as the strongest steels, yet hollow and so light an ordinary man could easily transport six twelve-foot beams, three on each shoulder, his only inconvenience the length, the weight barely noticable.

The advantage of polymer reinforced spun titanium was that it was essentially invisible to electronic detection.

Had anyone other than a person intimate with New Germany searched for the structure? The redoubt would never have been discovered except by the physical accident of walking into it.

On the day when Doctor John Rourke led the forces of liberation against the Nazi dictatorship, the records from which the data on the redoubt was derived were about to be subjected to magnetic degausing when anti-Nazi forces seized control of the computer center. The attempt to destroy the computer data was interdicted. At the time, so many other concerns had to be attended to, that Mann had never given a second thought to the redoubt or how it might provide a solid base of operations for Nazi forces.

The new plastic explosives would penetrate the synth-concrete which cocooned the facility, but Wolfgang Mann hoped not to be forced to use them. Instead, as much as any responsible military commander could allow himself to rely on a single gambit, he counted on the new generation energy weapons, several of which were mounted aboard a small number of the gunships in the air armada he would be sending against the Nazi stronghold.

Only recently field tested, in experiments at New Germany, the 'energy cannons' as they were popularly called, had shattered and burned their way through synth-concrete of equal or greater thickness to that utilized in the mountain redoubt.

But tests were one thing, and combat use another. If, however, the new weapons did perform as the field trials promised, the lightning strike into the redoubt that Wolfgang Mann so hoped for, could be carried out. On its speed, hinged the entire success of both of the mission's ultimate goals. Those two goals were to destroy Albert Heimaccher and Deitrich Zimmer's Nazi organization, ridding the earth of the plague of National Socialism forever; and, to rescue the newborn baby, who was the son of John and Sarah Rourke.

He thought of Sarah Rourke often since the terrible night of death; but, he had thought of her often before that night, too.

Wolfgang Mann realized that he loved her.

Sixteen

The blue light flashed and the synthetic concrete that looked identical to the rock surface of the mountain shimmered, then cracked, fragmenting everywhere with a sound louder than the detonation of a hand grenade.

Natalia Tiemerovna stood in the doorway of the German gunship, stripped of her black arctic parka, shivering in the wind, as her hands, gloved in black leather that was thin and strong, secured the strap for the sheath which lay across her back.

In the Chicago Espionage School deep within the Union of Soviet Socialist Republics, five centuries ago, she had immersed herself in the martial arts as she had once in ballet, and for the same reason, its physical release and its beauty. More than any of the other forms, she had come to love kendo, the use of the sword, perhaps because of its total lack of potential for use in the field—or so she had supposed.

As an officer in the Committee for State Security, she had come quite often to rely on a knife. And, to her surprise, she found that utilization of a knife in the same manner as a sword took an opponent totally by surprise and was marvelously effective.

When the War came to an end and she went to Europe to work with the children of the Wild Tribes, her body still craved movement and beauty. She returned to the sword. Bjorn Rolvaag led her to Lydveldid Island's finest swordsmith and she spoke with the man, drew out her desire on paper, and watched as he gave it dimension in wood. They talked, she tested the length of blade and handle. He refined it beyond anything she had ever dreamed possible when, in the fiery orange glow of his forge, he transformed an idea into steel.

It was the perfect sword for her height and weight and strength, and most of all for her style of fighting. Had someone told her at the Chicago School, that as a woman born in the twentieth century she would be going into combat five centuries later with a medieval style sword as one of her weapons, she would have considered the idea madness.

But in desparate close quarters combat, when a gun was empty or failed, a massive and intimidating blade could not only buy precious seconds in which to act, but neutralize an opponent totally. Although she was strong for a woman, a short-sword-sized knife such as John carried, his Crain Life Support System X, required more physical strength than she possessed, at least to use it to its full potential.

She shivered. With John's knife and a ferocity she never realized she possessed, she beheaded her husband, Vladmir Karamatsov, as he was about to kill John Rourke. To behead a man with an edged weapon that was anything short of an axe, required either phenomenal strength or great luck because the blade had to pass between the vertebrae.

A true sword, on the other hand, had a longer reach and its mass was distributed in such a manner that it was actually easier to deliver a more powerful blow, the blade itself accomplishing what strength alone would have to do with a mere knife.

The gunship banked and Natalia, secured to a safety line, kept her balance despite her extreme angle to the open doorway.

More of the gunships were firing toward the seemingly innocent mountain summit, but with each shot as the dust settled, the mountain's innocence was stripped away, revealing the Nazi redoubt within.

Their anti-aircraft defenses would be opening up in seconds, but hopefully not soon enough.

Her sword looked like something from a barbarian fantasy.

202

Its blade of D-2 tool steel was a full thirty-six inches in length, spear pointed and double-edged, flat ground from the median line of stock three-eighths-inch thick.

The handle, designed to accommodate both her hands and full tanged for strength against snapping, was covered in leather wrapped over black linen micarta. There was a broad double quillon guard of steel reinforced brass. The sword's pommel was a large, spherical skull crusher, also of steel.

But now was no time for swords. Once inside the redoubt, perhaps, but not now. Her M-16 was in her right hand instead, her left hand grasped to the security strap. Natalia Anastasia Tiemerovna stood ready to jump. Now was a time for guns.

Annie Rourke Rubenstein had a Remington 870 12-gauge taken from the Retreat just before she left for Lydveldid Island. She knew full well that some persons five centuries ago, who weren't really that knowledgeable concerning firearms, had abortively attempted to push the idea that the most shotgun a woman could handle was a .410. Annie laughed at the thought as she tromboned the action of the shotgun her father had always said was the finest American made pump to be had. The Remington was a 12-gauge.

Paul Rubenstein let the Colt assault rifle slip back on its sling, drawing back the bolt of the Schmiesser sub-machine gun he had carried into combat with a Rourke beside him for more than five centuries . . .

Michael Rourke leaned against the bulkhead beside the open doorway of the German gunship, the icy wind tearing at his face, clawing at his hair. He gave a goodluck tug to the two Berettas under his arms in the shoulder holster over the German flak vest.

His father hadn't liked the 9mm cartridge except for special purpose use, but had always told him that was personal preference only. Once wedded to the .45 ACP, always. Michael Rourke, on the other hand, liked the 9mm Parabellum cartridge a little better and preferred the larger capacity magazines.

There were many fine large capacity 9mms, of course, the foreign guns that had been imported before the Night of The War—the SIG-Sauer P-226, the Walther P-88, the TZ-75, the excellent Taurus PT-92 and PT-99 and many others—and even one American large capacity 9mm, the third generation Smith & Wesson 9mms, could be ranked as a world class gun. The Berettas, excellent, were also available.

He liked them.

Michael shouted to Paul and Annie and Natalia, "Gas masks up!"

Then he pulled his own mask over his face, popping the cheeks to make the seal.

He charged the chamber of the Colt M-16, and his right fist clenched around the pistol grip, trigger finger along the outside of the guard, ready.

Seventeen

Somewhere, there was pain, and words that were only vague rememberings brought pictures to him of Sarah, of fire, of death. And the pictures were terror because they were glimpses, like something seen between the blinkings of the eye.

The pain became a dullness, but it was there, above him, holding him down, relentless. On a level of consciousness he did not know he possessed, he knew that he was dreaming, and that there could only be one reason for dreaming. And both the reason and the realization held him in their grasp that was fear. And the dream began and although he tried to hold on to the realization that it was a dream, the dream took stronger hold of him and the awareness of unreality vanished, exchanged for a new reality . . .

Michael Rourke vaulted the few feet to the granite surface of the mountain. The wind from the German helicopter gunship's downdraft combined with the winds which scoured the rocks of all snow and ice; its intensity near the equivalent force of a gale. In pockets, where the rock formed natural shields against the high altitude blasts, there was snow that was feet deep at least, crusted over in shimmering ice crystals which caught the sunlight and threw it back brighter and more concentrated than before. He came down in a crouch, his M-16 in his hands.

Natalia and Annie and Paul jumped from the German gunship and surrounded him.

There was a hole in the rock surface a few yards from them and Michael Rourke started running toward it. On all sides, German Commando and Long Range Mountain Patrol personnel were reaching the mountain top, some jumping as Michael and the family had done from gunships hovering only a few feet above the surface, others rapelling from choppers hovering at higher altitude. The mountain redoubt's anti-aircraft defenses were coming into action, flak exploding in black, heavily textured bursts in the air all around the J7-V's coming in from both the north and the south, converging on the redoubt.

Contrails of surface to air missiles, gleaming white, streaked across the deep cold blue of the sky, some of them exploding in mid-air because of German counter measure weapons.

Flickers of pale blue flashed across the sky as well, originating at the muzzles of the helicopter mounted energy weapons, terminating against the rock surface itself.

Avalanches began, great chunks of rock and ice and tons of dislodged snow cascading down the mountainside into the cloud-shrouded valleys below.

Michael Rourke reached the opening, not knowing what lay beyond except in a general fashion from his study of the redoubt's blueprints. From a pocket of his battle vest, Michael took a handful of ground readers, as the Germans called them. They were flat, rectangular pieces of plastic, at the longest edge less than an inch, with sensors built into them that, when he activated their control unit, would cause them to detonate a harmless high-pitched noisemaker charge if they hit a solid surface. Michael flipped the lock, then the toggle switch on the control and tossed them though the opening. There was a high-pitched whistling sound that indicated they had struck a hard surface and he wouldn't be jumping through the hole into air space alone. Michael lobbed a gas grenade, then another through the opening, Natalia doing the same.

Paul flanked him on the right. Michael Rourke hurtled himself through the opening, stopping just inside and dodging right, firing a burst from his M-16 high over the head of any human target, since the gas was temporarily so thick anything beyond a few feet was obscured to him and for all he knew, he might have accidentally entered the redoubt in the same portion of the structure where his newborn brother was being kept.

Paul was through, then Annie and Natalia as Michael and Paul edged their way along the wall surface behind them. He could hear Paul speaking through the headset built into their gasmasks. "I can't see a thing, Michael!"

"Keep moving along the wall."

Natalia's voice came to him. "Annie and I will cross the room to the far sides. Watch out for us! Starting now."

Michael Rourke snapped the muzzle of his rifle high and away, saying into his headset, "Let us know when you're there!"

"I'm set," Annie's voice came back.

"So am I," Natalia said.

"Paul, up the middle. Should be a doorway."

"Moving now," Paul came back.

Michael Rourke was running, the gas cloud dissipated to the degree that there was a modest amount of visibility. The room was a storage chamber of some sort, crates—possibly food-stuffs—stacked everywhere.

They reached the doorway almost simultaneously, Annie and Natalia joining them in the next instant. The door was closed and locked, similar in appearance to the watertight doors on submarines. Natalia dropped to her knees before the wheel lock, setting a strip of the new German plastique to it, then a detonator. "Fifteen seconds! Get back!"

Michael Rourke ran back, turning his face away and shielding his head with his left arm against possible flying debris.

There was a crack, a pop and the sound of metal striking the wall surfaces.

As Michael Rourke looked back, the door was swung part way inward. He ran for the door, calling to Paul, "Crisscross through the door, Paul, Annie. You and Natalia use gas grenades, right and left." At the doorway, Michael took one flank, Paul Rubenstein the other, Annie behind Paul, lobbing a grenade through the opening left to right, Natalia behind Michael throwing her grenade right to left.

"Go!" Michael snapped, and he was through, Paul crossing near him in a blur, both of them taking up positions on the other side of the door.

There was an air evacuation system in operation, the gas being sucked out through vent holes in the upper portions of the wall, but still intense enough to cause an unmasked person discomfort and produce some disorientation.

But there was no time to lose.

A staircase at the far end of the corridor, nearer to the center of the mountain, looked like the obvious choice.

"The stairwell. Hit it. Annie, cover!"

"Right, Michael!"

Michael Rourke ran along the corridor, nearing the stairwell.

It was circular, winding, metal, going down into the bowels of the mountain itself. The corridor behind him was filling with more German personnel who had attained it through other holes blown into the exterior of the structure. Michael switched frequencies, linking up to Otto Hammerschmidt who led the ground forces. "Otto? Any resistance?"

"No, my friend."

"Send some men to cover us, then bring the rest with. We've gotta go down."

"Agreed!"

Michael crouched near the height of the stairwell, peering downward, the stairs seeming to go down forever. Natalia dropped to her knees beside him. She tapped him on the shoulder, and Michael nodded, telling Hammerschmidt, "We're switching to your frequency now."

Michael changed frequencies, telling Natalia and his sister and brother-in-law. "Switch to Hammerschmidt's frequency."

He switched, then Natalia's voice came on. "I started to tell you, this stairwell gives me a bad feeling."

"I know. That's why I'll go first."

"Then, I'm second," she responded.

He looked at her, would have smiled except that the mask he wore wasn't really conducive to it.

The gas masks they wore would not be enough if the Nazis were flooded the interior of the mountain with nerve gas, but it would have been impossible to function with total effectiveness in full chemical-biological-nuclear gear and it was hard to imagine even the Nazis using nerve agents as an intruder defense system, when it would be just as deadly to their own personnel.

Michael glanced over his shoulder, Hammerschmidt and two dozen or so German Commando and Long Range Mountain Patrol personnel ready and waiting. Michael Rourke's gloved left hand on the pipe bannister, his M-16 in his right, he started down the stairs, Natalia so close behind him she was almost beside him . . .

His twin stainless Detonics CombatMasters were in his hands and he stood in a vast hall, the walls covered with mirrors.

He started walking.

In one of the mirrors, he saw a flicker of movement, but it wasn't his own reflection. Yet, it was.

He began walking again, toward the mirror where he'd seen the movement. And he saw his own image, but there was something wrong.

And the mirrors were gone and there was blackness surrounding him, but his guns were still in his hands. Light, brilliant and bright, and within the light as he moved forward to be closer to it, he saw Sarah. She sat in a rocking chair, a baby in her arms.

"Sarah?"

"Is there trouble, John?

He looked down at the guns in his hands, then back toward the light and she was no longer there. The light was growing stronger and he wasn't walking toward it anymore, but it was surrounding him. His eyes squinted against it. "Sarah? Where are you?"

There was no answer.

He turned around and the light became desert and a sun, hot and glowing, glared down at him like some malevolent eye from a sky that was a brilliant blue.

He looked down and his guns were still in his hands.

He started walking.

Somehow, his sunglasses were on and the light was less bothersome to him because of that. This was a strange desert, because it had all the heat and desolateness of a desert, but there were houses ranked on sand covered streets and there were sand dunes everywhere. But sometimes, poking through from inside he could see parts of automobiles and trucks and airplanes.

But, there were no people.

"Sarah? Are you out here?"

He looked at the house on his right, saw movement from behind a porch window.

John Rourke started toward the house, the sand very deep here and the going slow. He was on the steps, the treads mounded with sand and piles of ash. He stepped onto the porch.

In the window, the same window, he saw movement.

It was his own reflection, but there was something wrong with it. "What's going on?"

Only his own voice echoed back to him, that and the lonely keening of a hot wind.

Eighteen

Each time there was an air strike, the staircase vibrated, and it vibrated regularly, meaning the J7-Vs, under the command of Wolfgang Mann, were doing their job well.

At a mid point in the stairwell, there was a landing, and leading off from it a corridor shaped like a large pipe, tubular and of gleaming metal.

"I'll check it out," Paul volunteered.

"I'm going with him," Annie said.

"All right, Paul, but be careful," Michael cautioned, the tube a perfect place for a trap. "We'll send a dumbass first Otto?

Hammerschmidt nodded, already ordering one of his men to unlimber his pack. The pack's seams were composed of a hook and pile fastening material, the pack body stripping away easily. The interior of the pack was foam formed, configured to the shape of the object within. That was a dumbass, a robotic device specifically designed to attract every possible danger, sparing the human operators behind it, the experience.

The dumbass was started along the tube. About fourteen inches high, with a telescoping mast and built in video relay capabilities, it hummed along on miniaturized tank treads.

Hammerschmidt, before Paul and Annie could start down the tube after it, ordered two of his men in a safe distance back from the dumbass, one of them the operator. Four more of Hammerschmidt's personnel fell in behind Paul and Annie, one of the Commandoes carrying an energy weapon.

Michael and Natalia at the lead, Hammerschmidt took the rest of the column down through the stairwell, continuing toward the bottom where there seemed to be some sort of vast stone hall.

"How's it going for Paul and Annie and your men?"

Hammerschmidt nodded toward a man just above them on the stairwell, the man—one of the Long Range Mountain Patrol people—monitoring a video display about the size of a twentieth century audio cassette. "All is in order, Herr Major," the corporal volunteered.

"Good," Hammerschmidt nodded.

They continued down the stairwell, more of the hall below them becoming visible. It seemed to have been carved from the mountain's fabric itself, or was perhaps a huge natural vault within the mountain to begin with, but there was nothing that seemed manmade about it.

The stairwell broke from within the natural seeming cylinder within the rock through which it passed, Michael Rourke and Natalia on the tread just above him, stopping there.

"The Hall of the Mountain King? perhaps," Hammerschmidt suggested.

The hall was vast enough that a small aircraft could have operated within it with considerable impunity. As Michael started to say something, there was loud click.

Natalia shouted, "Trap!"

Firing ports opened from hidden positions within the ceiling through which the stairwell passed, surrounding the stairwell totally. Michael Rourke shouted, "Hit the ropes!" And, as he said it, he dropped his already safed M-l6 to his side on its sling, clamping on the lead from his vest's rapelling pack to one of the verticals supporting the stairs. The muzzles of automoatic weapons began to protrude through the ports.

Natalia was helping one of the German commandoes whose gear was malfunctioning. As he clamped on, Natalia began to access her own rapelling kit.

Automatic weapons fire started from the firing ports and Michael Rourke vaulted over the railing, grabbing Natalia into his left arm and holding her against him, saying, "Hold onto me!" He jumped, gunfire everywhere around them now, bullets pinging off the metal substructure and the treads, some of Hammerschmidt's men going down.

A bullet tore across Michael's right shoulder, skating over his vest's ballistic layers. He nearly lost his hold of the rope, but held it, controlling their descent just enough that he could break their fall without snapping the rope.

Down they went, other ropes snaking out around them, men skidding along them, gunfire from the floor of the hall now, some of the German personnel under Hammerschmidt's command taking hits, some returning fire. Some men merely skidded along their ropes, out of control, others locked in place, dangling there, dead or wounded.

Natalia shouted through her radio, "Look down!"

Michael looked down.

The source of the gunfire from below was a group of men in a ragged circle around the base of the stairs, perhaps fifty men in all.

There was a voice over a loudspeaker system, shouting in German, "Hold your fire! Hold your fire!"

Michael Rourke slowly started their descent, Natalia still clinging to him. The men below them, in black BDUs with Nazi insignia armbands, held assault rifles, some fixed with bayonets.

Michael eased Natalia and himself down the remaining twenty or so feet, separating from the rope as Natalia let go of him, both of them standing there, back to back, surrounded by Heimaccher and Zimmer's Nazis.

Hammerschmidt and those of his men who survived the rapel hit the floor, weapons raised and ready.

Again, over the speaker system, came the same voice. "You will throw down your weapons and surrender to the forces of the Reich! Or, you will die!"

Hammerschmidt's voice came through the radio set into Michael's ear. "That is Zimmer's voice, I think."

Michael estimated the odds at slightly better than three to

one against them.

He looked at Natalia. Visible through her mask, he could see her eyes as she blinked, just looking at him then.

Michael Rourke nodded, licking his lips. He tore away his gas mask. He could understand some German, speak very little of it despite having slept with a native German speaker, Maria Leuden. So, in English, he shouted, "I am Michael Rourke. I have come for the return of my brother. Who is in charge here?"

Michael turned slowly around in a circle, looking at the faces surrounding them, the nearest of the Nazis encircling them was perhaps twenty yards away.

The formation broke and Michael turned and looked. A man, smallish-looking, dark haired, a classic Hitlerlian mustache centered like a small black blotch at the middle of his upper lip, stepped through the opening. Like the others, he wore black, but he had a better tailor, Michael thought.

"Is it Halloween?" Michael Rourke shouted to him. "I mean, you're dressed up like Hitler, and I certainly can't see someone doing that everyday. The fake mustache is really great, by the way."

The man—Heimaccher, obviously—stopped, hands on his hips, his jodhpured legs thrown slightly forward as he threw his head back and laughed. "If you and these traitors with you surrender, your lives will be spared."

Michael Rourke nodded his head, inhaled, then spoke, his voice barely a whisper. "Unless your people are very good, there's a superior military force all around and through this place, air power beating it apart and you've got about ten or twenty minutes before you're overrun."

The self-styled Fuhrer said nothing, merely smiled.

Michael Rourke continued. "I came for my brother, and I won't leave until I have him. And, of equal importance really, I came for Deitrich Zimmer, to shoot his God damned brains out. If I interpret your intentions, we surrender, you hold us hostage against Colonel Mann's forces taking you, then make some sort of dramatic escape, after which, of course, you'll kill us anyway, right?

Heimaccher started edging back.

"Well," Michael Rourke said, "not today." Michael's left hand rested on the butt of his cross-draw carried revolver, and he twist-drew the Smith & Wesson and double actioned the trigger, putting a single 180-grain jacketed hollow point into Albert Heimaccher's natural target, the mustache.

Michael's right hand swung up, the M-l6 at his side, its safety tumbler set to full auto as he moved the muzzle of his revolver right and killed the nearest man to him who was about to return fire.

As the Nazi went down, falling over Heimaccher's already sprawling body, Michael Rourke jerked back the trigger of the M-l6 and held it zig-zagging the muzzle of the assault rifle right and and left, killing as many of the Nazis as he could before one of them killed him.

Gunfire was everywhere.

A bullet creased along Michael Rourke's thigh, another across his right forearm.

The M-16 was already empty as the momentary shock caused him to lose his grip on the weapon. The Smith & Wesson revolver was emptied as well, and Michael Rourke crashed it down over the head of a Nazi less than a yard from him, smashing the nose and teeth.

There was a blur of motion beside him and he heard Natalia's voice, unfiltered by a gas mask, shouting, "Dodge right! Now!"

Michael Rourke sidestepped and ducked as he stabbed the revolver between his gunbelt and abdomen, his right hand, still a little numb, groping for the Beretta under his left arm.

He had it, but before he could use it, Natalia opened fire, hosing the phalanx of black-clad Nazis with 5.56mm from her rifle.

A Beretta 92F in each hand now, Michael Rourke fired into the men point blank, killing as many as he could.

Nineteen

Deitrich Zimmer had always prided himself on anticipating the moves of his enemies and countering them before they could be accomplished for his undoing.

He walked along the corridor now, the baby screaming its lungs out for food or because its clothes were wet or dirtied or because it had gas or for some other one of the myriad reasons why babies screamed and cried and always had.

None of that mattered. The National Socialist movement mattered and it was not confined to here, alone. In New Germany, there were partisans aplenty to aid him, and he had the means to get there; then start again. His sole purpose for coming to the redoubt had been accomplished, and gloriously.

As he turned a bend in the corridor, he saw a little mechanical contrivance moving along the floor. He recognized it at once as a dumbass, the robotic sacrificial lamb that was one of New Germany's most recent military developments.

But, before Deitrich Zimmer could turn back, there were soldiers, and then the Jew, Rubenstein, and his wife. "Freeze!" the Jew shouted.

There was a pump shotgun, rather primitive but devastatingly effective under the proper circumstances, in the woman's hands. Its muzzle did not tremble. Zimmer took it as a sign of maturity and skill that she did not bother to work the action but already had the chamber loaded and merely pointed the gun at him.

Zimmer's pistol was pressed against the baby's head. "No, I will not freeze, Jew, because I have the muzzle of my pistol and the little boy's head both, just where they should be. All that is necessary for me to do is to twitch my finger and the child dies. Even if you or your wife—she is a disgrace to her race—but if you or she should think that firing upon me will somehow negate my abilities to pull this trigger, then think again!"

Zimmer pressured the muzzle of the pistol so hard against the baby's head that the baby cried.

The Rourke girl, now the Jew's wife, shrieked at Zimmer, "Leave the baby alone, damn you! Try me! Afraid of a woman? Try me!"

"Annie, hold off," the Jew told her. Then he turned his gaze toward Zimmer. "You kill that baby and death will be something you'll beg for. Understand?"

"I am so terribly frightened," Zimmer laughed. "My hand is shaking so badly I might even pull the trigger of this pistol by accident."

The Jew and his bitch did nothing.

But, Deitrich Zimmer had to get past them to survive this, to make the future of the world secure, for him.

"We're at an impasse," the Jew called out. "Let the baby alone and you have my word that you'll walk out of here alive and unmolested. My word."

"The word of a Jew!?"

The military commander with them was a lieutenant of good family, the last person Zimmer would have suspected of associating with a Jew or harboring anti-Nazi sentiments.

"Kill the Jew, join me!"

The young officer spat onto the corridor floor as he stood shoulder to shoulder with Rubenstein. What better place for a traitor than standing beside a Jew, Zimmer thought.

The lieutenant announced, "If the child is killed, Herr Zimmer, you will have no leverage, and no other fate will await you but death. You must know that."

"I know, young man, that even a traitor must have sufficient

217

intelligence to realize that, in my position, I will not surrender the baby. The only way any of you will get the child is as a corpse. If that is your wish, I can kill the child now."

Zimmer drew back slightly on the trigger.

The Jew's wife screamed at him, "He's my brother, damn you! Don't do it!"

"Then, let me pass. Otherwise, I will spare this child the pain of growing up and discovering that his sister has defiled her race and her body by fucking—"

"You son of a bitch!" she shouted, starting toward him.

But Rubenstein ordered her, "Don't, Annie!"

She stood her ground, then, but the muzzle of the shotgun was shaking violently.

The Jew said, "Lieutenant, let him pass."

"But, Herr Rubenstein—"

"Let him pass, Lieutenant."

The young officer cleared his throat, ordered his men, "Let this vile being pass."

Zimmer smiled, the muzzle of his weapon tight against the right temple of the screaming infant as he continued along the corridor, the Jew and the woman and the others falling back to let him pass.

There was hatred in their eyes, and that was good, because when one acted out of hate, one acted less than rationally.

Twenty

The initial burst of gunfire had subsided because the weap
ons in the hands of the Nazis were ill-suited to close quarter
combat such as this and so comparatively powerful that severa
of the Nazis fell dead by shots from their own comrades
rifles.

In that alone, the Nazis were at a disadvantage. There were
so many of them that it was impossible to miss.

The revolvers in her hands were empty now, but she used
both of them to crash down across the neck and shoulders o
one of the Nazis who was locked in combat with Otto Ham
merschmidt. Jabbing the guns into her belt, her right hand
swept over the pocket along her thigh and she had the Bali-
song, wheeling it open, as her right arm arced outward and
downward, averting her eyes from the blood spray as the tip of
the Wee-Hawk patterned blade caught the carotid artery of one
of the Nazis and slashed it open.

Something struck her, driving her to her knees, a man's
weight crushing her. Natalia twisted her head to the right. The
man, one of the Nazis, was dead. She threw her shoulder
against his chest and rolled him off. She came up in a crouch,
her knife still in her hand. She thrust it forward, into the
chest of one of the Nazis. His hands grasped her wrist in a
death grip.

Natalia drew her body back and kicked her right foot into

his testicles. He lurched back, and her hand slipped from the knife.

It was as if fate were telling her to use the sword, she realized, because a Nazi, with a bayonet fixed below the muzzle of his rifle, charged toward her and it was either use the sword or die.

Natalia's left hand reached to the handle of the sword, starting it up from its sheath, her right hand grasping the hilt as she started to clear.

She stepped back, the toes of her left foot pointing forward, her right foot shifting so she stood in a T-stance, the sword in a high guard position. As the man charged, Natalia spun 180 degrees right, sweeping the blade in a long arc as she dodged the bayonet, the sword meeting the Nazi's throat at the adam's apple, killing him.

She backstepped on her right foot, the sword in a high guard position again, then cleaving outward and downward in a broad, fast arc across the left side of the neck of another of the Nazis.

Natalia turned half left, edging her left foot back, the blade alive in her hands now, spinning as her eyes sought a new target . . .

The heel of Michael Rourke's left hand impacted one of the Nazis at the side of the nose, splattering blood everywhere but not killing the man. Michael Rourke's gloved fingers gouged for a handful of flesh, finding it, twisting the man's head toward him as Michael's right arm punched forward, in his fist the knife made for him at Lydveldid Island by old Jon, the Swordmaker. Edge up, he drove the blade in well beneath the sternum and ripped as he pushed the man off his steel.

About a dozen of the Nazis, firing handguns sporadically, were running toward the doors at the far end of the vaulted stone hall.

Michael Rourke shouted as he wiped the blood from his blade across the back of a dead man, "After them! Come on!"

Michael slipped the knife into the sheath as he broke into a run, jumping the body of another dead man as he started a fresh magazine up the butt of one of his Berettas . . .

Deitrich Zimmer reached the end of the corridor, the doorway there, airtight, sealed.

Behind him, the Jew and his wife and the traitorous soldiers kept close watch, weapons ready for him to lose his concentration for that single second that would allow them a shot.

Zimmer smiled inwardly.

If he released the baby to open the door, they would have him. If he released the gun, they would have him.

And, beyond this doorway lay the future of mankind.

Carefully, his eyes on them every second, he shifted the baby downward, placing the muzzle of the pistol into the baby's mouth.

"You bastard!" It was the bitch who shrieked at him.

Zimmer let the smile inside of him show on his face. Carefully, he shifted the pistol from his right hand to his left, holding it awkwardly but well enough and obviously so that his ability to pull the trigger and blow the child's head to nothingness would not be impaired.

With his right hand, now, he opened the wheel lock on the door.

He stepped through and into the windy blast.

The air forces of New Germany pummeled the redoubt, gunships and J7-Vs everywhere.

The facade of synth-concrete covering the superstructure of the redoubt was largely blasted away now.

In moments, the redoubt would totally fall and the anti-Nazis would think they had won, which was even better than he could have planned.

Deitrich Zimmer approached the loaf-shaped structure set into the rocks, his now free right hand finding the control set in his pocket, his thumb flipping back the guard, then depressing the switch.

His eyes settled on the doorway, the Jew Rubenstein and the others waiting for him to make the slightest misstep.

He looked back toward the loaf-shaped rock; it was already rotated away, the powered half-track sled waiting for him as it had been for Albert Heimaccher before Zimmer had availed himself of the control unit. Within the enclosed vehicle were emergency rations, emergency weapons, and supplies.

Zimmer activated the next button, the cover of the sled rising upward and forward.

Zimmer eyed his enemies.

His timing would have to be precise.

Carefully, the baby turning blue with the cold, his own hands starting to numb, he approached the sled, then stepped up and inside.

Rather than closing the bullet resistant cocoon around him, he activated the sled controls, the engine purring to life. He started the machine moving slightly forward, glancing back to his enemies. They were through the doorway, weapons shouldered and ready.

The machine reached the edge of the snow covered ramp.

Deitrich Zimmer retook the pistol in his right hand, holding up the screaming child, the muzzle of the weapon still in the child's mouth.

Zimmer turned toward the Jew and the others, shouting to them, "I have won!"

He fired the pistol, casting the dead infant away as the hail of bullets started, his left hand hitting the cocoon control, his right hand discarding the pistol, working the lever to power the machine to full.

Bullets zinged off the body structure, a pellet from a shotgun blast tearing into his right shoulder.

The sled was already picking up momentum.

The Jew threw himself onto the cocoon, hammering at it with a rifle butt, then the rifle falling away, the Jew's fists pounding on the covering.

The sled was at the ramp, moving along it.

Zimmer, his right shoulder paining him badly, gave the half-track sled full power forward.

The Jew Rubenstein clung on for a few seconds longer, then fell off, into the snow, hopefully to his death.

The half-track sled was into the run now, and before air power could come after him, he would be gone.

Despite his pain, Deitrich Zimmer smiled.

The world would be changed forever.

Twenty-one

They cornered the dozen Nazis between their own unit and a group of German Long Range Mountain Patrol personnel, the Nazis throwing down their weapons and raising their hands.

Michael Rourke, a Beretta in one hand, his M-16 in the other, walked toward the twelve, Natalia beside him.

"Ask one of them in German where's Zimmer and the baby," Michael ordered.

Natalia repeated his question, but as one of the Nazis started to answer, Otto Hammerschmidt, who had been talking to someone on his radio, interrupted. "Michael. The infant child is dead and Zimmer has escaped. Zimmer murdered the baby."

Michael Rourke turned toward Otto Hammerschmidt.

Michael blinked.

Natalia Tiemerovna began to cry, then screamed, "God damn them!"

Michael Rourke turned toward the Nazi who had been about to speak, shoved the muzzle of his rifle against the man's face.

"Please, Herr Rourke! Please—"

Michael pushed the muzzle of the rifle into the Nazi's mouth.

Tears filled Michael Rourke's eyes.

His right hand trembled.

There was a strong fecal smell, and the Nazi's eyes were so wide that they looked about to somehow fall out of their sockets.

Hammerschmidt's voice. "Michael, do what you must."

Natalia screamed, "Do it! What is the use!? Do it!"

Michael Rourke pushed the muzzle of the rifle in deeper.

The man was gagging, choking.

Michael Rourke closed his eyes.

His mother.

His father.

Now the brother he had never seen.

Michael Rourke could feel his father's voice inside his head, but he couldn't hear any words.

He took the muzzle of the M-16 from the Nazi's mouth. His voice tight, the words hard coming, Michael Rourke rasped, "Thank the God you don't believe in, you're not Deitrich Zimmer."

Twenty-two

In days and nights of tireless searching, there had been no sign of Deitrich Zimmer.

The best specialists that New Germany had to offer in the field of mortuary science had done all that could be done, and still the little child's coffin was closed, most of the head disintegrated from the hydrostatic shock and concussive force of the bullet.

Deitrich Zimmer had planned the child's murder. That was obvious, because the round he used in the German pistol was not even intended for use in a handgun, merely the same caliber and dimensions, but a tracer that was fired from small tank mounted cannons out of an overbarrel spotting rifle.

It was a marvel that the gun, badly damaged as it was, had not totally shattered when Zimmer fired it.

The cemetery was a quiet place.

The Christian minister from Lydveldid Island, who spoke in a language Michael Rourke could not understand, performed the service.

Clouds gathered on the horizon, deep gray and menacing.

His sister and Natalia on either side of him, Paul with them, Michael Rourke stared at the open grave.

The casket was so small, the grave so small.

The child had never really lived, never known a kind touch.

In halting English, the minister said, "I commit the body of John Thomas Rourke, Jr., to this earth in the hope of everlasting resurrection."

Natalia and Annie wore black civilian clothes, as did Paul and Michael. Annie wept. Visible in Natalia's eyes were the tears she was holding back.

Michael Rourke was cried out for the moment.

The casket was lowered into the ground.

"He was a little child and he's with the angels now," Paul murmured.

Because of their upbringing, Annie, when first reaching the baby, had baptized him with the water of her tears in the hope of his soul being freed to enter Heaven.

Michael supposed he would have done the same. Annie whispered now, "I baptize you in the name of the Father, and of the Son and of the Holy Spirit."

She wept loudly, her body racked with tremors as Paul folded her closely into his arms.

Michael approached the grave, took up a handful of the soil of New Germany. He threw it into the grave, over the coffin. The vault lid was ready to be lain.

He stared at the coffin of the brother he had never known. "This is the wrong place to say this, John, and the wrong time, too, I guess. I can't even promise you I'll get your murderer. But I'll promise you that you'll never be forgotten."

Annie and Paul stood beside him.

Michael was wrong, because the tears came again and very hard, harder than he had ever experienced them.

Natalia put a hand on his shoulder and another on his arm.

Michael Rourke could not promise his brother revenge, but he would try.

Part Three

A New Order

One

Akiro Kurinami's office was spartan, and thus typically Japanese. A polished rock was the only adornment on the table that was his desk. The heat within the recently completed public building worked well, and Dodd was almost warm, but the heat was slightly noisy. Kurinami said, "Sit down, Commander."

"Thank you, Mr. President." Dodd took the folding chair opposite Kurinami's desk. Like many of the furnishings of Eden, the chair was from New Germany. What didn't come from New Germany or occasionally from Mid-Wake was scavenged from the shuttles themselves or put together from the Eden Project stores. There was talk that the Russians were interested in a trade agreement with Mid-Wake, New Germany and Eden and that Kurinami himself had suggested it because of the Underground City's vast manufacturing potential.

Kurinami smiled as he spoke. "I cannot help but wonder at the odd turn of events, Commander. As much as I puzzled over why you stepped out of the election I now wonder more why you have volunteered the idea that since more of this continent is habitable than Europe, we should open ourselves to immigration from the Russian cities and the Chinese First City. It is a remarkable idea, and noble as well, but—"

Dodd made himself smile. "I felt our young nation needed unity. I did what I felt was best for Eden in stepping down. Now I feel our young nation needs strength. It's the American tradition to open our shores to all who wish to come here in peace. But you still believe that I'm some sort of enemy, don't you, an enemy of Eden?"

Kurinami laughed. "Eden. The name sticks, does it not?"

231

"Yes."

"I do not know how to feel about you, Commander. I believe that a man can have a change of heart, that a man can sacrifice private ambition for public good, no matter how strongly that ambition drives him. I was speaking with the Chairman of the First Chinese City. As an ally, as a friend, he saw your proposal as one that would serve to end divisiveness in the future, make the whole world closer to being one."

"We have vast expanses of land within what was the United States, land which can bear life, be productive. There is industry to restart, building to do. For all of that, we need people. You must believe me, Akiro," Dodd said, nodding his head, smiling, "making a new world order is my ultimate goal. I know you've said that encouraging new thinking is just what we need. Well, I took that to heart. And with the returnees from Mid-Wake planning to move here to the western regions, well, it just seemed natural that this land should become an international homeland for all of humanity. My ambitions, however you interpreted them, however personal they may have seem, were other oriented, aimed at accomplishing the goal of rebuilding our planet in the most expeditious way possible. I hope you'll come to see that someday—in fact, Mr. President—I know you will, that the goals I outlined had a purpose greater than anyone imagined.

"I'm here to say," Dodd concluded, "that you can count on me to work for a new order with all my energies."

Akiro Kurinami leaned back and smiled.

Commander Christopher Dodd just smiled.

Two

Michael Rourke swung down out of the saddle, dropped to one knee and traced the outline of the horseshoe print with his finger in the dust.

"Is it the same shoe, Michael?"

"Cast off a little with a deformed nail head. Yeah." Michael Rourke stood and stretched. He stared toward the setting sun, but averted his eyes slightly, the glare bothering him. He was stiff and tired from horsebacking through these wastelands where once there was rain forest and now there was encroaching desert.

Paul's saddle creaked and he stepped down, rubbing his backside a little. "The Germans have a plan for this place."

Michael Rourke smiled. "Yes, they have a plan for everything, God bless them. Use plasma energy to melt sections of the mountain snows and bring water back to the land so the trees they want to plant will grow."

"All I know is that I'm tired of the air everywhere being as thin as something at the top of a mountain."

"It's even thinner there," Michael agreed. When they had attacked the Nazi redoubt, part of the reason for the gas masks was that they were connected to small compressed oxygen units which bled in a richer mixture to their normal air supply. Otherwise, unused to the horribly thin air at the higher altitudes, they would have been incapable of sustained physical exertion. "Maybe their plan will work, at least to start."

Paul bent over to stare at the hoofprints on the ground. "Still six sets. Has to be Nazis, to be out here."

"Has to be," Michael agreed.

But, as he looked up, he noticed Paul Rubenstein was no longer looking at the footprints, but was looking at him. "What happens if, assuming we nail these guys, none of them knows anything about Zimmer? You know I'll go on as long as you want to, so will Annie and Natalia.

But you can't spend your whole life in pursuit of revenge. Your Mom and Dad wouldn't want you doing it. For six months now, we've been alternately going through every Nazi era record in New Germany and all the stuff that was found at their mountain hideout, then going into the field to pursue the next set of leads.

"We've killed or captured twenty-six men," Paul continued, "and not a one of them, even under drugs, has known anything about Zimmer's whereabouts. I don't think we're going to get him, Michael, even if we devote the rest of our lives to it."

Michael said nothing.

Paul went on. "Like I said, we're all with you. You think we've got a chance of getting this schmuck, fine, you'll never see me quit. But, if we don't, just spend the rest of our lives doing this, then what?"

"What do you mean?"

"There's a world out there your father and mother would be busting their butts to rebuild if they were with us. You know that. All you're doing is becoming an expert on neo-Nazis and a great hand at tracking people down, but that's not doing anything to make this place a better place. If Zimmer surfaces anywhere, he'll be arrested or shot. With Akiro running Eden, we don't even have to worry about Dodd anymore."

"I wonder. Anyway, we still owe him."

"Kill Dodd and even Akiro will say it's too much, Michael. Akiro pulled the plug on the charges against Natalia and the rest of us. Sure, I'd like to twist Dodd's head off and crap down his neck, and if you say we should do it, I'm with you, just like Annie and Natalia are with you. All I'm saying is that maybe there are some better things we should be doing, things John and Sarah would have wanted us to do. Like, whatever happened to you pursuing a medical education?"

"So I can find out my father's and mother's conditions are hopeless? I already know that, Paul. Anyway, every time I'm in New Germany, almost invariably I bump into Maria. With her marrying, it's even more awkward than before."

"How about Mid-Wake?"

Michael Rourke shook his head. "No. I could give you a bunch of reasons why I don't want to live there, but in the final analysis, they're all an excuse. I want to see the world, see what's out there that we've missed. Being a doctor worked for Dad, but I can't save lives with one hand and take lives with the other. I could never be the doctor he—"

There was a silence. He'd almost said 'was'.

Paul broke the silence, saying, "You can do anything you set your mind to, Michael—"

Michael Rourke laughed, telling his friend, "Look, you may have been born a couple of decades before I was, but chronologically, I'm older than you are. And I'm not your seventeen-year-old nephew or something, who just decided to get a tattoo and drop out of high school."

Paul grinned, shook his head, said, "Touché, Michael."

"The point is, I know what I don't want to do. At least that's a start." And Michael looked along the trail, the hoofprints vanishing in the distance over the rise "And I know we probably won't find Zimmer, Paul. And sometimes I wonder what I'd do if I did. Mom and Dad never taught me to commit murder, but God, I'd never forgive myself if I didn't kill the bastard. How he could do that, murder a baby—Jesus, I'm—" Michael balled his fists, inhaled to keep the tears from coming, because sometimes they still did.

"If we find him, we'll kill him, and we both know that, whether it's murder or not, who cares? It can't be a moral consideration to kill a man like Zimmer. But if we don't find him, yet spend our entire lives looking for him, maybe we'll be giving him another kill to his credit, hmm?"

Michael Rourke rolled the reins of his horse between his hands, looked then at Paul. A man Michael Rourke had never heard of, before the attack on the hospital, was responsible for the near death state in which his father and mother now existed, would perhaps exist forever. And the murder of their child.

"A little longer?"

Paul just shook his head. "Yeah, we'll look a little longer. But, I tell you, if we're still saying this years from now, well—I don't know."

Michael Rourke caught the horn and swung up into his saddle Indian fashion.

Paul mounted more deliberately.

Then they both continued along the trail.

Three

The desert was gone and it was night and he was inside a house. He recognized it. It was the sprawling farm house they had lived in before The Night of The War.

But, it wasn't then, before The Night of The War, because at the dinner table, along with Sarah, there was a grown up Annie, a grown up Michael, and Natalia and Paul were there, too.

On either side of his empty dinner plate were his guns.

Sarah said to him, "Have you seen the baby, John?"

"No, I haven't."

She just smiled. When he looked down, his plate was no longer empty. John Rourke looked more closely at the plate, because what was there was not food, but the United States.

It looked like the outline of the North American continent as it would be seen from space, and there were lights twinkling everywhere and, as he looked more closely and started to mention what he saw to the others at the table, all around him there was blackness, except for the outline of North America in the distance.

And the lights.

But the lights were different now, growing in intensity. As he stared, the lights were flashes, mushroom shaped clouds erupting everywhere, brilliantly bright, more and more of them, their light obscuring the shape of the continent, one flash after another after another after another and John Rourke looked around him.

He was sitting in an airplane.

The airplane rocked, lurched, seemed almost to twist.

A woman screamed.

John Rourke knew what was happening.

It was The Night of the War and he was condemned to relive it.

Four

The city, of more than two thousand people, had grown up almost overnight; or, more accurately over sixty nights or so. Four months ago, there had been nothing but desert where the Amazonian city of Manaus had once been, a wasteland where alternately hot and cold sandy winds blew and nothing of great consequence besides insects and rats lived. Like all of northern and central Brazil, when the fires came which burned the sky in the Great Conflagration, the rain forest had been wiped out, and with it the moisture.

The Amazon and its major tributaries, like the Negro, still flowed, to be sure, but they were not rivers that were the arteries of a once thriving nation, not highways through the greatest green area on the face of the earth, merely water. There were fish, mostly bottom dwellers, but fewer species because the sun beat down without mercy in the daylight hours, since nothing grew here. At night was the cold. No life along the river, only eroded deserts too vast to contemplate.

Many tributaries no longer flowed, and it was part of the German plan for re-greening the Amazon and eventually re-oxygenating the atmosphere to free water frozen in mountain ice for irrigation of the high mountain deserts.

And what once had been Manaus on the River Negro, in north central Brazil, was now the boomtown for the new ecology.

The figure she was following, Armand Gruber, was a nonentity of a man, really, but for now he was the most important man in the world to her.

He turned into the little pub-like bar that was packed with mustered-out German soldiers working in the bio-project, some Chinese engineers and a few people who looked like they could be Americans from Mid-Wake. There was talk that soon there would be Russians here, and she did not long for their presence because when Natalia Anastasia Tiemerovna wanted to hear her native tongue that badly, she could always talk to herself.

Natalia glanced at her mirror image in the shop window and primped her light brown hair and adjusted her glasses. Then she looked back down the street. This was the bad area of Opentown, as the name of the new Manaus translated into English. The jobs as police/security for the city paid little compared to the hard labor or the tech jobs, so law enforcement personnel were hard to find and there wasn't enough lawlessness (openly) to bring in the army. Built of pre-fab units, with streets wide enough to easily handle four lanes of construction traffic if needed, the bad section of Opentown was the only place where the people who worked in the new industry which had arisen here, could come to unwind. Annie followed Gruber into the bar the previous night and got away with just a few black and blue marks from pinches on her posterior.

From Natalia's vantage point beside the shop window—cheap knives, cheap binoculars, cheap canteens, cheap everything (made in Russia) filled the display—she could see through the window constantly and the door of the bar every time the door was opened.

Annie had told her, "We should go back tonight together."

"Remember, you are a married woman. Your rear end is spoken for. On the other, I'm not and mine isn't. Anyway, Gruber might have noticed you."

There was nothing more said of the subject.

At New Germany, Natalia and Annie, waiting for Michael and Paul to return from their latest field trackdown, became privy to intelligence data concerning a new Nazi cell in Opentown. There were already agents of the government of New Germany working to infiltrate the cell, but their success potential was dubious. And, although Paul and Michael would have preferred to pursue the lead themselves, she was sure, there was much to be said for two women being vastly more able to dig out information in a wild boomtown, where men outnumbered women more than seven to one.

A trip for the right clothes (Annie was pathological about shopping) and some rinsable hair dye and they were on their way, both of them taking office jobs with the bio-industry, Annie as a bio-consultant from Mid-Wake and Natalia as a German national in environmental engineering. With her knowledge of computers and the fact that she had always been a quick study, she was able to fake being a specialist rather well.

Armand Gruber, after a week of observation, somehow seemed just right and the bar—brazenly called the Lightning Bolt—was a rumored hangout for neo-Nazi sympathizers. Because New Germany was a free society, thinking like a Nazi was not a crime.

Acting like a Nazi was, however, another story.

The sounds of her high heels clicking on the pavement died the nearer she came to the bar, the sounds from inside growing louder.

She opened the door and went inside . . .

Michael Rourke ran his hand over his face. Stubble so old it was almost a beard. But, water here was scarce, and shaving dry was something he had no desire to try.

There was slight movement in the darkness to his left and the Beretta that rested on his thigh was in his hand and pointed toward the origin of the sound. But, as he'd anticipated, it was Paul returning. His friend and brother-in-law dropped to the ground beside him, exhaling softly as he whispered. "We got 'em, all six of 'em. Gotta be the same guys we've been tracking for the last ten days or so. I mean, no Nazi armbands or anything, but they all look pretty well dressed, all things considered, and they're heavily armed."

"The thing I can't figure is what the hell they're doing riding around out here all this time."

"Beats me," Paul answered, Michael barely able to make out a shrug of the shoulders in the darkness. "Unless they wanted us to follow them."

"That's crossed my mind, too. But I figured if they were some kind of hit team—"

"You watched too many videotaped movies when you were a kid."

Michael grinned, saying, "I had pretty much nothing else to do for about a decade and half. But, if they are a hit team, it could be Zimmer who set them up. So maybe we'll get lucky."

"A lot of times, you remind me of your Dad so much it's scary, but then sometimes you don't, and maybe that's scarier," Paul whispered.

Michael Rourke shrugged his eyebrows and picked up his rifle. The sling and swivels were taped to prevent extraneous noise. If the six men they followed were a hit team suckering them into a trap, there was no sense making it easier for them to do their work . . .

Natalia eased up on her toes and slipped onto a bar stool, letting her dress ride up just a little to show some thigh. 'Golden Oldies' from Mid-Wake were the musical rage of New Germany, and here especially, it seemed. Over the sound system, as she'd entered, one of the Beach Boys' signature tunes was just ending and the Beatles' "You're Gonna Lose That Girl" began. By the time one of the three bartenders noticed her, Elvis was singing.

"Yes, Fraulein?"

"Vodka and tonic, please."

"Good. I get tired of women ordering things that ruin their plumbing and bar's, too." And he was gone, leaving her to wonder just what some of the women ordered.

Men were everywhere, some dressed in the trendy suits of New Germany which looked like 'sixties Nehru jackets, some in work clothes (coveralls) and some few in casual clothes. And there were a disproportionate number of women here, considering the sexual demographics of Opentown, some of them in obvious working clothes, too.

Under Nazism, prostitution had flourished no less than under other forms of government, merely keeping itself well below the surface to avoid direct conflict with the law. In Opentown, as it had been for centuries everywhere, prostitution was illegal, but Natalia had noticed no one seemed to care.

Lights, again very 'sixtiesish, flickered across the dancefloor while the dancing itself was more reminiscent of the Latin dance forms which had enjoyed some vogue before The Night of The War, men and women all but copulating in time to the music.

The song had changed, the Doors doing "Light My Fire," and just as if the song were a cue, a man took the bar stool next to Natalia and asked, "Buy ya' a drink, lady?"

He spoke English, obviously from Mid-Wake. She mentally shrugged and acknowledged she understood. "I already have a drink coming." As if on cue, as well, the bartender brought her drink and set it down beside her right hand. "See?" Natalia smiled.

"Name's Bob Jessup, ma'am."

He was long legged and had a face that looked like he'd seen a few fistfights in his life and blue eyes that smiled like a boy's.

"I'm Heidi Frobe." He offered his hand and she took it briefly. His flesh was warm and dry. "Are you an American?"

"Mid-Wake Marine until peace broke out, ma' am. You German?"

"Yes. Do you work with the bio-team?"

"Diver. I go skinny-dippin' in the river every day. Used to do the same thing with a gun back in the Corps. Same difference only the pay's better and the food tastes like shit."

She laughed in spite of herself.

"Whatchya do?"

"Here?"

"No, I mean, well, regular. Cinch you ain't one of the workin' girls."

Natalia took it as a compliment that Bob Jessup didn't see her as a prostitute. "I work in engineering, with computers. I agree, the money is very good, but the food is terrible, I think."

He was so American and it would have been so easy for her to drop into his accent, but she kept the German intonation and inflection to her English.

"Wanna dance?"

"I just met you."

"I have a dangerous job. There might not be a tomorrow night, lady."

She liked his style and she hadn't danced in a place like this in five hundred years. "All right," she told him, smiling. And, Gruber was on the dance floor and she'd be able to keep a better eye on him there . . .

Michael Rourke moved ahead on knees and elbows, his rifle in both fists at eye level, the crackling of the camp fire, the sounds of insects and birds and the soft hiss of the wind, the only noises.

He kept moving.

Their horses were tethered and hobbled almost a half mile away so a stray noise would not betray their presence to the enemy personnel.

Paul would be coming up on the far side the camp.

As Michael crawled forward, he stopped, beneath a piece of half dead scrub brush able to see the camp clearly. The fire burned too brightly. Aside from the fact it was a natural attention getter, something six men on the run would try to avoid, even this far from what civilization there was, the fire was also a waste of wood. The nights were cool, but not cold unless the winds blew right and wood for burning was hard to find, the area so arid.

A trap for him and Paul almost certainly.

But Michael Rourke had planned ahead. Four things he took off his father's body, to hold for his father, and use if he had to. His father's watch, the little A.G. Russell Sting IA Black Chrome, the Smith & Wesson Model 640 Centennial revolver and the old battered Zippo windlighter with which his father had always lit cigars.

His father's other equipment, along with his mother's gun, was confiscated by Dodd. Kurinami, after his election to serve four years as President of Eden, had ordered the return of the items and Dodd complied. They were now stored at the Retreat.

The Rolex watch was in storage at Mid-Wake for his father to redon if—when, Michael told himself—his father some day awoke from this new Sleep. The lighter he—Michael—carried as a memento. And the gun and the knife he carried in the event that he did find Deitrich Zimmer, to use them, if possible, to end Zimmer's miserable life.

Michael could see all six men, or what appeared to be six men, at least, sleeping bags filled with man shapes just close enough to the fire to be seen but not close enough to be seen distinctly.

He moved on, over the rough ground and toward his pre-selected position.

There were no trip wires, no alarms of even the most primitive type set as a perimeter alert system. This worried Michael Rourke still more.

He kept moving . . .

Natalia Tiemerovna, despite herself, was having a good time. Bob Jessup was a good dancer, his arms strong around her but he never once attempted to touch her in a way that was less than gentlemanly. And she could watch Armand Gruber, who had left the dance floor and sat deep in conversation at a small corner table with a woman of about thirty, the woman's clothes and manner in sharp contrast. She was dressed cheaply, but carried herself beautifully.

"Heidi?"

"Yes?"

"Old line, least at Mid-Wake, but what's a nice girl like you doing in a place like this?"

Natalia laughed. "You are right; it is an old expression. In answer to the question, though, I am actually a spy and I followed a very desperate character here."

"Right," he laughed.

Natalia smiled up at him.

"So, don't tell me," he said.

"Well, Opentown is very boring. All I do is sit around at a computer terminal all day long. Tell me about your job. It sounds very exciting," she said.

The song switched to a fast number and he started her back toward the bar. Her drink was still there, but she wasn't about to touch it after it had been left unattended. Bob Jessup signalled the bartender and Natalia asked Jessup, "Could you get me a glass of water?"

"Sure. I don't drink a lot myself. Couldn't when I was on duty and I never figured it made much sense to blow a weekend pass spending every dime I had for the first couple of hours, then throwing up the rest of the time, if you'll pardon my French."

She laughed, at him, at the expression—she hadn't heard it in years—and how thoroughly stupid a situation this was. What was she going to do when Armand Gruber decided to leave?

Her water arrived and Jessup had a beer. He raised his glass, saying, "To pretty German girls."

"To handsome American men," she nodded. They clinked glasses. "Is it very dangerous diving all the time?"

"Ever try it?"

She giggled. "Oh, no—I would be afraid to try."

"I'll take you, if you want."

"Oh—that would be nice, but I do not know." Armand Gruber and the woman—she was blonde and wore a tight black vinyl skirt and low cut black top—got up, starting toward the back where there were several doors.

"Whatchya lookin' at?"

"Looking at?"

243

"The little guy and the bleached blonde hooker. They interest you?"

Natalia looked at Bob Jessup, for once flat-footed and without a ready answer. So she said nothing, but still watched Armand Gruber and the 'bleached blonde hooker'. Natalia took her purse from the bar and clutched it in her lap. The Walther PPK/S was inside it, and so was the suppressor, but the bag wasn't long enough to accommodate gun and silencer assembled. Jessup just stared at her. She stared back.

"So, maybe you are a spy."

"I have to leave, Bob. Thanks for the dance."

He put his right hand on her left arm and Natalia's right hand moved to rest between her knees so she pushed up her dress and get to the Bali-Song knife strapped to the inside of her left thigh.

"If there's somethin' wrong, Heidi, maybe I can help," he told her.

The possibilities were limited: start a scene and attract Gruber's attention or take Bob Jessup along. She could always dump him later. "All right, but do exactly what I say. Come with me," she told him, slipping off the bar stool and smoothing down the straight skirt of her dress.

"Yes, ma'am," Bob grinned . . .

Michael Rourke plotted every conceivable spot for a trap, but when one of the six sleepers by the fire, turned out to be in the rocks to his left and whispered in awkwardly accented but syntactually correct English, "Do not move, Herr Rourke," Michael Rourke wasn't at all surprised. He froze.

"Now, drop the rifle in front of you."

He let the rifle fall from his fingers.

The route Paul would be taking into the camp was more involved, so they wouldn't have Paul yet, hence the man who had the drop on him still whispering.

Michael Rourke started to his feet, the Nazi starting to order him not to. But Michael stood anyway. The two Berettas in the shoulder holster he wore would take care of most close range situations if he could get to them. But, as his father had always insisted, Michael Rourke planned ahead.

He raised his hands, clasping his hands behind his head. "You've got me. Why don't you shoot and get it over with?"

"You will die soon enough, Herr Rourke."

Michael nodded, but didn't think so. The sleeves of his black German field jacket were wide, to accommodate the liner and heavy clothing beneath when weather demanded. Tonight, Michael Rourke wore no liner nor anything heavier than a black knit shirt beneath the jacket. Strapped in a skeletonized holster to the inside of his right forearm was his father's little Smith & Wesson revolver.

Michael, hands behind his head, had the revolver gripped in his left hand.

There was movement and the man with the drop on him emerged from the rocks. "I had expected more from a Rourke."

"Well, always tough following in your father's footsteps," Michael smiled. "Why are we whispering?"

"Because, it—"

"Ohh, so if I made some noise, your guys out there wouldn't be able to spring a trap on my friend."

"The Jew," the man snarled, spitting into the ground.

"Hey, lighten up. I mean, Paul's the only Jew I know well but he's like my brother. I met a couple of Jews at Mid-Wake. They seemed okay, too. Ever think you and your Nazi buddies got this all wrong?"

The man took a step forward, which was the best Michael Rourke could hope for.

Michael dodged left and dropped to one knee as he stabbed the little stainless steel .38 Special out at shoulder height and shot the man in the throat and forehead with a double tap.

The shots still echoed in the night as Michael reached to the dirt and caught up his rifle in his right hand. There was no need to shout to Paul, because they had planned for the contingency of unexpected shots.

Gunfire tore into the ground near Michael's feet and the rocks behind him, as he threw himself right and into the darkness behind some low rocks and scrub brush. His M-16 spoke in a long burst, but he was moving again before the answering fire could zero in on his muzzle flashes.

Five

The doorway through which Armand Gruber and the blonde woman in the black vinyl had disappeared, led to the outside. Bob Jessup seemed like a nice guy and, for some reason she didn't quite understand herself; Natalia liked him. She dropped the German accent from her English as she opened her purse. "Look, you might get yourself killed, Bob. Stay here. This is Nazi stuff."

"Nazis?"

She nodded her head.

He shrugged his shoulders. "You got a gun, huh?"

Natalia nodded again.

In the marginal lighting, there at the end of the corridor, she could see Bob Jessup smile when he said, "Me, too. I wasn't a Marine for nothin', lady. Hey—your name really Heidi?"

"What do you think?" Amateurs could get a person killed, but there wasn't the time for anything else, even an answer. Her hand on her gun, but the Walther still inside her bag, her left hand went to the doorhandle. "Ladies first," she told Bob Jessup as she pushed past him.

As she passed through the doorway, the Walther came out of her bag and down along her right thigh. With a straight skirt and no pockets, there was no better way to hide it.

Beyond the doorway was an alley, dirt only, no pavement. Trash compactors were ranked along its length in both directions. Humankind hadn't changed that much in five centuries, Natalia reflected.

There was an electric car with a badly damaged right rear

fender parked at the end of the alley and she saw it just in time to see a flash of blonde hair. As the passenger door closed, the car already starting to drive off.

She almost said a dirty word.

Bob Jessup said, "Wanna follow it?"

"You have an electric car?"

"Better, unless you were serious back there about being scared of things."

She didn't follow him and told him so.

"Hey, we got it knocked. Come on." And Jessup started running toward the alley's mouth.

Shaking her head, stuffing her gun back into her bag, Natalia ran after him . . .

There were three men near the fire, and Michael's gunfire toward their unprotected position, took two of them out, almost instantly. Gunfire from the opposite side of the fire—it had to be Paul—took out the third one.

"Hey, Michael!"

"Should be two more, Paul. I got one over here."

"One more. I got a guy with my knife."

Michael Rourke shifted position, slowly, carefully. The sixth man could have been two hundred yards away or more and had one of them under a starlight scope. Which gave Michael Rourke an idea. He shouted to Paul. "How do you think some eggs would go right now?"

"Egg" was a slang term he'd picked up from his father for flash-bangs, sound and light grenades. Through a starlight scope, the flash of a sound and light grenade would be as blinding as the flash of a nuclear weapon. He remembered the Night of The War, when the flashes from the bombs which destroyed Atlanta were like sunrises.

If Paul caught his drift—

"We could get killed." Paul caught it, apparently.

"Not we, me. Don't worry."

"Worrying's part of my ethnicity. You say when."

Michael Rourke studied the terrain surrounding them. Flat,

ideal for a sniper in almost any direction, but if the guy were really good—and this had to be a hit team—he'd take the best spot not only for a shot but also for a getaway in case things went wrong.

That meant the sniper was to the north, where there was a narrow pass that a well-thrown explosive device could block, if the need arose.

Michael Rourke put on his ear protection, then the glasses which, in darkness like this, made him almost blind. He kept his gaze trained on the fire, which through the protective glasses merely looked like a dull glow.

Taking up his rifle, Michael came from cover, starting toward the fire as if to examine the bodies of the three dead men there.

There was no timing this thing. If he waited too long, he'd be dead. When he was halfway to the fire, which should be just the perfect mixture of light and dark for the sniper's starlight scope, Michael Rourke shouted, "Now, Paul!"

In the same instant as the first grenade hit, there was a shot, catching Michael Rourke across the left kidney as he threw himself down at a tangent to what he anticipated—correctly—was the sniper's line of fire.

Michael Rourke squinted his eyes tight, the light flashes still visible through his eyelids despite the protective eyewear. His hands were cupped over his ears, but still the high pitched whistling made his ears ring and vibrate.

And he was in terrible pain . . .

Opentown wasn't large in area, high rise prefabs—four stories high—serving as housing and consuming several grid squares of the city, the recreation area where the bar was the only part which stretched out seemingly aimlessly into the wasteland. The factories and offices which supported the bio-project were on the opposite side of the housing area.

After a run to the end of the alley, across one of the ultra-wide streets and up along it for another fifty yards, Jessup turned a corner and stopped in front of Opentown's sole private gymnasium. He started inside. "What the hell are you doing?" Natalia called after him.

"Too many crooks. This is where I park my wheels."

He went through the door. Natalia, her gun back in her purse, pushed a lock of hair back from her forehead and followed him.

"You can sweat in here, pump real iron," Jessup said over his shoulder.

She was the only woman in a room full of men, all of them close to naked—gym shorts and athletic shirts—and their bodies dripping sweat. It wasn't climate controlled, large fans turning lazily overhead, just moving air, not freshening it.

What used to be wolf whistles came toward her and she was about to step back through the door onto the street, when she saw Jessup disappear behind a curtain. Then she heard a sound, familiar, yet not.

The curtain was pushed away and Jessup straddled out a motorcycle which looked hauntingly similar to the ones that the German forces sometimes used. "I love this thing," Jessup called to her.

But evidently the men in the gymnasium did not. "The damn synth-fuel stinks, Bob, damnit," another American voice called out. It belonged to a man doing inclined bench presses, his biceps and triceps so large they almost looked more than human.

Jessup rolled the machine slowly past her, stopped, looked at her and smiled, saying, "Wanna get the door, lady?"

Natalia got the door, stepped out onto the pre-fab synth-concrete sidewalk, letting the gymnasium and its smell of sweat fade from her consciousness. "Where did you get—"

"German guy, works in hydroponics. Wanted me to teach him diving. We kinda worked a trade. He says it's surplus. Ever ride one of these things?"

Natalia pulled three pins from her hair and shook it loose, put her hands down along her thighs and tugged her dress up almost to her hips as she straddled the machine behind him. "Yes."

"Fine. Electric car, it can't go too far into the wasteland, and it can't match this for speed. We go in a likely direction, and if we don't see the car, just circle the city until we do."

"It could be in the city, too. Let's go.

"This thing's damn fast, ma'am. You're gonna have to hold on tight." Jessup looked at her and smiled.

Natalia shook her head and laughed. "I suppose you are right, Bob." She put her arms around his stomach and held him. "Tight enough?"

"Ma'am, if you held onto me any tighter I might just start thinkin' about forgettin' about that electric car and your Nazis and ask you up to my room. Hang on, now!"

The motorcycle jumped the curb and was into the dirt street with a roar . . .

It was a deep crease in the fatty area behind the rib cage and, aside from bleeding a lot and hurting even more, didn't appear serious to him. Holding his side, he ran as best he could, in the direction of the rifle shot, relying on the sniper's temporary blindness to be total.

Paul, unharmed and starting out well north of the fire anyway, was ahead of him.

And he heard Paul shout, "I got him! Michael!"

Michael Rourke stopped trying to run and just stood there in the darkness, hurting. And he called back to Paul Rubenstein, "Keep him for me!" With considerable effort, he forced himself to walk.

Six

A circuit around the city showed no sign of the electric car with the damaged right rear fender, so they turned back in toward Opentown, toward the pre-fab housing units. Bob Jessup was a decent motorcycle rider, especially good considering he had to be a beginner. He took his turns very cautiously, which she considered a tribute to his good sense. Rather than trying to impress her with his daring, he was trying to get them to their destination, wherever that turned out to be, alive and uninjured.

The glasses she wore helped her eyes against the dust—they were coated with it—but her hair felt gritty and knotted as they turned into the housing area.

One of the units was reserved for office personnel and visiting military and civilian VIPs, the other units for the workers. And there was crime here, like there was on the recreation strip. Aside from the fact that the buildings were vastly shorter and she was five hundred years removed from the Twentieth Century, she was reminded of her one and only visit to an inner city Federal Housing Project. That was in Chicago, a few years before the Night of The War, and Vladmir had been negotiating with a Chicago street gang to precipitate summer rioting.

There was never a deal struck, the following summer going by peacefully in the city.

But she remembered the look of the place still, like a jungle with wild things preying on the inhabitants and the visitors equally.

It was that same look, that same feel here.

Bob Jessup stopped the motorcycle as they turned the corner of a dirt street.

Evidently, he saw the electric car with the damaged fender at the same time she did . . .

Michael Rourke sat on a rock, twisting the sling of his rifle in his hands as Paul cleaned the wound near his left kidney. "You are lucky, very lucky."

All skill; I practice dodging bullets for a half hour each day."

"Yeah, right," Paul laughed.

The sniper, bound hand and foot with plastic restraints, writhed on the ground, groaning.

"After I came up on him and realized he wasn't kidding, I put the restraints on him and put some salve on his eyes. Had to sit on him to do it, though. He must've thought I was trying to torture him or something. Asshole. There." And Paul stepped away.

Michael Rourke touched gingerly at his back, a large bandage in place and the smell of the German antiseptic/healant spray still heavy on the air. Michael started to stand, then thought better of it, pain and stiffness gripping his back when he tried to move, even a little. "Tell him who we are so he knows for sure we're going to kill him if he doesn't talk. At the distance, his hearing didn't get affected."

Paul looked at Michael in the light of the lantern, then nodded.

Paul dropped to one knee beside the sniper, grabbing a handful of the man's jacket front, telling him, "You know who we are; that's why you and your friends led us around, to try and kill us. If you know who we are, you know we'll kill you if you don't co-operate."

The sniper, a Nazi, simply managed to say the word, "Jew" and tried to spit at Paul, but Paul backhanded him across the face before he could. Paul looked over his shoulder, exchanged glances with Michael, then looked down at the sniper. "Yes,

I'm a Jew. And if you don't understand enough English to understand what I'm about to say, you're shit out of luck. If you know all about Nazis and Jews, you probably heard that your kind, five centuries ago, were blamed for killing six million of us. You were told that was a lie, that the photographs of the dead were from the bombings of Dresden. They weren't.

"Now," Paul almost hissed, "you may not believe that your kind killed six million of my kind, but I believe it and that's all that matters because I've got a gun and you don't. Aside from the fact you tried killing my brother-in-law and me, aside from the fact that your boss maybe killed my wife's parents, aside from the fact that your boss murdered an infant, aside from the six million dead Jews you fuckin' Nazis racked up five centuries ago, I just don't like your face.

"And, if you don't talk, tell us where Zimmer is," Paul went on, his voice more an animal-sounding snarl, "I'm going to shoot your balls off one at a time. Understand balls, Nazi? Testicles?" Paul looked at Michael and winked.

Michael Rourke looked away so he wouldn't laugh.

He heard the sound of Paul's Browning High Power being drawn and the hammer being cocked back, heard Paul say, "That's the sound of my gun. Wanna hear another sound?"

Then Michael heard the sniper say, "I will tell you, please. Please!"

Seven

"You said you had a gun."

"Yeah." Bob Jessup reached down to his left trouser leg and pulled something that looked like a chopped down version of the Mid-Wake issue Lancer 2418 A-2. "Got a friend makes these. A lot of Marines carried 'em for backup."

"Umm," Natalia nodded, stepping away from the bike, aware of his eyes on her. "What are you staring at?"

"Your legs, ma'am. God, they're the longest things I've ever seen." Her dress was still bunched up, but as she walked it would settle and to move to do something with it now would only be provocative. "Heidi your real name?"

"I'm Natalia Tiemerovna."

"You? Holy shit! I saw you once, but your hair—"

"It's dye that washes out." She took off the fake glasses and dropped them in her purse, taking out the Walther and its suppressor, then threading the suppressor onto the PPK/S's extended barrel.

"You really on the trail of some Nazis?"

"One in particular, and this man we're following might lead me to him. The man we're following is named Armand Gruber. The man I am after is Deitrich Zimmer, the man responsible for what happened to John and Sarah Rourke and the murder of their baby."

"We gonna kill 'im?"

Natalia turned and looked at Bob Jessup as she gave the suppressor a good luck twist. "When I find him. But understand this, that I will kill Zimmer. I am the only one who should."

"Why do you say that?"

Natalia ran her free hand back through her hair, feeling the grit and dirt, but tellling herself she would wash it soon. "If you know who I am, then you know why. We want to see who Gruber is talking with, and what is going on. You wait for me to tell you what to do or you wait here, understand?"

"You're a Major, right?"

"I was, yes."

"Well, ma am, I was a sergeant. So, I guess I'm used to takin' some orders. But one thing."

Natalia was studying the building in front of which the electric car with the dented fender occupied a space in the parking lot. She was only half-paying-attention. But she heard him and said, "What one thing?"

"You're a woman and I'm a man—" She started to groan, but instead of what he could have said, he said something that was almost sweet. "If there's trouble, anyway, don't go tellin' me to stand back or anythin', because Major or not, Bob Jessup doesn't let a woman take a bullet for him, see."

She looked at him, smiled, said, "All right, Bob Jessup."

They started walking across the parking lot, toward the main entrance to the pre-fab housing unit She ran the numbers in her head. Four floors, fifty apartments to a floor, it would be impossible to knock on every door with any hope of finding who Gruber had come to meet.

But there were only four stairwells, one at each corner of the building, and no elevators. From the center of the corridor, someone could watch all four stairwells (not easily, but satisfactorily, if the floor plans were like those used in the building where she stayed with Annie) and keep watch on the parking lot outside.

"Here is the plan, Bob. I will take the top floor. You take the second floor. If you see someone coming out into the parking lot and getting into the car—"

"The little guy and the hooker with the blonde hair?"

255

"Probably, but possibly just the 'little guy'. Anyway, if you see him but he didn't pass you we know he spoke with some-one in an apartment on the first floor. If you see him coming down toward the second floor and I didn't see him, we will know his meeting was on the third floor. You understand?"

"So, we let him go and go after whoever it was he met?"

"That is the idea. Fifty apartments on each floor, that still will not be easy."

"Twenty-five apiece," he grinned.

They had parked beside a fence and near one of the large electric trams which took men to the bio-project, so there was little chance they had been seen from one of the upper floor windows. "I will go in first," she said, setting down her gun, pulling her hair back and putting it up quickly in a little bun. "Follow me after five minutes or so. Keep your gun handy, but we cannot kill Gruber, just in case this leads us nowhere. Do you understand?"

"Any chance my buyin' you dinner?"

Natalia looked down at her shoes and her ruined stockings and then up into his face. She laughed, telling him, "If this helps me to kill Deitrich Zimmer, Bob Jessup, I will buy din-ner for you. And that's a promise."

Eight

The man had evidently been faking his discomfort, but when Michael Rourke moved his father's Zippo lighter back and forth a few feet from the man's eyes, the pupils did not track the flame. Temporarily at least, the man who, with his five associates, would have killed them was, indeed, blind.

Paul and Michael exchanged glances. Then Michael asked the question that had been eating away inside of him. "Were you part of the attack on the hospital? Tell us everything."

"I had nothing to do with the attack on your family, Herr Rourke. Believe me. I was hired by Herr Doctor Zimmer to get you to follow us here and kill you. That is all!"

"What's Zimmer planning and where is he?" Paul insisted. The man cleared his throat. After a long pause, he said, "You must promise me that you will protect me from Zimmer. You must promise me—"

"If you help us, we'll help you. What if we brought you back to New Germany and got your eyes fixed and made a big deal out of how you told us everything you could about Zimmer and his movement, hmm? What do you think Zimmer would do to you then? What's your name, anyway?"

"Decker, Horst Decker."

"All right, Decker. Stop wasting everybody's time. What's it gonna be?" Michael asked.

"Yes, yes, all right. But you must—"

"We'll see you get protection," Paul told him.

In the light from the lamp, as Michael moved it closer, he could see the man's face, sweat dripping down it despite the cool wind here. This was sheer terror, plain and simple.

"Herr Doctor Zimmer was leaving for the place called Eden." Michael Rourke swallowed hard. So did the Nazi. "One of the Herr Doctor's lieutenants talks a great deal when he drinks. Herr Doctor Zimmer was going there. But that is all I know, Sirs."

"Eden," Paul said slowly. "The perfect name, and the perfect place for a snake."

Michael Rourke only nodded, his wound hurting . . .

The whole evening was turning into an incident out of some piece of lurid hardboiled detective fiction, and ruefully Natalia realized she was the babe. When she heard the shot, she drew her gun from her purse and started running across the parking area and toward the front door of the four-story building. The shot was very light, from a medium caliber pistol, but very close.

She looked back once. Bob Jessup was mounting his motorcycle, not coming after her. "The hell with him," Natalia said under her breath, the sound of his motorcycle rising behind her.

She saw the blonde with the tight black vinyl skirt.

Where was Armand Gruber?

The woman was running from the foyer, into the dirt parking lot. Natalia shouted to her in German, "Stop where you are!"

The woman shrieked back, "They want to kill me!" And she kept running.

There was a blur of motion and Natalia dodged right, Jessup's motorcycle rocketing past her. Bob Jessup shouted, "You get her! I'm goin' in, lady!" And he cut the fork of the bike toward the entrance to the building. There were steps, to elevate the first floor, because of the problem in Opentown with roaches, rats and other vermin that followed human habitation.

Jessup jumped his machine and took it over the steps, getting the machine up on its rear wheel and using the machine like a battering ram to punch through the door; the door crashing down and part of the frame with it.

And he was gone from view.

The blonde in the tight skirt was running through the parking lot, but not toward the battered electric car, not toward anything, it seemed, just away.

Natalia stood on one foot, catching at her right shoe, then took off her left one, stuffing both shoes into her purse as she ran after the woman in earnest. "Stop. I will not hurt you!"

But the woman kept running.

Life as a prostitute, which Natalia was more and more convinced the woman was, evidently didn't breed physical fitness. The woman was slowing down, running clumsily. Natalia starting to overtake her.

There was gunfire from inside the building, but Natalia was committed to this now, chasing down the woman.

Natalia, her pistol in her right hand, closed the gap. The woman, as if on cue in some American monster movie, fell, sprawling into the dirt, and struggled to get up.

Natalia shouted, "Damn'!" as she jumped, catching the woman at the shoulders and knocking her down again. Natalia rolled past her, came up on her knees, pointing the gun at her. "Stay where you are!"

But the woman started running again, evidently more afraid of what she'd seen inside the domicilary unit, than anything another woman could do to her.

Natalia was up, running, overtaking the woman in a half dozen strides, grabbing at her. The woman shook her off, but Natalia grabbed for her again, hauling her off balance and knocking her to the dirt. Natalia dropped on her, Natalia's right knee into her abdomen, knocking the wind out of her. And now Natalia straddled her chest, the muzzle of the suppressor against the tip of the woman's nose. "What do you run from?! Answer me!"

"They killed him."

"Who was killed? The man in the bar?"

"Yes. Let me go!"

"Who killed him? Tell me, or so help me I will take you back inside."

"No! Three men. Nazis, I think."

"Why?"

"I do not—"

"Why?" Natalia screamed.

"He was selling information to them and they killed him." Natalia stood up, her dress torn at the skirt up the side-seam. She looked at the prostitute. "Get out of here or wait until the police come. Someone will have reported the shots. Your choice." And Natalia turned away from her and started running back toward the building . . .

The motorcycle was beside the base of the stairs leading toward the second floor and above. Natalia dropped her shoes to the floor, stepping in them, the bottoms of her stockings ripped through. As she started up the stairs, she heard two things almost simultaneously: the sound of a police siren in the distance and the sound of a pistol shot. Natalia ran up the the stairs, trying to pinpoint the sound, passing the second floor, reaching the third floor and noticing a partially open door midway along the length of the corridor.

She ran toward it, her purse slung cross body and back so it wouldn't get in the way, both hands gripped on the butt of the suppressor-fitted Walther. She slowed as she neared the doorway, moving along the wall now, listening.

She heard voices. One of them sounded like Jessup's voice, but there was something wrong with it. She licked her lips, her lipstick gone and her mouth dry. She took a short breath and turned into the doorway.

Bob Jessup was on the living room floor, a gun a few inches from his extended fingers, blood on his hand and covering the front of his shirt. Two men lay on the floor at the other side of the living room, one of them a stranger, the other Armand Gruber. And a third man, evidently one of the Nazis, stood over Bob Jessup, a pistol in his hand, his body weaving slightly as he aimed the pistol toward Bob Jessup's head and said in German, "You will never tell what we have transmitted."

As he made to fire, Natalia pulled the trigger on the Walther, double actioning the first shot into his neck, the second shot—single action—into the man's left eye at an upward angle that would strike the brain.

He swayed for an instant longer, then fell back, knees buckling under him and his pistol discharging into the small sofa, a cloud of stuffing rising around the hole.

Natalia's eyes scanned the room. There was a high frequency transmitter in an open suitcase on the small coffee table, still turned on, the frequency diode reader visible. She committed the numbers to memory as she crossed the room. The police sirens were louder now. There was a large ceramic ashtray, pieces of something that had been burned inside it, smoke still rising from it.

Natalia dropped to her knees beside Bob Jessup. He had at least two sucking chest wounds and there was nothing she could have done for him without an emergency room staff standing by. She set down her pistol and raised his head. He coughed blood as she rested his head in her lap. "Bob?"

He smiled with his pretty eyes.

"I'm sorry—I—"

He winked at her and her cheeks flushed. She leaned over him, kissed him hard on the mouth. He was trying to say something as she moved her mouth away. She couldn't hear him. She put her ear beside his lips, feeling his hot breath on her cheek and neck.

And then his body seemed to stiffen and his head lolled back.

Natalia raised her head.

Bob Jessup's dead eyes stared upward. She thumbed them closed, gently setting his head on the floor.

Natalia stood up, blood all over her dress and her bare arms. Bob Jessup's blood.

The police sirens were very loud now.

She wondered if she was a curse to men as she stared down at Bob Jessup.

She closed her eyes, shook her head, turned away and walked over to the ashtray. Natalia took the Bali-Song from her thigh and opened it. What had been burned was clearly a magnetic tape, because within the pile of ashes as she stirred it with her knife, was a cassette.

There was nothing marked on it.

Built into the transmitter was a high speed player for audio tape.

Whatever had been on the tape was broadcast at high speed, then the tape burned.

And Armand Gruber had brought it to the Nazis. But what was it?

Natalia looked at Bob Jessup there on the floor, the pool of blood around him still growing, but slowly.

He'd whispered a single word to her. The word was "Cry."

There were tears inside her for him, but there was no time to shed them.

Natalia ran from the room, along the corridor, down the stairs to the landing, then down the next flight and into the foyer. She mounted Bob Jessup's motorcycle, kick-starting it as she wrestled the machine toward the door.

She had nothing to lose except time if she waited for the police, and time might now be very valuable.

She gunned the machine through the foyer, through the doorway and down the steps, gearing up as she saw the lights from the slow moving electric police cars coming up near the complex entrance.

Eluding the police wouldn't even be a challenge.

Nine

Dodd disliked horses intensely, but they were occasionally necessary here because there were not enough vehicles to go around and, in some places, a vehicle could not successfully navigate the terrain. Despite his work to spur immigration from Mid-Wake, China and Russia, work which Kurinami heartily approved, Dodd had begun a detailed inventory of Eden stores in all the locations so far opened for use. It was inevitable that Kurinami with his duplicate computer records, would eventually send out parties to check the stores farther from Eden, near the nuclear no-man's land that surrounded what was once the course of the Mississippi.

And then Kurinami would discover that the construction materials were missing, as were the salt dome stored fuel reserves, as were the weapons.

And, eventually, although he had not found it yet, Kurinami would discover the location of D.R.E.A.D.

Something had to be done to prevent all of that, and so Dodd had tried to contact Deitrich Zimmer. Almost surprisingly, Zimmer was already in North America and, after several abortive contact attempts, Dodd was told that Zimmer would be contacting him.

Contact was made. So, Dodd borrowed a horse from among

the two dozen or so the Germans had donated for Eden's use, had it saddled and rode to his meeting with Deitrich Zimmer, about three miles from Eden, in a rocky defile which had once been a river course but was now dry.

Dodd's rear end was stiff and sore, and he felt like the insides of his thighs would never be the same. Walking along the defile after tying up his horse was almost a pleasure.

And, as he rounded a bend in the path, he saw Deitrich Zimmer, sitting calmly beside a synth-fuel stove, the smell of hot tea on the calm, cool air.

"Have some tea, Commander."

"You've got to kill Kurinami for me, before he keeps us from getting control of D.R.E.A.D.—"

"Defense Recovery Emergency Armed Deterrent—D.R.E.A.D. What a picturesque name. But even if your nemesis Kurinami locates it, he will be unable to deprive you of it. I have not been idle, you see. While you were unable to reach me, I have located the missiles which you so desperately want, Commander, and buried them where no one can find them unless I wish them found."

Dodd dropped to one knee beside the stove, looking Zimmer straight in the eye. "You cheated me, damn you!"

Deitrich Zimmer was oddly quiet.

"Say something!"

"What is it that you wish me to say Commander?"

"I need those nuclear warheads or—"

"Your plans will be jeopardized? But, you see, I have greater plans. And you have a single choice. You will cooperate with my plans, or you will never leave here."

"You—"

"What?" Zimmer smiled.

Dodd licked his lips "Your plan, uhh—"

"Why risk annihilation because of impatience when, if all the circumstances are perfect, victory will be assured?"

Dodd just looked at Zimmer.

Zimmer laughed. "I wish to hold the world inthralled to

National Socialism, while you merely wish to establish yourself as a dictator. If you co-operate with me, you will have your power and I will have my new world. If you do not co-operate, you will surely die."

Dodd could see no one else, and there was no sign of a plane or vehicle or even a horse. He could kill Zimmer, perhaps, because Zimmer had only a handgun in view, and this was holstered. Dodd looked at Zimmer's blue eyes and the eyes still held laughter, as if somehow Zimmer knew what he was thinking and found it humorous, amusing. Dodd realized that his hand had been moving toward his belt and he froze. He said, "What do you mean?"

"Great plans require great leaders to bring them to fruition, Commander. If you follow my plan, your troublesome Akiro Kurinami will be dead and you will be forever rid of the yellow man and his black wife. You will control Eden, bring Eden to a position of great power, living out your life in happiness and comfort. But you must do only what I say to do, and only when I say?"

"I don't understand, Zimmer," Dodd told him, speaking honestly.

Zimmer smiled still. "There is no reason to suppose that you should. Suffice it to say, were I to have your yellow nemesis, Kurinami, killed, while members of the Rourke family live, you would never know rest until you, yourself, were dead. If the Rourke family is out of the way, however, you will be able to function with impunity in the aftermath of Kurinami's death, because there will be no one to stop you, provided Kurinami's death cannot be so obviously linked to you that New Germany or Mid-Wake unilaterally intervenes."

"What remains, then, is to remove the Rourke family."

"Kill them? Yes!" Dodd said. But how?, he wondered.

"Killing them would be problematical at best, Commander. They will take themselves out of the picture, as it were, and then we can kill them."

"I don't follow you at all," Dodd said, shaking his head.

"Tea?" Zimmer poured a cup of steaming dark brown liquid for himself.

"No," Dodd told him.

Zimmer shrugged his shoulders.

"How will you get rid of them without killing them?"

"By using their sense of family against them."

Dodd didn't understand.

Zimmer, sipping at his tea, then blowing over the surface of the cup, said, "They have a quest, do they not? To see me dead for what I did to John and Sarah Rourke and for killing the child. And, they wish to see you dead, or punished, at least. If I am dead and you are dead, they will do the inevitable."

"Dead?" Dodd repeated.

Zimmer laughed aloud. "No one is talking about killing you, Commander, unless you choose to disobey me. No. I wish for us to appear to be dead. Then you will be able to go on with your work and I with mine."

"You aren't making any sense."

"My medical specialty is micro-surgery, but I always considered myself a devotee of motivational psychology. I perfected a computer model which predicts, with a degree of certainty in which I have full confidence, just what the Rourke family will do when they realize their quest is at an end. They will join John and Sarah Rourke in cryogenic sleep. It may be immediate; it may take as long as eighteen months, according to the model's most extrapolated predictions, but sleep they will."

"Why?"

Zimmer lit a cigarette, and speaking through exhaled smoke, said "Their very sense of family will undo them. And, if my model is wrong, I will still be able to destroy them."

Dodd shook his head. "You mean, if, uhh, if they don't go into cryogenic sleep, you still have a way —"

"Yes. A perfect way. And, the model allows for all or any of them not to take the cryogenic sleep. In either event, they

267

will die."

"But, what about—" Dodd was uncertain about this business of appearing to be dead himself.

"There will be an incident. Never mind what. Two bodies will be substituted for our own. I have already prepared my duplicate, a captured soldier of New Germany. Your duplicate will be ready soon."

"Duplicate?"

Zimmer laughed again, then sipped at his tea. "No, we are not dealing wibh science fiction, Commander," and he gestured expansively with his cigarette. "Their dental records will match our dental records, certain injuries—your chronic knee dislocation, for example, and the scar tissue built up because of it—will match. No one has performed plastic surgery to make a facial double, quite impossible to be thoroughly convincing at any event."

"And because they think you and I will be dead—"

"They themselves will die. Then, you will resurface and Kurinami and his wife will be killed and the blame will be put on me. You will proclaim your anti-Nazi sentiments and assume the leadership, carrying out my programs ostensibly as a means of making Eden stronger, which will indeed be the case."

"And D.R.E.A.D.?"

"I control it. To use nuclear weapons at this juncture would mean the end of all humanity. But, in the future, the threat and judicious use of nuclear weapons backing a conventional force of considerable capability with appropriate leadership, of course, will be a different story entirely. Consider yourself the interim government for a power which will one day realize man's oldest dream, the domination of the entire planet under one man."

"Who?"

"That is a very intelligent question, Commander," Zimmer said, nodding appreciatively to Dodd. "Very incisive. You will not live to know the answer, although I sincerely hope you live to a very old age. No, that is one secret you will not know."

"But, you're older than I am!"

"For the moment," Zimmer agreed. "Only for the moment, Commander." And then Zimmer laughed again and Dodd shivered.

Ten

It was the first time she had been to Eden since her outlawry had been declared by Commander Dodd. And, even though many months had passed since Akiro Kurinami's first act as President of Eden had been to rescind that declaration, Natalia had no desire ever to return. Too many memories, many of them very bad ones. But the current necesssity was inarguable.

The people of Eden had once been ready to hang her, but as she stepped from the J7-V, Annie, a tread above her; a tape began to play the Star Spangled Banner and Akiro and Elaine stood before the entire population of Eden and the people of Eden cheered her return along with Annie's. Paul and Michael, who recently picked up with a Nazi prisoner in the wastelands, would be arriving soon, as well.

The United States' national anthem played on as Natalia Anastasia Tiemerovna looked back at Annie, then said to her, under her breath, "Except for Akiro and Elaine, they're all hipocrites." And she felt Annie's hand touch at her shoulder . . .

Michael had grown a mustache. Natalia's favorite American film star, before The Night of The War, was Tom Selleck. Michael's mustache was very like his, accentuating the cragginess of Michael's face, making him somehow look older, yet handsomer, different than she had ever seen him. She imagined what it would be like if Michael were to smile, and she hoped that he did not.

"These the ones?" Michael said, touching at her arm but addressing the question to the young German military doctor who supervised the field morgue.

"Yes, Herr Rourke."

Michael nodded. She watched his eyes as he looked away from the doctor and back at her, then at Paul and Annie.

Natalia shivered, drawing her coat more closely around her.

They were inside the German base outside Eden. The German doctor drew back the hook and pile-closured flap and beneath the black synth-rubber, there was a face that was barely human. The shape of the head generally matched that of Commander Dodd, she supposed.

Natalia wanted to look away, but would not allow herself the luxury.

"We have checked all the dental records, Herr Rourke," the German military doctor—a young, severely expressioned man—began. "But, in the case of such men, dental records were not enough. The American, Dodd, had several times dislocated his knee. The right one. Logic infers there would have been considerable scar tissue and cartilege. We found both in the post mortem. An appendix scar, such as was the common result before the advent of modern surgical techniques, was also expected to be present. I had never seen one before, of course, but consulted with medical records at New Germany. And, of course, I verified surgically during the post mortem. The appendix is missing. Other small scars on the body, as noted in his records, were all present as they should be. The general shape of his bone structure, his musculature, all matches. There was no DNA typing five centuries ago, so there was no means by which to make a comparison. However, I am confident this is the corpse of Commander Dodd."

"What about fingerprints?" Annie asked.

"They were checked, of course, and they match. But fingerprints of themselves are not a valid technique for identification, Frau Rubenstein. With current techniques, they can be altered comparatively easily. There is a type of laser surgery on cloned

271

human tissue, where new fingerprints are grown and the old skin at the fingertips is merely removed, the new skin grafted in place, giving a new fingerprint. Again, a laser technique—there are no discernible scars if the procedure is performed competently."

"What about the other body?" Paul asked.

"Ahh! A much more positive identification, Herr Rubenstein," the young doctor said enthusiastically. He let the flap of the body bag fall back over the charred face of Commander Dodd, then moved along to the next drawer.

Natalia's breath steamed and for some reason, that at once thrilled and frightened her, she wanted Michael's arm around her.

She forced herself to stare at the next body as the flap of the bag was opened and drawn back. The face, only half burned, was much more recognizably human, and matched photographs she had seen of Zimmer.

Annie, who had seen Zimmer in the flesh, said, "My God, that's him."

The German doctor—his name was Belzer—added, "Indeed it is, Frau Rubenstein. We were able to check his retinal print, something unavailable in the case of Commander Dodd. As you can see, one eye was destroyed, the right, but the left is intact. Even with the most sophisticated techniques, retinal identification cannot be—what is the word?"

"Faked?" Michael suggested.

"Yes, faked, Herr Rourke. This can be no other than Deitrich Zimmer. Body scars, everything matches. DNA typing agrees one hundred percent. As, of course," and he smiled a little condescendingly, "do the fingerprints."

"So they just fell out of the sky?" Michael asked. "This is almost too convenient."

"The report is considerably detailed, Herr Rourke, but in summary, as I understand, the gunship on which both men flew—President Kurinami had ordered the arrest of Commander Dodd for expropriation of strategic materials and Herr Doctor Zimmer was aiding in the Herr Commander's escape—

the gunship Herr Commander Dodd and Herr Doctor Zimmer used, developed mechanical difficulties of some sort and there was an explosion. These bodies, as you may already know, were assembled from parts. I was at the scene of the crash. Finding the sufficient number of teeth in order to check dental records was challenging in the extreme. Herr Doctor Zimmer's head, for example—" And Doctor Belzer drew the bag back farther.

Natalia looked away in disgust. There was a difference between doing it in combat and watching it afterward, the clinical thing about it coldly, frightening.

Deitrich Zimmer's head rested over the shoulders where it belonged, but it was not attached to the body . . .

She stood alone, apart from Michael and Annie and Paul. The morgue which had been set up to store the bodies was a small pre-fab building at the far end of the German base's airfield.

The wind blew strong here.

Natalia was cold.

And she felt hollow, because it was all over. Vengeance, albeit of an impersonal kind that was not satisfying, was finally theirs. Yet, no vengeance could compensate for the loss of John and Sarah and the baby.

Part Four
Life Threads

One

Natalia laughed as she thought about it, that women only glistened and never perspired. Would that it were true. After helping with moving chairs and painting scenery and washing dirty children all day long, the moisture on her body was nothing more or less than sweat. "All right," she said, raising her voice to the children. "How many of you want to be shepherds?"

Not one of them raised a hand.

"What's a more or less atheist doing casting a Christmas pageant?" she asked herself under her breath. But that really wasn't true; she'd once been an atheist, simply because everyone around her was; but she was one no more.

After she'd seen the bodies of Dodd and Zimmer buried, she left Eden, telling herself she would never return. By the grace of Colonel Mann's J7-V, she'd flown to Lydveldid Island with Paul and Annie, staying with them there for several weeks and, while she was at it, studying Christianity under one of the country's many clerics. It was a way to pass the time and focus her mind on something else. And religion, Christianity and Judaism, hadn't seemed to have hurt the only real friends she'd ever had.

In the end, she said good-bye to Paul and Annie and told them to contact her in Europe as soon as Annie was pregnant. And she had herself baptized, but not without realizing there was never going to be any philosophy, religious or secular, which she would ever fully embrace, any but her own. Nor did she intend to conduct her life in any manner other than the way in which she had conducted it ever since she had abandoned the KGB and begun to aid the Rourke Family, in the fight for freedom.

She didn't delude herself that now, somehow, she would have a better chance of prayer being heard (she was convinced that someone was there to listen, but not that the likelihood of being heard was at all enhanced by water and the sign of the cross, only by the sincerity of one's intent; if God was Love, then God, unlike men, could not turn a deaf ear simply out of dislike for the petitioner). She prayed, whenever she thought to do so, however, for John and Sarah to recover.

And sometimes she prayed that she would be able to ignore the feelings which stirred within her every time she thought of Michael Rourke.

He was beautiful and wonderful.

John had intended that she marry him. That was obvious. But John loved her. That was implicit.

She loved John and—God help her, she prayed—she loved Michael.

Working with the children of The Wild Tribes was her only chance for salvation, and atonement as well. If there was a hell, she had already consigned herself to it. But that was no excuse to continue along a path she knew was wrong. Nothing could ever undo the evil she had done in the name of her native land. And she never prayed to God for herself.

Begging was not in her nature, at least not begging for herself.

Two ministers from Lydveldid Island and one from Mid-Wake had taken up residence in what was called 'Gaul', roughly the location of pre-War Strasbourg, France, along the German border.

They helped her with the school and managed the hospital (the man from Mid-Wake was a retired Navy doctor) and she, in turn, was helping them with this Nativity play.

She fancied the wisemen differently. Women, in those days, were bond servants and nothing more. But, had she been a man and in company of the Three Wisemen from the East, she would have killed Herod and been done with it. It should have been obvious the man was so obsessed with power, that killing the Holy Child or any child, would not bother him one iota.

The wisemen, like most true intellectuals, were innocents in the ways of the world.

Sometimes, Natalia thought she would have made a very fine avenging angel.

"If no one wants to be a shepherd, then who wants to be an angel?"

The little girl, Reverend Slaughter of Mid-Wake, had named Charity, raised her little hand.

Charity, like all of the Wild Tribes children to greater and lesser degrees, had a face that was distorted by normal standards, the nostrils so wide the nose seemed flat, the teeth larger than they should be in normal human children, the skin leathery looking and to the touch, and the color of cafe au lait.

Her eyes were blue and very beautiful when she smiled, though.

At first, Natalia had seen the children of the Wild Tribes as ugly. Now, she saw them only as children. And, as children, they were beautiful and unique.

She was reminded of a verse she remembered from her reading of the Bible (one could not even partially embrace a philosophy without reading its principal text) about the sins of the fathers being visited upon their children. The ancestors of the Wild Tribes children had planned for nuclear holocaust, but not planned well enough. Some were French, some German, some Austrian, none sufficiently well equipped to survive underground long enough.

The 'fathers' returned to the surface when the radiation was still too strong.

Their children—these children—paid for those sins with leathery skin, distorted faces, distended teeth, the occasional missing or extra digit, and a heritage of violence which had nearly eradicated them forever.

So far, twenty-eight hundred and some members of the 'Wild Tribes of Europe', as they were called collectively, had been found.

Seven hundred five of them lived and learned how to live better here at Strasbourg.

One hundred eighty-three of those were children, some of them teenagers, some of them infants, the remaining seventy-two, her children, none of whom wanted to be shepherds, one of whom—Charity—wanted to be an angel.

"All right; you are an angel."

"Thank you Natalia!" Charity, before Natalia could stop her, ran up to her and threw her arms so tightly around Natalia's thighs that Natalia nearly lost her balance. "I love you!"

Natalia dropped to her knees and hugged Charity. "I love you, too."

"And I love you, I finally realized."

Natalia stood up.

Charity clung to Natalia's skirt.

Natalia looked over her shoulder, then closed her eyes. The shoulders of his parka still spotted with snow, hair tousled — wonderful — it was Michael Rourke and she wondered if Charity were clutching at her knees again or if her knees just stopped working . . .

"That's the way it always is; never can get a shepherd when you need one."

"Why did you come here?"

Michael sat on the couch — he obscured it, she thought, his legs so long, his shoulders so broad. He lit a cigarette, but he didn't answer her.

Her pre-fab was as personalized as she could make it, but when she looked around it nothing even looked familiar, certainly not inviting. She poured a glass of the German taste-alike for Seagram's Seven Crown, John's favorite alcoholic beverage, one of her favorites, too. Natalia exhaled, her fists — God, they were small, she thought, compared to Michael's hands — balling tight on the counter as Michael was suddenly standing there on the other side. She looked up into his face. "You should not have come here."

"Why?"

"This can't be."

"What if my father never wakes up? And, what if he does? He has a wife. I don't. I came to correct that."

"You — you — " She wasn't breathing right.

The radio was playing Christmas songs, a program from Mid-Wake uplinked to a communications satellite put into geosynchronous orbit three months ago by New Germany; and now the whole civilized world, such as it was, had communications.

"Me? What?"

"No, it's — " Natalia began again.

Michael's hands reached out and covered hers. "I didn't come here to be a look-alike substitute for the genuine article. If you can't accept me as anything else but that, then I'll leave."

She looked up at him across her kitchen counter. "You don't know what you are asking, Michael."

"Oh, yes I do," Michael Rourke told her, his brown eyes smiling. "I'm asking you to love me."

She bit her lower lip. She swallowed and she had nothing to swallow. She took a gulp of her whiskey and it burned her throat, drinking it so fast. "I, uhh—" She turned her back to him, stabbing her trembling hands into the pockets of her skirt. "I already—" She told herself to shut her mouth and her mouth obeyed. He must have walked around the counter, because she felt hands—strong hands—touching at her waist, the fingers almost encircling her. "Let go of me, Michael."

"No."

His hands were on her shoulders and he turned her around and she turned her face away, but then his hands were on her face and lifting her face toward his.

His eyes, everything about him, his father, not his father. Tears started in her eyes. "Can't you see—"

"Maybe, maybe I see something else." He didn't kiss her, just held her face so he could and she could not stop him. Her arms were at her sides, limp, useless. She lowered her eyes. "I thought about you," Michael almost whispered. "I never stopped thinking about you. You were my friend. You still are my friend. I don't know a lot about things like this. Madison was an angel, like your little girl, Charity. I don't love Madison any less. But what I feel for you, I've never felt for anybody."

She shook her head, tried to speak, could not. "This is wrong, Michael. It's wrong for us—"

"Life, living? That's wrong?"

"Michael, I beg you—"

"No. Tell me to go away and I'll never be back. That's my promise. Look at me and tell me that, Natalia. Just look at me and say it. That's all you have to do and it's all over forever."

Natalia Anastasia Tiemerovna opened her eyes and looked up at Michael Rourke and opened her mouth and couldn't say it.

And he kissed her mouth and her body, without her letting it, melted against his.

And she knew what death was, in that instant, and life, too . . .

Natalia stood perfectly still, Michael's hands moving over her.

Her body trembled as he kissed her.

She had pictured this and, like a nightmare, it had terrified her. Because she had pictured herself fantasizing that the Rourke whose fingers now undid the button at the waistband of her skirt, drew down the zipper, pushed the skirt down over her hips, although she would know he was Michael, she would pretend was John.

281

But that did not happen.

He opened her blouse, pushing it down along her arms, leaving her arms bound within the fabric. He undid the hook and eye fasteners at the back of her bra, the bra sliding down over her arms on its straps. And she did not move.

When she looked into his eyes, touched her lips softly to his face, it was Michael and there was no dark fantasy within her that it was John. His hands pushed her slip and her panties over her hips and along her thighs and down to encircle her bare feet.

Michael lifted her up into his arms and carried her across the room.

"Tell me that you love me, Michael," Natalia whispered.

"I love you," he said softly, simply, as comfortably, she thought, as if he had said it countless times to her.

Michael set her down on the bed and she lay there, waiting for his will.

He undressed quickly, the muscles of his chest and shoulders and arms rippling easily.

And then he was beside her, freeing her arms of her clothes, freeing her heart.

She realized she was crying only as she spoke, saying, "I love you, Michael. I love you."

Two

"Mr. Rubenstein?"

Paul Rubenstein turned around to look for the source of the voice behind him on the path through the park. The face, which went wit' the voice, was open and smiling, blonde and fair. Stig was a sincer student of history, if not the most naturally gifted.

"Yes?"

"I was wondering, sir, if I might walk with you a bit and ask you few questions concerning today's lecture, please?"

Stig's English was a bit peculiar, but vastly better than Paul Ru benstein's Icelandic. "Certainly. May as well cross the park togethe What is it you wish to know?" And young Stig fell in at Paul Ruben stein's side.

But old habits died hard, and however long Paul Rubenstein live with his wife in the rebuilding Hekla community, he knew, he woul never quite lose the old habits. He kept the boy on his left so, if i came to that, he could shove the boy back with his left hand lon enough to get at the battered old Browning High Power, he still wor under his coat and probably always would.

He supposed a psychiatrist would call it paranoia, because noth ing here in Lydveldid Island posed even the remotest threat. But h remembered, on a path like this, before the volcano had erupted and destroyed everything, before the rebuilding of the Hekla Community had begun, the death of a very beautiful, very pregnant young girl named Madison Rourke, Michael's wife.

Paranoia or not, Paul Rubenstein would never risk his own fate or the fate of a loved one by going unarmed.

"I was wondered, sir—"

"Wondering—you were wondering, not 'wondered', okay?"

"Yes. Thank you," the boy smiled. "No matter how hard I understand, or try to understand, I mean, with men such as yourself and Doctor Rourke alive, it is incomprehensible to me that evil flourished so that the war could ever start."

Paul Rubenstein smiled, looking down at his shoes for a moment, then over at young Stig. "I believe you just gave me a very great compliment. So, I thank you for that. Before The Night of The War, like everybody else, I was so busy with having a 'normal' life that I thought anyone who planned for something I personally thought was impossible was a little crazy. I really did think that way, Stig.

"There was my job, my friends, a girl I was going with, the rush to the office every morning, the rush home every night, and not much time to sit down and think about what the world around me was really like, as opposed to what it seemed to me to be. John Rourke saw life differently.

"He was always on the edge, I suppose," Paul Rubenstein went on. "He looked beneath the surface, and he saw things most people would have refused to see, that some people even refused to see after the war had come.

"It was a much larger world then, more people, or course, so many nations most people—myself included—couldn't have told you how many, and everything was ordered and neat on the surface and boiling away beneath the surface. People chose never to look below the surface."

"I still do not—"

Paul Rubenstein shrugged his shoulders. "We were so concerned with getting to work on time, with taxes—remember I mentioned the concept?"

"Yes."

"Work, taxes, who said what to whom, trying to make a buck—make money. Anyway, all the little things that had nothing at all to do with really living, took up so much time there was no time for living. The more you value life, the more you try to preserve it. People were too busy to know what life was, many of them, maybe most of them, and so the thought of preserving it, if it ever entered their heads at all, was something to be shunted off to the police or the military or to anybody else but themselves.

"The city I lived in was called New York," Paul related, realizing he was deviating from answering the boy's question, but doing it anyway. "In New York, there were more people than there are on the

284

entire earth today. And people would put bars up, like a prison—a place for confining criminals—might have, just to keep people from breaking into their homes and businesses and hurting them. And people wouldn't go to Central Park, not at night, because there were gangs that would attack people for no reason at all, except to steal from them, or maybe just to get some pleasure out of hurting them. And if somebody tried to safeguard his own life or the life of a loved one with a weapon of any kind, he was violating the law usually.

"Life was upside down, with foreign dictators stealing from their countries and torturing and killing their own people, the cost of everything—the number of dollars needed—going up and up and some people working harder and harder just to stay even, while other people refused to work and expected the government to pay for their food and everything else, and raised their children to be the same way.

"There were people who hated other people because of the color of their skin, or the way they worshipped God or because they didn't believe in God or because they did. Women might do the same work as men, but often times they were paid less. The world was a lot less concerned about right and wrong than about profit and loss. There were even people who laughed at the concept of personal honor, of honesty.

"But the majority of the people, like people everywhere, were basically good, but basically uninvolved, too busy living what passed for life, to realize life was passing them by and that even what passed for life, might slip through their fingers."

"It sounds like hell."

"It wasn't. But men like Doctor John Rourke were few and far between, and didn't come along every day. And, when they did, people were too busy to listen, let alone do something.

"The coming of the War was easy," Paul Rubenstein concluded.

"The Russians must have been terrible people."

"No. The Russians were just people, not terrible or otherwise. The problem wasn't a problem between freedom and totalitarianism, good and evil, anything that simplistic. The problem was that people were too busy to care, or too beaten down to do anything, if they did care. The world was slipping away and we were all too busy to notice."

They reached the end of the path.

285

What five centuries ago would have been a city block away, lay the small house he and Annie occupied. There were still only two of them. Annie's menstrual cycle had just begun. But some day they would have a baby, both of them fertile, just not lucky yet. "I have to leave you here, Stig. Try that book I suggested from Mid-Wake I suggested. There are some copies at the library. If the library is out, call me and make arrangements to borrow mine. The author, as I told you, who survived the War, was an American submarine commander. He was closer to the situation than good historical scholarship allows, but the account is the best you'll find."

"Thank you, Sir. Very much, Sir." And young Stig offered his hand.

Paul Rubenstein took it, then turned off the path and along the row of small private houses, toward his. As he halved the distance, he saw Annie emerge onto the porch. She raised her right arm and waved at him. Paul waved back, quickening his step.

She was beautiful, as always, like a pretty gift wrapped in lace and ribbons, always his.

The trappings of life, as he'd suggested to young Stig, were tempting.

As he walked, Paul Rubenstein thought of his wife's father, John Rourke.

If/when—was hope embodied in a word?—John awakened in some future time, his friend would be totally alone in a world that was totally changed.

Paul Rubenstein stopped at the base of the porch steps, looking up at Annie in her ankle length floral print dress and white pinafore-style apron. She looked as delicate as a flower, more beautiful than any flower could have been.

She loved the everyday things of life, this house, the prospect of a child, the classes she taught, the classes he taught, the normalcy of waiting for him on the front porch every night while dinner cooked on the kitchen stove and the hot bread or a cake or a pie that was in the oven.

He felt his waistline. He kept fit, and the 'good life' wasn't showing on him, or at least not yet.

"I was thinking about your Dad," Paul said to her.

"I was thinking about him, too, today."

"I was wondering if maybe we should, uhh—maybe—"

She opened her arms and he walked up the steps, stopping a few treads below her, folding her into his arms, leaning his head against her breast, smelling the perfume of her, her woman smell, the sensual odors of what she had been cooking, just holding her and feeling her warmth through her clothes against his hands, against his face.

"Do you want me to say it, Paul?"

He didn't move his head, just hugged her. "Reading me?"

"I didn't mean to, honest."

He laughed, held her more tightly. "Well, to my unasked question, then?"

"He'd be so alone, especially if Mom—"

Paul Rubenstein nodded, touched his lips to her hand as her fingers caressed his cheek.

He loved the normalcy, too; but, perhaps, there really was fate, or destiny, and theirs was so inextricably tied to John Rourke's, that the bonds could not be broken if they tried.

Three

The spring would be very short, of course, because the summer was very short and the autumn was even shorter.

But the winter endured, within the last few days only, it seemed relinquishing its grip in Gaul, surrounding Strasbourg; the days a little warmer, green sprouting where the snow was melting.

But here, in the distance, it was always winter because the icesheet, the glacier, had not retreated more than an inch or so each summer for more than three centuries according to the records.

Lydveldid Island was not called the "land of ice" without reason.

"Hold my hand."

Michael Rourke turned in the pilot's seat and looked at Natalia. He needed only one hand for the controls of the J7-V at the moment and Natalia, a better pilot than he was, knew that. He took her hand in his. "Relax. There's nothing to worry about. Weren't they happy for us?"

"Yes," Natalia murmured, nodding her head. "When you told them, though, I think I was more frightened than I've ever been in my life."

"Why?" The ocean slipped away beneath them, the rocky beach and icefield beyond replacing it. The German base outside Hekla would not be coming up on his heads-up display for another two minutes, at their present airspeed.

"Russians are very strange people, Michael. We feel guilty for everything. That's why there was always so much alcoholism in the Soviet Union, I think. Depression."

"Hmm," he nodded, relinquishing her hand for an instant to manually check his landing gear controls. He retook her hand. "I guess I'm a little uptight, too. When I was a kid, I watched you in your chamber, always beautiful, never stirring. Despite the fact my childhood wasn't quite normal, you'll have to admit, I still remembered the stories Mom or Dad would read to me when I was little. I couldn't look at you with-

288

out thinking of *Sleeping Beauty*. But you hadn't eaten something that poisoned you and as much as I would have loved to awaken you with a kiss like in the story, I knew—I thought I knew—that somehow Dad had a wife waiting for me when I grew up enough."

He let go of her hand, the heads-up showing the outer boundary beacon for the base. He started running a pre-landing computer check. "I figured," he went on, "that Dad had it all figured out wrong, though. Just picture yourself as a guy in his teens," he told her.

"I can't," Natalia laughed.

He squeezed her hand for an instant. "No, I mean, well, there's this unaging goddess waiting for you to grow up and be old enough to—well, old enough. And you know that's what your Dad had planned all along, but you figure it'll never happen. So, I told myself it wouldn't."

"If John—your father—if—"

Michael Rourke looked at Natalia Tiemerovna. He nodded, saying, "I hope to God I would have, and you would have." He picked up the microphone—he hated headsets—and started to call the German-base . . .

The kitchen table was typical Annie, Michael Rourke thought.

Little salt and pepper shakers, pretty cloth napkins that matched the table cloth, fresh flowers not just in a vase but arranged with obvious care.

Paul brought him a drink and sat down opposite him.

"To—whatever," Paul suggested.

"Good toast," Michael nodded, clinking glasses, then sipping at his wine.

Michael's eyes drifted toward the opposite end of the long, narrow kitchen, where Natalia helped Annie. Annie was in a long dress and an apron, looking like a nineteenth century doll—he'd seen them in books—and Natalia looking considerably less formal and slightly perplexed.

"You look good for yourself, Michael. Natalia does, too. You seem to agree with each other."

Michael Rourke looked at his brother-in-law and friend. "I could say the same for you guys. Annie looks happier than I've ever seen her."

"I still can't figure out what she sees in me," Paul grinned, taking another sip of his wine. "She even cooks Kosher better than my mother did, God love her. I'm not implying the opposite, but you don't look like you're starving."

"He'll eat anything!" Natalia called out, laughing.

"This woman does not lie," Michael said equally loudly.

Paul laughed.

"Seriously, she's a terrific cook. I asked her once, you know, to make something Russian. She said she never learned how to cook Russian food."

"When I was on that job with—with Vladmir," Natalia said, looking toward them, the oven door half open. "Where we had to pretend to be Americans? I needed to know how to cook, so the KGB sent me to a cooking school. All they taught was American and Continental cuisine, so I never learned how to cook like a Russian."

"I had an aunt who was Russian," Paul said, laughing. "Trust me, if she was any indicator of Russian cooking—"

"No," Natalia responded, her potholdered hands clasped to a pie. "Russian cooking can be wonderful. I just never learned it."

Michael lit his rare cigarette, almost hating to do so because the kitchen smells were so good. He looked at the lighter in his hand, then set it down on the table and pushed it toward Paul.

Paul picked up the battered Zippo and turned it over in his hand. " 'J. T. R.'—wow." He put the lighter down.

"Tell him, Paul," Annie called over her shoulder.

Michael looked at Paul. "Tell me what?"

Paul's eyebrows shrugged. "I figured to talk about it later; may as well talk about it now. Annie and I have been giving this a lot of thought. Uhh, careful consideration. We, uhh—"

"You're going to join them," Michael said.

Paul looked at Annie, then back at Michael. "Yeah. I checked it all out. Yeah. We decided. Him, anyway. Someday, he'll come out of the coma he's in. Sarah, they still say, well, they still say it'll take a medical breakthrough—they can't even foresee to give her even a chance. But, someday, he'll come out of it. The monitoring system shows that with his brain wave patterns. I was talking to Doctor Munchen. They've done some experiments and they're certain. There shouldn't be any trouble telling when his alpha rhythms get into the normal range. Your Dad'd be, uhh—"

"Alone," Michael supplied.

"Yeah," Paul nodded. "So, well, you and Natalia have each other now. He would have wanted that. We can tell him all about you guys and everything."

"When I radioed, I said we had something special to tell you."

"Yeah, I, uhh—I figured maybe you guys were preg—Getting married, maybe, or—"

Michael inhaled on his cigarette, just looking at his friend. "We were going to tell you the same thing, Paul. Natalia and I talked about it a lot. And we came up with a lot of reasons. I don't know how good any of them are, but it's something we want to do. I haven't checked with Doctor Munchen or anything, but he was next on my list. We figured—Natalia and I—we figured that we wanted to tell Dad ourselves, be there when he wakes up, maybe find a way that doesn't exist yet to help Mom."

A glass broke, but Michael didn't look.

He watched his friend's face, instead.

Then Paul extended his hand, saying, "The Family."

Michael Rourke nodded, saying nothing, but taking Paul's hand.

And Annie and Natalia, as if they had rehearsed it (and with women Michael Rourke realized a man could never be quite sure) called out, "The Family!"

Four

His mother—only her left temple was bandaged—looked beautiful, at peace and timeless forever.

Michael Rourke looked at Paul, then at Annie, his sister.

They were already asleep, the blue-white gas suffused totally throughout their chambers.

Consciousness of his nakedness only a fleeting thought, he walked toward where Natalia sat, naked as well, but covered from her breasts downward with a sheet. She smiled, saying to him, "When you went into The Sleep, I gave you and Annie the injections. How things have changed but remained the same. You were the most beautiful little boy, and now—"

Michael Rourke leaned close to her, touching his lips to her mouth. "Lovers. When we awaken, I'll love you then as I love you now."

And Natalia put her head against his chest, her lips touching at his flesh, her arms clutched around him.

She trembled slightly.

After a moment that was not long enough, he helped her into her chamber, helping her with the light sheet which would cover her.

Doctor Munchen approached.

"Are you ready, Natalia?"

She looked at Michael.

Michael Rourke said, "She's ready."

Natalia smiled, then closed her eyes.

Doctor Munchen sprayed her arm with the antiseptic, then touched the needle to her skin.

Michael Rourke held her hand for a while longer, then looked at Munchen. Michael nodded.

The cryogenic chamber closed and Michael stepped away, going to his own.

He sat on the edge.

When he looked to his right, above his own chamber, he could see his father, when the gas swirled for an instant quite clearly.

"So, Michael. I will never see you again. But, do a kindness for me?"

Michael Rourke looked at Munchen's eyes. "Of course."

"Good," Munchen nodded. "Tell someone about me, that is all. That way, long after I am dead, I will know that I am remembered."

"Yes." Michael extended his hand to Munchen.

Munchen smiled, took his hand. "So, shall we?"

Michael Rourke turned around, bringing up his legs, then stretching out in the chamber.

The German models were more spacious, better designed to guard against blood clotting, suspending the sleeper. After a few seconds, Michael felt comfortable enough.

The spray was cool against his arm.

He looked at Munchen, then at Natalia, the gas already all but obscuring her.

Then, Michael Rourke closed his eyes. "I'll remember you as a friend," he said.

Kurinami was in power in Eden, Dodd and Zimmer were dead. The new world was a place of promise, the future bright.

The needle touched his skin, pricked his flesh.

Michael Rourke remembered that one dreamed in The Sleep, dreamed endlessly. So he focused his mind on Natalia and the love they shared, in the hope that his dreams would be good ones.

293

Part Five

The Legend

One

The hem of the pretty girl's sleeveless white mini-dress stopped well above the midpoint between hip and thigh. She wore a soft white cap with a bill on it over her past shoulder length straight blonde hair and, over textured white stockings, knee-high white plastic boots with large; industrial-sized zippers, like the one at the front of her dress, running up the sides. "Now, everyone aboard the bus, please! And mind your step!" And she looked over the rims of her big round sunglasses and smiled as she added, "Remember, Citizens of Eden and any foreign visitors, Retreat Tours, its employees and subsidiaries, cannot be responsible for any lost articles. So, keep your belongings with you in hand at all times!"

He had no possessions in hand, stepped aside to allow a woman with a small child in tow to board ahead of him, then climbed aboard himself.

The bus was jointed at the center and, after a hurried guesstimate, he judged it would carry one hundred people.

He took a seat near the center exit door and beside a window on the driver's side. The center rows were filling up fast, and most of the window seats were taken.

A girl, dressed and coiffed similarly to the tour guide, but with a different color scheme—brown hair and a blue dress and blue boots—sat down beside him. She wore round-framed glasses, too, but not for sun, and had pretty green eyes behind them. "You can have the window seat if you like," he offered.

No, I like to be able to move around. But, thanks, anyway. Taken the tour to Rourke's Retreat before?"

"No, I never have taken the tour. Is it exciting?"

"Oh, I guess, if you like history and everything."

"Don't you like history?"

"I'm taking a group of sixth graders here next week as part of

297

Rourke Day celebrations. I haven't been in years, so I figured I'd go up and have a look around." And she laughed, adding, "So the kids would think I know what I'm talking about. If you haven't been, give this a read."

And she reached into her smallish shoulder bag and took out a folded up brochure.

She offered it and he took it.

There was a pretty color photograph of a rather heroically posed statue atop a mountain summit. "That is a nice piece of sculpture, isn't it?" She was looking over his shoulder. "You know the story of course, right?"

"I know about John Rourke, of course, but all this—The Retreat Tour. It's all new to me. History wasn't my big subject either," he told her.

"Golly, hard to imagine anybody not knowing it." She shrugged her little shoulders. "That's supposed to be John Rourke, how he looked when he single-handedly fought off the last Soviet helicopter on the morning of the Great Conflagration. That's the old American flag supposed to be flying behind him, there. See?"

"Yes. Marvelous detail in the sculpture."

"He was a pretty handsome guy, the way they depict him, anyway. When I was a little girl, I used to look at his face on the dollar bill and think, wow, what a guy. Mom and Dad were into history, so I guess that's where I got it."

"The Retreat was his personal hideaway."

"Got all his stuff there, or most of it anyway. The guns that they display there—you'll like that part; most men do—they're supposed to be the same guns he really used before he was killed in that hospital explosion."

"I thought they survived that?"

"Well, I suppose you can look at it that way, but both of them were brain dead anyway. Poor people. But you're right, technically. They were still alive until those terrorists attacked the place at Mid-Wake where their bodies were being kept and burned it."

"Now, was that before or after Kurinami and his wife were assassinated?"

"The same day. Let me guess. You're from Mid-Wake, right?"

"I've spent a lot of time there," he smiled.

"Yeah, can you imagine that? John and Sarah Rourke were both killed—actually killed—and the first President of Eden and his wife were assassinated on the same day. Gosh, that would have been a recreationist's nightmare, wouldn't it?"

"Recreationist?"

"Now, come on, they've gotta use recreationists at Mid-Wake."

"I don't think so, but if you tell me what one is, I could tell you for sure."

The bus started and the tour guide announced, "Please make certain that your seatbelts are properly fastened. The road leading up Rourke's Mountain is very steep. For safety information, consult the monitors in the seat backs in front of you."

There was a small color television screen set into the seat back, and every seat back, playing now a demonstration on seatbelt adjustment, then moving on to how to properly position oneself in the event of an accident.

"What was I saying?"

He looked at the girl, smiled, said, "You were telling me what a recreationist is."

"Well, you know. On the news? When there's a crime or something, it's re-enacted so people can see how it actually took place."

"Like a play?

"Well, sort of, but nobody makes it up. It's just like the real thing, only better."

"I see. How long have you been teaching sixth graders?"

"Five years. I taught kindergarten for a year before that. "It must be wonderful to be a teacher," he told her.

"It's a living."

The tour guide's voice came over the bus' PA system. "In this the 125th year since the landing of the Eden Fleet," she began, "every citizen of Eden, every citizen of the World, should pause to reflect on the courage of Doctor John Thomas Rourke."

Automatically, it seemed, the windows of the bus tinted, obscuring exterior light. There was a flicker on the video screen in the seatback in front of him. An intricate electronic logo appeared for Eden National Television.

The logo was cut to the statue which appeared on the brochure, the young woman who sat beside him, had taken from her miniscule purse. But it was a close up of the statue's face. The camera drew back, moving on a track or a steady-cam mount, it seemed, starting to pan around the statue as an announcer's voice came on.

"One hundred twenty-five years ago, this man, Doctor John Thomas Rourke, risked his life to save the returning Eden Project astronauts. The world was still engaged in the bloodiest war of human history, a war which had destroyed almost all life on the planet, human, animal and vegetable.

"Under John Rourke's leadership, and with the help of the courageous Eden astronauts, a fighting force was forged, standing virtually alone against the land, naval and air forces of the Soviet Union . . ."

He recalled the line variously attributed to several historical figures, among them Napoleon: "History is a set of lies agreed upon."

The girl beside him whispered, "They say that Lance Stone almost begged the government to let him play John Rourke. Isn't Lance Stone just gorgeous?"

He didn't comment.

The actor, tall, with dark curly hair, stood atop a mountain, shirt ripped to shreds like "Doc Savage," and seemingly more muscles beneath the tatters. There was a pistol in each of the man's hands. The American flag blew in a stiff wind behind him.

Fire rolled across the sky.

Fast intercut of advancing helicopter gunships, all painted matte black, mini-guns firing, smoky white contrails snaking behind streaking red-tipped missiles—he imagined this was a very sophisticated form of digitized computer animation.

Back to Lance Stone. "You haven't won, Karamatsov! And as long as one free person exists on this scorched planet, you never will! Come and get me!" It should have been Rozhdestvenskiy to whom the actor hurled his challenge; because, at that time, Karamatsov was assumed dead.

The helicopters streaked over the mountainside and Lance Stone, as John Rourke, oiled muscles rippling, flag still flowing in the breeze behind him, fired his pistols from the hip. Fast cutaway to one of the Soviet helicopter gunships exploding in mid-air, fiery bodies tumbling from it.

Cut to the sky, fire rolling in from all directions.

Close up of Lance Stone as John Rourke. Somehow, he'd gotten a cigar in his mouth, a big one, half-smoked, and the way the camera and the lighting worked together, his eyes could be seen faintly be-

300

hind dark lensed aviator style sunglasses, squinting in determination as lightning bolts flashed all around him and machine gun fire barely missed him.

The announcer's voice returned, as there was a cut back to the continuing pan of the statue. "With the help of his faithful companion, Paul Rubenstein, John Rourke's heroism saw its finest hour when Soviet gunships attempted to shoot the returning Eden Project spacecraft from the skies."

Close up, was the face of Lance Stone, a cigar clamped in his teeth, aviator style sunglasses cocked back on his forehead, eyes squinted again. The camera drew back. Stone, as Rourke, was in the cockpit of a helicopter. "Eat lead, Commie bastards!" Fast intercut of a thumb depressing a red button labelled Fire Control, cut to tight shot of missiles on weapons pods, then streaking away. Cut to distance shot, showing missiles and contrails.

A black helicopter gunship with a red Hammer and Sickle symbol was blown out of the sky.

Obviously computer graphics again, but very good. Space Shuttles, Eden One in the lead, cracked the sound barrier and looped out of an icy blue sky. Soviet gunships zipped above the shuttles and below them.

Back to Lance Stone, a microphone in his hand, saying, "Eden One, this is Rourke! Come in! Take evasive action! Over and Out!"

It might possibly be easier for a boulder to take evasive action than for a twentieth century space shuttle to do so. But the shuttle craft did, anyway.

"I met Lance Stone once. Gee, he's terrific, isn't he?"

"Terrific, yes."

"And this is just the way it happened. It's all documented."

"Really? This is exactly the way? Right down to the stuff he said on the radio and everything?"

"Ohh, yeah."

"Exciting," he told her, his eyes never leaving the screen . . .

The headphone set he wore as he walked up the roadway from the bus, the pretty little mini-dressed brunette beside him, told him, "The historical importance of the Rourke shrine cannot be minimized. It was here, at The Retreat, that John Rourke set his plans to,

301

literally, save the world. Now on Eden-owned land in the absence of any descendents because of the terrorist atrocity, which claimed the lives of the entire Rourke family, The Retreat on Rourke's Mountain is a modern day Mecca for citizens of Eden and citizens of the World.

"On the very same day as the terrorist assault on the repository at Mid-Wake where the Rourke family bodies were held in cryogenic freeze, Eden's first president, the courageous Japanese astronaut, Akiro Kurinami, was assassinated along with his wife, the former Elaine Halversen, an Eden scientist.

"Commander Christopher Dodd, whom it had been thought had been the victim of foul play, was miraculously alive. Dodd returned in the aftermath of President Kurinami's death, heroically taking on the mantle of leadership he had rejected months earlier, when he refused to run for the Presidency. Christopher Dodd, against his pro-testations, continued as President of Eden until his death, at which time a successor he himself had selected was voted unanimously into office by the ever growing Eden population.

"That man, of course, Eden's third President, was Arthur Hooks, President Dodd's able assistant in the closing days of his history-making life.

"President Hooks' administration continued the great works begun under Christopher Dodd."

He wasn't interested, but there was no way of shutting off the wire-less headphones, really receivers. So, he ignored the words, not wishing to remove the headphones.

At last, as they reached the height of the road, the broadcast ceased.

Others removed their headphones and so did he. The girl beside him said, "You know, you look familiar."

"I do? I guess I just have that sort of face, common."

"No! You have a nice face. And I don't usually like beards."

He smiled.

"What are you doing after the tour?

He looked at her. "I'm sorry?"

"Do you have a health card?"

He had to think. "Yes," he finally said.

"Well, why not my place and we can see what develops over the evening, huh? I've got a spare toothbrush."

He started to try thinking of an answer when their tour guide began to speak. "All right, may I have your attention, please?" Evidently, she had it. She said, "We are about to enter The Retreat. This entrance before you was once a closely guarded secret known only to Doctor Rourke's closest friends, men like Akiro Kurinami and Christopher Dodd." Half-right, he thought. "The synth-glass electronic doors weren't in use then," she smiled. There was general laughter. "Now, remember, inside the Retreat there are real weapons, vastly more powerful than some that are in use by the outlaws in the Wildlands. They are all under unbreakable synth-glass, but please remember not to touch anything."

People started filing through. In the space between the outer doorway and the inner vault door, illuminated in red lighting, there was a jet black Harley Davisdon Low Rider. "John Rourke personally rode this motorcycle during many of his heroic exploits, usually parking it in this very spot. Now, watch your step, because this is real rock and sometimes gets very slippery."

Dutifully, he watched his step, taking the young lady's elbow—to her evident surprise—and helping her.

"Martin Zimmer, Eden's leader since the abolition of the presidency some ten years ago, personally rededicated this shrine as his first official act, it is said. And, he undertook to make certain that every item stored within was perfectly maintained out of his deep personal respect, for the heroic Doctor John Rourke." The tour guide always seemed to end every sentence, almost every word, with a big toothy smile. This time was no exception.

"I haven't seen any pictures of Martin since—"

The girl with him looked positively shocked, eyes like saucers behind her enormous glasses. "He's never seen in public. He was terribly disfigured, the poor man, during the war with the outlaws in the Wildlands."

"That's right. Silly me for not remembering."

The tour guide chattered on.

Down three steps and in the center of the vast central chamber there were illuminated cases.

As the people from the tour broke up, he started toward the cases, the girl still beside him. "Just like a man. Look at all the cowboy toys."

He smiled, shrugging his shoulders.

He took off his sunglasses, peering into the largest case.

There were two shiny stainless steel pistols, below them a printed label reading, "Detonics CombatMaster. 45 automatic pistols used by John Rourke on the day of the Great Conflagration, to shoot down the last Soviet helicopter gunship." There was a long barrelled revolver, .44 Magnum simply labelled, "Smith & Wesson Model 629." Below these there was a little black knife bearing the label "A.G Russell Sting IA Black Chrome," a large fighting/survival knife with a label beneath it reading, "Handmade Life Support System X by Jack W.Crain of Weatherford, Texas, circa late twentieth century." And there was a pair of dark lensed aviator style sunglasses.

He smiled, turned to the girl and said, "It's not that your invitation doesn't flatter me, because you're very attractive. But I'm afraid I've got something to do tonight."

"Hey, I've got a health card! I'm not hard up."

"I'm sure you're a real prize, honestly."

He looked back into the case, then put on his sunglasses.

Two

There were weapons detectors everywhere in Eden and its capitol, Eden City. Every public building (nothing was privately owned) was accessed by passing through an arch. Police surveillance cameras were located at every intersection, police vehicles – quite traditionally black and white – patrolling, and the police seemed heavily armed. As he walked from the station at the foot of Rourke's Mountain and toward the bullet train station that would return him to Eden City, he passed through two security arches.

Before they'd left The Retreat, the tour guide pointed out to them, one of the secret tunnels connecting the mountain summit above with the interior of The Retreat. She told the tourists, "It was this escape tunnel which Doctor Rourke used to re-enter The Retreat in the very instant the sky caught fire.

A little boy shook off his pretty young mother's hand and declared, "I can climb it!"

The escape hatch was open, but covered in synth-glass. The tour guide smiled indulgently, bending over to get her face even with the little boy's, showing everyone behind her what was under her mini-dress in the process. "You want to do it just like you saw John Rourke do it in the vid-movie, don't you? Well, remember, it wasn't really John Rourke who did it. It was Lance Stone, who played John Rourke!"

As she stood up, she quipped in a conspiratorial tone to the adults around her, "Or, maybe it was his stuntman."

Everybody laughed.

The pretty girl who'd invited him for dinner and sex – she hadn't really mentioned dinner – sat beside someone else on the way back down the mountain and walked away quickly when the bus returned to the departure station for the tour.

He left quickly as well, boarding the same bullet train, but in a different car, using his round trip ticket.

He studied the brochure the young woman had given him. The Retreat, owned by the government of Eden, tours leaving every hour on the hour every Monday, Wednesday and Saturday, first tour at ten, last beginning at six.

Under his breath, he murmured, "A real moneymaker."

The statue atop Rourke's Mountain was just as pictured on the cover of the brochure and in the video he'd seen aboard the bus. The end of the historical re-enactment, starring Lance Stone (who had played "John Rourke" in the vid-movie of the same name), showed Lance Stone in a pose identical to that of the statue, Lance Stone's face dissolving into the face of the statue.

He wondered if some day they would change the face of the statue—the statue's face looked nothing like Lance Stone's face—to match?

The man sitting beside him was evidently a shift worker, using the bullet train to get to his job, a plastic lunch box on his lap, the newspaper, "The Gates of Eden" open on his lap. The man's eyes were closed and, evidently, the man was asleep.

The train moved very rapidly, very smoothly, and the very rhythm of it would have made falling asleep very easy. He did not fall asleep, however.

John Thomas Rourke had slept enough to last him for a very long time.

Three

They were all present, except the one, after all these years, he realized mattered most to him.

Paul and Annie sat together. Michael and Natalia sat together.

John Rourke sat alone.

Far away, in China, the last place anyone would think to look, were the two chambers which were still unopened, Sarah, hovering between life and death, in one of them.

The man whom the head of German intelligence had said was his best agent, Manfred Kohl, smoked a cigarette. Kohl was tall, lean, athletic looking and young, but he sat with his shoulders slumped and his eyes closed behind his glasses, the very picture of an old man deep in thought.

James Darkwood paced the floor between where Kohl sat and John Rourke sat. How much like Jason Darkwood, whom John Rourke had fought beside, this young man looked. It was uncanny. Had this been a twentieth century motion picture, rather than a twenty-sixth century reality and they'd all been actors—like Lance Stone, a.k.a. John Rourke—this James Darkwood and his ancestor, Jason Darkwood, could have been played by the same man.

James Darkwood was still a commander, not yet a captain, and although he was likely quite at home on a Mid-Wake submarine, his business was Naval Intelligence.

Kohl, without raising his head, but opening his eyes, said, "So, you have seen the place, John. Everywhere, you are enshrined, but what you stood for is debased."

"Martin Zimmer," Natalia whispered, just shaking her head. "When the young American from Mid-Wake died in my arms, he said the word "cry", or at least I thought he did."

"From what we have been able to determine," Kohl said, at last looking up, "it would have been possible for the man you followed almost

307

one hundred twenty-five years ago, this—" He closed his eyes, looked at the room's ceiling as though consulting a notebook, opened his eyes again and continued, "His name was Armand Gruber, yes?"

Natalia nodded.

"What we have learned by sifting through computer records, indicates that Gruber could have had access to German and Mid-Wake research in cryogenics. The original Zimmer was a man well ahead of his time. When he died, most of the knowledge of his micro-surgery procedures and his research in genetic surgery went to the grave with him. It would not be stretching credibility to assume that if he had the basics given to him, Zimmer could have duplicated the cryogenic chambers and the all-important serum, have somehow survived."

"It couldn't be because we saw his body," Paul asserted. "And even if he could have rigged that in some way, there was his retina print. You said yourself that it couldn't have been faked."

"If Bob Jessup was trying to say the word "cryogenics" instead of "cry," Natalia began.

"What about the brother theory?" Michael asked.

"The DNA typing could, indeed, have been achieved through murdering his brother. Zimmer had one, who was also a Nazi, and there are no records of Zimmer's brother ever being arrested or any grave found for him. But that still leaves us with the eye," Kohl said. "Damnit".

James Darkwood stopped pacing. "I read the autopsy reports concerning Zimmer and Dodd. We know that Dodd's was faked, of course, because Dodd resurfaced in the aftermath of President Kurinami's death, telling some wild story about Zimmer kidnapping him and putting in a ringer for him, then the ringer and Zimmer getting killed."

"You still have the eye," Annie said, standing up, stabbing her hands along her thighs, looking for pockets, John Rourke surmised. But the attire worn by Eden women—essentially indentical to clothes worn in the 1960s—didn't include pockets because it fit so tightly. Her dress was shockingly short, he thought. Even though she was a married woman, she was still his daughter. "The eye thing is impossible to duplicate."

James Darkwood looked at her and smiled. "What if he actually sacrificed his own eye? The other eye was missing. Zimmer was a crack shot, the records say, a rifleman. Manfred found a photograph that showed Zimmer firing right-handed. He could have fired a pistol right-handed and had a left master eye, but not a rifle. What if he felt proving his own death actually merited the loss of an eye? After all, he was into micro-surgery, right? We can clone a human eye today and replace it. Maybe he could do it then, or figured the process would be an inevitable development he could wait for."

John Rourke just listened. Who was Martin Zimmer? That was the real question. All the rest, about Deitrich Zimmer and his missing eyeball, about cryogenics, all of that was essential, but could wait.

Martin Zimmer was building an arsenal of chemical and energy weapons that could unleash devastation that might parallel the Night of The War. He had the largest standing army in the world. And no nation on earth could stand up to him because he already had nuclear weapons—the ones from the Defense Recovery Emergency Armed Deterrent program, or D.R.E.A.D. Reportedly, even before those were deployed, he was already building more of the same, only the tactical nuclear kind, battlefield superiority weapons.

To have challenged the build-up, to have threatened interdiction might have forced Martin Zimmer to launch the old D.R.E.A.D weapons. In a century and a quarter, the environment was considerably restored, but still sufficiently fragile that Eden's capabilities under Martin Zimmer could have brought about annihilation of the species.

His armies and air forces were poised, ready.

And no one knew his face.

"What are you thinking, Daddy?"

John Rourke lit the thin, dark tobacco cigar in the blue-yellow flame of his old battered Zippo. When they were awakened, the Zippo was among Michael's things. Michael returned it to him. He looked at his daughter, smiled, said, "About how little things really change."

Manfred Kohl cleared his throat "If we announce your return, John, with the way in which Martin Zimmer has virtually deified you, the people of Eden would—"

"Think I'm an imposter, an actor, just like Lance Stone who played me in their damn movie. When the medical people in China saw that my brain wave patterns were back in the normal range, your government and the government of Mid-Wake figured your problems were solved. Awaken me, awaken Paul and Annie and Michael and Natalia. Gee, sorry nothing can be done for Sarah Rourke, yet. But we're still working on that. And you can go back to the Sleep if you want to later, but right now we want you to overthrow Martin Zimmer. No. It's not that simple.

"If Martin Zimmer somehow could be Deitrich Zimmer, or even if there's a connection, there's something considerably more important to me than world peace, to consider right now," John Rourke declared. "You said what little background data exists on Martin Zimmer indicates that he may have been a doctor. So, if he is Deitrich Zimmer, or Deitrich Zimmer's pupil, the micro-surgery techniques Deitrich Zimmer supposedly took with him to the grave, could be just what's needed to reach that bullet lodged in my wife's brain, free her.

"You—you want—" Kohl stammered.

James Darkwood laughed, looking at Kohl, saying, "I was right, wasn't I? Five generations ago, Jason Darkwood wrote his memoirs of a life at sea and his adventures with John Rourke in the closing days of the War. You should have read those memoirs, Manfred. I tried to tell you John Rourke doesn't take orders. He does what he thinks is best." Darkwood clapped Manfred Kohl on the shoulder, saying, "And you're shit out of luck."

Four

They rode in relative silence, a father and son who, at least once, were both in love with the same woman, and their faithful Jewish companion, as Paul Rubenstein often thought of himself.

He looked down at the journal page before him and began to write. "We are passengers in what these days passes for a delivery truck, taking fresh supplies of souvenirs and candy to The Retreat. Again, Manfred Kohl became considerably bent out of shape. He told John that breaking into The Retreat to retrieve his old weapons was silly.

"John was very patient with him, explaining that not only were the weapons he'd always carried the best to be had, even if there were more modern ones, but that the psychological value against Martin Zimmer was important. Martin would be wondering who had broken into the Retreat, and for what purpose? Putting the dictator of Eden even a little off balance was to everyone's benefit, John insisted.

"I don't know if Manfred Kohl agreed with him or not—and I suspect the latter—but he acquiesced.

"I was, frankly, very worried when we were first awakened from The Sleep, worried over the situation concerning Michael and Natalia. How would John accept this? It was always clear that John loved Natalia, but equally clear that, because of his personal code of honor, that love could never be consummated while Sarah lived. Does Sarah live?

"Her heart and lungs still function at the prescribed rate for cryogenic maintenance, and her brain wave pattern is normal considering the trauma inflicted upon her.

"I worry that, if Sarah is revived, she might not be the same person. What damage might have been done to her brain by the bullet? At the time, we were assured that the physical damage was very little and that the problem was that the bullet could not be removed. But what if those medical opinions were in error? And now, with Michael and Natalia lovers—and that is obvious—the possibility exists that John might be

311

forever alone.

"John constantly amazes me. Michael and Natalia approached him after the initial stages of our recovery from The Sleep. Michael held her hand. He let go of her hand, stepped in front of her and told his father that he and Natalia were in love, and had consummated that love. John sat there very quietly for a moment and I didn't quite know what to expect. My wife, Annie, John's daughter and Michael's sister, held my hand so tightly I could feel the circulation slowing.

"Then John said—and I think I'll remember his words until I go to the grave—I love you, Michael. And I love you, Natalia. Now I can love both of you as one. And he stood—with some difficulty because the body relearns movement slowly after the Sleep—and embraced Michael, then embraced Natalia, kissing her cheek. He shook his son's hand.

"I cannot imagine a man handling such a situation in a finer or better way than he did. Here, in Eden, John Rourke's praises are sung, regardless of the motive, for his heroism. His bravery is something I would never deny. But, the more I learn about my friend the more I realize that his real greatness is in his humanity, something no statue, no guided tour, no face on postage stamps or coinage or currency could ever convey."

The truck stopped.

John said, "Gentlemen." And he drew the Detonics Scoremaster, Annie had loaned him, from his trouser band.

The rear doors of the truck opened, one of Manfred Kohl's agents-in-place waiting with a gun in his hand. "You must hurry now."

Paul's journal was already closed. He left it, inside a musette bag, on the seat he'd occupied in the back of the truck. He took the battered old Browning High Power from beneath the sixties-ish turtleneck he wore under his hooded black windbreaker and started for the door . . .

Using the German climbing equipment, added to the fact that they were all intimately familiar with each face of the mountain, facilitated their ascent, despite the darkness and the fact that there was no moon.

The only electronic security they had encountered, perforce not overly precise because there was now abundant re-released wildlife in the area, was at the fence surrounding the base of the mountain itself. Bridging the fence without interrupting it's current allowed them easy access.

The new German climbing boots, the advanced crampons and the fact, that for better than fifty percent of the distance they needed no climbing gear at all and could essentially just walk, reduced the ascent time to under two hours.

"There's no electronic security on the summit, except for a video camera on the far side," John told them. "By keeping low and going in front of the statue, we'll be undetectable."

They approached the statue, Paul seeing it for the first time, as was Michael. Michael observed, "The face on the statue is pretty lifelike; I think you ought to lose the beard, Dad. Just a suggestion."

John turned around, saying nothing. And, in the darkness, Paul could not see his face. But, he agreed with Michael. The full beard John had grown to disguise his now very recognizable face, just wasn't him, somehow.

Keeping to knees and elbows, they crawled past the base of the statue past the escape hatch John had actually used before and after the event which the statue depicted, as if frozen in time, and to the far side of the mountain's summit, well out of range of the video surveillance.

There was a large, flat stone, surrounded by several smaller stones. Michael began moving the smaller stones away. "If we do this right," John said, taking one end of the large, flat stone, Paul taking the other, "we'll be in and out and they'll never know how we did it. That should make our Martin Zimmer even more upset." Michael joining them, they moved the flat stone onto the tarp John had laid out on the rocky surface beside it, so there would be no scuff marks on the stones.

"Where's this come out again?" Paul asked.

But John only laughed softly . . .

Michael Rourke knew The Retreat as well as his father, having been its master for all the years while his father returned to The Sleep. Michael and his sister had grown up there.

Going first through the tunnel, climbing downward in near total darkness except for the small flashlight he held clamped in his teeth, he reached the interior vault closure and began to work the combination.

"How are you coming, Michael?"

"Almost—got it, Dad.

"Where do we come out?" Paul reiterated. "Ohh—I remember. It takes a sick mind to think of something like that."

"I'll grant you devious," Michael's father said. Michael Rourke drew open the door and aimed his flashlight at the back of the object which masked the secret entrance. "Remember, push on your right side and swing it to your left."

"I remember." Michael pushed, the porcelain cold against his hands. The toilet's flush tank swung away and Michael Rourke drew back. There was no light, no sound. He decided to go for it, stepping through, feeling with his foot first that the toilet lid was down, only putting part of his weight on it, then stepping down to the floor. If there were motion or pressure sensors, their entry would be detected.

The flashlight in his teeth again, Michael held one of his Berettas in each hand.

His father was through the opening, then his brother-in-law.

"We can't risk lights because a power surge would be detected. There are motion sensors by the main entrance, but I can't get my Harley up the escape tunnel anyway, so there's no need to go to the main entrance. The video cameras probably aren't monitored continuously, so let's hope they don't catch the flicker."

And they started getting out of their backpacks . . .

Reaching the video camera without its seeing him was the hardest part, and he stood beside it now, balanced precariously on top of one of the gun cases, the A/B switch in hand. Coaxial cable was vastly changed over what he remembered, but he had rehearsed this, at the house on the outskirts of Eden City, which James Darkwood had secured as a very temporary headquarters for them.

Using the pliers from his Leatherman Tool, Michael Rourke worked loose the locking nut, then readied himself to jerk the coax free of the camera feed. He was double gloved now, rubber below leather, to avoid leaving fingerprints, which were still used occasionally for indentification, he'd understood from Darkwood and Kohl. But, these days, sophisticated laser scanners routinely picked up latent prints that were left through a porous glove, a technology pioneered in the late twentieth century.

He jerked the coax free and pushed the single feed end of the A/B switch into place, leaving the lock nut until later. In the next instant, he pushed the coax that was a moment before it disconnected from the camera onto one of the receptacles on the other end of the A/B switch.

No sirens sounded, no lights flashed on, but he didn't for a moment feel safe . . .

Paul Rubenstein had his A/B switch in position on the second video surveillance camera, then tightened the lock nut. The video equipment they were attaching would be their gift to the government of Eden. It was cheap Russian equipment, suited to the task but so ubiquitous as to be untracable, the Eden market flooded with identical units, only these with all serial markings removed.

Paul climbed down off the kitchen counter, checking his connection to the video recorder.

He hit the A/B switch's remote and the switch moved to the center position, the feed from the camera going to both coax lines, the one leading along to the main entrance of The Retreat and the one leading down to his recorder.

His fingers poised over the play and record buttons. In six centuries, apparently, no one had discovered a way to make one button which reliably did both.

When the camera reached its farthest rearward swing, Paul pushed play and record, the same feed that was going along coax to the security station going into the recorder as well.

He looked at his watch, timing a full rotation of the camera from starting point back to starting point at one minute and fifty-two seconds. He tapped out the numbers on a calculator, then leaned against the wall and waited.

Five

John Rourke had the alarms on the cases he needed to enter bridged in under ten minutes, the video of the interior of the Retreat's great room being fed back through the coax from the security cameras, so that anyone observing the video signal—watching it on a monitor—would see exactly what was expected, an empty room in darkness except for illuminated cases, not three men rifling them.

The alarms bridged, Paul and Michael aiding him, John Rourke began to open the cases.

The first things he took from the cases were the twin stainless Detonics .45s. He hefted them in his hands, nodding in satisfaction.

Carefully, he set both pistols onto the padded length of material he'd stretched across the floor. Michael handed him the two full-sized Detonics Scoremasters. John Rourke set those onto the length of fabric as well.

Paul set the 629 next in line and the suppressor-fitted 6906.

The knives—both the Crain LS-X and the A.G. Russell Sting IA Black Chrome—along with their sheaths, the leather surprisingly well-preserved, were stowed in an open pack.

John Rourke took his dark-lensed aviator style sunglasses from the case and placed them carefully in the hardside case in a pocket of his jacket. "Paul, get my SSG; never know when we might have to do some long distance work," Rourke whispered beside his friend's ear.

Paul nodded.

John Rourke went to the library shelves.

He set the open pack on the floor beside him.

Videotape was supposed to be wound periodically to guard against deterioration, but German scientists had assured him that if he could get it, they could salvage it.

Michael was beside him, whispered into his ear, "What are you getting?"

316

"Home movies. Annie's and Paul's children can see them someday, and yours and Natalia's, too."

"Dad, I, uhh—"

"What I said, I meant. You know I loved Natalia, but there was no way we could ever be together. You did what I wanted, and I'm happy for both of you that you did it on your own, without me prompting it. My daughter is married to one of the two finest men I've ever known, and some day Natalia will be marrying the other one." He touched at his son's arm, then went on with his work.

He left the video shelves and went to one of the book shelves.

"What book?" Michael asked him.

"What else?" John Rourke smiled. There were two books, one the Rourke Family Bible and the other was Ayn Rand's novel, *Atlas Shrugged* . . .

There were other items they took with them, extra Barami Hip-Grips and Pachmayr Grips for his father's revolvers, Pachmayrs for the .45s, as well. Spare magazines and speedloaders, were other gear that might prove necessary to them. From here, they would join Natalia and Annie, then travel into the Wildlands.

He didn't need sleep, but he needed rest.

Michael was last into the escape tunnel, pulling the flush tank behind him, then starting to work on the door. They had worn surgical slippers over their boots so no footprints would be left behind, at least none that would be recognizable, and he pulled his off now, stuffing them into a pocket of his coat so he'd have decent traction on the ladder rungs . . .

John Rourke reached the summit and climbed out into the cold night air, Annie's Detonics ScoreMaster in his right fist, the Smith & Wesson Centennial in his belt on its Hip Grip, one pack on his back, another in his left hand.

Keeping from sight of the video surveillance camera, John Rourke took a moment to look upward into the night sky. With no moonlight, and the only artificial light from hundreds of feet below, the star fields were brilliant diamonds set against black velvet.

He thought about the two women he had loved in his life. And perhaps both of them were forever lost to him. Certainly Natalia was. He'd wanted this to happen, intentionally used the cryogenic chambers after the Great Conflagration to bring his son and daughter to adulthood, so Annie could wed Paul, so Natalia could wed Michael. He'd wanted Natalia to belong to Michael, wanted it and feared it and now it had happened.

Happiness and sadness could sometimes be one.

Stars altered their paths slightly over the years, as did men and women, and had he the means, he would have calculated how much subtle variation their was between the patterns among the stars now and then. John Rourke watched the stars a moment longer. In the six centuries which had passed since he'd first viewed the stars from the summit of this mountain, his question was still unresolved.

Six

While they slept, Commander Dodd instituted a dictatorship, and during the long years of his dominion, resentment grew in Eden, so did its population. The former was a natural result, the latter was planned. Out of both grew a resistance to tyranny, forced into the Wildlands for survival.

John Rourke watched the terrain below the now-antique Jl7-V, Kohl at its controls. Eden lived up to its name, a garden of lush green, the summers still short and cool, the winters still long and cold, but the tree cover returned, looking like the Georgia that had existed in the latter decades of the twentieth century, rather than the barren wasteland he had awakened to after the first Sleep in the immediate aftermath of the Great Conflagration. In that respect—the re-greening—Dodd and his successors had done well.

John Rourke had always felt the devil was worth his due.

Rourke's eyes shifted back into the cabin. James Darkwood slept, but young Darkwood had been up nearly all the night and, unlike the rest of the cabin occupants, had not come out of a century and a quarter's cryogenic repose.

Annie did needlepoint.

Oddly, so did Natalia, although with evidently less practice. He smiled, thinking about that. Not something that was probably given great emphasis at the Chicago Espionage School six centuries ago in the Soviet Union, needlepoint. Perhaps cross-stitch instead.

Michael and Paul played chess, happily still a pastime for people everywhere.

John Rourke returned to his notes.

A century and a quarter's worth of history wasn't assimilated in a moment.

Dodd's plan—or was it Deitrich Zimmer's?—was to increase the population of Eden exponentially, through immigration of carefully

319

selected groups and through a rigidly enforced policy of sexual exploitation of women.

Today in Eden, women had no political rights. Like men, they owned little else but the clothes on their back. Today, economic incentives had replaced harsher methods. Today, women were given a cash payment and tax credit for every child they brought into the world. When Dodd was just getting started, women who refused to bear children were forced to do so.

He understood the woman who had tried to 'pick him up' on the bus. She wanted to be made pregnant. Although artificial insemination was available to any woman who chose it, it was forced on women of child-bearing age. If they did not become pregnant by more conventional means, the alternative punitive taxes were levied. Over half the young women he had seen in Eden were pregnant.

When Dodd took over, almost immediately he proceeded to activate D.R.E.A.D., but in secret.

Over the intervening decades, the Soviet Union, prohibited from building nuclear weapons, allied itself with New Germany and Mid-Wake for protection against Eden. Eden possessed the Soviet nuclear weapons seized after conquering the Soviet underwater complex. New Germany armed itself, a technologically simple task, comparatively, sharing the technology on a give and take basis with Mid-Wake.

The alliance between Mid-Wake and New Germany insistently reminded John Rourke of the relationship between the United States and Great Britain before The Night of The War, all but perfect mutual trust (tempered with a little espionage between good friends, to be sure).

There was resistance to Dodd's policies, and some of the Eden returnees, some of the immigrants from Mid-Wake (whom Dodd could not prohibit, although he apparently tried) and some of the Russians abandoned Eden proper, for the Wildlands.

Unlike the settlers of America's frontiers centuries earlier, these immigrant pioneers brought with them considerable technological sophistication, and most importantly the ability to duplicate it.

Meanwhile, the ranks of Dodd's supporters also grew, through the help of immigrants from New Germany who were Nazi sympathizers and through the educational programs installed at Eden. Children were brainwashed into Dodd's brand of National Socialism from the earliest possible moment.

Soon, all non-whites had either fled Eden or disappeared.

Dodd's replacement, Arthur Hooks, carried on in Dodd's footsteps almost as if one were the clone of the other, expanding the baby farming program, deepening the tyranny. The average woman in the fifty years following Dodd's accession to office, bore seven point five children each. The circumstance also contibuted to the decline in women's rights, because the life expectancy for women was generally lowered by almost nine years.

By Hooks' administration, Eden had full deployment of the nuclear arsenal of D.R.E.A.D. Although New Germany and Mid-Wake wished to crush Eden's tyrannical government and restore freedom there, the risk of nuclear devastation was too great.

Mid-Wake encouraged population growth, rather than demanding it, and Mid-Wake itself grew. No longer did citizens of Mid-Wake wish to return to their ancestral homeland in what was once the United States and was now, ironically, known as Eden. Instead, they re-populated the Hawaiian Islands, then Australia. But the undersea city of Mid-Wake was still the capitol.

Many Soviets from their undersea culture, once mortal enemies of the Americans of Mid-Wake, joined with the people they had once fought, creating no separate colonies, but comingling to swell the populations of Hawaii and Australia.

A small percentage of Germans from New Germany in Argentina set out to what was called 'Gaul', where the Wild Tribes of Europe lived. Their goal was to rebuild historic Germany. With the help of the people of the Soviet Underground City, not only did historic Germany become a reality, but the two peoples, in many ways, became one.

The world was arrayed now into two armed camps. How familiar that was.

On one side was the Trans-Global Alliance, led by Mid-Wake (including the states of Hawaii, Australia and New Zealand) and New Germany, including the state of European Germany. Committed to this alliance as well were the Russian Ural Republic (once the Underground City) and the Russian Pacific Republic (once the Soviet underwater complex).

On the opposite side stood Eden, the greatest power on earth, greater separately than ancient Rome, Nazi Germany or the Cold

War Union of Soviet Socialist Republics, perhaps greater collectively.

Eden extended along the eastern half of what was once the United States, from Maine to what remained of Florida after the great earthquake, but surpassed those boundaries into what had been Canada and the Caribbean nations, into northern Brazil.

The only neutral nation on earth (sympathetic to the Trans-Global Alliance, but not a member) was Lydveldid Island. Yet, Iceland's very borders were at risk, the southern tip of what was once Greenland was now occupied by Martin Zimmer's, Eden troops.

Periodically, Eden aircraft would incurse against Lydveldid Island's air space and Lydveldid Island would file a diplomatic protest. Only because the Trans-Global Alliance was committed to Icelandic freedom did the tiny island nation remain free.

But Martin—who was he really?—continually harassed Iceland.

Portions of the world were still radioactively hot, no-man's lands that only a lunatic with a death wish would enter. Other areas, in some ways inhospitable, had become havens for fragmentary population groups. The Wild Tribes of Europe were assimilated culturally into Historic Germany (John Rourke had been pleased to learn that Natalia's school was now the site of a Wild Tribes cultural center, the building and grounds named in her honor).

Other small groups, most notably the people who had left Eden and dissenters from the Russian Ural Republic, lived away from organized government, forming their own societies. Russian dissenters, still believing in Communism, had set up communal societies in western Europe and northern Africa. The Eden exiles, except for very small groups in the deep snows of the Tennessee mountains, lived in confederations of communities stretching from what once had been Montana to New Mexico and into northern Mexico.

The societies here were as diverse, Kohl and Darkwood had said, as thumbing through the pages of a history book, or perhaps a psychology book.

To the west of the Wildlands were the great salt marshes where the Pacific, in the aftermath of the destruction of California, had encroached upon the low-lying desert. To the east, between the wildlands and Eden, there was the radioactive wasteland which followed generally the course of the Mississippi River.

But, in the Wildlands, in the last decade, there grew a new menace, one more immediate than accidentally stumbling into a radioactive hotspot. That menace was the Land Pirates.

The Land Pirates, some of them said to be descendants of the Russians of the KGB Elite Corps and the Marine Spetznas, others of various ancestry, traded in precious stones and precious metals, for technology and flesh.

Slavery flourished in some portions of the Wildlands, sexual slavery the most prevalent and the most insidious. Everywhere, people were obsessed with increasing their numbers.

An easy and obvious comparison could be made between the Land Pirates of the twenty-sixth century and Comancheros of the nineteenth century. Although easy and obvious comparisons were sometimes as easily and obviously spurious, this one was not.

Intelligence data gleaned independently by New Germany and Mid-Wake suggested that Martin, who allowed the Land Pirates to exist, was effecting an alliance with them. His purpose was uncertain, although it seemed obvious, at least, that with the Land Pirates as allies, he could subdue the Wildlands without bothering to commit vast numbers of troops.

And there was a chance, however dubious, that Martin Zimmer was in the Wildlands now, conferring and working strategies with his new allies.

To see Martin Zimmer's face would be worth any personal risk. Because, if this man had somehow used cryogenics and was Deitrich Zimmer, then there was a score to settle for the murder of a child more than a century ago. And yet, Zimmer's talents as a surgeon, might be the only way to save Sarah from the living death in which she now existed.

John Thomas Rourke exhaled, tired but not ready for sleep. He lit a cigar in the blue-yellow flame of his battered Zippo.

The thought of knowing the face of Martin Zimmer at once drove him onward and frightened him more than anything had ever frightened him in his long life.

At times, John Rourke wondered if his life had been too long, but he would not allow himself the luxury of death; it would have to be forced upon him.

John Rourke put away his notes, the reached into the pack near him, pulling out one of the Scoremasters. He had detail stripped,

323

cleaned and oiled the little CombatMasters, but left the other guns for the long, slow, zig-zagging flight to the Wildlands. He removed the .45's magazine, drew back the slide and confirmed that the chamber was empty, then moved the slide in line with the disassembly notch and started to push out the slide stop.

The sun was up and, just about now, someone would be noticing that certain items within Martin Zimmer's little museum at The Retreat were missing. And, when Martin Zimmer learned just what was missing, he might experience the same uncomfortable feeling John Rourke had when thinking about Zimmer.

Seven

Also, in the Wildlands, aside from pioneers and Land Pirates, there were agents of Allied Intelligence. Three of these agents, a man and two women, bundled in heavy clothing against the sub-zero temperatures and high winds, met the J17-V as it touched down on the circle of ice. The pad had been cleared and iced over to keep blowing and drifting snow from accumulating.

As John Rourke stepped from the V-stol aircraft and pulled up his parka's snorkel hood, the ice beneath his feet was so slick he could barely stand. He stepped back, sat briefly on the accommodation steps and secured ice creepers to the soles of his boots.

Before The Night of The War, this had been suburban St. Louis, Missouri. The city was neutron bombed and, despite the fires of the Great Conflagration and five intervening centuries, some ruins still stood, visible from the air as they'd terrain-followed to stay under Eden's air defense net.

Not far from here were places where the radiation levels were still so high that exposure would mean certain slow death.

"Better put on ice creepers," John Rourke called back inside.

The creepers in place, he went aft along the fuselage to begin unpacking the gear stowed there. Michael joined him in a moment, assisting him.

Rourke looked over his shoulder, Paul with the two women going over to meet the reception party, Kohl and Darkwood with them.

John Rourke's skin tingled slightly where the full beard and mustache were shaved away just a few hours ago.

The gear stacked away from the aircraft in the event the J17-V had to take off rapidly, John and Michael Rourke started away from the plane to join the others.

The three agents—Rourke was told that one of the women was a German, the other woman and the male agent from Mid-Wake—

were just finishing shaking hands with Paul and Annie and Natalia. "This woman is the best field operative in the Wildlands," Jason Darkwood began. "And she's not even from Mid-Wake, darnit."

Annie laughed.

John Rourke turned to face the woman, the first time he had seen her eye to eye. And her gray eyes locked on his face in a mixture of terror and revulsion. She was somewhere in her late forties or early fifties, he surmised, long gray streaks in what little of her dark brown hair was exposed beneath the front of her parka hood.

"This is a sick joke, Jason."

Darkwood repeated, "Sick joke? Do you know who this is?"

"Him and this one," she pointed to Michael. "The mustache is really cute."

"What do you say, Hilda?" Manfred Kohl asked.

"You received my report a little earlier than I thought, I suppose. But where did you find these two—?"

"What do you mean?" John Rourke interjected.

"You know perfectly well what I mean, you damned fool. With that face if you are seen around here by any of the locals, you will be shot or worse for—"

Natalia interrupted her. "I thought the people of Eden revered the face of John Rourke."

"The people of Eden aren't the people of the Wildlands," the German agent told her.

Jason Darkwood said to her, "Tell me now, Hilda, what was in that report you think we've seen."

The woman—Hilda—looked at Darkwood oddly, then shrugged her shoulders. "If you have not read it, this is the strangest coincidence in history; and, like most people of my profession, I do not believe in coincidence."

"What was in the report, Hilda?" Darkwood insisted.

"The Land Pirates struck a town about a hundred miles north of here almost a week ago. We got there when the town was in flames, the children had been kidnapped and the men and the old people tortured to death, the women of child bearing age kidnapped, of course. We found a few people alive, older people, but all of them dying. Margie and Dan and I tried to get what information we could out of them, because the Land Pirates have been a lot more active in the last several weeks."

326

"Get to the point," Paul told her.

Natalia lit a cigarette.

"Fine. The point, Mr. — what was your name again?"

"Rubenstein."

"Part of the joke. I get it," the woman named Hilda said.

"The point, huh?" Michael suggested.

"All right. Good. I asked a dying old woman if she could tell me anything that could help us. She could not talk, I realized in the next instant, because they had cut out her tongue."

"Ohh, Jesus," Annie murmured.

"The old woman?" Darkwood pressed.

She drew with her finger in the snow, and drew the word 'Devil' in English. And then she opened the palm of her hand. There was an Eden half-dollar in her hand. It was the last thing she did before she died. Very carefully, she set the coin, face up, inside the letter 'D', and then she tried making a word, but she died."

"What did the word sound like?" Kohl asked her.

" 'Rourke' was what it sounded like. And it was John Rourke's face — his face, and his face, without that mustache." And she pointed to John Rourke and then to Michael Rourke.

"The Devil?" John Rourke queried. "Maybe."

His face on the Eden half-dollar, Michael's face exactly like it, except for the mustache. But, who else's face was it?

Eight

She got the feeling that the German woman, Hilda, still somehow doubted that the men sitting across from her, at the old table in the more than six centuries old police station's basement, were really John Rourke, Michael Rourke and Paul Rubenstein.

The question that Natalia was really Natalia Tiemerovna and Annie was really Annie had never even come up.

It was only logical, she supposed, for the woman to be unbelieving, accepting one hundred twenty-five years of disinformation, as fact.

After Annie and Paul and Michael and she had decided to join John and Sarah in cryogenic sleep, Jason Darkwood who was in charge of security for the original cryogenics operation that had placed John and Sarah in suspended animation out of medical necessity, determined that, someday, his own security would fail. Perhaps because security was not his profession—he was then and was, until he became Admiral of The Fleet ten years later—a submariner, perhaps the best there ever was. With the acquiesence of his then superior officer, Admiral Rahn, and key persons in authority in Mid-Wake, New Germany and the Chinese First City, Captain Jason Darkwood devised a plan. Then, with the help of Marine Captain Sam Aldridge, first officer of the USS *Reagan*, Sebastian, Field Marshal Wolfgang Mann and Han Lu Chen of China, Darkwood carried out that plan.

A portion of Darkwood's plan was rather grisly, she thought when more than a century later she read Jason Darkwood's personal account of what happened, left behind after his death to inform them. Duplicate cryogenic chambers were set up, and six recently dead bodies were acquired, three male and three female, all of approximately the correct size (this took a period of several months). They were fitted with prosthetic make-up to closely approximate the facial features of the six living persons for whom they substituted.

328

Then the entire Rourke family, with the help of the crew of the *Reagan*, was transported by submarine in total secrecy, taken to the last place Darkwood theorized potential killers would look, yet where he was certain proper security measures could be enforced. This was the Chinese First City. And, after Sam Aldridge's and Tom Stanhope's Marines put the six chambers and all necessary monitoring and spare parts equipment in place (Doctor Munchen the medical supervisor on the scene), Han Lu Chen and a hand picked team of Chinese security personnel took charge of their safety, eventually passing this charge along through the generations.

In China, within the Secret Service, there existed to this day a secret society, known simply as 'The Watchers', who until this new Awakening kept the vigil.

Natalia held these men and women in the deepest respect, because for over a century they had safeguarded the lives of the Rourke Family (and her liaison with Michael now made her membership in that family more legitimate than she had ever before felt it to be).

And Jason Darkwood's security measures proved prophetic. Less than thirty days after the transfer of the cryogenic chambers, two events occurred simultaneously.

A team of suicide commandoes, Nazis and former Elite Corps personnel working in concert, attacked the cryogenic repository at Mid-Wake. Apparently, revenge, even more than politics, made 'strange bedfellows'.

A similarly composed team (most of whom survived) attacked Eden while Akiro Kurinami was making a speech, killing Kurinami, his wife, Elaine Halversen, and eight other Eden returnees.

The suicide team which struck Mid-Wake was neutralized before they could have reached the cryogenic repository, all the members killed or taking their own lives. A tribute to Jason Darkwood's security arrangements, it was also the opportunity Darkwood needed to ensure the future safety of the Rourke Family in cryogenic sleep in China. News was leaked, then verified openly, that despite heroic efforts by United States Marine Corps personnel, terrorists were able to reach the Rourke Family and succeeded in precipitating their deaths.

She remembered the line John and Michael sometimes quoted concerning history, that it was ". . . a set of lies agreed on."

After linking up with the Allied agents in the Wildlands, Kohl and

Darkwood left, flying the J17-V they had used west. If it had been discovered by one of Eden's spy satellites or the occasional high altitude intelligence overflight, it would appear to have stopped for refueling or some sort of repair, rather than to drop off infiltrators.

The five of them were on their own with the three intelligence agents, Hilda, the German, and the man and woman from Mid-Wake, Dan and Margie.

It was warm here in the basement of the police station, and Natalia pulled her arms out of the cowl neck black sweater she wore, then slipped the sweater over her head. Annie helped her to set it across the back of the camp chair on which she sat.

"The popular theory is that there were vast oil refineries and storage areas where the great rift valley is, possibly more salt-domed strategic reserves," Hilda told them. "And there is evidence there were explosives plants in the area as well. Anyway, it's not radioactive there, but whatever happened altered the course of the river. And when the firestorms came in the sky, of course, the river's above ground sources dried up, so its volume was reduced.

"Whatever happened, between St. Louis, here to the north and Memphis, to the south of us in what was Tennessee, the river was diverted. Erosion and other forces gouged out the river bed, and some scientists theorize that the mid-continental fault ruptured and there was a quake. I do not know, but the result is a great rift valley where once the river flowed, but vastly deeper than the Mississippi river ever was, according to our best research."

"How deep?" Annie asked her.

Hilda looked over her shoulder, saying almost dismissively, "Three hundred meters in some places."

"Earthquake. It would have had to have been," John said.

"Whatever. It's there. And right in the center, between here and Memphis, is the stronghold."

"The Land Pirates'?" Annie asked.

"No, the bad fairy's. When I want to talk to a woman from Eden I'll—"

Paul stood up. "My wife, Hilda. Leave her alone before she rips your head off and craps down your neck. She's not from Eden and if Eden women are a waste of your time, that's your problem, not ours. I'm in a bad mood. And don't push it, because I know what's coming. The only way in or out of the Land Pirates' stronghold is through this valley, right? Tell me I'm fantasizing."

"The Land Pirates have a way of their own, a route, through the valley. There's no one who knows the way in, no one alive at least, except for the Land Pirates. That is why I told Jason Darkwood and Manfred Kohl that this was a fool's errand. No vehicle can get in or out of the stronghold because of the electrical activity. It is because of the radiation, I think. Something like what happened when the Great Conflagration occurred, the air itself charged with too much electricity. I am not a scientist. But even if you could survive the radiation, it would do you no good. The electrical storms, when they come, are so powerfully magnetic, they will bring down an airplane or neutralize any sort of land vehicle."

"How do the pirates get in?" John asked her without expecting an answer, Natalia guessed. "If they can get in, they must be going below the level of the storms. If the valley is as deep as you say it is in some places, they must have a route that keeps them deep enough within the valley that their vehicles are unaffected. Either that or shielding of some kind."

"I am sure you are correct, whoever you are. But no one but the Land Pirates knows that route, so there you are. It is useless. All of you would be well advised to wait here until Darkwood and Kohl return to pick you up."

"And you think that Martin is out there, conferring with the leaders of the Land Pirates?" Michael asked, dismissing her advice.

"I would bet my life on it," Hilda declared. "But, as I tried to tell Kohl and Darkwood, we cannot get to him in the stronghold. There is no chance."

Paul was pacing the room. He looked at Hilda and asked her, "Do the Land Pirates steal everything they have, or do they trade?"

"Well, of course they trade, my God! Why do you think they steal women of childbearing age? Even the Land Pirates couldn't use all of them themselves."

"Then how is the trading accomplished? Do the Land Pirates go to the customers or do the customers come to them?" Paul persisted.

"The customers sometimes come to them," Hilda said, her tone more subdued. "There is an active smuggling trade here, as you may know. Some say that Martin Zimmer actively encourages the trade to keep the Land Pirates occupied. The smugglers sell to the settlers, because they are the only source of things like certain antibiotics,

331

spare parts for weapons, like that."

Paul pressed, "They trade in women. The smugglers couldn't use all the women, either."

"Some of the women are ransomed back to their families by the smugglers, and rest of them are used for baby farming. There is a premium on children, as I think I have said."

"They smuggle women," Paul continued, as if thinking out loud, "which means they have to be able to get vehicles into the Land Pirates' stronghold, that are large enough to carry a human cargo back out. That means they have a route, maybe not the same one the Land Pirates use, but a route, nonetheless. Who's the top slave smuggler and where do we find him?"

Michael clapped Paul on the back, then looked at Hilda, the German agent. "Well?"

"The man is called Boris. Getting to see him is impossible. You do not know the Wildlands. The three of us—Dan and Margie and myself—we do. Boris doesn't just meet people."

John said, "What if we wanted to trade him a couple of women?" And he looked at them both and winked. "In wonderful condition."

Annie sucked in her breath so quickly it was almost a scream. Natalia just looked away, thinking she wasn't going to like this . . .

There was a map on the wall of what was once a cell there in the basement of the old police station, but the door had rusted off its hinges and where there had likely been a barred window, the opening was now closed over with some type of metal to keep out the cold wind.

On the map, crudely drawn, but likely accurate enough, Dan marked out a route with his finger. "East St. Louis, according to what I've read, was in another state before The Night of The War. States were political subdivisions within—"

"Illinois," John Rourke supplied. "It was a nice enough town."

"Sure. How was George Washington's inaugural party?"

"The champagne was flat," John Rourke smiled. "We shouldn't need radiation gear to get over there, should we." It was a statement, not a question. "So, is that bridge your map shows still useable? Looks the most direct route."

"It's guarded. Twenty-four hours a day, it's guarded."

"Anything sophisticated?" Michael asked. "Or people only?"

"People only, but they're tougher than you guys."

"Ohh, I don't know," Paul grinned. "We're pretty well-rested."

"Yes, we are indeed," John Rourke agreed. "I understand that the only plasma energy weapons out here in the Wildlands, generally, are in the hands of the Land Pirates. Just conventional stuff with the smugglers, this Boris?"

"Enough 'conventional stuff' to choke on, pal," Dan snapped back. "Sure, some of it's a hundred years old—Soviet AKM-96 assault rifles, shit like that—and maybe you guys don't know much about guns, the old kind, projectile weapons. But, they could hurt you."

"Just those little tiny things they called bullets?" Michael asked. "I mean, I wouldn't imagine they could do that much damage, could they?"

John Rourke realized his son had finally developed the Rourke family sense of humor, which had largely skipped him, he knew. His father, Michael's grandfather, a kind man and gentle except when the situation called for something more, was always noted for his wit . . .

It was good and bad, her ability, and the recent Sleep had only served to increase it. She could, without trying at times, read. At times, sometimes when a loved one was in extreme danger, but with frustratingly irregularity, the reading ability she possessed was empathic response. She could feel the pain, the anxiety, the loneliness. Sometimes, subconsciously she could tell her husband's thoughts and, when she did, would try to block them out, despite their love and their closeness, feeling something akin to the voyeur. Sometimes, she could make herself do it. Sometimes, she would just get an impression. It was this now, as Annie Rourke Rubenstein changed clothes. Her father, John Rourke, for some reason was thinking of his father, her grandfather whom she had never met.

But she knew the man, knew her father's impression's of his father, remembered the stories he would occasionally tell.

"Like father, like son," the old aphorism went. Her father's father had been in the OSS, the World War Two United States Office of Strategic Services. And, her grandfather had a sense of humor which had somewhat skipped his only son, his only child.

Once, during World War Two, deep behind enemy lines in Europe, he'd spent the night hiding out in a jeweler's shop. And, he hit on a rather bizarre idea. What would happen if officers in the Nazi high command thought there were assassins assigned to kill them? Would they try to make a lower profile for themselves, and could this reduce their efficiency and aid in the Allied war effort?

He didn't know, but he emptied the magazine of his .45 automatic and engraved the names of seven of Hitler's top general staff officers on the bullets at the mouth of each cartridge, one man per round.

Several days later, when he was in Berlin and posing as a German officer in the Wermacht in order to pick up information from an Allied agent working in deep cover, he left the first of the seven personalized rounds in a washroom.

A bullet with your name on it would not be pleasant to find, he theorized. And, correctly, it seemed.

Seven rounds were left to be found in conspicuous places around wartime Berlin. One of the officers committed suicide, another shortly afterward was hospitalized for some sort of mental disorder. Still a third was fired from the General Staff because of sudden inefficiencies in the performance of his duties.

"What are you thinking about? Reading someone?"

"No," she laughed, telling Natalia, "but I accidentally did. Daddy was thinking about his father."

"This sounds silly," Natalia began.

"What?"

"I always loved you like a sister, but—"

"Now we are, almost anyway." Annie smiled. And she went over to Natalia and hugged her.

Nine

John Rourke planned ahead. He realized the unique possibilities for women in clandestine work, something many men did not. Michael realized it too, and she was happy for that. Natalia Tiemerovna never wanted to be relegated to being someone who had to be sheltered, protected. Although the motivation behind such thoughts was pleasant to contemplate, and sometimes even more pleasant to enjoy, she had abilities and not to use those abilities would have been wrong.

Although, as John had once put it, "Not to sound vulgar, but I firmly believe that the only important thing a man can do that a woman can't do as well, is urinate standing up," John knew the single most important capability of women in clandestine work. Women, if they acted the part properly, could be ignored, almost invisible. Who pays attention to someone scrubbing his floor or dusting his desk or cooking his food? Who, if he ascribes to the more macho/stupid brand of popular wisdom, fears someone who, by her very nature, was bred to be helpless before him, her only possible defense to beg for his mercy?

Intelligence data from the Wildlands was, to say the least, bizarre. The human habitations which had grown up here were a mixture of ridiculous and sublime, communities where the level of technology was so low that conditions and attire were almost medieval; entire areas where fundamentalist beliefs held such terrible sway that spiritual and physical freedom were non-existent and the punishment for transgression was swift and deadly; societies which had intentionally retrogressed to eras that were perceived as happier, better.

Natalia was dressed in clothing that had been made in New Germany, but based on intelligence data collected, no doubt, by Hilda and Dan and Margie. She wore an ankle length dress, plain and of rough cloth, long sleeved and high collared, of the sort worn by women and girls in some of the strictly religious communities where freedom of thought was essentially non-existent.

Annie, on the other hand, was dressed like a woman of Eden, mini-skirted and booted.

The story when they were brought before Boris, the slaver, was that Paul, the only man among them whose face would not be instantly recognizable, was a fugitive from Eden City. Annie was kidnapped from the city. Natalia herself was a woman he kidnapped from the community known as Heaven, along what had once been the Canadian border.

And now, Paul wanted to sell the two women for some of the designer drugs and weapons Boris traded for women.

Natalia Anastasia Tiemerovna, Annie beside her, stepped out of the passenger compartment of the all-terrain vehicle Paul drove, Michael and John climbing down out of the rear cargo area.

"I'm freezing," Annie remarked, a blanket wrapped around her over her skimpy clothes "Why couldn't I be from the same place? This is the pits."

Natalia almost laughed.

John and Michael joined them. John said, "Once you're inside, just relax. We'll be there somehow."

"I was never cut out to be a drug dealer," Paul told him.

"Call it a career move," Michael laughed. They were twenty miles from the bridge leading over to East St. Louis. Natalia, cold as well, hugged her tattered blanket around her. "Are you ready?" Michael said to her.

Natalia laughed as she turned her back to him. "Would you be ready, Michael?" He started to bind her hands behind her with a piece of rope. "I'd like to see you do this?"

"Got your knife?"

"Up the crack of my rear end under my dress."

"Remember to tie a square knot," Paul remarked.

"Right," Michael said.

"Tighter, Michael," Natalia said. "If it's too loose, they'll notice it."

"Let me know if I'm hurting you."

"It's bad enough I won't have bruises. A little rope burn won't hurt for added authenticity," Natalia told him. Her hands bound tightly behind her—but, if her circulation didn't go, she could still reach her knife with her fingertips—Michael turned her around. "Promise me you won't get to like this, but kiss me."

Michael took her into his arms, his mouth coming down on hers and she let herself go limp against him as he held her.

After a long moment, she was looking into his eyes and they smiled down at her. "If you get hurt, I'll be upset."

"I wouldn't want to upset you. Finish me."

He turned her around, then gagged her with a handkerchief between her teeth. It was dry and, even though she knew it was clean, dirty-feeling against her tongue. Then he tied another handkerchief over her eyes as a blindfold.

Natalia felt Michael's lips touch her forehead, and then he started leading her toward the truck.

Annie would be bound and gagged and blindfolded in the same way, she knew, so the two of them would look the part of captured women about to be sold into slavery.

And Natalia told herself to start making herself appear helpless, feel helpless, to make their charade that much easier, more believable. She tripped on the hem of her dress as Michael helped her into the back of the truck, Michael's arms catching her before she fell. Then a blanket was thrown over her. She felt hands—Michael's hands she assumed—binding her ankles together.

Under the circumstances, feeling helpless wouldn't be that difficult.

Ten

Paul Rubenstein stopped the truck on the Missouri side of the bridge.

About two hundred yards away from him, six men with AKM-96 rifles stood behind a barricade of logs and barbed wire. Barbed wire was produced in Eden factories. The wire was shiny enough to be relatively new. Trade goods? He wondered.

"Hey!" Paul shouted to the armed guards, as disreputable looking a bunch of men as he'd seen, since the old days when he and John fought the Brigands in Texas. "I wanna talk with this guy Boris. I got some shit in the back of the truck I wanna trade him!"

The six men did nothing for a moment, then two of them moved off to the right side of the bridge and began to confer. After a minute or more, one of these two shouted back, "What kinda shit you got?"

"Pussy shit, that's what, man." Paul Rubenstein had come from a good home, and if his father—not to mention his mother—had heard him now, especially considering one of the women in question was his wife, he would never have seen the sunrise.

"We got plenty o' pussy, man. So take the fucks with ya' and get out."

"Not like this, you ain't. You pass this up and this Boris guy finds out what he missed, your ass is grass, pal! I ain't talkin' tradin' goods for him to pass off to somebody. I'm talkin' fine stuff, he's gonna wanna jump himself!"

Paul Rubenstein was trying to remember the dialogue from every third rate movie he'd every seen; so far, at least, he figured he was doing okay.

338

But he was walking a narrow line, because if he made the captive women sound too exciting, he might wind up facing the six men here at the bridge, inciting them to want to kill him to get their hands on the women for themselves or to make points with their boss.

Under his coat, he had the battered old Browning High Power, chamber loaded of course, and his right hand near it. The second High Power was in the same condition, but tucked into his waistband at the small of his back.

Three of the six men clambered over the barricade, ducking the barbed wire with practiced expertise it seemed, then started to approach the truck . . .

It was at once hot and cold under the blanket. The first time she'd moved, her legs starting to cramp, her skirt was up to her crotch. By now, it felt like it was up to her waist.

She could faintly hear Paul as he shouted, presumably to some of the men who worked for Boris.

And the words he said, even though she knew they weren't his words, would have frightened her if she had anything less than total faith in her husband. She didn't like being talked about as though the only thing she was good for was what was between her legs. Like Natalia, she had a knife, accessible to her when she needed it if her fingers, already a little stiff, didn't get too stiff.

The gags they both wore, were a wise idea, she realized, because a real outlaw would have gagged them to shut them up and, if they hadn't been gagged, she would probably have tried talking to Natalia. But as it was, all she was capable of were unintelligible grunts.

She heard new voices now, several of them, and it sounded as if there was an argument going on . . .

Michael Rourke smiled at the thought. He was, literally almost, following in his father's footsteps.

The river bank was very narrow here and, if he didn't place his feet in essentially the same spots his father did, he'd fall in.

They were nearly to where the support columns for the bridge could be reached. So far, they evidently went undetected from the bridge above. Michael Rourke had never seen Dan or Margie shoot, so he took little comfort from the fact that they were waiting on the roof on an abandoned building, about one hundred and fifty yards away with sniper rifles. Equipment, no matter how sophisticated, was no better than the man or woman who operated it.

His father reached the pylon, swinging back beneath the bridge on the gravel and dirt, Michael joining him in the next instant.

They both set to opening their packs. As they worked, Michael, his voice a low whisper, said to his father, "I felt like I was doing something behind your back, you know, but I told myself I shouldn't feel that way."

"You did the right thing."

"Still—"

"Is that why you and Natalia decided to take the Sleep again? So you could tell me together?"

"Yeah, but that's not the only reason," Michael told his father.

"Well, fine, consider me told. It was an insoluble situation, Michael. Natalia and I loved each other, and I don't think that will ever change. No offense."

"None taken," Michael nodded, checking the power for the charge that was in his hands.

"I was the fool to let it go as far as I did, and the longer it went on, the worse both of us felt, because it was hopeless. I loved your Mother and Natalia, and I'm married to your mother. You actually did me a favor. I could never figure out what to do about the situation the three of us were in." And Michael's father extended his gloved right hand. "Pardon the glove, okay?"

"Okay."

"You just remember one thing; treat Natalia the best that you can. And not only will both of you be happy, but you'll be making me happy, too. But, if she ever starts calling me 'Dad', you and I duke it out, right?" And he grinned "Right," Michael nodded, smiling.

He'd never expected anything less of his father, but now that everything was in the open, it was better, somehow.

"So? You guys going to get married?"

"Yeah, sooner or later. Neither one of us has anything against the idea, but neither one of us sees any reason why having some words said over us will make us any more married than we are."

"I agree," his father said "But, I'm old fashioned enough to think it's a good idea, anyway."

"We kind of figured, well, we'd wait until maybe Mom was—

His father put his hand on his shoulder. "She'd like that. Thank you. But you know that she might never—"

"Yeah," Michael said, swallowing hard. "But I'm like you that way, too damn stubborn to give up."

His father started to speak, inhaled, then nodded and looked away. And he realized his father was holding back tears.

Between them, in the packs they'd brought, there were six powerful charges of the latest German plastique. The bridge pylons were old enough that, as Michael Rourke rubbed his gloved hand over the one nearest to him, some of the concrete on the surface flaked away. They would be reinforced, of course, but the explosives would take care of the structural steel as well.

They began setting the charges, moving through the girderwork below the bridge, placing the charges on the insides of the pylons, so the pylons would blow outward into the river, and the bridge section would entirely collapse.

They hoped . . .

The long skirts of her dress were twisted around her legs, binding her almost as much as the rope on her ankles. And when the blanket was pulled off, aside from a sensation of light at the upper and lower edges of her blindfold, she was also instantly chilled.

"What color's this bitch's eyes you said?"

"Blue. Prettiest damned blue you ever saw. The other one—look at those legs, huh—she's got brown eyes."

341

"Boris likes broads with blue eyes. Let's see 'em."

"Fine, but that's all you see."

"Look at that one. Her dress is all the way up. Let's check out her—"

There was the click of pistol's hammer being drawn back to full stand. "Keep your fuckin' hands off her panties, man; I came here with two virgins and your boss gets to see 'em first."

"Shit, asshole, they's six o' us and one o' you!"

"You wanna die first?"

"Take her damn blindfold, off and let me see her eyes."

Natalia felt herself being manhandled into a sitting position, her back aching with the sudden movement. Under different circumstances, she would have found being called a virgin mildly amusing. Not now.

Then the blindfold was pushed down, and she squinted against the light. She felt hands at the back of her head and as the blindfold was ripped away, she lost a few hairs in the process. Her hair was longer than she'd ever worn it since she was a little girl, well past her shoulder's now and unbound, more than she could say for the rest of her.

When, at last, she opened her eyes, she sucked in her breath almost in a scream. It wasn't acting. The light hurt her eyes, but it was the sight of the men standing beside Paul, who nearly precipitated the scream. Dressed in rags and new clothes combined, but nothing fitting properly, long dirty hair, scraggly beards, each of them armed to the teeth, they looked like barbarians.

Beside her, Paul was sitting up Annie, taking the blindfold from over Annie's eyes "Good lookin, huh. This one's my personal favorite. Look at those legs, so long they could wrap around you twice, I bet."

Annie's eyes were as wide as saucers. Except for her panties, she looked naked from the waist down, her stockings shredded (intentionally).

"The truck stays here," one of the men growled. He was taller than Michael or John, and easily one and one-half times the size of either of them. As he reached toward Natalia, the smell of his body was overpoweringly strong. "I'll grab this one."

"They'll walk. And we ain't goin past the middle of the bridge. Now back the fuck off," Paul threatened. Paul produced a knife, put it in his teeth, grabbed at Natalia's dress and pushed it up to her knees, then cut the ropes at her ankles "On your feet, bitch," Paul rasped.

If she made it out of this alive, Natalia thought, she wasn't certain whether she would congratulate Paul on his hitherto concealed acting talents, or feel like slapping him in the face.

As he pushed her out of the truck bed, her feet were too numb to support her and she dropped to her knees.

Annie was beside her in the next instant, flat on her face in the snow.

Paul dragged first Natalia to her feet, then Annie.

Natalia swayed, still not certain that her feet and legs would support her.

But she was flexing her fingers. The man with the body odor twisted her around roughly and she almost fell, narrowly keeping her balance. His skin felt like leather as he grabbed at her wrists. "Tied tight enough." And then his face was near hers, his mouth odor so bad she nearly vomited in his face. "Girlies like you don't be real good, we take some of that barbed wire and tie 'em up in it. Then we kick 'em around for a while. Feels real good!"

She cast her eyes down, for two reasons: it was probably what he expected her to do and, if she looked at him much longer, she would throw up.

"Boris ain't gonna like comin' down to the bridge. He's got shit to do."

"Yeah, and I go walkin' in there with these," Paul laughed evily, "and I don't come walkin' out again. You tell this Boris that I want plenty of antibiotics, some nose candy and six AKM-96 rifles.

"Six! For pussy?"

"Six for each one; tell him. Or I pack up the truck. He hears what he missed with these two, hell, I wouldn't wanna be you guys. Probably get six or eight kids outa each one of 'em before he'd throw 'em away."

She watched the two with whom Paul bargained.

They walked some distance away, Paul keeping his old Browning High Power on them while they conferred.

The key to the plan's having any chance of success at all was that they didn't go into East St. Louis, never got off the bridge, that Boris came to them.

And, although she didn't like it, she realized that Paul was making a last gambit. He shouted to the two men, saying, "Look at this, man!" And his fist closed over the front of Natalia's dress and ripped it open almost to her waist.

She wore a bra underneath and that was all. He went to Annie and did the same thing.

Natalia stood there, watching the men as they watched her, watched Annie, their eyes going farther than Paul had ripped. "All right. Get 'em up to the barricade. Boris ain't gonna like it. I tell ya that, man."

Paul only nodded . . .

All of the charges, three on each side of the bridge, were in position, set to detonate when the radio signal was made.

John Rourke looked across to the other side of the bridge. Clinging to one of the girders there, as he did on this side, his son, Michael, was ready.

John Rourke looked at the black-faced Rolex Submariner on his left wrist.

All they needed was Paul's signal.

His eyes drifted back to the face of his watch.

This was taking too long, and the longer it took, the more chance there was it would go wrong.

Eleven

Natalia's fingers had full flexibility now, if not full feeling, the tips still tingling as she moved them. As soon as the two men had retreated toward the barricade, Paul walking on with them for a moment; she turned her back toward the truck and caught up her skirts, pulling them up until she could slide her right hand inside the waistband of her underpants. When she pulled on the Bali-Song that was taped between the cheeks of her rear end, the tape took a little skin with it. She was grateful for the gag to bite down on to keep her from making any sort of sound in the instant of pain. She let her dress fall back.

But she had the knife, the lock off, the handle in her right hand, shielded by her left. She desperately wanted to cut the bonds from her wrists, but to do so now might be premature. From a distance, if the ropes were seen not to be connected, the deception might be blown. Instead, she let one handle half drop, sawing with the Bali-Song's primary edge against the ropes but not cutting all the way through. The rope was old, so it would be dry and cut away more easily, and only twisted around her wrists three times. Once one turn of the rope was cut through, she could pull her wrists free. Michael tying her, they had experimented with it several times to make sure that it would work.

Natalia looked at Annie, Annie nodding that she had her knife as well.

Paul, his voice gruff sounding, shouted, "Move your asses, girls! On the double!" Bowing her head slightly, Annie beside her, Natalia started moving off slowly toward him. "Hurry it

345

up, damnit!"

She quickened her pace.

When they neared Paul, he grabbed them both and pushed them forward roughly. "Move it!"

The blanket that had been wrapped around her against the cold fell from her shoulders. When she looked back toward it, Paul gave her another shove, saying through his teeth, "Sorry." Then he shouted at her, "Stupid! Don't want the damn blanket? Then freeze your ass!"

They were nearing the barricade, Paul grabbing Annie and then her, pulling them together back to back. This was so they could help each other with the ropes on their wrists, if need be.

She looked toward the barricade. The two men who had accompanied Paul and then gone back ahead of him were gone, presumably to get Boris. She lowered her eyes, sawing through the turn of rope all the way.

Twelve

She was cold and stiff from standing there in the cold. And she really didn't know just how long it had been, but her wrists were free and she could tell by feeling behind her, that Annie's wrists were free as well.

A truck, from intelligence data she had seen, almost a brand new Eden Army issue, was pulling up on the far side of the barricade.

The two men she'd seen with Paul jumped down from the back, the truck parked at an angle across the bridge. She could see quite clearly.

Then a man climbed down out of the passenger side of the cab.

He was big, fat, and dirty looking. He wore a heavy coat that looked to made of sheepskin, cinched at his enormous waist with a wide belt, a pistol holster on either side in front, the pistols set for crossdraw. Cartridge belts were crisscrossed over his chest.

He wore a black beard, so long, it was nearly to the center of his chest. As he started forward, toward the barricade, she could properly assess his height as well over six feet. She guessed his weight at close to three hundred pounds.

"And who the hell are you to order me to come and see two damn pieces o' ass? Yeah, you, damnit!"

Paul kept his cool. He shouted back, "Hey, you don't wanna see 'em, no big deal! I'll move on and sell 'em someplace else."

"The hell ya will!"

Paul stood his ground, his pistol still in his hand.

The big man was coming through an opening made for him in the barricade, his stride so long, it looked almost as if he could have crossed from one side of the river to the other without even needing a bridge to keep his feet dry.

"Blue eyes, huh? And he walked straight up to her, past Paul, grabbing Natalia by the neck with his right hand and almost lifting her off the ground. "Let's see 'em bitch!" She looked right at him. If he held her like this much longer, she'd have to try to kill him, because she couldn't breathe.

"Keep your hands off til ya own her, man," Paul said from behind him.

The big man started to laugh, his breath when he opened his mouth—his teeth were yellow, except for the ones that were black—more malodorous than anything she'd ever smelled in her life.

Then he let go of her neck and she almost fell, deciding to let herself fall, dropping to her knees, leaning forward and making a show of gasping for breath. On her knees, she was even less to be noticed, less of a possible threat.

Above her, Paul and the big man—she hoped he was Boris—argued. "I don't give no six rifles apiece for no damn piece o' ass. I can take these from ya right now. Three rifles for both o' 'em and the drugs you wanted. That's my deal, man. Take it or leave it."

"Boris, huh? You a Russian?"

"So what? You want the three rifles or you wanna be dead?"

"What if I can get you more women like this?"

"If they're virgins?"

"Virgins," Paul said.

"Hell, for a steady supply of virgins—which you ain't got, asshole—but I'd swap ya a rifle apiece and all the drugs ya want. Get high as the moon, I don't give a shit."

Paul touched his left hand to the back of his neck, as though rubbing away a cramp.

Natalia was waiting for the signal . . .

348

John Rourke heard the beeping in his left ear, one beep, then two, then one, then two. Paul was activating the radio signalling device located under the collar of his shirt.

John Rourke gave his son a "thumbs" up signal and they both started to climb . . .

Paul said, "You know, these two women. They're worth a lot to me. Maybe I oughta take 'em to the Land Pirates."

Land Pirates was the signal.

Paul stabbed his pistol toward Boris.

Natalia's right hand moved forward, the ropes falling away from her wrists as she made it to her feet, her left hand pulling away her gag, then clawing across Boris's face, grabbing his right ear and twisting his powerful neck left, as the Bali-Song went click-click-click in her right hand and she had the point of the knife against his carotid artery behind and below his right ear. "Unconscious in five seconds and dead in twelve, if you move. I'd just as soon you moved."

Thirteen

John Rourke flipped the railing on his left hand, the Score-Masters coming into his hands as his feet hit the bridge surface. "Hold it!"

As expected, the men who were starting to react to Paul and Annie and Natalia—six by the barricade and four beside the truck and one just climbing out from behind the wheel—turned toward him, starting for their weapons.

But John Rourke had planned ahead, arranging with his son that he would come onto the bridge the instant after he heard him shout.

Michael was on the bridge, an assault rifle in his right hand, the 44 Magnum Model 629 four-inch gleaming in his left. "Move and you die!"

Two of the men moved anyway, the driver of the truck and one of the men beside the barricade. John Rourke shouted as he fired, "Truck!"

The Detonics Scoremasters bucked once each in his hands as Rourke wheeled toward the barricade, the man dropping before his assault rifle could fire. Annie, one of Paul's High Powers in her hands, fired at the man in the same instant, his body on its side, on the floor of the bridge.

The report from Michael's assault rifle still echoed off the bridge's metal struts.

No one else moved. Rourke shouted, "Natalia! Get that thing into the truck. Annie! Get his weapons and toss them over the side into the river. Shoot his kneecaps out if he

350

causes any trouble. He just needs to be able to talk, not walk."

Michael, a gun still in each hand, started herding the remaining nine men toward the center of the bridge. In minutes at the most, the rest of Boris, the slaver's men, would be coming and John Rourke didn't care to wait around to see them . . .

She locked three sets of disposable plastic restraints around Boris's massive wrists, her knife to his ear as Annie secured his ankles. "You need a tongue to talk and one ear to listen, so this one is expendable if you move."

"You—"

"Go ahead," Natalia hissed through her teeth. "Call me something and see how fast you start losing body parts!"

He shut his mouth. Annie finished with his ankles and jumped down from the back of the truck, a blanket wrapped around her shoulders.

Natalia caught up her skirts with the same hand in which she held her knife and jumped to the bridge floor. "Go up to the cab with Paul. I'll join you in a minute."

"All right."

"But give me Paul's other Browning."

Annie passed the 9mm to her, saying, "It's hot."

"Right." Natalia's eyes glanced down at the pistol as she settled it in her hand. Cocked and locked. There had been thirteen rounds plus one in the chamber, and Annie fired two.

Twelve rounds, nine men. She flipped Bali-Song closed lefthanded and dropped it in the side seam pocket of her dress. Natalia, her left hand holding together the top of her dress, started toward the nine men at the center of the bridge. One of them was the man who had talked so big, while she'd been bound and gagged.

Michael and John were looking at her as she approached. Michael cautioned, "We're running out of time, Natalia."

"Then these things who call themselves men had better

351

hurry or I will shoot each one of them." And she shouted now at the nine men who stood with their hands clasped over their heads "Hear that? I am in a hurry. Remember how you shed your weapons?" Their guns and knives were in a pile on the bridge, near the far railing. "Let's see you shed your clothes the same way. Be quick or be dead!"

Some of the men looked at one another, then looked at her. Natalia pointed the High Power at the biggest of the nine men. "Guess where I will shoot you!"

He started to undress . . .

Michael Rourke started hurling the guns and knives taken from the slavers over the bridge rail and into the river. Most of the guns were post-War and in terrible condition. There were a few Beretta 92F military pistols, but in such a condition of neglect that their value for parts would be dubious. The knives were big and flashy and of poor quality.

The last of the weapons tossed away, he looked back toward the center of the bridge.

Natalia was tall for a woman, but very slender. In the torn long dress she wore, she looked almost frail, her left hand holding her clothes together, her right hand holding a gun.

The last of the nine men was down to nothing.

Time was running out, but Natalia owed herself this, Michael Rourke realized. "Now, I want all of your to hold hands and form a circle, backs to the center. Move!

The nine men did as she ordered, looking stupid, just as she wanted, he knew.

Michael looked at his father. John Rourke, a .45 still in each hand, as he was standing beside the rear end of the truck, laughing out loud.

"Now," Natalia ordered. "You will walk that way toward the far end of the bridge. The first man who breaks the circle, dies. Start walking! Go on! Walk!" Tripping over each other, but holding hands as though their lives depended on it, they started moving. "Faster! Come on!"

Michael Rourke, shaking his head, smiling, started for the truck . . .

Michael helped Natalia up into the cab of the truck Paul had driven here. The gesture, however unnecessary, was the gentlemanly thing to do.

John Rourke ran forward along the passenger side of the Eden military truck they were stealing from the slavers, toward the cab, climbing aboard, one foot inside, the other hanging free, his body weight on the open door, his right hand holding the radio detonator.

"We're rolling!" Paul shouted, the truck starting forward, grinding through the gears of its automatic transmission as it picked up speed.

The truck carrying Michael and Natalia was already off the bridge and on the semi-paved excuse for a road leading to it, gathering speed.

John Rourke looked back. The nine naked men were running for their lives now, vehicles of all descriptions coming onto the bridge from the far end, some of the naked men pointing behind them, toward the near end of the bridge.

The vehicles were entering onto the bridge, driving four across, filling the bridge from one side to the other. Shots rang out, the range too great for any accurate effect.

John Rourke looked at the detonator switch in his right hand. The stolen truck was clear of the bridge, onto the road. "Daddy? Are you going to—"

"I'm holding out for maximum effect, Annie. Just another few seconds," Rourke told his daughter.

The wind of their slipstream tore at Rourke's face and hair and ears.

The lead element of the enemy vehicles was approaching the near end of the bridge, coming up fast.

John Rourke flipped the release from the protective cover.

He put his thumb over the red button.

He depressed the button and counted, "One thousand one, one thousand two, one thousand three—" John Rourke didn't throw away the detonator because doubtless, he would need it again.

The near end of the bridge buckled upward, the supports beneath it flying outward to right and left, the sounds from the six explosive charges all but blocked by the sound of twisting and tearing metal.

The near end of the bridge collapsed inward, men and equipment careening through the air, where seconds earlier the bridge had been falling, now the bridge collapsing around them.

John Rourke swung into the cab and pulled the door closed. He put his arm around his daughter's shoulders and said, "On to bigger and better things.

Fourteen

The trail used by the smugglers and slavers who dealt with the Land Pirates was not through the rift valley but along the plateau to its west. Much of the land here was radioactive or chemically contaminated. By trial and error, the smugglers and slavers had found a safe route.

But it could be traveled by horseback alone, the electrical storms which whipped across the plateau on either side, coming without warning, sometimes lacerating the barren ground with heavy rains. Sometimes electrical activity alone, would neutralize the electrical system of any vehicle the smugglers and slavers possessed. So, teams of horses, four abreast, as many as twelve animals in all per vehicle, were used to tow engineless trucks which carried in plunder and carried out women, from the stronghold of the Land Pirates.

Boris was left to Natalia and Annie to interrogate, and whatever they threatened to do to him—Paul Rubenstein did not want to know—Boris proved a font of information. Like bullies everywhere, without his friends to back him up, he was a coward. The tapes made of his answers during the interrogation provided even more information that they had expected.

Indeed, Martin Zimmer was with the Land Pirates. For years, Zimmer had let them exist, even helped them, but now he was forming a formal alliance. With promises of the latest in Eden military equipment and a steady supply of women and anything else they wanted from Eden, he was consummating an arrangement by which the Land Pirates would systematically hit every settlement in the Wildlands.

The objective, as far as Boris knew, was to kill anyone who might oppose Martin Zimmer, kidnap the usable women and kill the rest, along with the children who were too young for sexual or other uses. Then he would impress the healthy men into the service of Eden. Boris knew many of the details, he revealed, because he was trying to work an alliance with the Land Pirates where he could "get in on the action" and make a profit.

Martin wanted to assemble an army in the west before he attacked the Allies, an army that would cover his back.

Boris also revealed that route used by the Land Pirates through the rift valley was secure not so much because it was a secret, but because of the plasma energy weapons that were installed along its length. The weapons—energy cannons—were programmed to fire automatically when motion sensors hidden along the walls of the rift valley, detected movement.

When the Land Pirates exited or entered, the defense system was shut down in stages, but never completely off.

The larger vehicles used by the Land Pirates—and intelligence data corroborated this—were enormous, mobile fortresses almost the size of World War Two aircraft carriers, moving over any obstacle their sheer momentum and weight did not crush, on a system of independently operating treads, each of these many times larger than those used in twentieth century tanks.

Paul had wondered, from the intell data and again after Boris's interrogation covered them, how such machines could operate without just sinking into the ground out of sheer weight.

But the tread design and independent drive for each tread system, John theorized, allowed the vehicle to tow itself out of anything, without ever becoming stuck or bogged down.

The Land Pirates possessed insufficient technology to build such vehicles, or program computer controlled weapons. But, Eden did. According to Boris, agents of Eden actually controlled the Land Pirates. And the vehicles were built in Eden. Even if no one knew, Boris had said, Eden had hundreds of these vehicles, built in secret, ready to deploy against the allies.

Paul Rubenstein had studied Latin five days a week in high school (and Hebrew over the weekend, of course). At last, he finally remembered something he'd been trying to recall since the first data on Eden was given to him, after this last Awakening.

It was about Martin Zimmer's name.

In Latin, Martin meant the warlike.

It seemed to be a name that fit.

Fifteen

It was good to be back in her own clothes, her skirt a respectable length.

She remembered the lovely young Chinese agent who had ridden sidesaddle, and tried to teach her to do the same. Annie Rubenstein could have done it, she supposed, but what was the sense? Riding astride had once been considered terribly unfeminine, she knew, from the books she had read, the video tape movies she had watched. But, riding astride was the most practical way to get from one place to another on horseback.

Someday, there might be a world in which she could ride for pleasure, because she genuinely liked riding horseback. But not in this world.

After two nights of camping in the Wildlands without even so much as an hermetically sealed tent, she felt positively grubby and didn't even want to think about her hair. But this was her job as much as it was her father's job or her husband's job or her brother's job—or Natalia's.

She had noticed it subconsciously, feelings from her father, about this man named Martin Zimmer. And the nearer they came to the Land Pirates stronghold, the greater sense of unease she felt.

Last night, in their dark and cold camp, the electrical activity in the sky becoming maddeningly intense and cold rains washing down on them, her father had spoken of their plan. "This Martin Zimmer, whoever he is," her father began, "is getting ready for war. If he attacks the allies, eventually it will come to nuclear weapons. Intelligence data indicates he has gas and biological weapons as well. The allies won't have any choice but to defend themselves with their own nuclear weapons. Parts of the earth are starting to return to life. Other parts may never come back. If there's another nuclear war now, we all know what that will mean.

"And Martin has to be counting on that."

Why did her father call this man by his first name, rather than calling him "Zimmer"? The feelings were stronger in her, as if someone were invading her thoughts without trying.

She urged her horse ahead along the track that paralleled the rift valley where once the Mississippi had flowed.

This was once the land of Mark Twain and his Huck Finn and Tom Sawyer and his Becky.

But in another few hours' ride, it would be the stronghold of the Land Pirates . . .

He had already formulated a plan, and if the terrain, as the talkative Boris had described it, were close enough in reality, they would have a decent chance of making it inside. Escaping the stronghold was another question, but he had plans for that as well, again very dependent on Boris's information.

Martin Zimmer.

John Rourke was already beginning to understand that. He could see it in Annie, almost sense it in her. But, even if he had Annie's ability (gift or curse)—and he thanked God that he did not—he would have fought it, rejected it.

Martin Zimmer.

It was not that sort of feeling, any sixth sense message. It was something that to him would always be more powerful and inevitable.

It was logic.

It was necessity.

John Rourke urged his mount ahead with his knees and

359

heels.

To travel anywhere near the rift valley, Hilda and Dan and Margie required horses. These animals, she understood, were in part the descendants of horses given to Eden by New Germany over a century ago. The animals given to them by the Allied agents were a curious breed.

Natalia had ridden horseback all over the world, only occasionally for pleasure. The German horses were very strongly Arab in their lineage. But these horses of Eden were only partly Arab and part American quarter horse. Aboard the Eden shuttles, there were cryogenically-frozen embryos of all the domestic animals that could concievably be useful in the retaking of a devastated earth.

The horse, after the camel, was the ultimate form of four-legged transportation, and far easier to control, not to mention more comfortable to ride.

When they reached their destination, the stronghold of the Land Pirates, the horses would be left unsaddled and tethered so that, with a little effort, they could work their way free after a time. That way, if the horses were necessary for escape, they would be there. If the horses were left behind and John's plan for getting hold of one of the Land Pirate mobile fortresses worked, the horses would eventually get free and have a chance at survival. More than likely, the animals would try to return to their home stable.

Natalia's mind settled on the question of Martin Zimmer. John had begun calling him "Martin" and nothing else.

And there was the question.

The old woman about whom the German agent, known as Hilda, had told them. She had scrawled the word "Devil" into the snow and then carefully set a coin with the image of John Rourke in the center of the "D".

The cult of personality that Martin Zimmer had built around John's legend. It did not make sense that an evil man would so exalt a man who was good. Martin was clearly a Nazi, even bore the surname of Deitrich Zimmer who had been responsible for the woes which beset them now. Why would a Nazi, spawn a cult of personality around a man who, philosophically, could most closely be described as an Objectivist, a man who had spent his entire life fighting the very sort of tyranny Martin himself stood for?

What seemed irrational, she had learned very long ago, to someone, somewhere, was rational.

Why did Martin elevate John Rourke to the rank of some historical demi-god when they were so diametrically opposed philosophically?

Was it just a cruel joke?

In a very little while—she checked the ladies Rolex on her left wrist—they would know.

Sixteen

It was a citadel, the stronghold of the Land Pirates.

He had watched it now for nearly twenty-four hours, memorizing every feature of it.

If evidence had at all been lacking to involve the government of Eden with the Land Pirates, here it was. The structure that was the fortress itself was fabricated of modern synth-concrete, not something whipped up in the Wildlands by men who were little more technologically advanced than Middle Ages barbarians.

During the late twentieth century, there was considerable furor concerning state lotteries, some talk of a national lottery as well. John Rourke did not see gambling as a moral issue. If people wanted to gamble, they should be free to do so. He did not gamble, simply because he thought it was a stupid waste of hard-earned money. If others wished to do so, good for them.

But now, there was no choice but to gamble, and considering that the lives of his wife, Sarah, and his son, Michael, and perhaps all their lives hung in the balance—it was the biggest gamble of his life.

Michael, although promising Natalia faithfully that he would grow it back, had promised that he would shave his mustache . . .

Michael Rourke walked down along the path, his parka open despite the cold, so that he would be visibly armed. He wore no assault rifle.

If his father's plan did not work, he wanted access to his

guns even though he would die. At least he would kill a few of the Land Pirates before he went down.

The two Berettas were in their shoulder rig, slingling a .92F below each armpit. The four-inch Metalife Custom Model 629 was in the crossdraw holster between his navel and his left hip. He wore the knife made for him by old Jon, the Swordmaker, as well.

He came down from the path and started walking toward the guard post on the north wall of the citadel.

Eventually, someone would notice him.

The electronic security which comprised the early warning system of the stronghold's integrated perimeter defense was disarmed in two locations, thanks to Natalia and Paul. Bridging it, rather than interrupting it; it was extremely unlikely anyone monitoring the system knew anything had been done to it.

Within the next second or two, the guards on the wall would notice him, he told himself.

And then it would start.

And he hoped his father was right.

There was a shout. "Hey! What the—"

Three guards on the wall had assault rifles to their shoulders and, from within the stronghold, an alarm began to sound.

Before anyone could shoot, Michael Rourke shouted up to the wall "I am Martin Zimmer! The man who negotiates with your leaders is an imposter. Shoot at me and all of Eden will crush you!

The "crush you" line was something he extemporized on the spot and he thought it was rather effective.

The alarm which had begun sounding fifteen seconds ago still sounded as John Rourke, using the modern German equivalent of ninja climbing claws, scaled the synth-concrete wall of the citadel.

He reached the top, peering over. As he had predicted, human security was all looking toward the north wall where Michael would be announcing himself just about now.

The cameras, as high altitude photographs taken by German satellites indicated, were aimed at the outside perimeter, to compensate for poor vigilance on the part of human guards, not on the height of the wall itself. Every such video system had dead spots, and after a day's worth of observation, constantly comparing data arrived at on the ground with the aerial photographs, he had plotted a route to the wall that one man could follow, taking advantage of the dead spots; hence remaining undetected by the cameras.

That part was not difficult.

But getting up the wall, which all observation indicated was not, itself, fitted with sensors, was the trick. In white snow gear, the German assault rifle he carried painted white, working his way through the snow before dawn, then lying here at the base of the wall and waiting, had been comparatively simple. That was why he had waited for Michael.

John Rourke went over the wall and down, ridding himself of the climbing claws. To remove a sentry now would be a tactical error. Quickly, he moved along the wall and into the shelter of a cupola which his observation indicated covered a stairwell.

From one of the musette bags he wore strapped crossbody from shoulder to hip, Rourke took an electronic probe sensing device. It was merely a more sophisticated version of bugging detectors in common use during the latter part of the twentieth century, designed to pick up electronic activity. This one had a much greater scanning radius range between low and high end signals and could detect activity up to a distance of fifty yards. It was developed at Mid-Wake.

Rourke held the German assault rifle in his right fist, the probe in his left as he first tested, then started down the staircase.

Five steps down, he detected an electronic sensor pulsing intermittently near the base of the stairs.

He kept moving, more slowly though. And, as he neared the sensor, he was able to determine the position. There were actually two transmitters and two receivers, located on the sides of the stairwell.

Slung around his neck below his chin were a set of goggles. These too were developed at Mid-Wake, designed to allow divers to penetrate electronically secure areas. Rourke pushed down the hood of his snowsmock and his parka, then pulled up the goggles, activating their power unit.

Like night vision goggles, the image they presented appeared digitized (which it was) and wasn't ideal for detailed viewing. But these goggles were designed to receive electronic signals and translate them to visual signals.

With the goggles in place, he could monitor the patterns of the signal beams. They looked like pencil-thin beams of light, and they crisscrossed. If he could had not have seen them, it would have been impossible to evade them. Interrupting one of the signals would doubtlessly sound an alarm of some sort at the security center.

But, with the goggles, and with extreme caution and considerable difficulty considering his height, John Rourke dropped to hands and knees on the stairs and began to crawl between the beams . . .

Michael Rourke was surrounded by men who gave the concept of looking evil a whole new meaning.

"You dead, mother fucker!"

Michael Rourke looked at the man—well over six feet, bearded and burly, armed with a pre-War shotgun and two pistols—and forced himself to smile. "The next man who says something like that to me loses his tongue or his life. Whichever amuses me more. Take me to where this impostor pretends to be Martin Zimmer." And then Michael Rourke let the smile fade. "Now!"

Seventeen

She was frightened for Michael and for John, but there was no time to worry. Because, if she and Annie and Paul failed, no matter how successful Michael and John were, they would all be doomed.

Natalia Anastasia Tiemerovna flipped over the synth-concrete snow fence and ran along it toward the massive doors. Evidently, the Land Pirates had a raid planned. In some ways, this was bad, but in others good.

There were more personnel in the incredibly massive garage complex at the rear base of the stronghold than she had thought there would be. But, on the plus side, out of the six incredibly huge vehicles garaged in the system of structures, two of them had engines running.

The stronghold of the Land Pirates was almost a mile square, walled entirely around. The northern approach, which John had taken, was set on higher ground. The southern approach stretched out over a valley, the foundation formed by the garage structure into which she now looked. The mobile fortresses of the Land Pirates were not the size of World War Two aircraft carriers. That would have been impossible, she knew, the moment their size was brought up.

But they were larger than anything she could have imagined. Their main decks were easily the size of an American football field, in length and width. There were helicopter landing pads, it appeared, although she could not see beyond the main deck's perimeter. But there were at least two Eden gunships visible to her on each of the mobile fortresses. For what purpose? Surely, none of the Land Pirates knew how to fly. Below the main deck where smaller vehicles—the size of conventional tanks—were parked, there was a system of subdecks, gun mounts visible at various locations.

These would be plasma energy cannons.

There were missile arrays as well. The Land Pirates might conceivably need energy cannons to do their work of plundering, but not missiles, because these were obviously of the surface to air variety and no one in the Wildlands had airpower.

But the Allies did.

Huge cranes, attached to the main decks of the fortresses, were raising more gun batteries into position.

She saw men in military uniform moving about within the complex, some uniforms clearly those of the Eden armed forces. The other uniforms, black, bore Swastika armbands.

The Land Pirates themselves seemed a disgusting lot, as foul appearing as the slavers had been, but better armed in many cases.

There was movement behind her and it startled her, even though the source of movement was what she had expected, Paul and Annie joining her. Paul, except for his play-acting with the slavers and an occasional burst of anger, was very temperate of speech. But under his breath, he murmured, "Holy shit!"

Natalia could not have agreed with him more . . .

Michael Rourke was surrounded by a dozen sentries as he crossed the stronghold's courtyard. But, so far at least, they weren't one hundred percent certain he was not Martin Zimmer, he surmised, because not a one of them had dared to attempt or even suggest that he be disarmed. Under the circumstances, he was no danger to them.

What worried him most was that his father's plan was working as well as it was, because that meant that the premise for the plan had to be correct.

Martin Zimmer had to be his—their—physical duplicate. But

how? He threw his shoulders back and kept walking.

Paul Rubenstein settled his cap on his head, looked from side to side to be certain he was unobserved, then stood up and immediately started walking toward the nearest of the mobile land fortresses.

His Browning High Powers were under the Eden uniform tunic that he wore.

John had planned ahead, as he always did, and as it usually worked out, he was correct. Bringing the Eden armed forces uniforms in the first place, then wearing them under their arctic gear and snow smocks when they'd made their pre-dawn infiltration, paid off.

The land fortress toward which he walked, like the five, was of incredible size. The treads themselves were nearly half his height thickness. The wheels on which the treads were set were as tall as a small house from before The Night of The War, it seemed. The main deck towered more than a hundred feet above him.

There would be several entrances to a vehicle of such size, but the one he walked toward, gangplanked like a battle ship, was busy, men going in and out constantly. There were no guards.

He passed an Eden officer wearing lower rank designation than he wore and the officer saluted him, mumbling, "Hail Martin!"

Paul Rubenstein returned the salute, the green uniformed man disappearing round a stack of crates marked "High Explosive." There were other uniforms here, those that were black and sported Swastika armbands on the left sleeve, but he encountered no one wearing such a uniform.

A half dozen Land Pirates, grubby looking men, heavily armed, exited the land fortress along its gangplank. Paul kept walking toward the entrance. The Land Pirates, dressed in pieces of Eden battle uniforms and a motley collection of mismatched garments, walked past him, one of them nodding. Paul nodded back.

He reached the foot of the gangplank, pausing for a split second to take a breath.

Annie and Natalia would be coming along as soon as he created his diversion, the cover of a diversion necessary to get them aboard, despite the Eden uniforms they wore. Because, on close inspection, they would obviously be noticable as women, and there were no women in the Eden armed forces, nor certainly among the forces of the Land Pirates. Women held positions as teachers, secretaries, factory workers, but nothing beyond that in Eden, a dramatic step backwards.

Paul Rubenstein started up the gangplank . . .

The interior of the Land Pirates stronghold was much as he'd imagined it would be. There were long corridors, dormitory style sleeping rooms leading off from these corridors, and storage rooms and weapons vaults. Women, dressed in rags, some visibly shivering in the cold and dampness, slunk about the place carrying loads of wash or food, the one commonality among them, the look of terror in their eyes.

At the end of one of these corridors, there was a large assembly hall, dining tables ranked along it, with chairs enough to seat more than a thousand men.

With his twelve man escort surrounding him, Michael walked along its length, large doors set at the center of the far wall . . .

Paul had deferred to Natalia for advice on a diversion. Crouched beside Natalia now, shivering with the cold because she wore no arctic gear, just a man's Eden military uniform, her eyes were on the main deck of the nearest of the mobile fortresses.

If her husband reached the main deck without being challenged for papers or identification he did not have—when, she told herself, when—he would drop a plastique charge into one

369

of the tanks located there, turning it into a giant shrapnel grenade.

In the ensuing confusion, she and Natalia would get aboard, she hoped.

Eden tanks, like tanks ever since tanks first saw fuel battle use in World War One, were only armored on the outside.

John Rourke stopped. The detection unit he carried revealed no further electronic barriers, at least not within range, but his hearing and normal night vision, the goggles slung below his chin again, revealed something else. For the past several minutes, he had been moving through a huge basement storage area, a synth-fuel dump, enormous tanks full of it on all sides of him.

But the sound he heard was not mechanical. It was the sound of men, talking, the guttural quality of their speech as he slowly, silently, approached the origin of the sounds, suggesting they were Land Pirates.

Under the circumstances, he was happy they were here . . .

Paul Rubenstein stepped out onto the main deck of the enormous vehicle. At least as big as a football field, he thought. There were helicopter gunships, six of them, secured to the deck, of the type that were the latest addition to the growing Eden arsenal. Each of the gunships seemed equipped with a full missile array in pods located to port and starboard. He doubted any conventional explosives would have a sufficiently serious effect against one of these vehicles. In pre-War dollars, to build even one of these would cost well over a billion dollars, he guessed.

But Eden was big on taxation.

He started walking toward the nearest of the rows of tanks. The deck plates below his feet seemed somehow different and, as he walked, he looked at them more carefully. He realized he was walking across a massive ramp. The ramp, set into the deck, could apparently be extended outward and downward, like a pre-fabricated military bridge section, for the use of the tanks as they left the main deck and returned.

He made a mental note about the ramps, trying to think of a way to sabotage one at some future date, if there ever were a future date.

The immediate job at hand was to blow up a tank.

Eden military personnel, Land Pirates and the occasional black clad, Swastika armband-wearing Nazis were everywhere, all busily engaged in what seemed like last minute preparations for an operation.

This was not going to be a raid against some hapless hamlet, but a full-scale military deployment. Was Martin Zimmer on the brink of beginning his war against the Allies?

Paul Rubenstein reached the tank.

Beneath his uniform tunic, he had several charges of the latest German plastique, in various sizes for various contingent uses.

He selected the largest of the charges, then started to climb aboard the tank.

"You!"

Without turning around, Paul Rubenstein knew it could only be a Nazi who would shout like that to a man wearing a captain's uniform. Paul looked back. The man wore some sort of SS officer's rank, probably a major or the equivalent. Although he might well be forced to take it up for future reference, studying World War Two SS rank wasn't the sort of thing, as a Jew, he had ever enjoyed. "Yes?"

"What are you doing there?"

"I am climbing up onto this tank's superstructure. I have to inspect the hatches on each tank and see they are satisfactorily locked down. That is my job. I learned that if I do not check such work myself, the men under me will become lax."

"You will let me see your orders. Now!"

The man in the Nazi uniform was slightly built, blond haired, dark-eyed, sallow complected, as if somehow he never got out into the fresh air. Paul Rubenstein debated his possible courses of action. He was, after all, looking for a diversion.

"Just a moment. While I am up here, I will check this hatch." Paul turned his back to the man, clambering up the superstructure to the hatch itself. He looked back, the Nazi just standing there on the deck, hands on his hips like he was getting ready to dance or something, Paul thought. Paul opened the hatch with some difficulty, the lock tricky but the weight considerably less than he had expected. Using his body to shield the work of his hands, he reached under his tunic, pulled the charge from the hook and pile fastener belt he wore, then flipped back the safety cover. He set the toggle switch and closed the cover, dropping the charge down into the tank's interior.

He stood to his full height and closed the hatch.

As he looked back, the Nazi had been joined by two Land Pirates.

"You will show me your orders and you will show me what you placed inside the tank."

Paul's body was still turned away from the Nazi and the other two men. His hands closed on the butts of the Browning High Powers beneath his jacket.

As he turned around, he said, "Sure I will," then opened fire. Two shots per man, then two more—he dropped both Land Pirates who were flanking the Nazi. There was total silence on the deck for a split second. The Nazi looked up at him, incredulous. Paul Rubenstein pointed both Browning High Powers at the Nazi's chest and fired.

Gunfire started hammering against the tank's superstructure, but Paul Rubenstein was already jumping clear, running, toward the cover of the other tanks. In a few seconds, if a bullet didn't catch him, he'd be protected enough to activate the detonator and send shrapnel flying all over the deck.

If a bullet didn't catch him.

Eighteen

Killing one of the two Land Pirates with his knife, then placing the muzzle of his suppressor fitted 6906 against the forehead of the second, John Rourke got the information he required.

"Martin Zimmer's in the Chief's meeting room, probably."

"The Chief?"

"The boss, ya' know?"

"What's his name?"

"We just call him 'Chief', that's all."

"All right. This meeting room. Is it where the Chief briefs you on your raids and everything?"

"Yeah!"

"What's on?"

"What?"

"What's on, I said. Is there a raid planned?"

"Somethin' big. They got Eden Army guys here and some of the Nazis, too."

"Martin's in the briefing room, then. Where is that?" John Rourke shoved the muzzle of the suppressor a little harder against the man's forehead.

There was the sound of the man's bowels releasing, and a smell even worse than the Land Pirate's body odor, but he gave excellent directions. And, true to his word, John Rourke didn't kill him, just slipped him an injection from the kit in his musette bag, putting him to sleep for a few hours.

Quickly, because time might already be up for Michael, John Rourke moved through the maze of fuel tanks, toward a staircase that would take him up to the level of the briefing room . . .

When gunfire erupted on the main deck of the fortress, Natalia shouted, "Come on!"

And, Annie beside her, she started running toward the fortress.

This was more than they had bargained for, she realized, more activity, more enemy personnel. It was time to change the plan. From a pocket of her uniform tunic, she took some of the marble-sized German anti-personnel grenades, flipping their security covers, depressing their fuse starters, then throwing them toward the largest groups of enemy personnel she could find . . .

Michael Rourke, his twelve guards still surrounding him, waited in what looked like an enormous briefing room, a table long enough to comfortably handle two dozen people, at its center. On the stone walls there were maps of the Americas, North, Central and South. There was a detailed map of the Wildlands, with positions marked on it in large, circled X shapes.

This was a war room.

After he heard the sound of a door opening, he turned toward his right.

Seven men entered, one of them a Land Pirate, two in black uniforms with Swastika armbands on the sleeve, three more in Eden field uniforms, each of these wearing the rank of a colonel or better.

The seventh man wore civilian casual clothes.

He was speaking to one of the Nazis as he entered, then stopped and turned around.

"You must be Michael. What a pleasant surprise! Or, are you John?"

Michael Rourke just stood there. He didn't know what to say.

"We can't steal this thing! We'd never escape! Destroy everything behind you!"

Natalia ran ahead of her, up the gangplank, Annie firing her assault rifle into a knot of Land Pirates and Eden enlisted personnel, a hail of gunfire pinging against the hatchway's superstructure as she cleared the gangplank.

She reached into her uniform tunic pocket, taking out some of the German anti-personnel grenades. She activated one, threw it, then another, then another.

Then, she reached to her head, snatching off the uniform hat she wore and shaking her hair free.

She threw the hat away, then started to run after Natalia.

The tank into which he'd dropped the plastique exploded, strips of razor-edged armor plate flying everywhere across the deck, a ball of fire rising, stopping at the ceiling of the garage structure, then billowing outward in all directions as a wave of fire and smoke.

There had been no choice to any of this. If he had climbed down from the tank and conversed with the Nazi, he had no orders to show. If he had surrendered, once the charge was in place, he would have been forced with either, never activating it or committing suicide by standing there, waiting for it to explode.

Gunfire rippled along the deckplates, Paul Rubenstein ducking back, nothing to answer assault rifle fire with but his two 9mm pistols. Things were going wrong, but he had to find a way of making them go right or else all of them would die. Sirens sounded, smaller explosions starting. But in seconds, someone on deck would organize the now random resistance and there would be a charge against his position.

As he reached into his pocket for some of the marble-sized German anti-personnel grenades, his eyes stopped on something twenty yards away. It was one of the Eden gunships, its main rotor blades twisted and deformed by a piece of shrapnel from the destroyed tank.

But, a considerable distance away, the next closest gunship seemed in perfect condition.

Unlike the last time he had decided that taking up a gunship by himself was his only choice of action, this time he knew how to fly.

Paul Rubenstein flipped a handful of the grenades toward the greatest concentration of enemy fire, waited for the explosions—they came in rapid succession—then ran for the chopper . . .

"You look like me."

Martin Zimmer smiled. "Or is it that I look like you? Really, we both look enough like John Rourke to be John Rourke, don't we? You are Michael, I take it. John Rourke would probably have had something intensely witty to say, I mean."

"I'm Michael, yeah."

A beeper sounded faintly. Martin Zimmer took a pager sized unit from his belt and said, "Excuse me a moment." Then he spoke into the machine, evidently a two-way radio of some sort. "This is Martin . . . Oh, have they really? . . . Probably just the relatives stopping by . . . No, damnit! Don't let them get one of the helicopters airborne!" He tossed the radio onto the table. "Annie and Paul and Natalia, I assume? And John? Causing some trouble with the fortresses. But three or four people couldn't cause that much trouble, even Rourkes. What was the plan, Michael? You don't mind if I call you that, do you?"

"Who the hell are you?"

"I'm Martin Zimmer! And I'm about to take over the world. Nice of you to stop by, to congratulate me, no doubt."

"Who are you, damnit?! Why do you look like—"

"Like you? Like your father? Where is your father, Michael? Was this some sort of diabolical plan to get in and assassinate me?"

"That was the general idea, I think."

"Well, it didn't work." Martin Zimmer smiled. "If John Rourke is lurking around somewhere ready to spring out and do something heroic, he'll find he's shit out of luck. I have him outnumbered and outwitted. The only way out of here would be with one of the fortresses, which he won't get. And he'd never leave you behind, which means he'll be showing up—"

The door through which Martin Zimmer and the six other men had entered, opened.

Michael's father said, "Just about now?"

Martin Zimmer wheeled toward him. The other men in the room—the twelve who had accompanied Michael and the six who had entered with Martin Zimmer, turned toward the door as well.

Michael Rourke stepped back, drawing both Berettas, ready to go down in a hail of gunfire.

Instead of an order to shoot, Martin Zimmer just laughed.

After the laughter died, he said, "Daddy."

Michael held his pistols, but realized his hands were shaking.

Not counting Martin Zimmer, there were eighteen enemy personnel in the room. At any second, someone would start shooting.

This was it, unless his father had something up his sleeve.

From where he stood, he could see Martin Zimmer and John Rourke. They were identical in features and coloring and height, except for their clothes, each the mirror image of the other, as he was their image and they were his. A except for little bit of gray in his father's hair.

No one spoke.

Michael couldn't stand it anymore. "Who the hell are you, damnit!?"

Martin Zimmer didn't look at him, only at John Rourke. But he said, "I'm your long lost brother. After you both drop your weapons, maybe, Mike, you and I can go outside and toss around a ball or something with old Dad here. And then Dad can tell me all about the birds and the bees or something."

"Do you have Deitrich Zimmer's surgical skills, Martin?" Michael's father asked. "Because, if you do, you can save your mother's life."

"My mother!?" Martin Zimmer doubled over with laughter. And then he abruptly stopped. "Mom's not well, is she?"

"There's a bullet in her brain that son of a bitch, Deitrich Zimmer put there," Michael shouted, the urge to kill stronger in him than it had ever been in his life, no matter who the enemy had been. "Tell me he isn't our brother, Dad! Tell me he isn't our brother! Dad?"

Michael's father, apparently expecting this all along, seemed very calm, didn't even answer him. Instead, he said to Martin, "He is the infant that Deitrich Zimmer killed more than a century ago when he escaped from Michael and the others, from that redoubt in the Andes. That little boy was Lieutenant Martha Larrimore's child who was born the same day you were, wasn't it? Deitrich Zimmer took both infants out of the hospital the night he firebombed it and got both Sarah and me.

"I don't know the woman's name, but you guessed right, Dad. I'm really impressed! Now, since you could never get out of here alive, hand me over those slick looking pistols of yours. Call it my inheritance, Dad. I have a war to start."

Michael Rourke's fingers tightened against the triggers of his Berettas.

This would be it.

"And Zimmer used cryogenics, didn't he? He wanted a real world for you to conquer, one full of people, so he used cryogenic sleep until population caught up. That's why Dodd and his successors farmed babies. That why you still do it. No fun ruling an empty planet. But Deitrich Zimmer's still alive. He wouldn't miss this. He's got to be alive."

"Give me the damn guns, Daddy dear! They belong in my fucking museum! Just like you belong in the grave!"

For a moment, Michael almost shouted at his father, because his father rolled both ScoreMasters in his hands and offered them, butts forward, to Martin.

But then the momentary sickness Michael Rourke had felt in the pit of his stomach, a momentary light-headedness, was gone, replaced by an adrenaline rush.

A smile crossed his lips.

Martin reached for the guns.

John Rourke's hands dropped slightly, the guns moving in his fingers as if they somehow had a life of their own.

A double road agent spin.

Both pistols fired, taking down the Nazis standing on either side of Martin.

Michael Rourke opened fire, both Berettas firing into anything that moved, the boom of his father's .45s reverberating along the synth-concrete walls of the room. A bullet tore across Michael's left thigh and he stumbled to his left knee, but kept firing.

The Beretta in his right hand was empty.

As he drew the 629 from his belt, he saw a blur of movement, his father, the six-inch barreled '44 Magnum he carried out, firing, then suddenly Martin was in front of him like a shield and Michael heard his father's voice booming, "Drop your guns or he's dead!"

"Don't listen to him! He wouldn't kill his son!"

A tightness came into Michael Rourke's throat, not from the pain in his left leg, but from what his father said in the next second "That man over there is my son. You could have been, but you aren't."

Michael leaned back against the massive table leg, keeping the revolver and the one Beretta that still had a few rounds in the magazine, trained on the ten men who were still alive, some of them wounded, the others dropping their guns, raising their hands. His ears rang with the gunfire still. In seconds, half the Land Pirates in the stronghold would be beating down the doors to the briefing room.

John Rourke smiled. He said, "I heard your end of that radio conversation, Martin. You're going to get to meet the rest of the family, all right, because they'll realize that we can't get one of the fortresses out of here, so they'll take one of the helicopters and land it right in the courtyard. Reunion time, Martin." And Michael's father pressed the muzzle of the .44 Magnum Smith & Wesson revolver against Martin Zimmer's right temple.

Michael Rourke started changing magazines in his pistols, giving himself a few seconds before he tried to stand.

Nineteen

The controls on the Eden gunship, although she had studied Allied intelligence reports on the craft, were hard to get used to, so much computer assisted that getting the feel for the machine was virtually impossible.

With less grace than she liked, they had the craft airborne, for a moment terrified that with the low ceiling clearance above her in this vast hangar-sized garage complex, she would hit and crash the machine, killing them all.

Paul and Annie huddled inside the open fuselage door, hurling anti-personnel grenades in the machine's wake, firing the door gun as Natalie let the gunship slip, the main rotor starting to drag. She increased power, the gunship's downsweeping arc suddenly changing, the craft accelerating so rapidly that for an instant she thought she would crash them into the structure's ceiling.

But she brought the machine level, banking as she cleared the doorway and was into the open. There was no chance to try to disable the gunships left behind.

She started to climb.

"If John and Michael don't realize this is what we're up to, you and Annie pull out," Paul ordered. "I'll go in, and you back me up with some of those missiles. Make a real mess and then get the hell out of here before they send up some more choppers after us!"

As much as she didn't like the idea of being protected, Paul made sense. If they were all captured or killed, then there would be no chance for any survivors to be freed—or the dead to be

380

avenged.

They had grossly miscalculated the manpower of the Land Pirates, but there was no intelligence data to indicate that Martin Zimmer was about to start a war.

She banked the helicopter to starboard in a long arc, checking the arming of her weapons systems. "Paul, help me up here! Annie, be ready by that door if we go in!"

"I'm ready!" Annie called back.

Paul slid into the co-pilot's seat beside her. "What do you want me to do?"

You read the same captured manuals I did. Try to arm the missiles."

"All right."

She could see the courtyard now, a crowd of figures that were indistinguishable at her current altitude coming out of the main structure within the courtyard. "Annie! Be ready with that machine gun!"

"Ready!"

"Paul, hurry those missiles."

"I'm trying!"

She started descending, coming down in a tight circle over the courtyard. There were men on the walls, armed men, but no one was shooting at her.

Through the chin bubble, she could make out something about the figures below her. Some women, mostly men.

She thought she could see John or Michael. It was Michael, and he was limping.

Now she could see details clearly. About two dozen women were in the courtyard, dressed in tattered rags, herded together, Michael urging them along, it seemed.

And there was a veritable army of Land Pirates and Eden personnel, and some in black uniforms as well.

She saw John, but blinked.

She looked back, saw Michael.

John and Michael and someone John had a gun on, who looked just like both of them.

"Who is that?" Annie shouted forward. "He looks like—ohh, my God."

Natalia said, "Just be ready with that doorgun!"

"Missiles armed. I'm going aft."

"Right, Paul."

She let the machine turn a full 360 degrees on its main rotor.

Then she eased slightly forward on her control stick and skated the machine down about twenty-five yards from the women.

"How many people will this thing hold?" Paul shouted forward to her.

"Supposedly two fully equipped squads with light weapons," Natalia answered. These raggedly dressed creatures were some of the captured women. It would be tight, getting them aboard, but she wouldn't leave any of them behind.

She saw Michael clearly now, saw him limping but otherwise seemingly unhurt. She wanted to get out from behind the controls, run out to him, hold him. Natalia stayed where she was.

John Rourke's left forearm was clamped tight over Martin's neck, his left hand knotted on Martin's right ear, the muzzle of his gun against Martin's right temple.

Paul and Annie were in the fuselage doorway, Paul helping the women inside, Annie behind the doorgun, ready to use it.

Through the cockpit bubble, he could see Natalia.

Michael limped past him. "Come on, Dad."

John Rourke knew what he would do, if he could do it. It would be the only way to save Sarah's life, to bring her back.

He was grateful that this offspring of their bodies didn't know him any better. As John Rourke edged himself and Martin back toward the gunship, Martin tried to break away and John Rourke told him, "Do it and I'll blow your brains out!" He would never have shot any man that way, least of all this man.

"I got him!" Michael shouted, the muzzle of his revolver going to Martin's head as Michael and Paul hauled Martin up and into the machine.

John Rourke jumped aboard.

"Get us out of here, Natalia!" Michael shouted.

The machine lurched, rose, slipped to port a little and was airborne.

They wouldn't be followed, because they had Martin, and Martin was their leader.

The enemy—the Armed Forces of Eden, the Nazis who aided them, the Land Pirates—would expect a deal, a bargain.

John Rourke remembered the words of Winston Churchill when Churchill commented on making an alliance with Stalin to defeat Hitler. John Rourke would not make an alliance with the devil, but he would bargain for the devil's life.

Michael said, "We made it."

John Rourke said nothing, just reached out and took his son, Michael's hand, for a moment. His son . . .

JERRY AHERN

THE SURVIVALIST 19: FINAL RAIN

Eight men dead. The gale-driven snow already beginning to cover them.

The rear man of the marine Spetsnaz patrol had died first as the 12-inch blade of the LS-X stabbed through his arctic survival gear. The others, half-frozen, began to react, their AKM-96s firing wildly.

Too slow. John Rourke, CIA-trained weapons and survival expert, took out another three with controlled bursts from his M-16. Ahead, Paul Rubenstein opened up with his Schmiesser submachine gun. Two more down, another and another . . .

Too easy. But the hard part lay ahead. Particle Beam weapons, a nuclear death-tide of advanced technology that could destroy not just John Rourke and his allies, but the entire fragile earth.

HODDER AND STOUGHTON PAPERBACKS